POINT OF NO RETURN

POINT OF NO RETURN

Book Five in The Kathleen Turner Series

Tiffany Snow

Montlake
Romance

The characters and events portrayed in this book are fictitious. Any similarity to real persons, living or dead, is coincidental and not intended by the author.

Published by Montlake Romance, Seattle

www.apub.com

ISBN-13: 9781477822579
ISBN-10: 1477822577

Library of Congress Control Number: 2013921710

Printed in the United States of America

For Maria, my amazing editor.
This book is better because of you.

PROLOGUE

I hated hospitals.

Sickness and death. Grief and worry. The endless antiseptic corridors of a hospital were filled with them.

Which was why I was standing in the maternity ward, gazing at the newborn babies through the window.

It was the middle of the night or really early in the morning, depending on your point of view. Since I hadn't gone to sleep yet, I guess it felt more like the former than the latter.

It had been only a bit over twenty-four hours since my world had nearly ended.

Since Kade had almost died.

Kade Dennon. Ex-FBI agent, assassin-for-hire, cyber hacker with no fear of ever getting caught. He'd seemed larger than life. Unstoppable. Then he'd stepped into the path of a bullet to save his brother.

A few inches higher and it would have been the last thing he did.

The babies swam in my vision and I gasped for air, just then realizing I'd been holding my breath. My nails cut into my palms as I clenched my hands into fists. Holding myself together was getting harder and harder the longer Kade was unconscious.

I'd left the hospital earlier today for a few short hours. Mona had made me. A surrogate mother to Kade, she'd taken me under her wing as well, making me go home to change and eat something.

I hadn't wanted to take off the bloodstained brides-maid's dress I'd worn. It was stained with Kade's blood, and I felt an irrational fear that taking it off would make it seem as though I'd forgotten about him.

But I forced myself to put the dress carefully aside, shower, and pull on fresh clothes. I wasn't sure what—I just grabbed the first thing I touched when I opened my closet. Eating was out of the question. If I'd had any food in my fridge, which I didn't, there was no way I could've eaten it. My stomach was cramped in knots, and the thought of try-ing to get something down made me nauseous. All that mat-tered was getting back to the hospital. Back to Kade.

It was surreal, the people I passed as I drove back to the hospital. Everyone acted as though life were normal. My world had fallen apart, but the sun still shone like it was any other day.

Mona frowned when she saw me return so quickly. I gave her a wan smile and she sighed.

"He's going to be okay," she tried to reassure me. "The doctor said he'll recover. Trust them, Kathleen."

That's me. Kathleen Turner. It had nearly been Kathleen Kirk until my fiancé, Blane Kirk, had broken our engage-ment. He'd accused me of having an affair with his brother. His brother being Kade.

Blane Kirk was a Navy SEAL turned attorney and poli-tician. He was an expert at reading people, and it was nearly impossible to lie to him. Blane's accusation and our

2

subsequent breakup had broken my heart. He'd been wrong about Kade and me. We hadn't been having an affair . . . then.

Now, I wasn't so sure.

Kade had swept back into my life months after Blane and I broke up. He'd taken me to Las Vegas, shown me the town, partied with me Vegas-style. Then he'd made love to me. Told me he loved me. I hadn't realized until later that I was in love with him, too.

Now he lay unconscious in a hospital bed with two gunshot wounds, and he had no idea how I felt. Because I hadn't told him. Afraid it would only drive Blane and Kade further apart, I'd pretended to feel nothing, to want Blane only for his money and Kade for sex, practically daring them to hate me.

I'd prayed it would be enough to repair their relationship, broken because of me, and I had nearly succeeded. If Blane had been less intuitive, if both of them hadn't known me as well as they had, it might've worked. But they'd seen through my lies, my desperate gamble to remove myself from their lives.

I didn't know where things stood now, not really. A grief-stricken father had precluded any discussion, and Kade had stepped in front of a bullet intended for Blane, sacrificing himself for his brother without a second's hesitation.

Yes, they said Kade would recover, that he had made it through surgery okay, but that didn't relieve the guilt gnawing at me for how I'd treated him. And until he opened his eyes—until I could see for myself that he was still the Kade I knew—I could think of nothing else, *do* nothing else.

Blane and I sat through the day at Kade's bedside. We watched as they removed the ventilator, our hands tightly connected as we saw Kade's chest rise and fall on its own. We took turns running home, at Mona's behest, to change. Occasionally, one of us would take a break, leaving the other to keep vigil for a short time.

Which was how I found myself standing in the maternity ward staring at the babies.

One of them, a little boy, by the pale blue cap on his head, was fussing. Somehow he'd gotten his arms free from the blanket swaddling him, and his tiny hands were curled into fists as he cried.

A nurse walked over to him, scooping him up in her arms and settling him on her shoulder. She wandered closer to the glass as she shushed him. When she turned her back, I could see he'd quieted. He was wide-awake, his blue eyes open and taking in the world around him. He was beautiful, perfect, and it seemed as though our gazes met through the glass as he began sucking on his fist.

Pulling myself from my reverie, I glanced at my watch, surprised to see I'd been gone from Kade's room longer than I'd intended. Blane was probably wondering where I was.

Hurrying back, I was both relieved and disappointed to see that Kade was still unconscious. They wanted him to wake up on his own and I prayed that would be soon. The pain medication they had him on was heavy-duty.

Blane had fallen asleep in the corner armchair while I'd been gone, but even in sleep, his face was creased with lines of worry.

I sank into the plastic chair drawn up next to Kade's bed. His lax hand rested on top of the sheet covering him.

I curled my palm into his, carefully scrutinizing his face for any reaction.

His hair was inky black against the stark white pillow, the silky strands mussed. Reaching forward, I pushed back a lock that had fallen across his forehead. My fingers brushed his cheek, the stubble from two days' growth softly abrading my skin. I ached for his eyes to open, to hear his voice, for his lips to curve into that knowing smirk I knew so well—the kind that said he knew exactly what you were thinking. And it seemed he had always known what I was thinking, had always been looking out for me, from the moment we'd first met.

Carefully, I rested my head on Kade's arm, savoring the feel of his warm skin against my cheek. I closed my eyes and breathed in. Kade's scent was faint, the smell of medicine and antiseptic masking him. I let out a long sigh. I wished I could sleep—I was so tired—but I knew I wouldn't.

Kade's fingers twitched slightly in mine and I sat up with a start, my gaze flying to his face. His eyes were open, his gaze steady.

Emotion clogged my throat and I couldn't speak, my face crumpling into tears.

Kade's hand slowly lifted to my face. I covered his hand with mine, tipping my head into his palm cradling my cheek.

"Don't cry," he whispered. The ventilator had been rough on his throat and his voice was a low rasp.

Kade had always hated to see me cry, so I tried valiantly to stop. Turning my head, I pressed my lips to his palm, then forced a watery smile.

He opened his mouth again, but I pressed a finger to his lips. "Shhh. Don't try to talk."

He ignored me. Big surprise.

"C'mere," he said, the word barely audible. He tugged on my hand.

"I can't," I said, wondering if the pain medicine was making him a little loopy. "I'll hurt you."

"Bullshit. Need you."

Kade tugged again and this time tried to sit up, too. A grimace crossed his face. Alarmed, I put my hand on his shoulder to still him.

"Okay, okay," I said quietly. "Just lie down, all right?"

He lay back down on the bed with a sigh. I kicked off my flip-flops and climbed into the bed, carefully arranging myself on my side and trying not to disturb any of the equipment still hooked up to him. Kade wrapped one arm over my shoulders and pulled me closer.

It was him. He was alive, and judging by how he was already bossing me around, he was the same Kade. And despite everything I'd said—all those things that had hurt him—he still wanted me. Everything was going to be okay. Somehow.

Kade's lips pressed against my forehead. I looked up at him. His blue eyes were clear as he studied me.

"I love you," I whispered. "I'm sorry that I didn't tell you before. But I do. I love you."

Kade didn't react for a moment, and I was suddenly afraid that he hadn't understood—that the pain medication and being unconscious for so long had made him too groggy. But then he spoke, his words a low rasp in my ear.

"You would have to tell me that when I'm laid up in the fucking hospital," he said.

I huffed an unexpected laugh, and his soft smile made my heart feel lighter than it had in weeks. My whole body relaxed into him and my eyelids drooped. God, I was so tired . . .

~

Blane Kirk watched the scene from the shadows in the corner. He'd woken when Kat had settled into the chair by Kade, but had remained quiet. His heart had leapt when he saw Kade's eyes open, relief flooding him. Kade was okay, was going to recover.

Blane couldn't have lived with himself if his kid brother had died while saving his life.

The whispered words that Kat and Kade spoke had traveled across the room to Blane. Hearing Kat tell Kade she loved him had been like a hot knife sliding between Blane's ribs, even though he'd known for far longer than she had.

Where did the three of them go from here? Blane couldn't say. All he knew was that he loved Kade and Kathleen beyond anyone and anything else—and he'd do whatever he had to in order to see them both happy. If that cost him Kat forever, so be it, but he wasn't going to give up until he heard it from her own mouth that they were over. She loved Kade, but she loved him, too, which meant he still had a chance.

Blane could tell that Kat had fallen asleep, her body relaxed as she lay tucked next to Kade. Fiddling with the bed controls, Kade eased the bed up slightly so they weren't lying flat, but Kat didn't stir. Blane was glad she was asleep. She'd been awake for nearly forty-eight hours straight, almost dead on her feet from sheer exhaustion. Dark circles marred the delicate skin underneath her eyes, and her face was drawn and pale. The only thing Blane had seen her consume was coffee.

Not once had she blamed him, or had even hinted that she knew the whole reason Kade had nearly died was because of him. But then again, it wasn't in her character to think that way. If only Blane had realized that months ago. So many what-ifs . . .

What if Blane hadn't been so jealous of what he'd so clearly seen between Kade and Kathleen . . . If he hadn't listened to his uncle . . . If he had believed Kat instead of Robert . . . If he hadn't given in to old habits, using Kandi in a way that left him feeling ashamed now . . . If he hadn't been so angry that night, the night after he'd realized Kade and Kat were in Vegas together, sleeping together . . .

The *what-ifs* could paralyze him with regret.

Kade was stroking Kat's hair now, his fingers combing slowly through the long, strawberry-blonde locks. His expression was rapt as he gazed down at her, and if Blane had had any doubts as to the depth of Kade's feelings for Kat, they would have been washed away in that single, unguarded moment.

Suddenly, Blane felt like an intruder. The naked adoration on his brother's face was something private. Kade wouldn't appreciate that Blane was spying on them, even if it was unintentional.

Blane closed his eyes, then gave a big sigh and yawn. He stretched before opening his eyes again. As he'd expected, Kade's expression had shuttered, his gaze now on Blane rather than Kat.

Rising from the chair, Blane rubbed an imaginary crick in his neck as he walked toward the bed. It didn't escape his notice that Kade seemed to instinctively draw Kat closer, as if to claim her as his.

"You're awake," he said softly, so as to not disturb Kat. "How're you feeling?"

"Like I got shot," Kade deadpanned.

"That tends to happen when you get in the way of bullets."

Kade's lips twitched.

"Thought I was going to have to wake your ass up myself," Blane said. "She wasn't going to make it much longer if you didn't." He nodded toward Kat, who slept on, oblivious to the conversation taking place.

Kade glanced back down at her, his face softening.

"She's one tough chick," he whispered, brushing his knuckles gently down her cheek.

"In some ways," Blane agreed. "In some ways not."

Kade looked back to Blane, who met his gaze.

"Are we going to do this now, brother?" Kade asked, his voice deceptively smooth, though Blane could see a flicker of fear in his eyes. Kade's hold tightened on Kathleen, as though he was afraid that Blane would take her from him.

"You mean talk about the elephant in the room?" Blane said dryly, cocking an eyebrow.

"She'd get pretty pissed off if she heard you call her an elephant."

Blane grinned. Kade never failed to amuse him, even when they were talking about something so serious. For a moment he just reveled in the knowledge that Kade was alive, was going to be fine. Thank God.

Blane couldn't help reaching out, his fingers lightly grasping Kat's lax hand. She didn't stir. Kade's eyes narrowed, but he didn't protest Blane's touch. It seemed as though each of them wanted to mark her as his.

"She told me she loves you," Blane admitted, "and me. What that means, I have no idea. But we can talk about that later. For now I just want you to get better."

Kade's grip on Kathleen loosened, just a fraction.

Blane pretended not to notice, though his gut twisted. Too many mistakes and, eventually, you couldn't go back. He vowed not to make any more.

Blane glanced at his watch. "It's late, and I'm beat," he said with forced nonchalance. "Since you've reasserted your presence among the living and coherent, I'm going home to get some shut-eye. I'll be back in the morning."

"Sounds good," Kade said, resting his head against the pillow. His eyes slipped closed.

Blane turned away and headed for the door. Pulling it open, he glanced back one more time.

The dim lights cast a faded, golden glow over Kade and Kat. He'd resumed stroking her hair and she still hadn't moved.

"Kade," Blane said.

He glanced up.

"Thank you. For saving my life."

The ghost of a smile flitted across Kade's lips. "The least I could do," he said. "You saved mine first, remember?"

Blane shook his head sadly. "No, I didn't. Not really." He paused. "But she may have." His gaze fell on Kat as Kade's brow furrowed, then he turned and left, quietly closing the door behind him.

~

Sunlight streaming in through the window woke me in the morning. I squinted, and it took a moment for my sleep-fogged brain to realize where I was and who I was with.

Kade.

He'd finally regained consciousness last night, and now I lay curled into him, his arm slung over my shoulders and mine draped low across his abdomen. The heart monitor beat a quiet, reassuring rhythm while the IV hooked to Kade's left arm steadily dripped its fluid down the plastic tubing.

His eyes were closed, the evenness of his breathing signaling that he was sound asleep. I dearly wanted to wake him, see his eyes and hear his voice again, but I resisted the temptation. I knew he needed to rest.

Being careful not to disturb him, I eased out of the bed and slipped on my shoes. After using the bathroom and splashing water on my face, I felt more awake. The few hours of sleep I'd gotten by Kade's side was more than I'd had in days, though I was still tired. I felt like I could lie down and sleep for a week.

As I came out of the bathroom I suddenly realized . . . Blane wasn't there.

Maybe he'd gone downstairs for coffee or something? I prayed I was right, but knew it was more likely that he'd woken, seen me in bed with Kade, and left.

I hadn't meant to fall asleep. I'd just been so tired and so relieved to speak to Kade, but now I regretted climbing into bed with him. I didn't want to dwell on what Blane must be thinking.

The thought of Blane and Kade still being at odds, even after everything that had happened, had my stomach churning with nausea. Grabbing my purse, I decided to go get some coffee. Everything would look better once I had some caffeine in my system. Even hospital coffee was better than nothing.

Unfortunately, I didn't spot Blane in the cafeteria as I'd hoped I would. My heart sank. I must have been right in guessing that he'd left. Was he angry with me? He couldn't be angry at Kade, not after what he'd done to save Blane. I'd much rather have him mad at me, though I didn't want to hurt either Blane or Kade—I loved them both too much for that.

I sipped my coffee, loaded up with cream and sugar, as I headed back to Kade's room. The sound of voices greeted me as I drew closer to his partially open door. I recognized Mona's voice as she spoke, and her husband, Gerard's. Kade must have woken. They would be overjoyed to see him conscious again.

I paused outside the door, glancing in just long enough to see Kade sitting upright in the bed while Mona, Gerard, and Blane surrounded him. Mona laughed, likely at something Kade had said. I could hear his voice, a low rasp when he spoke, but it was too quiet for me to understand what he was saying. They were all smiling, even Blane.

I thought about going in—I wanted to go in—but my feet wouldn't obey.

They were all there together, happy. A family. If I went in, there'd be tension, putting a strain on everyone. Blane's smile would become forced. Kade would be stressed, the last thing he needed as his body tried to recover. Mona and Gerard wouldn't know what to say, since no one would want to talk about the elephant in the room.

Me.

I didn't want that, for any of them. So I did the only thing I could think of doing.

I turned around . . . and I left.

KATHLEEN

CHAPTER ONE

Counting. Counting minutes and hours until time passed, because the more time that passed, the less I'd hurt. Or at least, that's what everyone always said: *Time heals.* I wasn't sure how much I believed that.

I was in an unwinnable situation. In love with two men—two brothers—and the consequences of that would hurt us all. So I'd taken myself out of the equation, again, but that didn't stop the ache in my chest or the acid eating in my stomach as I unlocked my apartment door and let myself inside.

Tigger wrapped himself around my legs, nearly making me stumble. I guess he'd missed me. I reached down to scratch behind his ears and was immediately rewarded with loud purring.

Aimlessly, I went to the refrigerator, staring into its lit depths. Nothing seemed appealing, not that there was a lot to choose from anyway. Going to the cabinet, I grabbed a bag of animal crackers and retreated to the couch.

I munched, trying not to think. Yet I couldn't stop myself from seeing Blane and Kade inside my head. The first night Blane had brought me home when my car had died, the night he'd stayed when Sheila had been murdered. The

Christmas tree we'd decorated together and the many meals we'd shared while curled up on the couch.

And Kade. The morning he'd been there in the nick of time when I was being chased by a man who would have killed me. He'd sat with me, staring daggers at me, a sneer curling his lips. Playing bodyguard when he'd seemed barely able to tolerate my presence. The night he'd been wounded and collapsed on my couch, to when he'd shown up on my doorstep just a few weeks ago, his mere presence breaking through the ice encasing my emotions.

What was I going to do?

A part of my mind asked a question I wasn't sure I wanted to answer. If I had it all to do over again, would I have gotten involved with Blane? If I hadn't, I wouldn't be hurting like this.

The truth was something I didn't want to face, because I cringed from what it said about me. Yes, I would do it all over again . . . because I'd not only fallen in love with Blane, I'd also fallen in love with Kade.

My nearly nonexistent appetite disappeared completely and I set aside the crackers.

Even as I loved Blane, Kade had also made his way into my heart. That had become crystal clear in the hours I'd spent waiting to see if he'd live or die. So what did that make me? The kind of person I swore I'd never be—someone who could come between Blane and Kade.

What would happen to the three of us? Kade loved me— he'd told me so—but had offered me nothing that he hadn't rescinded. When he'd been lying on the hard ground, his blood coating my hands and each breath possibly his last, all the worry and heartache over what I felt for Blane—what my admitting that I'd fallen in love with Kade would do to him—had paled in significance to the very real possibility that I might lose Kade forever.

Priorities tend to shift in the face of death. While I'd faced my own mortality before, I hadn't until that moment faced Kade's.

I couldn't pinpoint where or when it had happened. It wasn't like one moment I hadn't loved Kade, and the next I had. It had been gradual, creeping up on me when I wasn't looking.

I shouldn't love him, not like this. By all rights, I should want to be with Blane. Blane was the good guy, the white knight. He wanted the same things I did—a settled life together and a family. His career had great potential and he was good at what he did. We were a good pair, had a good time together. Blane loved me, and yes, I loved him, too.

Yet Kade and I clicked, like two puzzle pieces fitting together. It shouldn't work, shouldn't be like that. Kade had done awful things. He'd been paid to kill people, and I'd never been brave enough to ask how many. He broke the law on an almost daily basis and displayed an alarming lack of concern as to what would happen to him if he ever got caught. My parents would roll over in their graves if they knew I'd fallen in love with such a person.

But I'd seen firsthand that there was more to Kade than what he allowed people to see. He'd let me in through the chinks in his armor. He did care, had cared about me right from the start, no matter what his mouth had said to the contrary. Kade may have been insulting me and cursing me six ways from Sunday, but he'd protected me from harm and saved me from certain death many times over. Whether it was as simple a thing as carrying me across a gravel lot so my feet wouldn't get torn up, to pulling me from a car set to explode, to doing the impossible and finding me chained in a shed in the middle of nowhere.

It was dangerous, loving Kade. My run-in with Garrett had taught me that. Using me as leverage, Garrett would have killed me, if not for Kade's timely arrival. Who was to say that wouldn't happen again? There were probably a dozen people or more who could want Kade dead. I would be a weakness, an Achilles' heel that could end up hurting him. Who's to say that he would want to be together, even now? He'd once told me, *You're the most vulnerable part of me. A year ago, I would have killed you myself if I'd known.* And I hadn't doubted him.

But what would I do if Kade *did* offer me something? Would I take it? Hurting Blane in the process and losing him from my life? Or could I spend my life with Blane and hope my feelings for Kade would fade over time? No matter what I did, I'd be that person who came between two brothers. I didn't know if I could live with that, but neither could I live without them.

I was too tired to think anymore, so I got off the couch and crawled into bed. The apartment was sweltering as the sun climbed into the sky. My head hit the pillow and I sighed, closing my eyes.

In the end, the only thing I might have to show for falling in love with Blane and Kade was a lonely bed and a broken heart.

I woke when it was late afternoon. Shadows were long in my room as I opened my eyes. I was cool and comfortable, and it took a moment for me to realize I was mostly lying on top of someone, my leg nestled between his. I jerked my head up in surprise, and green eyes met mine.

Blane.

The gentle affection in his gaze made words die on my tongue.

My heart ached at the warm strength of him and I rested my head on his chest with a sigh. One arm was curved around me, holding me in place. The other lifted to touch my hair, his fingers combing slowly through the strands.

"How long have you been here?" I asked quietly. I slid my hand over his shoulder, savoring the opportunity I'd just been handed to nestle more closely to him.

"Since shortly after you left the hospital," he said. His voice rumbled in his chest. "Why did you leave?"

I gave a little shrug. "I didn't belong. Don't belong."

Blane's hand stilled, then moved to my chin, turning my face up to his.

"You belong with me."

The absolute certainty in his voice made my insides warm. I opened my mouth to reply but didn't get the chance.

Blane started kissing me, his tongue stroking mine. There was no urgency in his kiss, it was languid and sweet, as though nothing had broken between us. And just when my thoughts caught up with my actions and I was about to pull away, he did.

I stared at him in confusion, but he just smiled and brushed the hair back from my face.

"What are you doing?" I managed.

"Kissing you," he said simply.

I was utterly confused. I'd told Blane I was in love with his brother. He should be yelling at me, looking at me in loathing and disgust, not holding me, gazing at me as if I were the most precious thing in the world.

"Why?" I asked.

"Because I wanted to."

I couldn't think what to say, still bemused by his actions.

"I'm not giving you up without a fight, Kat," he said. "Until you make your choice, I'm not going anywhere."

My eyebrows flew up at that and I scrambled off him and out of the bed. "Choice?" I asked as he sat up. "What do you mean, 'your choice'?"

"Me or Kade," Blane answered, looking at me as though this were obvious.

I was already shaking my head. "No, I'm not doing that." I backed up rapidly, hit the wall, turned, and hurried into the kitchen. Blane was right behind me.

"What do you mean?" he asked, latching onto my wrist and pulling me to a stop.

"I'm not doing that!" I exclaimed, horrified at the thought. "You make it sound like I'm picking which pair of shoes to wear or what movie I should go see. You and Kade are *brothers*. I am *not* choosing one of you." Though the thought had occurred to me just hours ago, hearing Blane spell it out made me cringe in mortification.

Blane's expression was unreadable as he stared at me. He let go of my wrist, pushing his hands into the pockets of his slacks as he leaned back against the wall.

"You have to," he said with a shrug.

"Forget it," I shot back. My mind was already playing the scenario in my head, me choosing a brother, forever alienating the one who remained. The one I chose resenting me for coming between them. Losing them both from my life, forever.

"I'm not . . . I can't . . ." Suddenly, it was hard to breathe, anxiety swelling in my chest.

Blane was next to me in an instant, his hands wrapped around my arms to hold me steady. Worry and concern now creased his features.

My voice was a choked whisper. "I can't . . . lose . . . both of you. I just . . . I can't." I shook my head, trying to dislodge the images in my mind. I stared up at him, willing him to understand.

It was the best I could do to explain it, the terror and despair that loomed at the mere thought of Kade and Blane no longer being in my life. I'd be alone, having lost the men I loved—the men who'd come to be my whole world. What I'd felt when Blane and I had split up four months ago would be a mere shadow compared to the agony I'd feel now if I lost them.

"What do you think is going to happen, Kat?" Blane asked with a frown. "It's not like we can share you." He seemed genuinely confused.

"I know it's not fair," I admitted, "but I'm not going to be what breaks you and Kade. Not now. Not after all that's happened. We can be . . . friends." A laughable goal, but it was all I could come up with.

"Do you need more time?" Blane asked, completely ignoring my friends comment. "Of course. It's too soon. Kade's still recovering and you've been pushed to the edge of your endurance." He looked vaguely relieved, brushing the back of his knuckles down my cheek. The sweet touch made me ache inside.

Time. That sounded good. I latched onto that. "Yeah. I just need . . . some time." I ignored that it'd be borrowed time. I was sure it wouldn't take long before they'd tire of waiting for me to make a choice that my conscience wouldn't allow me to make.

Blane studied me intently, as though seeing through my pathetic desperation. "You should know I won't just walk away, Kat. And I know my brother. Neither will he."

I swallowed, my stomach clenching into a hard knot. I didn't believe him, not really. Eventually I'd lose them both, and all I wanted right now was to put that moment off for as long as possible. It made me incredibly selfish, but I couldn't seem to stop myself. Holding on to Blane and Kade felt like an act of self-preservation.

"Are you going back?" I asked, anxious to change the subject. "To the hospital?"

"Yes."

I eased out of Blane's hold and he let me step away. "Tell him . . . tell him I said hi, would you?"

"You're not coming?"

"I have to go to work," I explained, glancing at the clock. I had to get moving if I wanted to shower first. "Did you turn on the air-conditioning?"

"Yes," Blane said, snagging me around the waist as I made to pass by. I looked up at him in surprise. "Don't turn it off," he ordered. "I'll pay the fucking bill. Just leave it on."

"I can't—"

"Leave it," he ordered again, interrupting me. He seemed pretty adamant about this, and considering the conversation we'd just had, I wasn't anxious to test his patience further. I nodded.

"Okay."

Before I could say anything more, Blane had me pressed against the wall, his body hard against mine, his mouth pressing my lips apart. I sucked in a breath, my pulse kicking into high gear as Blane proceeded to remind me of just how well he did this sort of thing.

It was several minutes before we came up for air and I found my fingers pressing hard into Blane's shoulders.

"Sooner or later, you'll choose," he whispered. "You'll want one of us more than you don't want to hurt the other. And you'll choose. I want to be the one you can't live without."

I stared up into his eyes, a brilliant green boring into mine. Then he was out the door and gone, leaving me trying to figure out what the hell had just happened.

~

Work was slow, which made it hard to stay awake. Even my nap today hadn't been enough to curb how tired I was. I ate a little, not really having a choice when Jeff set a plate down in front of me and glared until I took a bite. Nothing seemed to taste good. I chalked it up to too much stress.

"What's up with you?" Tish asked, leaning against the bar and watching me dry glasses.

"Just tired. Stressed," I replied.

"Boyfriend trouble?" She grinned. "Please tell me you took tall, dark, and dangerous for a spin."

I gave a small laugh even as my face heated. Her description of Kade was apt.

"Good for you," she said, easily reading my embarrassment.

I shook my head. "No. Everything's just . . . completely complicated now."

"Sex has a way of doing that," she commiserated. "You seeing him tonight?"

I hadn't told her that Kade had been shot, so I explained what had happened. When I finished, her eyes were wide.

"He took a bullet for Blane?" she asked. I nodded. "And now Blane wants you to choose, him or Kade?" I nodded again.

She rolled her eyes, unsuccessfully trying to hide a grin. "Girl, to have such problems. I'm finding it real hard to be sympathetic."

I smacked her lightly on the arm even as I laughed. "This is serious," I said. "I have no idea what to do. I told Blane I wasn't going to choose, that we could, you know, all be friends." It still sounded ridiculous and Tish must've agreed, because she gave a snort of derision.

"What'd he say?" she asked.

"He kissed me."

She whistled. "Gotta like his style, girl."

"You are absolutely no help whatsoever," I complained.

Tish spotted new customers walking in and pushed away from the bar. "I know," she said, "but if you need pointers on a threesome, you just let me know." She winked.

"Tish!" I exclaimed, but she was already sashaying toward the new table.

I rolled my eyes, sliding the now clean and dry martini glasses into the freezer before turning away to fill another order.

I was the last one to leave after we'd closed, though Jeff had hung around until it was time to go. Since I'd been attacked by James Gage, the district attorney for Indy, a couple of weeks ago, Romeo had insisted that there always had to be at least two people to finish up after closing.

Once I was in my car, I sat for a moment, thinking. I was exhausted, but I wanted to see Kade. I didn't know how many times it would take of seeing him awake and talking before the worry eased in the back of my mind, I just knew I wasn't there yet.

Twenty minutes later, I was parking in the hospital lot and heading inside. Visiting hours were long since over, but I managed not to run into any staff on my way to Kade's room. The hallways were dim and I stepped as lightly as I could. When I reached Kade's door, I paused and peeked through the window.

It was dark inside and I knew he was probably sleeping. I'd just pop in for a minute, then leave.

Carefully easing open the door, I slipped into the room. The door drifted closed behind me and I waited, letting my eyes adjust to the darkness. After a moment, I stepped farther inside, listening intently.

I could hear machines, their quiet whirring as they monitored Kade's vitals and dripped fluid into his arm. My eyes had adjusted and now I could see the outline of his form on the bed. Without even noticing I'd moved, I realized I stood beside him. I watched carefully as his chest rose and fell with even, deep breaths.

My whole body relaxed. My fingers itched to touch him, but I curled my hands into fists so I wouldn't. What if he hadn't made it? What would I have done then? I couldn't think about it. I'd drive myself crazy.

I had to touch some part of him, so I settled for resting my palm near where his hand lay on top of the covers. If I tried hard enough, it seemed I could feel the heat from his body through my skin.

"About fucking time."

I started violently at the sound of his voice, jerking my hand away. "I . . . I didn't realize you were awake," I managed to stammer. My face flushed and I was glad the room was dark.

"So I gathered."

The dry note in his voice made my lips hover in a smile, but I was inexplicably nervous and embarrassed that Kade had caught me unawares.

"I, um, didn't mean to disturb you," I said weakly. "I was just on my way home from work."

"You live in the opposite direction."

I pressed my lips together and didn't speak. I didn't have to. We both knew why I was there.

Kade reached for me, his hand catching hold of my elbow and tugging. I obeyed the silent demand, slipping off my shoes before climbing into bed beside him. His arm wrapped around my shoulders as I nestled into his side.

"How are you feeling?" I asked.

"Confined."

I smiled. Yes, Kade would feel that way.

"Are you being nice to the nurses?" I asked.

"One of them tried to give me a sponge bath," he replied.

I could imagine the fight it had been to determine who got the honor of giving Kade a sponge bath. "Was she pretty?" I asked, hearing the bitchy in my voice too late.

I felt more than heard Kade's huff of laughter. "Is that jealousy I hear?" he teased.

I didn't answer, instead burying my burning face into his side, which just made him laugh again.

"Would you still be pissed if I said she was ugly?"

"Who said I was pissed?" I protested.

"I love your jealous, bitchy side," Kade whispered in my ear. The touch of his breath against my skin made me shiver. His hand drifted down to my waist, his fingers tugging my shirt free until he could touch my skin. "Blane said we're all supposed to be friends now, that supposedly you're not going to pick a side." I could hear the amusement in his voice.

I stiffened, wondering what exactly from our conversation Blane had repeated to Kade.

"Need I remind you of what a bad idea the friend zone is for us?" he continued. His fingers trailed a feather-light path along my side and up my rib cage.

I swallowed. "It's the only solution. I'm not going to pick one of you over the other."

"So what are we then?" His fingers traced the outline of my ribs while my pulse beat a rapid staccato in my chest. My breath was much too fast and too shallow. "Friends with benefits?"

"I don't want to lose you," I whispered, tears stinging my eyes.

"I'm not going anywhere."

We fell asleep like that, the warmth of his palm pressed against my side, his thumb lightly brushing the tender skin under my breast.

When I woke up, the sun had just peeked over the horizon. Kade was still sound asleep, no doubt the timed pain medication had taken hold at some point, sending him into a deep slumber. Reaching up, I brushed a lock of inky-black hair from his forehead before easing out of the bed.

I put on my shoes and used the bathroom, splashing some cold water on my face to wake up. While I'd been relieved to be with Kade last night, I hadn't slept well. Each move or noise he made had caused me to come awake, my subconscious still steeped in anxiety about him.

To my chagrin, I ran into Blane in the hallway. He looked surprised to see me.

"Did you come by this morning or last night?" he asked.

I wondered what the correct answer would be, as his tone had definitely changed when he'd said "last night." I decided to be honest.

"I came by after work," I said.

Blane gave a brief nod, then took a sip of the coffee he held. "That was kind of you to keep him company."

There hadn't been anything "kind" for the reasons I'd had. I'd needed to see him, especially after what I'd said to him when he'd woken up. Since the daytime would mean running into Mona, Gerard, and Blane, the nighttime was preferable.

"I, um, I gotta go," I said, the awkwardness getting to me.

"Sure," Blane said easily. "I'm sure you're exhausted."

Okay, I was positive I heard a slight note of bitterness in that last part, but he was already past me and stepping into Kade's room.

I headed home, where I showered and did my laundry. I had to go to work earlier than usual because I was filling in for Scott this week. He was out of town and had asked if I'd cover his shifts. Since he'd done the same for me on more than one occasion, I didn't mind saying yes, but that meant I'd be spending the bulk of my days and evenings at The Drop for the next several days.

I went by the hospital again that night after work, crawling into bed with Kade without being asked. The pain medication was easing up so he was awake, and we talked.

We didn't talk about Blane, or the future, or being friends. We talked about ourselves and our past, me more so than Kade, though he did tell me a couple of things from his childhood, like how he'd gotten the scars on his back and the one on his chest. Tears had dripped from my face onto his chest as he talked, his voice quiet in the darkened room. My imagination painted too vivid a picture of a child version of Kade, and the pain he'd endured made my heart hurt.

He told me about the first time he'd killed a man, and why. I told him the story of the night my dad died. He told me of the morning his mother didn't wake up. I spoke of how hard it had been to sell my parents' house and move away from home. He finally told me the story of the dragon tattoo on his arm, and I confessed how I'd almost gotten my navel pierced on a friend's dare my senior year of high school, but had chickened out. Kade had chuckled at that.

Eventually, we fell silent, the rise and fall of his chest under my cheek lulling me to sleep in the wee hours of the morning.

The aroma of fresh coffee greeted me when next I opened my eyes. I sat up from where I'd been slumped, wincing as my neck and back gave sharp protests. I automatically glanced next to me, but Kade was gone.

"They took him for another X-ray."

I jerked around to see Blane leaning against the wall, sipping a cup of coffee. He looked put together, his hair perfect, his jaw freshly shaven, clothes clean and unrumpled. I self-consciously combed my fingers through my hair, knowing I had to look a mess.

"Here," Blane said, handing me another cup.

"Thanks," I said. I took a small sip of the steaming brew, grateful Blane must have stopped at a coffee shop on the way rather than getting the hospital's version. I didn't think too hard about how he'd obviously known I'd be at the hospital.

I disappeared into the bathroom, trying to make myself look like I hadn't spent the night scrunched next to Kade in a hospital bed. I didn't think I was successful. Without makeup, I looked paler than usual and the circles under my eyes added ten years to my age. My stomach was complaining, too, though I didn't really feel like eating.

When I came back out, Blane was still there and Kade still wasn't.

"I, ah, guess I'll head home," I said, feeling incredibly awkward. Blane and I hadn't really talked since he'd kissed me in my kitchen, and I was unsure how to behave around him. I couldn't read if he was angry with me, had changed his mind about us being friends, or was just taking all this weirdness in stride.

Blane nodded. "I'll let him know."

I turned and left without another word.

The days seem to speed by, each one mostly like the one before, until they blended together in my exhausted brain. I spent what time I could at the hospital, going by after I got off work. And I had to work almost every night, covering my shifts as well as Scott's. I'd crawl into bed with Kade and we'd talk for a while. I'd tell him about my day while he played with my hair. In the morning, I'd leave, trying to be gone before Blane got there without being obvious about it. I didn't want to run into him again, couldn't handle his seeming indifference and the awkwardness between us.

My schedule played havoc with my sleep patterns, and it seemed that no matter what I did, I was always tired. When I came home from the hospital in the mornings, I showered, ran errands, and did chores. Most days I had to be at work by four, so it was like each one passed in the blink of an eye. Eating was an afterthought. Guilt tarnished the happiness I felt about Kade and me growing closer, and the only respite I found was in the dark of night when I was in his arms. When I could pretend nothing outside of that room existed.

Kade was asleep this morning as I slid from the bed. I slipped quietly out the door and into the hallway, turned, and nearly ran right into someone.

"I'm sor—" I looked up into Blane's eyes and my words died mid-apology.

"Morning, Kat," he said, seeming completely unsurprised to find me there. He handed me one of the two cups of coffee he held. "You look a little tired."

Self-consciously, I tried to smooth my hair. My pony-tail had loosened during the night and I knew from the bathroom mirror that my makeup was long gone. I'd just climbed out of bed and I looked it. Whereas Blane was again impeccably dressed in full suit and tie, the knotted silk perfect at his throat against the crisp white linen of his shirt. His jaw was smooth and freshly shaved, and his dark blond hair didn't have a strand out of place. I could smell the scent of his cologne, which made me want to lean closer for a better whiff. A bad idea.

"Um, yeah," I said nervously. "Hospitals aren't exactly conducive to sleep." I took a quick gulp of the coffee, immediately regretting it when the hot liquid scalded my tongue. Shit, that hurt.

"How's he doing?"

"Good," I said. "He seemed good."

"They said he's healing really well," Blane said.

"I'm glad," I replied. This was different, Blane talking to me again. He didn't seem angry that I was spending so much time with Kade. I was glad. I missed Blane, but could do nothing but take my cue from him on our relationship status.

"Do you have to work tonight?" he asked, leaning his shoulder against the wall. Somehow he'd moved closer to me.

I thought for a minute, then shook my head. "I'm covering for Scott this week so I'm working through the weekend, but I'm off tonight." I'd planned on sleeping.

"Why are you covering for Scott?"

"He's out of town and he asked," I said with a shrug. "I don't mind." And I needed the money.

"Of course you don't," Blane muttered with a sigh, glancing away.

I frowned. "What's that supposed to mean?"

His gaze returned to me. "It means you've been through a lot. You look like you can barely stand because you're so exhausted, and you must've lost ten pounds that you couldn't afford to lose the past couple of weeks. You need rest, not to be covering Scott's shifts."

I was sorry I'd asked.

"Go home and take a nap," Blane said, taking a sip of his coffee. "I'll be by later and take you to dinner."

Dinner? That sounded alarmingly like a date.

"I can't . . . we shouldn't . . ." I stammered.

Blane stepped even closer, halting my words and forcing me to tip my head back to see his eyes. The warm scent of him wrapped around me like a blanket. "If you're spending your nights with Kade, I should at least get dinner, don't you think?" The low rasp of his voice made my pulse jump.

I didn't know what to say. I swallowed hard and nodded.

Blane smiled. "Good. Then I'll see you tonight." He brushed a kiss to my forehead, then moved past me into Kade's room. The door closed behind him, leaving me alone in the hallway.

∽

Mindful of Blane's comments about my appearance, I made a concerted effort to buy some groceries, eat lunch, and take a nap. It pricked my vanity, the things he'd said, so I took great care as I dressed for dinner.

"It's not a date," I muttered to myself as I flung hanger after hanger of clothes onto my bed, discarding each outfit in turn. And yet I was as nervous as I'd been that first night when Blane had given me a lift and walked me to my door.

Finally, I settled on a deep navy dress with cap sleeves and a V-neck. The skirt was why I'd bought the dress. It ended right above my knees, but from mid-thigh down, it was made of tulle with two thin strips of fabric that wrapped around the skirt. The result was that it was kind of see-through, because of the tulle, but not tacky, because of the fabric.

The color brought out my eyes and contrasted nicely with my long hair, which I curled and left loose. As I stood in my bedroom, surveying the results in the mirror, I caught sight of my jewelry box.

I opened it, eyeing for several long moments the sapphire pendant and earrings Blane had given me. They would go much better with the dress than the gold locket I was wearing.

Hesitantly, I removed the locket, setting it carefully aside before I added the sapphire jewelry. I felt odd, as though somehow I was betraying Kade.

The doorbell rang and I shook off the feeling, slipping on a pair of navy heels before going to answer the door.

It was déjà vu, opening the door to see Blane filling the space. His suit looked as fresh and polished as it had hours earlier. Light glinted briefly off one cuff link as he pushed his fingers through his hair and smiled wide enough to show the dimple in his cheek. The white of his teeth gleamed in the dusky light.

"You look . . ." He shook his head, as though any adjective he might use was inadequate. His voice trailed away as his gaze swept me from head to toe and back, lingering briefly on the pendant nestled in my cleavage. Appreciation and lust gleamed in his eyes, which, I decided, was compliment enough.

"These are for you," he said, handing me a bouquet of red roses.

Surprised, I automatically took them. It had been a long time since Blane had brought me flowers. Their heady fragrance was divine and I buried my nose in the velvety depths.

"Thank you," I said, stepping back to let him in. I went to the kitchen and reached for the cabinet above the stove for a vase.

"Here, I'll get it," Blane offered, and I had to suck in a breath.

He was standing right behind me, so close I could feel the brush of his body against mine as he stretched up to retrieve the vase. My hormones kicked into high gear and I bit my lip hard. Whatever problems Blane and I had, they'd never been in the bedroom, and my body was forcefully reminding me of that fact.

Blane took his time getting the vase down, his hips pressing lightly into my backside as he moved, then he gently set the vase on the counter and took a step back. I couldn't tell if he was doing it on purpose, or if I was imagining things.

I arranged the roses and added water to the vase before grabbing my purse.

"Ready?" Blane asked.

"Ready," I said too brightly.

He opened the door and I stepped through, not at all sure if I was ready for my non-date with Blane.

CHAPTER TWO

That feeling of déjà vu got stronger as Blane took me to the first restaurant we'd ever been to together. Now, though, he knew of my distaste for stools and we were led to a booth instead of the bar area. It was on the top level in a cozy corner.

"Good evening, Mr. Kirk."

It was even the same waiter we'd had that first time, I realized, my eyebrows climbing.

"Evening, Greg," Blane said. "I'd like a Dewars and water, please, and the lady would like . . ." His eyes were on mine as he said, "The lady would like a manhattan." The hint of a smile tugged at Blane's lips.

"You remembered," I said, somewhat surprised. Bourbon wasn't usually my drink of choice, but it had been what I'd ordered that night.

"Of course I do," Blane said, settling back in the chair. "You were suspicious of me, and wary. And every time you evaded my questions, my curiosity grew tenfold."

"You can hardly blame me," I retorted with a grin, blushing. "I'd seen you go through women the way you go through ties."

"Not anymore," he replied, his voice soft. "Not after you."

My blush grew warmer and I had to look away from his intent gaze. Picking up the menu, I pretended to look it over, though I didn't really read a thing printed on it.

"And just so we're clear," Blane said, "I'm *taking* you to dinner, so order what you want."

He hadn't bothered with the menu, probably because he already knew it by heart.

"You don't have to—"

"I know I don't have to," Blane interrupted. "I want to."

Greg came back with the drinks, and after a moment's hesitation I ordered the scallops. Blane ordered a steak and added a shrimp cocktail appetizer.

Blane loved good food and when the appetizer was set between us, he dug in. I watched with too much interest as his long fingers dipped a shrimp and carried it to his mouth.

"You have to have some," he insisted, dipping another piece and offering it to me.

I reached to take it from him, but he pulled it back.

"Uh-uh," he said, a teasing note in his voice.

I lowered my hand and he held the morsel out again. My eyes narrowed. I didn't think I'd ever seen Blane quite so . . . playful before.

Giving a mental shrug, I leaned forward and let him feed me. The cold seafood combined with the heat of the sauce on my tongue, but it seemed I barely tasted it at all, too consumed was I with how Blane was watching me.

"Did I ever tell you about when I beat up James that first time?" he asked out of the blue.

I shook my head, recalling all too clearly how furious Blane had been when he'd seen the bruise on my face from when James had hit me.

"Well . . ." he began, settling back again. His fingers toyed with his drink as he told me the story of ruining James's golf outing, provoking a fight so he could kick his ass, and managing to get James thrown out of the club. By the time he'd finished the story, our entrées had arrived.

I laughed as Blane described his feigned outrage that'd had the club's manager falling all over himself apologizing for James.

Blane kept me entertained and laughing all through dinner, ordering a bottle of wine when our cocktails were empty and making me split dessert with him. When we finally left the restaurant, I was pleasantly tipsy and in a better mood than I'd felt in weeks.

I wasn't too steady climbing the stairs to my apartment, and Blane kept his arm locked firmly around my waist as I giggled my way to the door. When I reached it, I leaned my back against the wood with a sigh.

"I had a nice time on our non-date," I said with a smile.

Blane braced his hands on either side of my head as he leaned into me. "Me too," he said. His eyes gleamed in the dark, the corners of his lips tipping up ever so slightly.

His cologne was a faint trace of scent now and I inhaled greedily.

"You smell nice," I breathed, then realized I'd said that out loud. Maybe I was a bit more than tipsy?

"So do you," Blane replied, his body moving closer to mine. The deep timbre of his voice washed over me, doing funny things to my insides.

Blane's tie caught my eye. It dangled between us, the knot slightly loosened at his neck. I reached up, the silk soft between my fingers, and tugged.

Blane needed no more urging and I whimpered when his lips met mine, heat flaring between us immediately. He tasted of wine and his own unique flavor. My hands pressed against the hard planes of his chest, creeping up to wind around his neck until my fingers were buried in his hair.

My mind was a complete blank, thoughts incoherent as Blane's mouth moved to skate down my neck, nipping and sucking until my blood was on fire. I tugged at his hair and he obeyed my silent request, his lips returning to mine.

His body was pressed against me, his hands spanning my waist, and the hard length of his erection prodding my abdomen made the flesh between my thighs ache.

Light flooded the terrace and I blinked in the sudden brightness. Blane pulled back, his body protectively shielding mine as he glanced around.

"Oh, I'm sorry," Alisha said, peering out her door. Bits was in her arms. "I was just taking Bits out for his evening toodles." Her voice said she wasn't a bit sorry and the look she gave me had a flush creeping up my neck.

"Um, that's okay," I said, lightly pushing against Blane's chest until he took a step back. I took a shaky breath, trying to regain my equilibrium.

Alisha and Bits headed down the stairs. We watched them in silence, then Blane turned back to me, his expression slightly sardonic.

"I'd better go," he said, and I nodded.

"Thanks again for dinner," I said, my voice a little too breathless.

"I'll call you," Blane said. Leaning down, his lips brushed mine again, then he was jogging down the stairs to his car. A moment later, the Jag was roaring out of the lot.

I wanted to be in my apartment before Alisha came back up, but I wasn't quick enough.

"What the hell?" she said, rushing up the stairs. Poor Bits was dragged the last few steps. "Since when are you seeing Blane again?"

Alisha still held a grudge against Blane for breaking our engagement, not that I blamed her. She'd seen me fall apart and hers had been the shoulder I'd cried on.

"I'm not," I protested. "Not . . . really." Finally, I managed to unlock my door, but Alisha followed me inside. Bits ran to greet Tigger, who acted like he wasn't pleased as could be to see his canine buddy.

"Did I not just see you making out with him?"

"Yeah, but we just went to dinner, and there was wine, and I dunno . . ." I avoided eye contact as I tossed my purse onto the kitchen table.

"So he got you drunk?" Alisha asked, appalled.

"No, of course not," I protested. "I don't know what's going on. He knows I slept with Kade, but—"

"You slept with Kade?" Her voice was a near screech. "And didn't *tell* me?"

I collapsed on the couch, laughing a little at her incredulity.

"It was in Vegas," I explained. "After Blane and I broke up. But then he didn't remember, so it didn't matter, and then he did, and then he got shot." I sighed. Recounting the recent history between Kade and me had sobered me right up. "Now Blane seems intent on making me pick him, even though I said I wouldn't choose between him and Kade."

I covered my face with my hands. "Oh God, what am I going to do?" I moaned.

"Don't care," Alisha said, plopping down next to me. "I want details."

"Alisha!"

"Kade seems like he'd be really good, lots of stamina. Was he good?"

I laughed at the eager excitement on her face. "I can't believe you're asking me that," I said.

"Are you kidding?" she protested. "He's stunningly gorgeous, saved you from being blown up, and oozes sex. Of *course* I want to know how it was!"

Alisha was completely unrepentant about her avid curiosity, which made me laugh despite myself.

"It was . . ." I searched for the right word, images replaying inside my head of Kade and me making love in Vegas, and again in the warm sunshine of an Indiana July afternoon. "It was . . . the best," I said simply, shrugging. I couldn't help the small smile tugging at my lips.

Alisha squealed in delight, throwing her arms around me in an exuberant hug, but then she suddenly pulled back, a frown on her face.

"So then why were you making out with Blane?" she asked.

My smile melted away. "Because a long-term thing with Kade is out of the question," I said. "The closest he ever got to it was asking me to stay with him when we were in Vegas, but then he took it back."

"Took it back? What do you mean?"

"He said it was too dangerous for me to be around him," I explained. "So, yeah, I'm in love with him, but what's the point? It's not like he proposed."

"And Blane?"

I remembered what Blane had said outside The Drop when we'd both been afraid he was heading to jail for Kandi's murder: *If I get out of this, if I still have a name worth giving to you, please tell me you'll give us another chance. I can offer you more than Kade ever can or will.*

"Blane still wants to marry me," I said. "I think. Maybe."

"Is that what you want?"

I thought about it. Part of me longed to settle down, build a home, a family, a life. But the other part of me wavered in indecision, and I wasn't sure if it was because I didn't think I was ready for that, or if I didn't know who I wanted to settle down with.

"I don't know," I finally answered. "I don't want to choose between them. It just seems wrong. They're brothers."

Kade wasn't exactly a "settle down" kind of guy. Would being with him mean I'd have to give up having a family? Kids? But then again, I had to remember that he hadn't offered me anything. Despite all we'd shared with each other in the darkened hospital room, future plans had not been discussed.

Whereas Blane had been clear about a future with him. He wanted to get married and start a family. When I'd apologized months ago for a pregnancy scare, he'd simply smiled and replied, *I wasn't scared.*

Alisha sighed, sitting back against the couch and staring off into space like I was.

"Well, we could make a list of pros and cons?" she said, making it a question.

I turned and looked at her.

"It was just a suggestion," she muttered. She thought for a moment. "I guess it comes down to . . . who you love more, doesn't it?"

"I'm not choosing," I said again.

We sat in contemplative silence for a few minutes, then Alisha stood.

"Well, I don't have to tell you who I'd pick," she said with a snort. "And as captivating as the soap opera of your life has become, I've still got to get to bed. Let me know if you need anything." She gathered Bits in her arms while I stood, then gave me a hug. I walked her to the door.

"Love you," she called as she left.

"Love you, too," I replied, closing and locking the door behind her.

I cleaned the makeup off my face, brushed my teeth, and ran a brush through my hair. After changing into pajamas of knit shorts and a tank, I crawled into bed.

As tired as I was, though, I couldn't sleep. I watched the minutes tick by on the clock, my mind refusing to quiet. I was doing my best to ignore the voice in the back of my head that was insistent on wanting to see Kade.

It was after midnight when my cell phone rang. I looked at the caller ID and my pulse leapt as I answered it.

"Did I wake you?" Kade asked.

"No. Can't sleep."

"Why not?"

"I don't know," I lied. I closed my eyes so I could concentrate on the sound of his voice in my ear.

"Are you boycotting the hospital?" he asked.

I frowned, unsure what he meant. "No . . ."

"Because I haven't seen you today."

"I'm sorry," I apologized. "I . . . I know you need to rest, so you can get better, and I didn't want to come by tonight and wake you again."

"You're lying."

I didn't reply. I never could get a lie past him, so there was no sense denying it.

"Why aren't you here really?" he asked. "And don't lie to me, because I'll know."

I sighed. There was no hiding it. I might as well just tell him and let the chips fall where they may. "Because I was out to dinner with Blane tonight," I confessed, flopping onto my back. "And it felt . . . wrong for me to see him, then come see you."

Kade was quiet for a moment while I held my breath. Would he be angry?

"Do you *want* to see me?"

My answer was immediate. "Yes."

"Then come to me." The low growl of his voice sent a delicious shiver through me.

My smile was wide as I said, "I'll be there soon." I ended the call and bounded out of bed, slipping on flip-flops and grabbing my purse before bolting out the door.

I made record time to the hospital and was now an expert at avoiding nurses as I crept to Kade's room. When I slowly pushed open the door, I realized the machines had been removed. That was a good sign. That meant they'd be releasing him soon, I hoped.

I tiptoed into the room, conscious that Kade might have fallen asleep. My eyes hadn't adjusted yet when I felt hands descend on my shoulders. I yelped in surprise, spinning around to see Kade standing behind me.

"You scared me," I said, slightly breathless.

Kade's face was steeped in shadow, whereas the meager light filtering in through the window in the door fell on me.

"You're out of bed!" I said, a wide smile breaking across my face with the realization. "That's fantastic!"

"Took a shower. Sick of sitting on my ass."

I took a step or two back to put some space between us, then promptly forgot everything I was going to say.

Kade was completely naked.

Oh God.

"Wh-where's your . . . your . . ." I stammered, my mind coming up empty. Bandages still covered the wounds in his chest, but it didn't detract from the hard lines of muscle. His arms were relaxed at his sides, the veins standing out in stark relief from hours of pumping iron. My eyes dropped lower to see that being shot hadn't affected Kade's libido in the slightest. My mouth watered at the sight.

He did nothing to cover himself as my hungry gaze devoured him, and when I finally jerked my eyes back up to his, the smirk I knew so well curved his lips.

"See something you like?"

Kade's low drawl had heat curling low in my belly.

"C'mere," he said, crooking a finger to beckon me. His hair was still damp, the dark locks a midnight black, and he'd shaved.

I stepped forward, unable to resist the compulsion to obey him.

His hands rested on my hips and he tugged me closer until our bodies touched. Leaning down, his lips grazed my cheek, then whispered down my jaw to my neck.

"You smell like him," Kade murmured against my skin.

I stiffened, my eyes flying open. I tried to step back, but Kade's fingers bit into my flesh, holding me still. I didn't know what to say. Should I apologize? My face grew hot and that squirmy feeling came back into my belly, the feeling like I was doing something wrong.

"I don't care if you go to bed smelling like him, so long as you wake up smelling like me."

Kade's words had barely registered before he was kissing me. His taste was dark and dangerous. Addictive. I couldn't get enough, and it seemed he couldn't, either. Our tongues dueled while his hands roamed, sliding inside my shorts to cup my backside and hold me closer to him. The heat of his palm seemed to brand my skin. I couldn't resist the temptation any longer and reached around him to squeeze his amazing ass. He groaned, the sound quickly consumed by our mouths. His cock grew harder as it pressed insistently against me. It took everything I had not to shove my shorts and underwear down my legs and climb him like a tree.

"You shouldn't be doing this," I gasped, pulling my lips from his. "You're not well yet."

Kade took my hand from his ass and wrapped it around his straining erection. "Does that feel like I'm not well?"

Desire pooled between my legs, soaking my panties.

"We can't," I said, though my words seemed a far cry from my actions as I gripped him, my hand sliding up and down his length.

"Then you'd better stop doing that," Kade rasped.

Somehow, I managed to make myself release him and step away. I devoured him with my eyes, the fire burning in his gaze making me want to rip off my clothes and damn the consequences.

"Probably wasn't the best idea to come here," I admitted, forcing my eyes to look away. "I should go."

"Don't," he said, taking a step toward me. "Don't go. I'll be good."

I glanced at him and the skepticism must have shown on my face, because he followed up with "Scout's honor."

I rolled my eyes—Kade had never been a Boy Scout—but watched as he slid back into bed, pulling the sheet up to his waist. It didn't hide the fact that he was still aroused, but at least it provided something of a barrier between his skin and mine.

"That better?" he asked, quirking an eyebrow.

Not really, I thought with an internal sigh of disappointment. It seemed a shame to waste his . . . energy. Shoving the errant thought aside, I climbed into bed beside him, nestling against his side while he curled an arm around my shoulders. I rested my hand on his chest, careful to avoid the bandages. The strong beat of his heart echoed against my fingertips, reassuring me.

"So Blane took you on a date tonight," Kade said rather than asked.

"It wasn't really a date," I said. "Just dinner."

"Did he pay?"

"Yes."

"Did he kiss you?"

A bit of a hesitation this time. "Yes."

"Then it was a date." He paused for a moment before he spoke again. "It seems it's going to be an all-out war for you, princess," he mused.

I lifted my head, alarmed. "No," I denied. "I don't want that."

"You say that as if you have a choice," he replied, his tone derisive.

"I won't have you two fighting over . . . over me," I stammered, struggling to sit up and slide out of the bed. Kade's grip tightened on me. "It's ridiculous."

Kade moved, turning so he lay half on top of me, pinning me to the bed. The sheet slid away and his leg pressed between mine.

"I want you," he growled. "And I'm not giving up. Not now. Blane's going to wine and dine you? That's fine with me. I'll just use sex to make you mine."

I opened my mouth to argue that there was no point to it. Kade himself had said there was no future for us. But before I could, his leg moved and his hand was inside my shorts, his fingers slipping between my thighs. My words strangled in my throat.

Kade's lips brushed mine, his tongue tracing my lower lip before he drew it into his mouth to lightly suck the tender flesh. His hand stroked me and my nails dug into his shoulders. "You're so wet for me," he murmured. "Like liquid silk."

"I thought you were going to be good," I managed to gasp.

"It will be," he whispered. "Just spread your legs for me, baby."

I couldn't reply, forming words as far from my current ability to function as it was for me to perform cold fusion. Obediently, I opened my thighs to him, then I was lost in his touch, the taste of him as he kissed me, the feel of his body over mine. My fingers were buried in his hair, the long strands soft and damp.

He slid a finger inside me, then two, pumping them with slow, deliberate strokes while his thumb teased my clit. I moaned into his mouth as the blood in my veins pulsed in time to his fingers.

I had to tear my mouth from his so I could breathe, my panting gasps and moans filling my ears. Kade shoved my tank up, baring my breasts. His mouth fastened over a nipple and I cried out. My body was on fire, every sense focused utterly on what he was doing to me. His teeth tugged and his hand moved faster. A keening cry fell from my throat as stars exploded behind my eyes. I could feel my body convulsing, gripping his fingers as my orgasm washed over me. I pulled at his hair and his lips came back to mine. I sucked his tongue into my mouth, arching my back so my overly sensitive nipples grazed his chest.

Kade groaned, his fingers still buried inside me. It took a long moment before sanity returned. Kade's mouth moved to my neck, nuzzling the tender skin beneath my ear.

My body felt boneless, the aftershocks still rippling through me. In the dark room with just us, nothing seemed more right than Kade's and my bodies pressed together.

"That . . . that was . . ." I couldn't come up with words that didn't sound . . . inadequate. How to describe the way Kade made me feel? Not just sexually, but how happy I was when I was with him?

Kade's breath was warm against my neck. He slowly withdrew his fingers, making me whimper. Though his fingers had been a fabulous substitute, I wanted him.

"This hasn't exactly left you satisfied," I said, my voice throatier than usual. I could feel his cock, still hard as a rock against my thigh. It had to be uncomfortable for him.

"Well, this wasn't about me," Kade said, stretching back onto his side next to me.

"What was it about?" I asked, tugging my shirt back down.

His smirk made my stomach flutter. "It was about reminding you of how good we are together," he said.

Yes, sex with Kade was very, very good. And yet . . . "Is that all?"

His brows furrowed slightly. "What do you mean?"

I didn't want to say it, didn't want to push. I knew only too well how quickly Kade could run hot and cold. The last time I'd asked him to offer me something, he'd walked away. My heart sank.

I shook my head. "Forget it. Never mind." I scooted out of his hold. "Listen, I'd better go. Let you get some sleep—"

Kade latched onto my arm, pulling me back. "What's wrong?" he demanded. His eyes narrowed as he studied me.

"Nothing," I insisted, avoiding his gaze as I tugged on my arm but was unable to break his grip. "It's just late, that's all." Exhaustion was creeping over me. I'd made out with Blane just hours ago, then I'd just done . . . that . . . with Kade. I was turning into someone I despised.

"Bullshit."

Tears stung my eyes. I had to get out of there. "Let me go?" I pleaded. Reluctantly, Kade released me. His expression was pained and I had to look away. "Get some rest, okay?" I babbled. "I'll . . . uh . . . I'll see you later."

"Kathleen, wait—" Kade called, but I was out the door and hurrying down the empty hallway, my flip-flops echoing in the silence.

Tears were tracking down my cheeks as I hurried to my car. This was getting out of hand and I had no idea what to do. When I thought about losing Blane and Kade, the pain was nearly overwhelming. But when I considered the events of the past couple of days, how I was leading on both of the men I loved, I died a little inside.

Something had to break, before I did.

CHAPTER THREE

Bad dreams plagued me that night, with images of Kade lying on the ground and blood everywhere. It coated my hands and my clothes as I tried over and over to wake him. His sightless blue eyes stared at nothing as I screamed and screamed . . .

I came awake with a start, the tang of blood still in my nostrils, and launched myself to the bathroom. The seafood from the night before combined with a gut-wrenching nightmare apparently didn't agree with me. *So much for having a nice dinner,* I thought, wiping my mouth before stepping into the shower.

When I got out and went into the kitchen to pour a cup of coffee, still wrapped in a towel, I saw I had a missed phone call on my cell.

Blane.

I dropped the phone back onto the counter as though it burned, turning away to pour my coffee. I couldn't see Blane, not after last night. I had hardly been able to look myself in the mirror this morning, much less face him knowing I'd gone straight from his arms to Kade's.

I pulled on a pair of shorts and a tank top and decided I'd tackle cleaning my apartment. I didn't have to go to work until four, so I had some time. It kept my mind off things, cleaning and scrubbing. The last thing I wanted to do was think. If I started thinking, then I'd have to come to terms with not only what I'd done last night—with Blane and Kade—but I'd have to face making the decision I didn't want to make.

It was when I was scrubbing out the kitchen sink that I felt water touch my bare toes. Jumping back, I saw the reason for it all too clearly.

"Oh no," I moaned, hurriedly shedding my rubber gloves and turning off the water. But it didn't matter. The water kept oozing from the cupboard under the sink. I hurriedly pulled it open, watching in dismay as water sprayed from the pipes, coating everything. Another gush of water came out and soaked the floor. Now I was standing in water.

"Shit-shit-shit!" I ran to get towels from the bathroom, layering them on the floor and crouching on my hands and knees to get under the sink to turn off the water valve. The damn pipe sprayed water all over my face, hair, and chest until I was soaked. The stupid valve was stuck and refused to turn. I hauled everything out from under the sink and climbed in farther, using both hands now to try and turn the valve.

"Goddammit!" I yelled in frustration, backing out from under the sink. I raised my head too soon, though, and smacked it on the counter. I yelped in pain, tears springing to my eyes.

It was the last straw and I fell back on my butt in the middle of the watery floor and started bawling, my face buried on my wet knees. Not the most logical response, but the most I was emotionally capable of at the moment.

The noise of my front door opening had me lifting my head.

Blane had let himself in, his eyes wide with surprise as he took in the water spewing from under the sink and me, sitting in the middle of the floor, crying and looking like a drowned rat.

He seemed to collect himself pretty quickly, though, and grasped what was happening. Hurrying in, he said with a soft smile, "Plumbing problems?"

I sniffed and nodded, a hiccup escaping.

Discarding his jacket and tossing it onto a chair, he walked over to the sink.

"No! Wait! Blane, you'll ruin your suit!" But it was too late or he didn't care. Leaning under the sink, he turned the valve, shutting the water off in seconds.

"There," he said, standing back up. "That's better."

I swiped a hand across my cheeks, but it was pointless trying to wipe away tears. I was soaked. My hair hung in a wet ponytail and my clothes were so sodden, they were dripping.

Blane looked down at me, the corners of his lips tipped up slightly. He held out a hand, which I took.

"You all right?" he asked as he helped me to my feet.

"It's okay to laugh," I grumbled. "I know I look ridiculous."

Blane chuckled. "I didn't say that. Why don't you get cleaned up and I'll see what I can do about your problem?"

That sounded like a good idea and I hurried into the bedroom, anxious to get dry. I toweled my hair before changing my clothes, then headed back to the kitchen. Blane was finishing mopping the floor.

"Well, this is a sight I never thought I'd see." I couldn't help but tease him.

He looked up and grimaced. "I can think of only one person I'd mop a floor for, and I'm doing it now."

He said it jokingly, but my smile grew strained.

"I'll just call the super and tell him to come by and fix it, now that you've got the water turned off," I said, heading for the phone. A few minutes later, I'd reported the leak and the super said someone from maintenance would be over later.

Blane helped me take the waterlogged towels down to the washing machine, then followed me back upstairs.

"So, um, what did you need?" I asked, taking a seat on the couch. Realizing that didn't sound very gracious after he'd just stopped my leak, I added, "Not that I'm not grateful you're here."

"You didn't answer your phone this morning," Blane said, sitting down next to me and resting an arm on the back of the couch. "I thought I'd come by, see if you wanted to go to lunch." His hand dropped, the backs of his knuckles brushing the bare skin of my arm.

"I'm not dressed very nice," I said, wondering if lunch was a good idea. My skin tingled where he'd touched me and I thought I should move away, but I didn't.

Blane shrugged. "It's just lunch."

My conscience was screaming at me to tell him no, that I had to end things with both him and Kade, but I couldn't obey.

"Um, okay. Just give me a minute." I got up and headed back to my bedroom to brush out my hair. I avoided my eyes in the mirror. I could have lunch with Blane. There was nothing wrong with that.

A flash of Kade in my mind, his fingers inside me, his mouth on mine.

The brush clattered as it hit the dresser, dropping from my hands as I clutched the sides of my head, squeezing my eyes shut.

I was lying to myself, and I knew it.

"It doesn't matter," I muttered. "Your time is ticking away. Enjoy it while you can." I just wanted to spend a little time with Blane, enjoy being with him, his company. It seemed like the time we'd had together had been fraught with danger and drama. Now that it seemed things had finally settled down, I was loath to put an end to our relationship. No matter the many reasons why I should.

Putting on some sandals, I went back to the living room where Blane was waiting. He got to his feet, not seeming to mind that I was in a pair of white shorts and a black T-shirt.

"I'll drive," he said.

I followed him out the door, locking it behind me. I jogged down the steps after him, then stopped short in surprise.

"Oh my God! You got a new car!"

Blane had slid his sunglasses on and he grinned at me. "What do you think?"

It was another Jaguar, but brand-spanking-new and just . . . wow. Silver metallic, it was a four-door, sleek, and gorgeous.

"It's amazing!" I enthused.

"Wanna drive it?"

My jaw dropped and I stared at him. "Are you kidding me?"

Blane tossed me the keys. "Let's take her for a spin."

I squealed with delight, hurrying to the driver's side as Blane slid into the passenger seat. He tossed his jacket in the back and I noticed the Glock wedged firmly in its holster at his side.

The engine turned over with a purr and I adjusted the seat for my considerably shorter legs. I took a deep breath, glancing at Blane. He was smiling and so was I. I looked up and was shocked again. The entire roof was made of tinted glass.

"Wow . . ." I breathed.

"Let's go," Blane urged.

I tore my gaze away from the roof and carefully backed the car up. I was almost too nervous to drive. Almost. With a gleeful laugh, we tore out of the lot.

Blane told me where to drive and I barely paid attention where we were heading, being too wrapped up in how amazing an experience it was to drive a car like this.

We were soon on an open country road, and Blane said, "Open her up."

I glanced over. "I can't do that! What if I get a ticket?"

Blane lowered his glasses, peering at me over the tops. His grin was wicked. "I know a great lawyer."

I laughed and gave in to the urge to go just a little faster. Okay, maybe a little more—it was just so easy and the car seemed to grip the road as it ate up the miles.

Finally, Blane directed me onto an exit and had me pull into what looked to be a park. It was nice, with huge shade trees and manicured grass. Since it was the middle of the week, no one was there at this time of day.

"I don't know what kind of hoity-toity restaurants they have in this itty-bitty town," I teased. "You may have to settle for a fast food cheeseburger for lunch."

Blane got out and so did I. "No, I won't," he said, popping open the trunk. "Surprise."

Curious, I stepped toward the trunk to see what was inside. Oh God.

There was a picnic basket and a blanket.

"I thought we could have a picnic," Blane said.

I swallowed. The last picnic I'd been on had been with Kade, and we'd—

"Um, yeah, sure," I said brightly, cutting off that thought.

Blane frowned. "Is that okay? Because if it's not, we can—"

"No, no, it's fine," I interrupted. "A picnic sounds great." So what if it made me feel like I was cheating on Kade? I wasn't. He and I weren't together. I was his go-to booty-call girl and yes, he loved me and I loved him, but you couldn't build a life together out of a booty-call relationship.

I grabbed the blanket while Blane took out the picnic basket, then followed him into the park. Finding just the perfect spot took a few minutes, and I hid a smile as Blane dismissed certain areas for "not enough shade" or being "too rocky." Finally, he designated the spot.

"You're sure?" I teased. "Before we spread the blanket and everything, because if you're not sure, we can keep looking."

"Smartass," he retorted, setting the basket down and taking the blanket from me. A few quick snaps of his hands, and the fabric floated perfectly to the ground.

I slipped off my shoes before settling down, then waited as Blane sat down, too. He looked a bit incongruous, sitting on a blanket under a tree with a shirt and tie on. I watched as he dug into the basket, producing two bottles of water and sandwiches.

"Where'd you get this stuff?" I asked, taking a chicken salad sandwich from him.

"Mona made it," he said, unearthing more food.

I'd skipped breakfast after the puking incident, so was starving now. Mona's cooking was good incentive and I ate the sandwich embarrassingly fast. She'd also packed strawberries and I eyed Blane as I ate those more slowly.

"Blane, when was the last time you went on a picnic?" He just didn't seem like the picnic kind of guy. He'd finished his sandwich, too, and was now resting back on his elbows, his long legs stretched out in front of him, ankles crossed.

His smile was a bit sheepish. "Years, I'm sure. I've probably not willingly sat on the ground to eat since I was deployed."

"So why now?" I asked. "Why today?"

"I thought you'd like it," he said. "And I wanted to see you."

I gave an inward sigh and lay down on my back, looking up at the puffy clouds drifting across the sky.

"Is that wrong? Am I not supposed to want to see you?" A defensive note had crept into Blane's questions.

"Of course not," I said. "I want to see you, too." Which was true. If I could just get Kade out of my head, maybe the feelings I had for him would go away and I could feel what I should feel—what I used to feel—for Blane.

It was quiet for a few minutes, each of us seeming lost in our own thoughts. The breeze rustled the leaves on the

61

trees. I could so take a nap right there. My eyes had just drifted closed when Blane spoke.

"I've decided to pull out of the governor's race."

My eyes shot open and I twisted so I could see him. "What?" Surely I'd misheard.

"I'm dropping out," Blane repeated, discarding his sunglasses.

"But . . . but why?" I stammered, stunned. "You've been working for this for years. Why would you drop out?"

"I told you before that I wasn't sure I wanted it anymore," he said. "Kade getting hurt, losing you. It just showed me how badly I'd prioritized the things in my life, people in my life." He paused. "Plus I want to break from my uncle. He has a lot to answer for."

I couldn't disagree. Keaston and his interference had nearly cost both Kade and me our lives.

"So what are you going to do?" I asked.

"In my career or about my uncle?"

"Both."

"I'll keep practicing for now. I might run for office again someday, maybe. It's all well and good to have ambitions and success, it just took me a while to realize that they don't mean anything if I don't have someone to share it with." His eyes were on mine as he said this, and I had to glance away.

"And your uncle?" I asked, not wanting to address the implication in his words.

Blane sat up, bending one leg to hook an elbow over his knee. He stared into the distance. "When I think about what he did, how Kade could've died. How I might not have gotten to you in time, nearly didn't. I want to kill him." He gave a bark of bitter laughter. "My own uncle. I've idolized him since I was a boy. To find out that he betrayed me, hurt me, all for his aspirations for my career . . ." He shook his head as though he still had trouble wrapping his mind around it.

The nearly palpable anger and pain emanating from Blane struck a sympathetic chord in me. I reached over, grasping his hand that rested on the blanket between us. He lifted his head and his eyes were a brilliant green as they searched mine.

"I'm sorry, Kat," he said. "You tried to tell me, and I didn't listen. I'm sorry for that. I'm sorry for everything that's happened to you . . . because of me." His lips twisted in a parody of a smile. "Ironic, isn't it? I turned out to be the worst thing that ever happened to you."

"Don't say that!" I sat up, quickly moving to kneel beside him. "That's not true," I said.

Blane shook his head slightly, glancing away, and I knew he didn't believe me.

I cupped his cheek in my hand, forcing him to look at me. "That's not true," I repeated. "I wouldn't trade the time we had together for anything. If I knew then what I know now, I'd still have gotten in your car that night." And I meant it.

Blane searched my eyes. He leaned forward and I knew what was coming, but I didn't pull away. His hand curved behind my neck and his mouth met mine.

It was as sweet and tentative as a first kiss. His lips were soft and coaxing, the gentle brush of his tongue against the seam of my lips a silent request I couldn't resist. He deepened the kiss, wrapping an arm around my waist and pulling me into his lap until I was cradled in both arms, my body wedged between his chest and his bent knees.

He didn't try anything more or attempt to take things further. He just . . . kissed me. Gradually, I relaxed against him, my body pliant and clinging to his.

I lost track of time and when Blane finally lifted his head, I was languid with desire. Our faces were inches apart and Blane just looked at me, his hand cupping my cheek. His eyes were a beautiful, deep green, the gray nearly invisible now.

"I love how your eyes do that," I murmured.

His lips twitched. "Do what?" His thumb brushed my cheekbone and I could feel the beat of his heart against my ribs.

"One minute, they're gray like an oncoming storm," I said. "The next, they're the vibrant green of spring grass."

Blane didn't reply. I didn't think he much cared about the color of his eyes. He seemed as though he were memorizing my face, his gaze drifting from my brow to my cheek, my nose, my lips and chin. His thumb brushed my lower lip and he leaned down, pressing a tender, chaste kiss to my mouth.

"You should probably get back to work," I said. I lifted my hand, unable to resist the temptation to push my fingers through his hair. The blond locks always fell perfectly back into place, no matter what I did. It made me smile. That was Blane. Unruffled and in control. Always.

"I don't want to," he said, making me smile even wider.

"I doubt your clients would approve," I teased. "Besides, I have to get ready for work soon anyway."

Neither of us made any move to get up. Blane wrapped a lock of my hair around his finger, his gaze focusing on it rather than me as he asked, "Have you been back to see Kade?"

I stiffened, immediately wary. "We probably shouldn't discuss Kade," I hedged. All the guilt and doubts I'd managed to push to the back of my mind came flooding back. I squirmed, easing out of Blane's arms and getting to my feet.

"We can't really *not* discuss him, either," Blane said. He stood as well.

"Then yes," I said, averting my gaze. I slipped my shoes back on and started to pick up the blanket. "I've been to see him. Is that what you want to hear?"

"Not really, not if I'm honest," he replied.

I folded the blanket over my arms, holding it against my chest like a shield as I faced him. "What do you want from me, Blane?"

"Fine, I'll lay it on the line," he said, moving closer until he stood right in front of me. "I want you, just you, all to myself. I don't want you seeing Kade anymore. I want you to want to be with me, and only me."

I swallowed. "You're asking me to choose. I can't do that. Not right now." The thought of giving Kade up caused a physical pain inside my chest.

Blane cursed, turning to pace away, his hands resting on his hips.

"I'm not asking you to stick around," I said. "I'll understand if you don't want to be friends anymore, see me anymore." The words sounded selfless, but that was far from how I felt. I'd really enjoyed being with Blane today. I didn't want to lose him.

Blane gave a curt nod, which I had no idea how to interpret. He picked up the basket and took the blanket from me. I followed him in silence to the car.

The drive back to my apartment was rife with tension. Blane had an iron grip on the steering wheel, sunglasses again covering his eyes. His expression was like granite.

I fidgeted, nerves getting the best of me.

When we pulled into my parking lot, Blane put the car in park, but made no move to turn off the engine. He stared straight ahead.

"Um, thanks for lunch," I murmured as I fumbled for the door handle. I felt absurdly like I wanted to cry. Absurd because, really, what had I thought would happen? Eventually, my feelings for Kade would drive Blane away, and vice versa. This tension with Blane shouldn't have been a surprise.

"Wait," Blane said, his hand shooting out to grip my wrist, catch me just as I was about to exit the car.

I stilled but didn't turn.

"I'm sorry, Kat," he said. "I've lost you so many times. I'm scared to death that this time, if I lose you, it'll be forever."

I looked around at him, his words breaking my heart. "I love you," I said. "You know that."

"But are you still *in* love with me?"

I hesitated before answering. "I don't know."

~

We were busy at The Drop that night, and with Scott gone, I didn't stop moving until it was nearly closing. I was restocking when Tish bellied up to the bar.

"Hand me a beer, Kathleen?" she asked.

I pulled a bottle from the fridge and popped the top before handing it to her.

"You're not going to have one?"

I shook my head. "Nah. Not tonight. I'm tired enough as it is." Beer didn't sound very appealing, and I wasn't exaggerating about being tired. It was an effort to put one foot in front of the other, and I couldn't wait to crawl into bed.

"How's the love triangle going?" she asked with a wink.

I groaned. "You make it sound like it's funny, when it's awful. It really is."

"I'm sorry," she said, immediately contrite.

"It's okay," I sighed. "I just don't know what to do. Every day it seems I'm being pushed one step closer to choosing between them, and I don't want to do that."

"In all seriousness, Kathleen, that would be the kindest thing to do."

I glanced over at her, frowning. "What do you mean?"

Tish shrugged. "Well, if it was me and I was in love with a guy who loved me and someone else, I'd want him to pick. It'd just be a waste of my time to try and hold on to a relationship that may never happen."

She had a point, and yet . . . "I don't want to lose them."

Tish reached across the bar and took my hand, giving it a squeeze. "This isn't you, Kathleen. You're not selfish. I know you're not. I think you're just scared. A lot has happened the past few months. But you're strong. You're a good person. You'll do the right thing, and you'll be glad you did."

Her words echoed in my head as I sat silent in the chair in Kade's room. They must've given him more pain medication, because he hadn't stirred when I'd snuck inside.

I watched him—thinking about him, me, and Blane—until I could hardly hold my head up. Tish was right. I had to be strong, had to make the right choice, even if I was so exhausted and confused right now that I had no clue what that choice should be.

It was closer to morning than midnight when I finally trudged up the stairs to my apartment. The late nights at the hospital were taking a toll. However, when I reached the top of the flight, I got an unwelcome surprise.

"What are you doing here, James?" I asked, backing away from where he stood leaning against my door. My hand scrabbled inside my purse for my gun.

James looked at me, his hands in the pockets of his jeans. "I hear you and Kirk are over," he said. "Again."

I swallowed. "What does it matter?"

"You're too good for him," James said. "I think that's why I hated seeing you with him."

"You need to leave," I said, wishing my voice weren't shaking. James scared me, our every encounter marked by pain.

James ignored me, taking a few steps in my direction. I hurriedly backed up while pulling my gun from my purse.

"Don't come any closer," I warned him.

He paused at the sight of the gun in my hand.

"Maybe if Kandi'd had a gun that night, she wouldn't be dead," he mused. "She means . . . meant . . . something to me." He gave a sudden, bitter laugh. "And we both hated you. Our common bond."

"Go home, James," I said. "It's late."

"Kirk deserved to die for what he did to her," James said. "But you were there, weren't you. Protecting him." His eyes

68

fixed on mine and he moved closer. Alarmed, I retreated until my back was to the wall.

"You're like a guardian angel for him and Dennon," he continued. "That's where you were tonight, right? With Dennon?"

He was close enough now that the gun was nearly touching his chest.

"That's none of your business," I said, fear crawling up my spine as I fought panic. "I don't want to hurt you. Just go."

He reached out and I flinched as his fingers gently grazed the side of my face and cheek.

"I can't stop thinking about you," he murmured. "Can't stop trying to figure you out—figure *us* out."

"There is no *us*, James!" I was frantic to get through to him. I didn't think I could pull the trigger, no matter how afraid I was.

"Fate brought us together, keeps bringing us together," he insisted. "If you think I'm wrong, then shoot me."

My hand tightened on the gun's grip, the weapon trembling slightly. James looked completely unafraid, his gaze weirdly serene as he stared at me. After a moment, he spoke again.

"You can't do it," he said softly. "You can't kill me, because that's not who you are. You're not a killer, like Kirk and Dennon. You're an angel."

Before I could say anything to that, he leaned forward and kissed me, a quick hard press of his lips against mine, then he was gone, heading down the stairs. A moment later, I heard a car start and pull out of the lot.

I was shaking like a leaf in the wind and could barely put my gun back into my purse. It took way too long to unlock my door and when I was finally inside, I hurriedly relocked it, then leaned against it and just breathed. As if I didn't have enough on my mind, James's unexpected reappearance in my life felt like the last straw for my tenuous composure. A hysterical laugh bubbled up in my throat but I swallowed it down.

Stripping to my underwear, I was too tired to do more than pull on a white tank, leaving my work uniform where it lay on the floor. I fell into bed and slept like the dead.

CHAPTER FOUR

I woke to the sound of someone knocking on my door. Blearily, I rubbed my eyes, glancing at the clock as I stumbled out of bed. I groaned. It was just after seven-thirty. I hadn't slept for even four hours.

Cranky now, and only half awake, I still remembered my late-night visitor and checked the peephole before opening the door, but it was Blane standing there.

"Um, I . . . I . . . wasn't expecting . . . you," I stammered, blinking in the morning sunshine. I belatedly remembered how I must look, with tangled hair and last night's makeup. Of course, Blane was in his customary suit and tie, sunglasses hiding his eyes.

"Brought you some coffee," he said after an awkward moment, handing me a cup.

"Um, okay, thanks," I said, taking it from him. I stepped back and he followed me into my apartment.

The coffee smelled heavenly, though my stomach lurched a little, reminding me that not enough sleep wasn't good for the digestive system. I took a cautious sip and let out a sigh. I might forgive Blane for waking me up at this ungodly hour since he'd brought really good, really hot coffee.

I turned around to thank him, but the words stuck in my throat. He'd taken off his sunglasses and his gaze was raking me from head to foot with a familiar glint in his eyes. I abruptly realized I wasn't really dressed for company. The white tank and bikini underwear left little to the imagination, and though Blane had seen it all before, it wasn't exactly the look I was going for right then.

"Give me a minute," I said, setting down the coffee. "I'll be right back."

I hurried into the bathroom, brushing my teeth and scrubbing my face. A brush through my hair did wonders and I pulled on a pair of knit shorts. I was back out in the living room in mere minutes.

"Sorry about that," I said. Blane was sitting on the couch, so I picked up my coffee and sat in the chair across from him.

"It's fine. Sorry to wake you."

I shrugged. "I worked last night." And had spent a few hours sitting at Kade's bedside, but chose not to mention that. It was on the tip of my tongue to tell him about James, but my problems weren't Blane's anymore, and James had always been my problem. I kept my mouth shut.

"I want to apologize," Blane said. "For pushing you yesterday. I said I wouldn't, and I did."

"You had every right," I replied.

"No, I didn't. You gave me your terms and I didn't abide by them."

I winced. When he said it like that, I did sound like a selfish bitch. Tish's words flashed through my mind and I took a deep breath.

"I can't do this, Blane," I blurted. "I can't . . . be with you one minute, and with Kade the next. It's wrong, and it's not fair to either of you."

He frowned. "What are you talking about?"

I swallowed, my voice quiet as I confessed. "You know I went to see Kade the other night, in the hospital, after you left."

Blane's face was carefully impassive. "Yes. I never said you couldn't."

God, I really didn't want to go into detail. I set down my coffee, noticing that my hand was shaking. I clenched my hands together in my lap.

"We kissed, Blane," I said. "You and me. Then I saw Kade, and . . . I kissed him, too." Surely that was enough. I could feel my face burning, but didn't give in to the temptation to look away and not meet his eyes. "I can't do that. I can't . . . be that person. I hate it. And I can't trust myself not to be."

The Adam's apple in Blane's throat moved as he swallowed. "So you're choosing Kade after all."

"No, I'm not. You were right, Blane. I can't have what I want with Kade. But you and me, we can't go back." It was the hardest sentence I'd ever had to say and my heart hurt just forcing the words out. "I can't . . . make myself feel about you the way I once did. And I'm sorry." Tears started halfway through, but I kept talking even as my voice grew quieter, the syllables harder to say past the lump in my throat. "I should want to, I know that. You're wonderful and I love you, I really do—"

"But you're not *in* love with me anymore," Blane cut in.

I shook my head. "And I'm so, so sorry," I whispered. I felt my face crumple and gave in to the tears, covering my face with my hands so Blane wouldn't see. My shoulders shook with silent sobs. I'd known this was coming, had known the three of us wasn't going to work out, but a tiny part of me had hoped I'd have longer with them. With Blane.

"Shhh, don't cry." Blane was suddenly crouched down in front of me, his arms wrapping around me and pulling me out of the chair and into his lap. He tucked my head underneath his chin.

But it seemed I couldn't stop. I no longer felt what had been inside of me for Blane, and being in love with Kade was pointless. Kade's words had proved prophetic. My heart was broken for what Blane and I had lost, and loving Kade was as futile as chasing a rainbow.

Losing them both was going to be as devastating as I'd imagined.

"D-do you h-hate me now?" I hiccupped through my tears.

"Of course not," he soothed.

"You sh-should," I said. "I've been awful . . . selfish. And I'm g-going to m-miss you."

The tears started again, dampening his neck, and I clutched the lapels of his jacket. I was one step closer to being alone again.

"I'm not leaving you," Blane said softly. "I'll still be around, okay?"

I wished I could believe that.

It seemed wrong for Blane to be comforting *me* at this point, so I pulled myself together and made the tears stop.

Blane was lightly stroking my hair, both of his arms around me as I rested against his chest. Neither of us spoke. I knew this would be the last time he'd hold me like this, ever, and I wasn't ready for him to stop.

"If I'd known our last kiss was going to be our *last kiss*," he murmured thoughtfully, "I'd have made it better."

I sucked in a breath as the pain of those words sank in, and pulled back. He looked down and our eyes met. I caught a glint of wetness on Blane's lashes, and his eyes seemed unusually bright. Then he blinked and I thought I must have imagined it.

"I, um, I'd better go," he said.

I took the hint and clambered off his lap. He got to his feet and absently smoothed his jacket and tie before adjusting his cuff links. It was as though I was watching him don his politician's armor right in front of me, and it made me unbearably sad.

He slid his sunglasses back on and ran his fingers through his hair. I followed him to the door, not knowing what to say or do. It seemed he didn't, either, because although he cleared his throat, he didn't speak.

The sunlight was glaring as I stood in the doorway. Blane gave me a hug and his lips brushed my hair.

"It'll be okay," he said, and I couldn't tell if he was saying those words to me, or himself.

He jogged down the stairs to his car and I hurried forward to watch him over the railing, like I'd done so many times before. He glanced up and gave me a smile before disappearing inside his car, and pain twisted like a knife inside me.

It was that politician's smile, the one that never reached his eyes. I used to be the one who he didn't have to hide his emotions from, didn't have to use that smile to conceal what was going on inside his head.

Not anymore.

Tears clogged my throat again and I swiped my wet cheeks with the back of my hand. Endings were hard, even more so when they faded away rather than exploding into dust.

I watched Blane drive off and it felt as if a hole had been ripped in my chest. The only thing harder than acknowledging to myself that it was over—really over—between us had been telling him.

My stomach heaved and I only just made it to the bathroom in time.

~

Kade had been blowing up my phone all evening. I hadn't had a chance to even glance at my phone, so when I finally listened to the voice mails, they went like this:

I want to see you. If you're not answering, that must mean you've been kidnapped by another psycho, because I'm sure you wouldn't just ignore my call.

Twenty minutes later.

Of course, if you are ignoring my call, then you're going to miss me telling you this great story about how this smokin'-hot girl showed up in my room the other night. I've been thinking about her all day.

Thirty minutes later.

That girl, she left too quick. I think she's mad at me. Or maybe sad. Yeah, she looked sad when she left. I'm not sure why.

Forty minutes later.

I think we had a fight, maybe. I'm not a hundred percent sure. I'm afraid that—a pause, and then a huff of humorless laughter—*I'm afraid. There's two words I haven't strung together in a long fucking time, princess.*

Twenty minutes later.

I hope she knows that I love her. A pause. *Yeah, just that. I love her and . . . I don't want to lose her.*

That had been the last message two hours ago. I'd cried when I listened.

I could see through the window that Kade was stretched out in bed and part of me hoped he was sleeping. I'd gain a reprieve. But he wasn't, and the moment I stepped through the door, his head turned and his piercing blue gaze met mine.

Time seemed to stop as I froze, right inside the doorway. I didn't even breathe as I crossed over to him. When I was near enough, he grabbed my arm and hauled me closer. Without another word, his hand curved around the back of my neck and he pulled me in to kiss me.

It wasn't sweet, it wasn't elegant. It was the kind of kiss you give someone you'd thought you might never kiss again.

Our lips and tongues entwined as his hands moved to gently hold my head, his thumbs brushing my cheeks. I buried my fingers in his hair, the taste and feel of him more precious than my next breath.

When we finally parted, we were both breathing hard. I rested my forehead against his, closing my eyes and concentrating on the touch of his hands, the sound of his breathing, the warm feel of his skin against mine.

"I love you," he said, his voice a low rasp.

Pulling back slightly so I could look into his eyes, I said, "And I love you, Kade Dennon." I hadn't said those words since he'd first regained consciousness, and it was almost a relief to be able to say them once more.

Then he was kissing me again until my breath was gone. He pressed light kisses to my cheeks, my closed eyes, my forehead before returning to my mouth.

"I thought you might not come back," he breathed against my lips.

"I can't seem to stay away." Which was the absolute truth. Kade exerted a pull on me that I couldn't resist.

Our eyes met. I could get lost in the clear blue depths of his gaze.

Kade tugged on my hand and I climbed up next to him. His arms curved around me, tucking me in close to his side.

"We can't go on like this," I said after a while. "Me. You. Blane. It needs an ending."

His fingers had been combing through my hair. Now they stopped.

"What kind of an ending did you have in mind?"

"The only one there can be," I said quietly. "I need to go my own way, and you two go yours."

Kade's grip on me tightened. "That's bullshit."

I shifted so I could see his face. "Then what, Kade?" I asked, exasperated.

"What do you mean?"

"You told me a month ago that we couldn't be together," I reminded him. "That it was too dangerous for me to be with you. Have you changed your mind?"

Kade studied me, his brow furrowed. His hand brushed my cheek. "I'm insane to want to keep you," he murmured, "but I can't let you go."

And it seemed that's the only answer I was going to get, because then he started kissing me and I didn't have the heart to push him away, not when our time was limited.

~

The aroma of fresh coffee greeted me when next I opened my eyes. I sat up from where I'd been slumped in the hospital bed, wincing as my neck and back gave sharp protests. I automatically glanced next to me, then froze when I saw the space was empty.

"They took him for some more tests."

I jerked around to see Blane leaning against the wall, sipping a cup of coffee. Shit. I hadn't left in time to avoid him, and after our conversation yesterday, I was all about avoiding. He looked put together and perfect, his slate-gray suit one of my favorites. The scent of his cologne wafted toward me, reminding me that I still smelled like stale booze. Nice.

I disappeared into the bathroom, splashing some water on my face and trying to make myself look like I hadn't spent the night again squished next to Kade. I didn't think I was successful.

I had no idea what to say to Blane when I came out, though I felt like I should say something.

"Do you have court today?" I asked, desperately searching for small talk.

Blane's steely gray gaze slid my way. "Yes." He didn't elaborate, taking another sip of coffee and glancing back out the window.

Okay, well, it wasn't like I couldn't read that "fuck off" message.

The tension was like thick cotton pressing on my lungs. I wanted to say something else, but didn't know what could possibly break through the wall between us. Blane was shutting me out, his face absolutely blank as he sipped his coffee. He glanced at the clock on the wall and then out the window, ignoring me completely.

But there was nothing I could say to or ask of him. He owed me nothing. Now I was merely one among the many exes that littered his history.

I'd known it would be bad, despite what he'd said to the contrary. I just hadn't realized *how* bad, or how much it would hurt.

~

It was the morning of the thirteenth day that Kade had been hospitalized. The doctor was optimistic about releasing him the next day. I'd slept fitfully and was groggy, though it was later in the morning than when I usually left.

"You all right?" Kade asked, his brow furrowing as he looked at me.

"I'm fine," I said automatically, adding a smile. He was doing so well, his healing progressing perfectly, and looked much better. "I'm just going to splash some water on my face and go."

"You don't have to jump up and leave so fast," he said, grabbing hold of my arm as I made to get out of the bed.

But I knew Blane would be there soon, and glancing at the clock I realized it would be sooner rather than later. My stomach knotted at even the thought of seeing him again.

"I've got to feed Tigger," I lied, slipping out of his grip. "And do laundry. But I'll be back tonight."

"Don't come back," Kade said.

That made me pause. "What?"

"You look exhausted," he said bluntly. "Go home. You'll sleep better there."

I shook my head. "Forget it. And since you're still lying in a hospital bed, you can't make me."

But Kade didn't smile at my teasing. His hand reached out to cup my cheek. The concern in his eyes made me relent.

"I'm just tired," I said. "But I want to be here. I *need* to be here. Don't make me stay away."

The desperation I couldn't conceal leached into my voice and Kade must've heard it, because he nodded, though the worry I saw in his eyes didn't ebb.

I couldn't really put into words how much Blane's utter disregard bothered me. What I did know was that if I was cut off from Kade, too, I felt like I'd fall apart. I'd grown to need the both of them so much—too much—and now it seemed I would be crippled without them.

And it wasn't anything I could say aloud. The feelings didn't make sense. It was selfish of me, needy, and yet I felt what I felt. So I tried to hide it the best I could. I deserved nothing from Blane, actually deserved far worse than his cold indifference. He was being kind just to tolerate me.

All those thoughts and more assailed me as I stood in the bathroom. They'd taken Kade for more tests, the last he'd undergo before he'd be discharged. I'd heard Blane come in just as Kade was leaving, heard them exchange a few words. I'd been hiding in the bathroom ever since. I felt strange this morning, weak. But I'd skipped dinner again last night, so that was probably why.

I looked at my watch for the fifth time. Ten minutes had passed. I was such a coward. But the longer I took, the weirder it would seem when I came out, so I took a fortifying breath, forcing myself to turn the knob and open the door.

Blane glanced around from where he stood by the window, sipping coffee as usual. He seemed surprised to see me and I realized he hadn't known I was there.

"I-I was just leaving," I stammered.

His gaze shuttered as he gave a curt nod, not even bothering to speak to me. He was dressed for work, of course, in a black suit and tie, the linen of his shirt a stark white that contrasted with the golden tan of his skin. As always, I felt like the poor relation, with my slept-in clothes and tousled hair. It seemed he had the same thought, as his eyes traveled a path down to my worn flip-flops before he turned back to the window.

Cheeks burning, I hastily turned away, a move I instantly regretted as the room tilted in my vision and I had to grab on to the bathroom door to keep from falling. A wave of dizziness swept over me and I swayed on my feet. Distantly, I heard my name spoken right before my knees buckled, and then the sound of something hitting the floor. Everything went dark.

～

Yelling. Lots of yelling. But it was muffled, like cotton was stuffed in my ears.

I opened my eyes and saw Blane's face above me, dismay etched on his features. He called out something, and I realized it had been him yelling.

"What . . . ?" I managed to ask, glancing around. I was mostly lying on the floor, though Blane had his arm around my back, holding my head in the crook of his elbow. Coffee was splattered in a puddle on the floor by the window, an empty cup lying on its side.

"You fainted," Blane said, the words not quite as muffled.

I felt like I couldn't move, my limbs so heavy it seemed they were held to the floor by invisible weights. I closed my eyes.

"Kat! Wake up, baby. Can you hear me?" Blane's urgent voice penetrated my haze and I opened my eyes again.

My head was beginning to clear and now embarrassment crept over me. I made myself sit up. This was what I got for not eating or sleeping enough. I'd made a fool of myself in front of Blane. The desperate need to get out of there had me scrambling to my feet, forcing my weak knees to work like they were supposed to.

"Take it easy," Blane said, hovering close enough that I suspected he thought I might faint again.

Just then, a nurse poked her head in the door. "Is everything all right?" she asked. "I heard someone yelling for help."

"She needs a doctor," Blane replied.

"I'm fine," I said.

"You just fainted," Blane retorted, his eyes narrowing. "You're not fine."

"I'm tired," I said. "I skipped dinner last night, so probably low blood sugar or something. I'm fine."

Our eyes were locked in a battle of wills.

"How are you feeling now?" the nurse said, heading purposefully toward me. She scrutinized my face.

"Better," I lied, hoping she'd just let it go. Blane had paid my last hospital bill, albeit without my knowledge or consent, after I'd gotten hit by a car. But I doubted he'd be doing that again. I couldn't afford a bunch of tests that would end up telling me what I already knew: I was overly tired and hadn't been taking very good care of myself. "I'm just tired."

"I can't let you leave without having a doctor take a look," she explained. "Liability reasons. Can you come with me?"

Shit.

I glared at Blane, who blandly smiled.

"As a lawyer, I'd have to agree with the nurse," he said. "You leaving would put them at risk should something happen on your way home."

There was nothing I could say to that and Blane knew it. I gritted my teeth and followed the nurse from the room.

She led me to another room not far away and asked me to sit on the bed and wait while she got a doctor. Twenty minutes later, they'd taken a blood sample for tests while I answered fifty thousand questions from the doctor as she shone a light in my eyes.

"The tests should be done shortly," she said, pocketing the light. "Why don't you rest here and I'll be back?"

I reluctantly agreed and she left. After staring at the wall for twenty minutes, I got bored. Fishing my cell from my pocket, I called Alisha.

"Hey," I said when she answered. "Are you at work today?"

"Unfortunately," she said. "Why?"

I bit back my disappointment. "Nothing. Just wanted to say hi."

"What happened?" Alisha was pretty perceptive.

I told her about Blane showing up and me passing out. "Now I'm stuck waiting for them to finish so I can leave," I said. "Besides feeling like a complete idiot."

"It's not like it's your fault," Alisha said.

"I know, but still." I sighed.

"He's still controlling your life! God, I swear! Can't he just leave you alone? If you didn't want to see a doctor, then that's your decision." She paused in the midst of her anti-Blane tirade. "Though I think it's a good idea that you are."

"Traitor," I said without heat.

"Well, I know I'll feel better about it if a doctor gives you a clean bill of health," she said. "So just this one time, I'll agree with Blane."

"You were just all mad at him for making me do something!"

"I have a lot of hidden anger," she protested.

"Hidden? Really?" My sarcasm was thick though I was grinning, too.

"Okay, maybe not so hidden," she allowed.

A knock on the door had me saying, "Doctor's back. Gotta go."

"Okay, call me and tell me what he says."

"It's a she."

"Whatever."

I ended the call just as the doctor entered.

"That took a little while," I said.

She smiled as she pulled a little stool on wheels over next to where I sat. "I apologize," she said. "We like to be thorough."

Something about the way she said that, the way she smiled, set off alarm bells in my head, and the leftover grin from my conversation with Alisha faded.

"What is it?" I asked. "What's wrong?" It hadn't occurred to me that something might actually be wrong with me. But from the look on the doctor's face, I knew she had something to tell me.

"I'm not sure if this is welcome news or not," she said carefully, "but the tests show conclusively that you're pregnant."

I stared at her, shock rippling through me. My mouth was hanging open and I snapped it shut.

"But-but that's impossible," I stammered. "I'm on birth control."

"No birth control method is one hundred percent effective," she said, her voice sounding much calmer than mine. "I'd also say you're suffering from exhaustion and malnutrition," she continued. "You'll need to be more aware of your body's needs the next few months. Eat right, get plenty of water and rest."

I barely heard her. "But . . . I can barely afford to pay my own rent. How am I going to pay for a child?" I was reeling, the implications and fallout hitting me with the force of a Mack truck.

"May I ask, is the father in the picture?"

Kade. Oh my God. He wasn't even sure *I* could be a fixture in his life, what would he say when he found out I was pregnant? And Blane. Oh God . . .

The room tilted again and the doctor jumped to her feet. "Lie down," she said, easing me backward on the bed.

I squeezed my eyes shut as tears threatened. I would not cry in front of the doctor. I felt her take my hand, but she said nothing until I'd regained control. When I opened my eyes, her face held only compassion.

"If this was unplanned," she said, "there are things you can do. Terminate the pregnancy, of course. There's also adoption, if you want to give the baby up."

This was too much. Her saying those things, it made it all too real.

"I have to get going," I said, sitting up. "Um, where do I pay the bill?"

"The bill's been taken care of," she said. "The gentleman who I believe helped you earlier?"

Blane.

Panic struck. "You're not going to tell him, are you?" I asked.

"Your records are confidential," the doctor assured me, "though if he's the father, I would encourage you to consider telling him."

Hysterical laughter bubbled up in my chest and I swallowed it down. This felt like déjà vu. Just a few months ago I'd been afraid I was pregnant with Blane's child. Now I *was* pregnant, but with his brother's.

I hurried out of the room, intent on getting away as quickly as possible. I couldn't think, couldn't begin to process the abrupt turn my life had just taken. I felt inches from falling apart. If I could just make it to my car . . .

"Hey."

I was suddenly brought to a halt by a hand on my arm. I looked up to see that Blane had stepped into my path.

"What did the doctor say?" he asked.

My eyes were wide with panic. I swallowed, forcing my voice to be calm when I replied. "She said I was fine," I said, pasting a fake smile on my face. "Just like I told you."

Blane's eyes narrowed. "You're lying," he said flatly. "And I'm not in any kind of mood to be playing games with you. What did she say?"

Suddenly, it was all too much, and I snapped.

"Oh, now you've decided that you care? Listen, Blane, I don't give a *shit* what kind of *mood* you're in! It's my life and you made it quite clear that you're no longer in it. So don't threaten me, and don't push me!"

Blane's face could have been carved in stone as my words echoed in my head. I was breathing hard, my fists clenched at my sides, as I stared up at him. I took a couple of steps backward, then turned and hurried away. I saw other people in the hallway staring, but I kept my gaze straight ahead and didn't stop until I was locked safely inside the steamy oven of my car.

I started the engine but paused as I went to shift into drive. My hands were shaking, and it hit me all over again.

I was pregnant.

Leaning against the steering wheel, I started to sob.

CHAPTER FIVE

I drove home mechanically, everything on autopilot. My head throbbed from crying and my stomach was rolling. I trudged up the stairs to my apartment and unlocked the door.

Like a robot, I started sorting through the stack of mail sitting on my kitchen table, tossing three bills in a row into a separate pile. Two ads and a coupon book later, I saw an envelope that jerked me from my stupor. I'd been dreading this.

My grades had arrived.

I'd missed all my finals. I'd been kidnapped, then had attended Blane's hearing, all of which forced me to skip the exams. The money I'd spent on the classes had been wasted.

I opened the envelope, steeling myself for what I'd see, then sat staring in astonishment.

Straight As.

But that was impossible! The final exam counted for half my grade in some of these classes. By all rights, the highest I could have possibly gotten was maybe a C, if the professor had been kind. They must have gotten things mixed up in the computer or something—wait.

Computers. Of course.

Kade had done this. That's what he'd meant when he'd told me not to worry about it.

I wasn't sure how I felt about that. I disliked cheating, but what was I going to do? Go in there and tell them my friend had hacked their computers and changed my grades? Right.

Tossing the paper onto the kitchen table, I heaved a sigh. I'd just have to ask Kade to change them back, that's all. But later. Not right now. Not until he was better.

My bed beckoned, so I lay down and shut my eyes. I didn't want to think, didn't want to face the fact that I was pregnant.

So I slept, not waking until the insistent buzzing of my cell phone on the table beside me wouldn't stop. I glanced at the caller ID. Alisha.

"Hey," I answered tonelessly.

"Where are you?" she asked immediately.

"Home."

"Well, come let me in then. I've been banging on your door for ten minutes."

Obediently, I ended the call and climbed out of bed. I walked through the kitchen and living room to the front door, then opened it. Alisha stood there.

"You've had me worried sick," she complained, following me inside. "You didn't call me back after you talked to the doctor. I've been imagining all kinds of horrible things." She plopped down next to where I'd settled on the sofa. "So what did he say?"

"She," I automatically corrected.

Alisha rolled her eyes. "Just tell me."

Part of me, the irrational part that still hoped this was all a nightmare, didn't want to tell her because that would mean it was real. I forced myself to speak.

"She said . . . she said I'm pregnant," I stammered, my eyes filling with tears again.

Alisha looked as stunned as I still felt, but when she saw me start crying, she wrapped me in a tight hug.

"It'll be okay," she crooned to me as I sobbed.

"N-no, it w-won't," I sputtered through my tears.

"Of course it will," she soothed, patting me on the shoulder as I eased back from her. She grabbed a tissue box from the coffee table and handed it to me. "So, do you, um . . . know . . . who the father is?"

"Geez, Alisha!" I said in exasperation. "Please tell me you did *not* just ask me that."

"Hey, no judgment," she said, putting her hands up in a gesture of surrender. "I'm your friend here, remember?"

I sighed. "I know. And yeah, I know who the father is." I swallowed. "It's . . . it's Kade."

"Yes!" Alisha hissed, squeezing her eyes shut and pumping her fist.

I laughed a little at her antics. "Nice," I said dryly, though she smiled innocently at me.

My smile faded. "I don't know what I'm going to do. What's Blane going to say? And Kade—he's just going to totally freak out."

"What does Blane have to do with anything?" she huffed.

"They're brothers, Alisha," I sighed. "It's bad enough I fell in love with both of them. Slept with both of them. When I think of how they're going to react to this news . . . ?" I shuddered, unable to finish the thought aloud. I swallowed.

"Blane's going to hate me. Kade will pretend he doesn't care what Blane thinks, but we both know that's not true. Not to mention the fact that Kade and I haven't discussed anything long-term, and now I have to tell him he's going to be a father. The longest I've ever seen him stay in one place is a few weeks."

Alisha seemed to digest this before asking, "So what're you going to do?"

"I have absolutely no idea." My throat closed up again, but I forced the next thought out, putting my worst fear into words. "What if he leaves, Alisha? What if he just leaves me?"

She took my hand. "Hey," she said, forcing me to look at her. "You're not alone, no matter what Blane and Kade do or don't do. You have me. You have your friends. You won't be going through this alone."

I couldn't speak through the lump in my throat, so I squeezed her hand, hoping she understood what I was unable to say.

"I'm hungry," she said, sitting back and abruptly changing the subject. "I think I have a pizza in my freezer. Want to come help me eat it?"

My stomach growled and I realized I was famished. I hadn't eaten all day and frozen pizza sounded like heaven.

"Yeah, let me just run a brush through my hair and I'll be over," I said.

She agreed and left after making me promise I wouldn't take longer than a few minutes. I was just finishing brushing my teeth when my cell rang.

It was Kade.

I took a deep breath before I answered. I wanted to sound normal. I wasn't ready to tell him yet, especially not over the phone.

"Hey," I answered, making my voice bright and forcing a smile.

"I hope you're taking it easy tonight," Kade said.

"Um, yeah, I . . . uh . . . was going to visit with Alisha for a while, maybe go to bed early." I winced, remembering how I'd practically begged him to let me come back to the hospital tonight. Now I knew there was no way I could see him. I wouldn't be able to hide this from him. He'd see through me immediately.

"Good," he said. "I'm worried about you."

"No need," I replied, keeping my voice light. "I'm fine." And I was. The doctor said I was perfectly fine . . . for a woman growing another person inside her.

I smacked my palm against my forehead. *Stop thinking about it stop thinking about it stop—*

"Doctor says I get to blow this joint tomorrow, finally," he groused.

"Want me to pick you up?"

"Blane's coming to get me. You don't have to."

I let out a silent sigh of relief. Alrighty then. That'd be a big, fat *Hell no*, at least on my part. A car ride with all three of us? No way could I handle that.

"Okay, that's good," I said, then realized how that sounded. "I mean, that you're getting out."

Kade was quiet for a moment, then said, "Blane said you collapsed from exhaustion this morning."

I forced a laugh. "*Collapsed* sounds so dramatic! No, I just had a . . . a spell, that's all. Shouldn't have skipped dinner last night, I guess." Another fake laugh that petered away into awkward silence.

"Wow. You are really bad at that."

"At what?" I asked, stung.

"At lying." I could hear the eye-roll in his tone. "But since I want you to get some rest and I'll get it out of you tomorrow anyway, I'll let it pass."

Now it was my turn to roll my eyes. "Whatever," I muttered, channeling my inner teenager.

"Catch you on the flip side, princess." The line went dead.

I stood there a moment, trying not to acknowledge the panic rising inside me. Alisha had helped a little, but now the doubts and fear came rushing back.

What was I doing to do? Like, really? Was I really going to greet Kade tomorrow with *"Hi! So glad you're out of the hospital! Guess what? I'm pregnant! Congrats!"*

My hands started to shake as my head continued playing out the drama.

"Congratulations, Blane! You're going to be an uncle! I know it was just eight months ago when we thought I was pregnant with your baby. This time the test came back positive!"

My knees started knocking as I imagined the look on both of their faces.

"Oh my God," I moaned, sinking onto my couch. I couldn't do it. Literally. I could not face Blane and Kade and tell them this. Would Kade even want the baby? What if he didn't? It had been hard enough for him to accept what a liability *I* had become in his life. What would a baby, his own flesh and blood, do to him?

I started seeing spots and realized I was hyperventilating. I bent over, sticking my head between my knees, and tried to breathe. After a few minutes, my vision cleared.

Suddenly, I wanted to be close to Kade, but going to the hospital was out of the question. What I *could* do, though, was go to his apartment. All his things were there, I'd feel better, and he'd be none the wiser.

Grabbing my keys, I headed out the door, stopping by to tell Alisha I'd changed my mind on the pizza thing. She looked concerned but let me go. I think she realized I needed more time to come to grips with the new twist my life had just taken.

Kade lived only minutes from my apartment, and in no time I was parking in the garage and letting myself into his place. He'd given me his keys last week, in case I needed "something other than a piece of shit" to drive.

Kade's apartment was dark, save for the soft glow of the two lamps that hung over the bar. They were glass shades handmade in amber hues. The penthouse loft was quiet and still, the low hum of the refrigerator and the ticking of a clock the only sounds.

I felt the knot in my stomach ease as I stood there. Going into his bedroom, I stripped and took a shower, taking too long sniffing his shampoo. When I got out and dried off, I searched his clothes, grabbing a black T-shirt he'd worn and discarded. Holding it to my nose, I inhaled deeply. It smelled of Kade.

Dropping the towel, I pulled the shirt on over my head before crawling into his bed. Nuzzling my face into his pillow, I let out a deep sigh, drifting off to sleep.

~

My blood pounded in my veins and I moaned. There was the most delicious sensation between my legs. Warm and wet, a gentle nudge pushing my knees farther apart. Hands slipped between my folds for a touch even more intimate.

Pulling myself out of a deep slumber, I realized it wasn't a dream. The sheets and blanket had been tugged down to my feet and a man's head lay between my thighs, his mouth and tongue on me, inside me.

Jerking fully awake, I squeaked in alarm. Then he raised his head and the piercing blue of his eyes met mine.

Kade.

I didn't know how he'd gotten here or why he was no longer in the hospital, since they weren't supposed to release him until tomorrow, and I didn't care. I sat up quickly, my hands gripping his bare shoulders and pulling. I needed him. Now.

Our lips met in fevered passion and I was gratified he'd already shed his clothes. Moving up my body, our mouths still connected, he settled between my thighs. We parted only long enough for him to jerk my shirt over my head and toss it aside, then he was kissing me again. He pushed inside me in one strong thrust.

Mewling and sounds I couldn't control emanated from my throat as I wrapped my legs around his waist. Each stroke of his cock pushed me closer to the edge and my nails dug into his shoulders. My hips lifted to meet his thrusts until I couldn't keep up with his pace. Harder and faster and deeper until I was on fire. My orgasm seemed to reach all the way to my toes, Kade swallowing my cries, his length growing thicker inside me. His hips jackknifed into me as a hard tremor shook him, pushing me over the edge again, my body convulsing around his. He gave a masculine moan that was one of the best sounds I'd ever heard.

My legs were still wrapped around him, my heels resting on his ass, as we both lay there, panting. My heart thundered in my chest and I could feel that his pulse wasn't exactly normal, either.

Propping himself up on his arms, Kade looked down at me. I smiled—I couldn't help it. What other reaction could I possibly have to being woken by Kade making love to me?

He leaned down, pressing a hot, wet kiss to my lips, his tongue dipping inside to stroke mine. His hand brushed the hair back from my face as he cupped my cheek. My internal muscles tightened reflexively and he groaned.

"Best get-well present ever," he breathed against my lips.

I snorted a laugh, pushing against him a bit so I could see his eyes. "Best waking-up present ever," I teased.

His eyes smiled at me as he placed a gentle kiss on the tip of my nose. I lifted my hand, tracing the contour of a dark eyebrow with my thumb, my palm resting against his cheek. He turned his head slightly, pressing his lips into the center of my palm.

Easing off me, he rolled to the side, taking me with him so we lay face-to-face. He propped his head on one hand, leaning on his elbow, and I mirrored him.

"I thought they weren't letting you out until tomorrow," I said.

Kade found my hand, lacing our fingers together. "I decided to leave early," he said.

A twinge of alarm ran through me. "What do you mean?" I asked. "You left against doctor's orders?"

"Calm down," he said. "I'm fine. I couldn't stand being in there another minute. The stitches are healing well and everything looked good. So I left."

I heaved a sigh, falling onto my back and looking up at the ceiling. I couldn't blame him—I hated hospitals, too—but I worried.

"Besides," he said, making me look back over at him, "how could I stay in the hospital when I could be here? Doing this?" He leaned down, bracing himself as he lowered his head to my breasts. His lips brushed one acutely sensitive nipple and I sucked in a breath, watching as his mouth closed over me. His tongue began doing things that made heat pool again between my thighs, his fingers tweaking and rolling my other nipple until I was gasping.

"You have," he said, switching his mouth to the other breast, which seemed to tremble with want for the same lavish attention, "the most amazing breasts. Have I told you that? I should tell you that. Every. Day." Then his mouth was again working its magic and my eyes slammed shut. I felt his hand move down between my legs, his fingers becoming slick with our fluids as he stroked me.

"Oh God oh God oh God," I moaned, my hips lifting to meet his now thrusting fingers.

"You can call me Kade," he whispered against my lips.

I buried my hands in the thick softness of his hair as he kissed me. His hand moved faster, his touch gentle but persistent. Kade's mouth moved to trail down my neck, his teeth settling around my nipple with a soft tug. Stars exploded behind my eyes and I cried out, a wave of pleasure pulsing through me.

Kade was still nuzzling my breasts when at last I could again breathe normally and opened my eyes. My limbs felt languid and heavy.

"That was . . ." I began, but trailed off. Words couldn't describe it.

"Amazing? Mind-blowing? The earth moved?" Kade asked, pressing light kisses to my neck and shoulder.

I laughed. "Modest, aren't you?"

"I've never claimed that as one of my virtues. Actually, I've never claimed any virtues at all. They're overrated." He pulled me into him, tucking my head against his chest. "Go to sleep, princess," he said. His lips brushed my forehead.

I was too exhausted and sated to even contemplate all the things I should be worrying about. Kade was here. I focused on that. I hadn't realized until now how much it had bothered me that he'd been in the hospital and how relieved I'd be when he was out. But it was as though a weight had been lifted from my shoulders.

And I slept.

~

When I woke, I was alone in bed and sunlight was filtering in through the windows. I stretched, feeling a familiar soreness between my legs. Getting up, I went to the bathroom, eyeing the grin on my face that I couldn't seem to help. I took a quick shower and pulled on one of Kade's clean T-shirts before venturing to find him.

He was in his office, seated in front of his computer. Four large flat-screen monitors sat on the desk, obstructing my view of him. I sidled around the desk and he glanced up at me. He wore only a pair of pajama bottoms, leaving his chest deliciously bare. I noticed his hair was damp. He must have showered as well.

"Good morning," I said with a smile, sliding between his chair and the desk. Kade quickly reached out and hit a key on his keyboard. All four screens went dark.

I sat sideways on his lap and his hands settled on my hips. Leaning down, I gave him the best kiss I could before having my morning coffee. It must have been pretty good, because I could feel the surge of his response beneath me. When I pulled back, he was looking at me. His brows were drawn together, an emotion I couldn't read on his face, and his hand came up to cradle my cheek.

My smile faded at his expression. "What is it? What's wrong?" I asked in alarm. "Are you in pain?" I started to climb off his lap, but his grip tightened, holding me in place.

He shook his head. "I'm fine."

I studied him, frowning, but couldn't be sure he was telling me the truth. Suddenly, the blank monitors at my back reminded me.

"Hey," I said, "we have a problem." Kade's body stilled. "You changed my grades," I continued.

Kade relaxed slightly, his breath releasing. "I don't know what you're talking about," he said blandly. His hands were creeping underneath my shirt and I grabbed his wrists.

"You need to change them back," I insisted.

Kade cocked an eyebrow. "Make me." A smirk teased his lips and I couldn't be mad at him. I'd been so afraid I would never see that smirk again, hear him tease me again.

"C'mon," he said, standing and setting me on my feet. "I'm starving."

Enfolding my hand in his, Kade tugged me with him to the kitchen. I sat at the dining table while he peered into the refrigerator. A few minutes later, he was cracking eggs into a bowl while coffee brewed.

I got up and went over to watch him, hopping up to sit on the counter.

"I didn't know you cooked," I said as he scrambled the eggs and dumped them into a sauté pan.

"One of my many talents," Kade said, shooting me a smile. "Though if you want to strip down and make some muffins, I won't stop you."

I laughed, remembering when I'd last tried to cook for Kade and had forgotten a key ingredient. He'd walked in on me bare-ass naked as I tried to save the muffins.

"I'll spare you having to stomach my cooking," I retorted with a grin.

A few minutes later, he'd slid two omelets onto plates and poured two cups of coffee. I sat beside him at the table as he dug in, smiling to myself. His appetite was back, that was good.

Forking a bite of omelet, I popped it into my mouth, then froze. I loved eggs, but something about the omelet was . . . off. The texture suddenly seemed very, very wrong.

My stomach heaved, and I shot up from my chair and ran for the bathroom. I made it just in time.

I threw up, bent over the toilet, until there was nothing but dry heaves, noticing only then that Kade stood behind me, holding my hair back from my face. My eyes were watering and a wet washcloth suddenly appeared in my line of vision.

"Here," Kade said gently.

I took the cloth and wiped my face, sitting back against the wall in exhaustion. Kade flushed the toilet and shut the lid, then crouched down beside me.

"Is there something you want to tell me?" he asked.

His blue eyes stared intently into mine and I abruptly realized the truth.

"You already know, don't you," I managed to say. It wasn't a question.

Kade's gaze was steady. "That doesn't mean I don't want to hear you say it."

This was it. The moment I'd been anticipating and dreading. So much depended on his reaction to this news, though I supposed if he already knew and wasn't running for the door, that was something.

"I'm having a baby," I blurted. "Your baby." Then I held my breath.

Kade smiled, a real one that lit up his eyes, and he said the most perfect thing I could imagine.

"You mean *we* are having a baby."

Tears filled my eyes and I threw my arms around his neck just as he gathered me close. It was exactly the embrace I'd hoped to experience when I'd dreamed of having children and imagined telling the father the news that I was pregnant. The fact that Kade was that man staggered me, especially as

I considered how he and I had begun compared to where we were now.

"Feeling better?" he asked, loosening his hold on me. I sat back and nodded. "Good. Let's get you some crackers or something—how does that sound?"

"Okay," I agreed. "I'll be out in a minute."

Kade helped me to my feet and left the bathroom. I quickly brushed my teeth, glad the nausea had abated, though I didn't think I'd be eating eggs anytime soon.

By the time I came out, Kade had finished off both omelets and was putting the plates into the dishwasher. I noticed he'd thoughtfully put some soda crackers and dry toast at my place setting. I sat in the chair I'd abandoned, pulling my knees to my chest, and nibbled on a cracker.

"How did you know?" I asked.

Kade turned around to look at me, leaning back against the counter while he sipped his coffee. My gaze drifted down to the way the muscles in his chest and arm moved. The pajamas he wore rode low on his hips. A line of dark hair that began just below his navel and disappeared behind the waistband drew my eye.

"If you expect to have an actual conversation, you'll have to keep your eyes above my waist."

I jerked my gaze up to his, the mischief in his eyes and knowing tilt to his lips made my breath catch. I was still overwhelmed by the sheer beauty of Kade.

"Sorry," I mumbled around the cracker I'd stuffed in my mouth. My hormones seemed to be working overtime, even after our middle-of-the-night lovemaking, and the last thing I wanted to put in my mouth was another dry cracker.

I chewed and swallowed before asking again, "So how did you know?"

"Hacked your medical records," he replied with a careless shrug before taking another sip.

My hand froze halfway to my mouth, the cracker I held, forgotten. I suddenly remembered the computer screens that he'd caused to go dark the moment I'd stepped into his office. He must have been looking at my records right then.

"You *hacked*—"

"Now don't get all pissed off," Kade interrupted, setting his coffee down and walking over to me. "Stop and think. Does it *really* surprise you that I'd do that?"

Well . . . no. It didn't. But I felt like I *should* be mad—it was an invasion of privacy, after all. Then again, we were having a baby together. Was the privacy of my medical records from my baby's father really a top concern right then?

Nope.

"If you weren't still wearing bandages, then I'd be mad at you," I said loftily.

"Then I'll have to make sure to wear them at all times," he shot back, pulling me to my feet. His hands drifted under the hem of my shirt, cupping my bottom through the thin pair of boxer shorts I'd found to wear.

"Oooh, boy's underwear," Kade breathed against my lips. "Sexy."

My giggle was muffled by his mouth as he kissed me, then his fingers slipped inside the shorts and I stopped laughing.

~

Afterward, we lay in companionable silence on Kade's bed, me on my back and Kade between my legs, his cheek resting on my stomach. My pulse was slowly returning to normal as my fingers threaded leisurely through Kade's hair, the strands soft as corn silk.

He turned his head and placed a gentle kiss low on my abdomen, right under my navel, and my heart turned over in my chest.

"I was so afraid you'd be angry," I said softly.

Kade looked up at me, laying an arm across my stomach and resting his chin on it.

"Why would I be angry?" he asked, frowning.

I shrugged. "Bad timing, I guess. And I just . . . didn't know how you'd feel about it."

Kade looked at me for a moment, his blue eyes seeing too much, then he crawled up my body until he hovered over me.

"I love you," he said. "How could I possibly be mad about the best thing that's ever happened to me?"

I reached up and curled my arms around his neck, pulling him down to me. My vision was blurred with tears.

"Don't cry," he whispered in my ear, his lips brushing away the wet tracks down the side of my face.

"I'm not crying because I'm sad," I whispered back. "I'm crying because I'm happy." I smiled through my tears.

"Oh. Well, I guess that's all right then," he said, his cocky grin returning. He flopped onto the bed beside me, swiping the wet trails from my face. "So, I have a business thing I have to do in Boston. Want to come with?"

My heart leapt. He was taking me with him. "Absolutely," I said, my smile so wide it almost hurt, then I remembered something and my smile faded.

"What?" Kade asked, frowning.

I hesitated. "Are you—" I began, then cut myself off. I wasn't sure how to ask what was inside my head.

"Am I what?" Kade repeated.

"Are you going to keep doing the same job?" I blurted, my face heating. I didn't want that, didn't want Kade to continue taking contracts as an assassin. I'd always felt that a little of his soul died every time he killed someone. He was better than that, deserved better than that. And I didn't want to think about how dangerous his job was or how many close calls he'd no doubt had over the years.

"I told you in Vegas that I was starting something new," he said, reaching out to play with a strand of my hair. He idly twisted the long curl around his finger.

"I know," I said, "but after what happened, I wasn't sure if—"

"Shhh." He placed a finger against my lips. "I'll make it work. I'll keep you and the baby safe. I won't let anything happen to you. I'm through doing what I used to do. I promise."

Kade did not make promises. Ever. The fact that he'd just done so momentarily robbed me of speech.

"You'd do that for me?" I asked.

Kade leaned over, resting his body half atop mine, and kissed me. When he pulled back, his blue eyes stared into mine. "I'd do anything for you."

Tears flooded my eyes again and I wrapped my arms around him, holding him as tight as I could. Finally, we parted.

"Before we go," I said, "we have to tell Blane."

A heavy silence fell between us at the mention of his name. Kade turned onto his back, his gaze on the ceiling.

"I'll do it," he offered.

"No. I should be the one to tell him." He turned to look at me. "He deserves that much," I said. Though I quaked inside at just the thought of that conversation.

Kade wasn't smiling, and his brows were drawn together in a frown. The deep blue of his gaze held mine for a long moment.

"All right," he said finally. "Tell him tonight. We leave tomorrow."

I swallowed. "Okay."

∼

I tried to remember the conviction I'd felt earlier that I should be the one to do this as I stood outside Blane's house in the deepening twilight shadows. I'd driven around the block at least half a dozen times before I finally mustered up the courage to actually park, then had taken another ten minutes before I'd convinced myself to get out of the car.

Now I stood staring at the forbidding front door, trying to persuade myself to knock. It was nearly dark and if I kept standing there, the mosquitoes were going to eat me alive.

I raised my hand just as the door suddenly swung open. I jumped back, startled, then saw it was Mona.

"Kathleen!" she exclaimed in surprise. "I wasn't expecting you there." She smiled and reached out to hug me. "So good to see you."

I hugged her back. "Good to see you, too," I replied.

We parted and I cleared my throat, glancing nervously over her shoulder into the darkened hallway.

"Um, is Blane home?" I asked, the coward in me fervently wishing he wasn't.

"He is," she confirmed, dashing my hopes. "I believe he's in the library. Shall I announce you?"

I shook my head. "That's okay. May I come in?"

"Of course." She stepped back to let me in, then passed me as she moved out the door. "Just heading home for the evening. Good night!"

"Night, Mona," I said.

She closed the door behind her, leaving me standing in the empty hallway.

Memories assailed me and I wondered, not for the first time, if I was doing the right thing. There was so much history between Blane and me, my feelings for him so confused, that I nearly turned around and walked out.

But I couldn't do that. He needed to know, and didn't deserve hearing it from someone other than me.

The door to the library was closed. I raised my hand and knocked.

"Come in," I heard after a moment.

Tentatively, I turned the knob and pushed open the door.

"Leaving for the night, Mona?" Blane asked, his voice flat. His back was to me. He sat at the piano, smoke from the cigarette in his hand curling as it drifted upward. Only one lamp was lit in the far corner, leaving much of the room in shadows.

I couldn't speak. The loneliness of the scene broke my heart.

When I didn't answer, Blane half turned, and spotted me. He froze for a moment, then deliberately stubbed out his cigarette and stood.

The sleeves of his shirt were unbuttoned, the cuffs turned back. His hair was mussed slightly, and he quickly ran his fingers through it to arrange it properly as he walked toward me.

"Kat," he said when he was close, "I wasn't expecting you."

I forced myself to speak. "I'm sorry to intrude, to be here uninvited," I began, the stilted formality between us making my voice shake.

"It's all right," he interrupted. "Come in. Sit down. Let me get you a drink."

"No, that's—"

But he was already moving to the sideboard, pouring two glasses of scotch. Returning, he handed me one and I laid down my keys to take it from him.

"Sit down," he encouraged, but I remained standing.

"Blane—" I began, but he interrupted again.

"I apologize about yesterday," he said gruffly. "I was worried, and I had a shitty way of showing it."

"It's okay," I said, guilt rising like nausea. His eyes were a brilliant green as he watched me, seeming to drink in my presence.

Although I wanted nothing more than to swallow the liquid courage in my hand, I carefully set aside the glass he'd given me. "Blane, I came tonight to tell you something," I said.

He didn't answer. He just looked at me.

"Kade and me—" My voice faltered and I had to force the words out, cringing inwardly as I did so. "Blane, I'm pregnant."

Blane's whole body went still as stone. I waited, expecting . . . I don't know what. But he did nothing for several moments.

"Please," I said in a broken whisper when I couldn't stand the silence any longer, "say something."

My words seemed to jar him and he lifted his glass to his lips, taking a long swallow of the amber fluid.

"Congratulations," he rasped.

I waited, but he said nothing more. "That's it?" I asked. "That's all you're going to say?"

"What more do you want from me?" he yelled, making me jump.

I stared at him, wide-eyed, but he didn't yell again. Instead, his jaw clenched tightly before he turned away and headed to the sideboard to refill his glass. His voice was toneless when he said, "I'm sure you can see yourself out."

My throat closed off as I choked back a sob, his coldness cutting me so deep it felt like ice had buried itself in my stomach. Turning, I rushed from the room, flinging myself out of the house and half running toward my car.

I leaned against the metal, still lukewarm from the day's heat, and cried. I hadn't known what I'd expected. There was no path back to what Blane and I had once been.

After several minutes, I regained control of myself and got in the car. Only then did I realize I'd left my keys inside the house.

"Dammit!" I exploded, slamming a hand against the steering wheel. I roughly brushed my hands across my cheeks and cursed six ways from Sunday over what I knew I had to do.

Getting out of the car, I walked back inside, only to stumble to a halt inside the doorway.

Crashes. The sound of breaking glass.

My feet moved until I was standing in the open door to the library, aghast and staring in dismay at what Blane had wrought.

The room was demolished. Everything breakable was smashed, glass and shards of wood littering the floor. Books from the shelves were strewn everywhere. The flat-screen television had been ripped from its alcove on the wall and thrown onto the floor. The only thing that remained untouched was the piano, which stood, pristine, in the midst of chaos.

Blane stood in the center of the room, his shoulders heaving from exertion. I watched in silence as he pulled a pack of cigarettes from his pocket and removed one. He set it to his lips with hands that shook slightly. I heard the rasp of a lighter, and then he saw me.

He seemed to hesitate for a moment, then finished lighting the cigarette and took a long drag.

"Was there something else?" he said on an exhale. "You wanted revenge? Congratulations. You got it."

"How could you possibly think that?" I asked, sudden anger rising in me. "*You* ended us first, Blane, *not* me. Was I supposed to come running back to you every time you broke my trust? Did you think there wouldn't be consequences? Or did you just think you could control those, too?"

Our eyes held and Blane was the one to finally glance away, taking another drag of the cigarette.

I sighed and rubbed a hand across my forehead. A headache was coming on. "I'm sorry, Blane," I said. "I'm sorry this happened. I never meant to fall in love with Kade, never meant to hurt you in this way. I know you may not believe it, but it's killing me, seeing you like this. I just—" I broke off and had to swallow, then took a deep breath. "Please forgive me."

Blane stubbed out his cigarette and sighed. He pushed one hand through his hair while the other rested on his hip.

"It's just so sudden, Kat," he said, his voice edged in bitterness. "A few months ago, I thought maybe it would be us starting a family, and I wanted that so goddamn much. Then everything went to shit. I thought I might get you back, that I still had a chance, and now that's shot to hell, too." He paused. "I can't forgive you. Not yet."

I nodded, unable to speak. Moving forward and avoiding his eyes, I snagged my keys off the table.

"Kade and I are leaving town tomorrow," I said. "Heading to Boston, I think. Kade has business there."

Blane didn't say anything, just nodded and turned away. Hesitantly, I moved toward him, my steps muffled by the carpet. When I was close enough, I slid my arms around his waist and rested my cheek against his back, squeezing him in a hug. His body was stiff, unyielding, and he gave no sign at all that he even noticed me.

Stepping away from him, I left without another word.

CHAPTER SIX

It was hard to concentrate on packing. Kade had said we'd be gone for a while, so obviously I needed to take a decent amount of clothes, but all I could see in my head was the way Blane had looked at me when I'd told him I was having Kade's baby.

I prayed that Kade's and my departure would help, that being out of sight would make it easier on Blane. But I couldn't pretend I wasn't going to miss him.

I was nearly finished when I heard the knock. I dropped the shirt I'd been folding, hurrying to the front door. Hopefully, it was Kade. I'd tried calling him after I'd left Blane's, but he hadn't answered and it had been hours since then.

Hastily pulling open the door, my welcoming smile froze when I saw who it was.

Blane.

The expression on his face was stark, his lips set in a grim line. Remembering how he'd demolished the room earlier, I took an instinctive step back, my pulse jumping with nerves, but he made no move toward me.

"I need to talk to you," he said.

I swallowed. Was he still angry? Kade was supposed to come by and pick me up along with my luggage. It would be bad if he showed up while Blane was still here. I couldn't handle a confrontation between them.

"Um, I'm kinda in the middle of packing," I hedged. "Can it wait? I can call you tomorrow."

At my words, a hint of pity flashed across Blane's face.

"No, Kat," he said softly. "It can't wait."

Something about the way he said that made the blood drain from my face and I started to shake.

"What happened?" I asked. "Is it Kade? Is he okay?" Panic clawed at me.

Blane hurriedly stepped inside, taking my hand as he shut the door behind him. He led me to the couch and I gratefully sank down onto the cushions when he tugged on me, my knees suddenly weak.

"He's okay," Blane said. "Kade's not hurt."

His reassurance made the breath leave my lungs in a rush and I slumped over, relieved. I didn't know what I would've done if something had happened to him.

"Kat—" Blane began, then stopped. I glanced up at him. He paused, the look on his face twisting into one of regret. My stomach dropped.

Suddenly, I didn't want to know, didn't want to hear whatever it was that Blane couldn't even bring himself to say. I jumped to my feet.

"I really need to finish packing. Kade's going to be here any minute and you know how he hates to wait . . ." I babbled, turning and walking back toward the bedroom.

"Kat—"

Blane was following me, but I kept going, not stopping until I was back in front of my suitcase. I grabbed the shirt I'd dropped, my hands trembling as I tried to fold it.

"Do you think Mona would keep Tigger for a while? I don't know how long we'll be gone. He didn't say. But Tigger likes it over there and Mona loves him, so I can't imagine that she'd mind—"

"Kat!"

I jumped, my mouth snapping shut.

Blane stepped up to me, removing the shirt from my fingers and then taking my hands in his.

"He's not coming," Blane said much more gently. "Kade. He left."

My heart seemed to stutter and my hands turned to ice.

"Wh-what do you mean?" I asked. "Of course he's coming. He said—"

"He's not coming," Blane repeated.

I jerked my hands out of his grip. "Stop saying that! You're wrong!" I hurried to my bureau, yanking open a drawer and pulling out a handful of shorts. "He'll be here. Any minute now. He said he'd come." I avoided looking at Blane as I piled the shorts in the open suitcase sitting on my bed.

Kade wouldn't leave me. He just . . . wouldn't.

"He came by the house," Blane said. "He said . . . he said he was leaving. Alone. And he's not coming back."

I let out an involuntary gasp from the pain that lanced through me at Blane's words. The clothes in my hands dropped to the floor. I turned on Blane.

"Why would you say that!" I screamed at him. "Why are you telling me such . . . such lies!" I spun away, but Blane snagged me around the waist and pulled me into him.

"I'm sorry," he said, his voice breaking. "Listen to me. He's gone, and I'm so, so sorry."

I fought him, pushing and struggling to get away, agony building in my chest while tears poured down my cheeks. Finally, I ran out of fight, of denying what I knew was the truth, and I sagged limply against Blane, my body shaking with sobs I couldn't control.

Blane's shirt grew damp, my tears leaking through the starched white cotton, but he kept holding me. His strength was the only thing that kept me on my feet, his arms holding me tight, a hand cradling the back of my head while I cried.

My breath hiccupped in my chest when I finally stopped crying. I felt exhausted, my emotions numb. Kade had left me, didn't want me. Why? What had I done wrong? He'd seemed so happy when I told him I was pregnant. Had he been lying to me? Or just had second thoughts once I'd left?

I looked up at Blane, needing some kind of answer. "Why?" I managed to ask, my voice a hoarse rasp from crying. "What did I do?"

"Kat, listen to me," Blane said, his palms cradling my cheeks. "It's got nothing to do with you. You didn't do anything. It's Kade. And I can't pretend to understand why he does the things he does."

But Blane was wrong. It had to be me, had to be that I was pregnant. Kade hadn't really wanted me, or at least not now that I carried his baby. I'd sprung it on him out of nowhere after we'd only slept together a few times. We hadn't even had an official relationship and I'd tried to tie him to me for life. How could I have expected him to react any differently?

I stepped out of Blane's arms and he seemed reluctant to let me go. I sank down to sit on the bed, staring straight ahead at nothing. I felt numb.

I was going to have to do this alone. The shock of being pregnant had faded when I'd been with Kade earlier, his open acceptance easing my worry and fears. Now it all came rolling back with a vengeance, and I felt if I even breathed too deep, I'd shatter into a million pieces.

"Kat," Blane said, crouching down in front of me. He rested his hands on my knees. "Come home with me. Even if it's just for a few days. I don't want to leave you here alone."

Absently, I looked at Blane. The pity in his eyes was almost more than I could bear. I was his ex-girlfriend, pregnant with his brother's child and abandoned by him. Yet here Blane was, offering me solace and comfort.

But there was no way I could accept. I'd put Blane through enough.

I shook my head. "I'll be fine on my own." Somehow.

Disappointment flashed across his face, then was gone. Searching my eyes, he finally gave a nod and stood.

"Did he say where he was going?" I asked, my voice small. "I'm not going to . . . bother him, if that's what you're thinking. I just . . . wondered."

"He didn't say," Blane replied.

Tears sparked my eyes again and I couldn't speak, so I nodded.

"I'll come by tomorrow," he promised.

I forced the next words out. "And you'll call if you . . . hear anything?" The request sounded pathetic, but I couldn't help it.

A pause. "Yeah. I will."

Blane bent and I felt his lips brush the top of my head. My eyes slipped closed, more traitorous tears leaking from my eyes. I heard his steps recede, and a moment later the front door opened and shut behind him.

I sat there, the agonizing ache in my chest squeezing my lungs like a vise. I had no thoughts, no plan for what to do other than taking my next breath. It seemed impossible that my heart could still beat when I was in such pain. How was this not killing me?

Kade was gone. I would probably never see him again. Blane hadn't even sounded like *he* would see him again, and they were brothers. And worse, Kade didn't *want* to see me.

There had to be some mistake. Something had happened. Or maybe he thought I wanted to get married and that had spooked him. If I could just talk to him . . .

I jumped to my feet. I had a key to his apartment. Maybe he wasn't gone yet.

Grabbing my keys and cell, I hurried to my car, not even stopping to put on shoes. I broke the speed limit on my way to Kade's apartment, screeching into the parking garage and slamming the car into park. Seconds later, I was jamming my finger repeatedly on the elevator call button.

My hands shook as I unlocked Kade's door. I pushed it open and stepped inside, flipping on a light switch.

The place looked exactly the same as it had hours earlier, as though Kade had just stepped out. Dishes from breakfast were still in the sink. But I could tell immediately that no one was there. The apartment held an emptiness that I could feel.

Hoping against hope, I ventured farther, back to the bedroom. The bed was unmade, the sheets, blankets, and pillows where we'd left them when Kade and I had climbed from the cottony cocoon earlier. Making my feet move, I went to the closet. Kade's clothes remained, hung neatly on wooden hangers.

Nothing gave any kind of an impression that Kade had left in a hurry, or permanently. Maybe Blane had been wrong, but then, where was Kade?

Pulling my cell from my pocket, I dialed him.

The number had been disconnected.

My legs wouldn't hold me anymore and I sank onto the bed. Kade was gone. Really gone. And I knew it, deep down inside, in the place where you just know that the bad thing tearing your life apart is real, and isn't going away.

Something broke inside me then, though I couldn't say what it was. After everything, all that had happened, what I'd been through—Kade's blood on my hands, almost losing him, kidnappings, beatings, too many close brushes with death. All of it had been for nothing.

I was alone and I was having a baby. It terrified me. How was I supposed to raise a child when I didn't want to face another day?

Sitting with my back to the headboard, I pulled my knees into my chest. I was cold, though it was warm in Kade's bedroom. I didn't think, didn't feel, and didn't care. I stared at the wall, listening to the deafening silence of the apartment. Kade would come back. He had to. If he didn't, for the first time in a young life already filled with too many bad things, I didn't wonder *how* I'd go on—I wondered if I even wanted to.

~

My phone was buzzing. I opened my eyes, blinking blearily. Sunlight streamed in the room now. The phone lay on the floor a few feet from me. I vaguely remembered dropping it.

I stared at it until it stopped.

~

Voices.

I opened my eyes. The room was dark. My body ached from being in the same position for so long. I didn't care. Then it hit me all over again. Kade was gone. A fresh wave of despair washed over me.

The voices grew closer, but I didn't care enough to listen. The light flipped on and I winced in the sudden glare.

"Kathleen!"

A woman's voice. Alisha's, I thought.

"She's in here!"

She sounded panicked, and I wanted to tell her that I was okay, but couldn't summon the energy to speak.

Alisha dropped onto the bed beside me. "Kathleen, we've been searching all over for you. God, I was so worried—" She was fighting tears now.

A man's torso suddenly appeared in my vision, then Alisha moved and he took her spot on the bed.

Blane.

The moment I saw him, tears started leaking from my eyes.

"He's gone," I whispered. "He left me. He left the baby. He just . . . left us."

The look on Blane's face was stark, then he pulled me close to his chest. "I know," he said softly, his lips moving against my hair. "But I've got you." He stood, lifting me in his arms. My head was buried against his neck, my tears wetting his skin, as I fisted a handful of his suit coat and held on.

∼

"How did you find me?" I asked later. Blane had taken me to his house and placed me in his bed. I hadn't protested.

"I stopped by Alisha's after I left," Blane said, "asked her to check on you in the morning, but you weren't there. When you hadn't come back by the afternoon and didn't answer your cell, she finally called me."

My face heated in embarrassment, and I looked away from Blane's steady gaze. "I'm sorry," I said. "I didn't mean for anyone to worry."

"It's my fault," Blane replied, taking my hand in his. "You were in shock and I shouldn't have left you alone."

I swallowed hard, tears swimming in my eyes when I looked back at him. "I hate feeling weak," I whispered.

Pain flashed across his face, then he was moving to lie down beside me and gathering me in his arms.

"You are *not* weak," he said fiercely. "Don't ever think that."

Blane's fingers combed lightly through my hair as he cradled me close. I breathed in the warm, familiar scent of him, easing into the strength of his body. I could hide away here, in the circle of his arms, and the pain was a little easier to take.

"Thank you." My words were a small breath of sound, but I knew Blane heard them.

"I don't need to be thanked," he said softly.

I gripped him tighter, my throat closing. We stayed that way for a long time, until I drifted to sleep.

~

It was the middle of the night when I woke again. Mechanically, I rose and went into the bathroom. My mind started spinning and I had to force myself not to think. I didn't want to think. If I did, I would feel, and I couldn't handle the pain. Not yet.

I stepped into the shower, standing under the hot spray of water, and let it wash over me. I scrubbed, rinsing my hair until the strands squeaked. Drying off, I found a toothbrush and brushed my teeth, then wrapped myself in Blane's rarely used robe that hung on the back of the door.

When I emerged from the bathroom, I could see Blane was sitting on the side of the bed. He'd changed into pajama pants, his shirt discarded. The soft glow of the bathroom light illuminated him when he glanced up at me. He stood as I approached.

"Feel better?" he asked.

I shrugged. "Yeah. I guess."

"You didn't brush your hair," he said.

I shrugged again, not caring about my tangled hair.

Blane moved past me into the bathroom, returning in a moment with a brush in his hand.

"Sit down," he said.

I climbed into the bed, sitting cross-legged while he knelt behind me. In a moment, I felt the bristles gently pull through my wet hair.

It was a scene oddly reminiscent of that night so many months ago, when Blane had brushed my hair while we sat in my bed. He was just as gentle now as he had been then, easing through the tangles he encountered.

The huge gaping hole inside my chest didn't seem like it was going to consume me, not with Blane there.

When he was finished, he set the brush aside and helped me under the covers, tucking them around my body, then he turned away.

I caught at his hand. "Where are you going?"

"I'll sleep in the other room," he said, giving my hand a squeeze.

Disappointment flooded me, but I understood. What, was I going to ask him to sleep in his own bed with me when I'd rejected him for his brother? Was I that selfish?

I bit my lip to keep from saying anything and just nodded, lowering my hand.

Blane seemed to hesitate. "Did you want me to stay?"

Our eyes met. "Only if you want to," I said.

He gave a small nod, then went and switched off the bathroom light, plunging the room back into darkness. It took a moment for my eyes to adjust, but Blane didn't seem to have a problem navigating his way back to the bed. He pulled back the covers and the bed dipped from his weight.

Blane's arm rested in the curve of my waist, drawing me back against him spoon fashion. I felt small next to his bulk, and my body relaxed.

$\sim$

When I woke again, the sun was up and Blane was no longer in bed with me.

I sat up, hearing the sound of his razor coming from the bathroom. The robe I'd been wearing was all askew and I rearranged it.

The heavy weight pressing on my chest wasn't any lighter, but at least I felt I could stand again. Even if it was inch by inch, I had to keep going. Having another breakdown wasn't an option. Even now, my face burned with embarrassment at what I'd put Alisha and Blane through. I needed to call her later, to apologize and thank her.

The razor stopped and I heard the sound of water running. After a moment, Blane stepped out of the bathroom. He was shirtless and barefoot, wearing just a pair of gym shorts. I thought he must have worked out earlier, when I'd been sleeping.

"What time is it?" I asked.

"A little after ten," he answered, walking over to me. "You need to eat something."

"I know." I looked up at him. "Aren't you supposed to be at work?"

"The police finally released Kandi's body. The funeral is today," he said.

My eyes widened. "Are you going?"

He nodded.

"Alone?"

"Mona and Gerard will be there," he said, heading to his closet.

I hesitated. "Do you want me to go with you?"

Blane paused from sorting through his dress shirts. "You would?"

"Of course," I said. "I mean, I don't want to intrude—"

"You're not an intrusion," Blane cut me off.

"Then I'll go get ready." I climbed out of the bed, trying to ignore the way Blane's gaze dropped to the length of thigh I'd unwittingly exposed.

An hour later, I'd forced down a bagel that Mona had brought me—my stomach was still not feeling normal and I didn't know if the nausea was from the pregnancy, Kade leaving me, or a combination of the two. I'd pulled on a black sleeveless dress and black heels, pinning my hair up into a French twist.

Checking myself over in the mirror, I frowned at the drawn, pinched look to my face. The shadows under my puffy eyes were immune to makeup. An oversized pair of black sunglasses would help that, though.

My gaze caught on the gold heart-shaped locket that hung between my breasts. Kade had given it to me at Christmas. I'd said that the reason I'd hardly taken it off since was because it held a photo of my parents, but I was through lying to myself.

I kept it on because Kade had given it to me.

Lifting my hands to the catch, I hesitated, then lowered my arms. I couldn't take it off. I knew I should, but not yet. I wasn't ready.

My stomach knotted and I thought the bagel was going to make a reappearance. I grabbed the bedpost to steady myself as a wave of anguish rolled over me.

Kade was gone, and this time he wasn't coming back.

That black hole threatened to engulf me and it felt like I couldn't breathe. I was pregnant, with the baby of a man who'd lied to me, then walked out on me.

What was I going to do? I was a bartender with no money, no family. School was out of the question now—no way could I afford an education *and* a baby. Who would take care of it while I worked? I could barely feed myself, so how was I supposed to feed a baby?

I couldn't breathe, the air choking in my lungs. Black spots danced in front of my eyes as I clutched the bedpost.

"It's okay. Kat, it's okay. Just breathe. Look at me."

Blane's hand under my chin forced my head up until I met his green gaze.

"Breathe, okay? Look at me. Breathe." Blane gently pried my hand from its vise grip on the bedpost, moving it to his shoulder. "Hold on to me, okay?"

My hand fisted the black suit coat he wore, and I focused with difficulty on the rhythm of his breathing, forcing myself to echo it. Gradually, the spots cleared, the weight against my chest easing.

Blane's face was grim, his mouth set in a tight line. "You need to lie down," he said.

"No, I'm fine," I protested, resisting his tug on me. "We've got to go, right? Can't be late."

His brows furrowed. "Maybe it's not a good idea for you to come."

"I'm fine," I said again, my voice stronger this time. "I just . . . had a moment, that's all. It's been a rough few days. Let's just go."

I grabbed my purse off the bureau and headed for the door, feeling Blane's eyes on me, but he didn't say anything more and followed me.

It was sunny outside and I dug my sunglasses from my purse. Blane held the door of the Jaguar for me and I slipped inside. A moment later, we were heading north on Meridian.

"You want to tell me what the panic attack was for?" Blane asked.

I glanced at him. Sunglasses hid his eyes, but the hard set of his jaw raised a red flag.

"I'm sorry," I said. "It's just a little . . . overwhelming."

"I'm not mad," Blane clarified. "But if you're panicking because you think you're alone, you're not. You have me."

I shook my head, turning to stare out the window. "I'm not going to do that to you, Blane," I said. "You deserve better. I'll be fine on my own. I just need a plan, that's all."

Blane pulled into the cemetery, finding a place to park among the cars already there. Once he had, he turned to face me.

"I don't want you on your own. I want you with me."

Stunned, I didn't have an opportunity to reply before he was out of the car, rounding to my side and pulling open my door.

There were people walking by, also clad in black, so I refrained from saying anything as I got out of the car. Blane offered his arm and we walked up a sloping hill to where a large number of people were gathered.

We stayed toward the back and a little bit apart from the others. Though Blane had been cleared in Kandi's murder— the real killer had confessed and was now behind bars—I could tell he was trying not to draw any attention to us.

Another freshly dug grave was nearby, and I realized it was for Kandi's father. I couldn't feel remorse for his death. He'd tried to kill Blane, had nearly killed Kade instead.

The service started, though we were too far away to hear the words spoken. After a while, someone began playing a melody on a flute. It sounded ethereal and lonely, a stark contrast to the sunny day and the flowers that dotted the lush, green landscape. Members of Kandi's extended family passed by the casket, placing pink roses on top.

Blane stood stiffly beside me and I reached for his hand, lacing our fingers together. He said nothing, but his grip was tight.

When the service was over, we turned to go, but someone blocked our path.

"You've got some balls, Kirk, showing your face here."

I sucked in a breath. It was James. He was also dressed in a black suit, and he looked livid.

"I've known Kandi all her life," Blane said evenly.

"It's because of you that she's dead," James spat.

Blane gripped my hand so tight it hurt. "Every time I speak to you, I find fewer and fewer reasons for you not to be in a grave, Gage."

"Speaking of which, so sorry to hear about your buddy Dennon getting shot," James retorted in mock sympathy. "Was a close call, wasn't it?"

Blane lunged and I shoved myself between them. "No, Blane!" I said, trying to push him back. It was like trying to move granite. "Not here!"

"Better listen to her," James sneered. "Tell me, does she screw both of you at once, or does Dennon fuck you in the ass while she watches?"

I spun around, my fist coming up and crashing into James's nose. There was a crunching sound, a look of shock on James's face, then blood began pouring. He stumbled back, his hands flying up to cover his nose.

Blane grabbed my arm and hauled me none too gently back to the car, moving so fast I had to run to keep up. In no time flat, we were in the Jaguar and speeding away from the cemetery.

I glanced at Blane, trying to read his expression. Shit. He was pissed.

"Listen, Blane—" I began, wanting to apologize. Well, not really. James had deserved it. Maybe I couldn't shoot him, but apparently I had no qualms about punching him. Yet I'd made a scene at Kandi's funeral and that was just wrong.

"That was fucking incredible," Blane interrupted. "You've got one helluva right hook, Kat." He shot me a grin.

I laughed, relieved he wasn't angry.

"So were you defending my honor?" he teased.

I thought about it. "I guess so." Huh. "James is disgusting," I said. "He deserved it." And now maybe he'd finally leave me alone.

"Couldn't agree more," Blane said. "How's the hand?"

I realized that my hand was killing me. "Hurts like hell," I said. "But worth it."

Blane drove us back to his house, opening the car door for me when we arrived. His hand settled on my waist as we walked up the drive.

He led me to the den, then went to the kitchen. When he reappeared, he was carrying an ice pack wrapped in a thin dish towel.

"Come sit down," he said, and I perched next to him on the sofa. He took my hand, gently laying the ice on my aching knuckles. I hissed a breath. I'd seriously have to rethink it if I ever wanted to punch someone in the nose again.

Blane raised his head and our gazes met, his eyes a stormy gray, the green mere flecks now. The black suit he wore was expertly tailored, like all his suits, encasing his wide shoulders in the expensive fabric. He still wore his tie, silver-and-black-striped silk knotted perfectly at his throat. His blond hair didn't have a strand out of place. He was so perfect, I was momentarily without words as I studied him. When had I started seeing Blane as ordinary? When had I begun taking him for granted?

Discarding his jacket and tie, he crouched down to remove my heels, then sat next to me on the sofa. Wrapping an arm around my shoulders, he drew me toward him until I was nestled comfortably against his chest.

Blane reached for the remote and flipped on the television, clicking through the channels until he hit a movie. We'd both seen it already, but it was one of those you can watch again and again and still enjoy it. My knuckles were numb now, which was better than how they'd felt before, and I set aside the ice pack. Blane's fingers combed idly through my hair as we sat comfortably in silence, watching TV. I tucked my legs beneath me on the sofa, releasing a deep sigh. My eyelids grew heavy.

I woke slowly, too comfortable to jerk awake. I'd slid down and now my head rested on Blane's lap. The television was muted and I saw that the movie was over, something else now playing. It was dark outside and I realized I'd slept for a while.

Blane's hand rested in the curve of my waist and I twisted a little to see his elbow braced on the arm of the sofa. He'd been staring off into space, but now glanced down at me, his lips tipping up in a tiny smile.

"Feel better?" he asked. His hand stroked a stray lock of hair back from my face, then rested lightly on my head.

"I'm sorry I fell asleep," I said, moving to sit up. I was a little embarrassed to have used him like a pillow.

"It's fine," Blane said, pressing lightly on my stomach to still me. I looked up at him. "You've been exhausted the past few weeks," he said. "You deserved a nap."

My stomach chose then to complain loudly that I hadn't eaten since breakfast. My face got red and I groaned with embarrassment. "Sorry," I muttered.

But Blane only chuckled. "Sounds like it's time for dinner," he teased. "Why don't you go freshen up and then meet me in the kitchen?"

I nodded. "Okay."

I changed out of the dress I'd worn to the funeral, pulling on a pair of shorts and a T-shirt, which were much more comfortable. I washed off my makeup and ran a brush through my hair, then headed back downstairs.

I expected to see Mona and Gerard in the kitchen with Blane, but it was just him.

"Where's Mona?" I asked.

Blane was chopping vegetables on a cutting board.

"It's their anniversary," Blane explained. "Gerard took her to dinner to celebrate."

"Oh. Okay. Well, can I help?" My cooking skills were notoriously lacking, which Blane was quite aware of, though he'd never seemed to mind.

Blane set down the knife and wiped his hands on a dish towel. "Yes, you can," he said. Then he grabbed me around the waist, picked me up, and set me on the counter. "You can keep me company." His gray eyes twinkled at me.

I laughed. "I get it. I wouldn't want me around a hot stove, either."

Tigger nosed around Blane's legs, probably hoping for something to drop, while Blane resumed chopping vegetables. A pot of water was boiling on the stove.

Blane had fixed dinner for me a few times before, though it was rare. He usually came home from work between six and seven, and if Mona was off for the evening, it was just easier to go out. His days at the office were often ten hours or more, so I could see why he wouldn't want to cook dinner when he got home.

"What are you making?" I asked, watching his hands deftly use the long, sharp knife.

"Pasta primavera," he replied. "Thought you could use something healthy."

His thoughtfulness made me smile. He glanced at me.

"What?" he asked. "Do I look funny chopping zucchini?"

I laughed. "No. I was just thinking how different you are from what I'd first imagined you to be."

"Oh no, here we go," he said with a grin. "Dare I ask?"

"All the girls at the office are in love with you," I teased. "They like to watch how you move."

"How I move?" he asked, raising an eyebrow.

I couldn't hold back a laugh. "Yeah. They'd watch you walk across the lobby to the elevator. It was like a morning ritual. Then we'd all discuss what suit you were wearing that day. We named them, you know, kind of like how Elvis named his suits."

Blane stopped chopping. "You named them?"

"Well, not me personally," I said. "It was kind of a . . . group activity."

Blane frowned. "I have over two dozen suits," he said.

"I know." I nodded sagely. "It was a very serious endeavor, especially if you were in a hurry and we didn't get that good of a look."

Blane shook his head as he again resumed chopping. "So now I'm curious. What were some of the names?"

"Okay, I'll tell you, but you have to promise not to let on that you know," I said, pointing sternly at him.

Blane stopped again and just looked at me.

"I mean it," I insisted. "I'm breaking the Woman Code by telling you any of this."

He snorted. "Fine. I promise I won't tell anyone that you broke The Code."

I grinned. "Okay, well, you know the gray pinstripe? I think it's Dolce and Gabbana?"

He nodded. "The wool and silk one? Yeah."

"Well, that one's called *Coming for You.*"

"That's not too bad," Blane said. "I expected worse."

I hid a grin. "That Armani light-gray stripe?" Blane nodded. "That's *FML.*"

"Fuck My Life?" Blane asked.

"Nope. *Fuck Me Later.*"

His brows rose and his lips twisted. "I see."

"And let's not forget one of my favorites," I continued. "The double-breasted three-piece Tom Ford. The one that's so dark gray it's nearly black? Yeah, that one's called *The*

Panty Dropper." I giggled. It was funny and ridiculous to be telling him these things.

Blane shook his head, but he was smiling, too. He dumped a box of pasta in the water, then put a big cookie sheet filled with chopped veggies in the oven and set the timer before heading my way. Reaching around me, he grabbed a bottle of wine that he'd opened. He was very close for a moment and I breathed in the scent of his cologne.

Refilling his glass, Blane said, "So did you ever name one of my suits?"

The heat flooding my cheeks gave me away before I could say a word. Blane chuckled. "Okay. Give. Which one and what's the name?"

Although I knew I shouldn't answer, I found myself saying, "The single-breasted charcoal Tom Ford."

Blane gave a slow nod, his gaze turning calculating. "I wore that suit the first time I kissed you."

As if I needed reminding. "Yeah, I named that one."

He cocked an eyebrow. "And?"

I hesitated. "I called it *Leave Me Breathless.*" Which actually was exactly how I felt at the moment.

Blane took a slow drink of wine, his eyes still locked on mine. "So tell me something," he said at last.

I raised my eyebrows in silent question.

"The night Sheila died, the night I stayed with you in your apartment, you had a nightmare, remember?"

I nodded. I remembered that night vividly, not only because of Sheila's horrible death but also because of Blane's comforting presence.

Blane leaned one hip against the counter next to me. "So the next morning, when we woke . . ."

My pulse sped up. That morning was burned in my memory. Blane's eyes were a stormy gray and I couldn't look away from them.

". . . I had my arm around you," he continued, his voice lowering. "And I was touching you. You didn't fight me, didn't tell me no, and I always wondered if it was because you were scared, or if you thought you owed me something—that I was your boss, something like that. Or if you didn't say anything . . . because you didn't want me to stop."

Memories came flooding back, making my heart twist inside my chest.

"I've always wondered," Blane said with a soft smile and a shrug. "Thought maybe you might put my curiosity to rest."

I swallowed before answering. "I was scared, a little," I admitted. "But mostly . . . I didn't want you to stop."

The air was thick in my lungs and neither of us moved. With me on the counter, we were the same height, and he'd moved closer. His gaze dropped to my lips and my mouth went dry.

The oven timer buzzed, shattering the spell woven around us. I jerked back, tearing my eyes away from him.

Blane. More potent and dangerous than the most addictive drug. The pull between the two of us was still there, no matter how heartbroken I was over Kade leaving.

Kade.

The thought of him was like a bleak cloud settling over me and I didn't say much as we sat down to dinner. Blane was a good cook and I was ravenous, a combination that meant I cleaned my plate and snuck another helping. Okay, two more helpings, but they were on the smallish side.

I wanted to do the dishes, but Blane insisted on doing them himself. A bath sounded really nice, so I asked Blane if I could use the tub in his bathroom, since it was way bigger than the one in mine.

"You don't have to ask," he chided me. "What's mine is yours."

His matter-of-factness brought a lump to my throat. Whatever mistakes Blane had made in the past, he'd more than made up for them since.

I almost fell asleep in the bathtub, I was so relaxed. Only when my fingers and toes began to wrinkle did I finally get out. I dried off and pulled on the white nightgown I always wore, brushing my hair and leaving it to trail wetly down my back.

When I came out of the bathroom, I saw Blane with his back to me as he took off his shirt. He peeled off the white linen dress shirt, then pulled the T-shirt he wore underneath over his head. The muscles in his back and arms flexed as he moved, rippling beneath perfect golden skin. I saw his hands move down to the front of his slacks.

I must have made a noise, because he turned suddenly.

"I-I'm sorry," I said, hastily averting my eyes from his very naked chest. "I'm done in the bathroom." No kidding, really? Nothing like stating the obvious. I headed for the door.

"Wait, Kat, where are you going?" Blane latched onto my wrist.

I turned, only to see his chest mere inches away. I gulped, then forced my gaze upward. He was frowning.

"If you're not tired, we can go watch another movie," Blane said. "Or I can find you a book to read or something. Whatever you want."

I cleared my throat nervously. "I was just going to bed," I said, my voice much too quiet.

Blane looked slightly hurt. "Oh. I thought—I just assumed—you'd stay in here with me."

My eyes widened. Last night had been one thing. I'd been upset, still reeling from what Kade had done. To stay with Blane another night seemed . . . wrong. And yet, the look on his face had guilt crawling inside me.

"Unless you don't want to," Blane added, his expression shuttered.

"No, that'd be . . . nice," I said, and it was worth it to see Blane's face smooth into a smile.

I headed for the bed, crawling underneath the covers. My nerves were jangling. I was too raw, too vulnerable to share a bed with Blane, and I knew it. I was deeply worried I'd do something I'd regret, but it didn't seem I had a choice. I didn't want to hurt Blane.

Blane switched off the light and I heard the rustle of clothing before he slid into bed. I was firmly on "my" side, though Blane took up his own space and then some.

I lay stiffly on my back, staring up at the black ceiling. My feelings were in a turmoil. I missed Kade so much, his absence was a physical ache, yet Blane's presence next to me was deeply comforting, easing the pain inside. The future scared me and I couldn't see what I was going to do, where I'd go from here.

Blane turned on his side to face me and I felt his hand settle over mine in the space between us. I closed my eyes as a tear tracked down my cheek to the pillow beneath my head. His kindness was sweet. Unexpected.

"Will you tell me more of the suit names tomorrow?" Blane asked, his voice quiet in the dark.

I smiled in spite of myself. "I've already broken The Code, so I guess it doesn't matter now."

Blane's soft laugh sent a shiver through me, which was bad-bad-bad.

"Good night, Kat," he said.

"Night, Blane," I replied, relieved that he wasn't going to try and pull me closer, which then made me feel guilty. Despite my heartache and guilt, I drifted to sleep.

~

It was still dark when I woke, and it didn't take me long to realize I was sprawled nearly on top of Blane. One of my legs was lying between his, my head and torso resting on his chest while his arm curved around me.

Blane was only wearing a pair of boxer briefs. My night-gown had ridden up and the skin of his legs was warm against mine. I could tell that even if he was still asleep, his body was very much awake.

Heat shot through me, pure hormones laying waste to logic and common sense, and I lay utterly still. I took a deep breath to get myself under control, then found my breath robbed as Blane's mouth covered mine.

It was sudden and overwhelming, and it was like setting a match to tinder. His fingers were buried in my hair, holding my head as his tongue stroked mine. The desperate urgency in his kiss drove every thought out of my head. I couldn't see anything—the room was too dark—and all I could do was feel. His mouth and hands were everywhere, dragging my nightgown over my head and turning me onto my back.

Blane's erection pressed between my thighs and I moaned into his mouth. His lips and tongue moved to my breasts. My fingernails dug into his shoulders, my heart racing as my body instinctively responded to Blane's touch. It had been a long time, but not so long that our bodies didn't recognize the other's in the dark. Blane's touch and kiss were dragging me down a familiar path of desire and want.

His hand moved between my legs, sliding under the satin of my panties to slip between my folds. I gasped as he stroked me, the wetness he found betraying my arousal. It wasn't until he pushed a thick finger inside me that reality intruded.

Oh God. This was going to happen. If I didn't do something, Blane was going to make love to me right here, right now. It was so wrong that we were doing this—so wrong that a part of me wanted it, but I was terrified I wouldn't be able to live with myself afterward.

"No, Blane, wait!" I said, reaching down to grasp his wrist.

The thrust of his finger paused immediately, though still inside me, curved and leisurely stroking a spot that made my legs tremble and had me biting back another moan. Blane kissed his way from my breasts up to my mouth.

"What is it, Kat?" he asked, his lips moving against my skin.

"We can't do this," I gasped, straining to keep hold of my thoughts against the raging tide of desire. "*I* can't do this."

He stilled.

"I'm sorry," I babbled. "I'm horrible—I know I am. Forgive me, but I just . . . I can't do this." I was up and out of the bed like a shot, stumbling for the door. Somehow I made it to my room. I dug for a T-shirt in the bureau and pulled it on over my head. My stomach ached and my heart hurt, not to mention my conscience, which was taking a painful self-flagellation while my hormones were throwing one hell of a temper tantrum.

Blane didn't follow me, which I thought was a good thing overall, though I fiercely missed his presence and my body craved his touch.

I lay under the covers and stared out the window for hours, unable to sleep, until the room was flooded with early sunlight. I dreaded facing Blane and had no idea what I was going to say to him—or why he'd done what he had. I'd told him how I felt, that he and I were over. Did he think we'd work it out now that Kade was out of the picture? Is that what I wanted?

I loved Blane and I wasn't going to kid myself into thinking that we couldn't have what we'd once had, given enough time. He was a good man—a decent, honorable man—who loved me. We'd had our problems, but if last night was any indication, I had it in me to fall back in love with him.

But I was having a baby . . . and it wasn't Blane's. That changed everything.

Once I was dressed and as ready to face Blane as I'd ever be, I headed downstairs. As I'd expected, he was in the den. He looked up when I cautiously knocked on the partially open door.

"Come in," he said, beckoning me. He was dressed in jeans that hugged his hips and a steel-gray button-down shirt that matched his eyes. The cuffs were turned back and his hair was still slightly damp from the shower. "We need to talk," he said.

I bit my lower lip, my knees practically knocking together. Was he mad at me?

"I'm really sorry," I managed. "About last night—"

"This isn't about that," Blane interrupted. "Well, maybe it is, but not directly."

"Okay." My nerves started jangling at that. God, what else did he have to tell me? Had Kade called? Based on Blane's tone, whatever he had to say couldn't be good. "Then what do you want to talk about?" I asked.

"The future," he said simply.

My breath caught and my eyes widened. I couldn't do this right now. I'd just gotten my equilibrium back yesterday, after my panic attack. If I started thinking about everything, I might fall to pieces again—and I didn't want Blane to see me like that. It was bad enough that he'd already seen me fall apart more than once.

"I don't know—"

"Just hear me out," Blane interrupted. "I know you're worried. I know you're scared. But you don't have to be."

"That's easy for *you* to say," I replied softly.

"Kade didn't leave you empty-handed," he said.

I frowned and my stomach lurched. "What do you mean? Have you heard from him?"

"No, but he left this for you." Blane slipped his hand into his jeans pocket. He removed a piece of paper and handed it to me. It had a bunch of numbers scrawled on it.

"What's this?" I asked, confused.

"It's the number of an account in Cayman National, a bank in Grand Cayman. It's your account now. I checked it. Kade put ten million dollars in it for you."

I nearly choked, shock hitting me hard. I stared at Blane, my jaw agape.

"He didn't want you to have to worry about money," Blane continued.

The ache in my chest was back, slicing through wounds that had only just stopped bleeding. Kade would give me a fortune, money he'd sold his soul to acquire, but he wouldn't give me himself.

"So, I guess that's the Kade-equivalent of leaving some money on the bedside table." Bitterness edged my voice. "I don't want his money."

"Don't be stupid," Blane said. "You need it. The baby needs it."

That shut me up. I'd been trying not to think of that word. *Baby.* It was easier, less personal, for me to just think *pregnant.*

"Oh God." I sank onto the sofa, my elbows resting on my thighs as I covered my face. I couldn't look at him. Kade's acceptance had helped me hold my head up when I'd had to tell Blane. But his leaving had me feeling ashamed. Embarrassed. Rejected.

"Hey," Blane said softly, prying my hands away from my face. "I told you that you're not alone, and I meant it."

I made myself look at him.

"I love you, and this baby shares my blood, too." His hand lifted to cup my cheek. "Stay with me. Marry me. You loved me once, you can love me again. I promise that I will *never* leave you. We'll be together. Always."

I was speechless. The enormity of what Blane was offering overwhelmed me. Safety. Security. His name. His love.

Blane slowly leaned forward, his gaze dropping. I had plenty of time to move away, but I didn't. His mouth met mine with a tender reverence that made my heart skip a beat. His lips moved coaxingly and his tongue softly brushed mine. His hands curved around the back of my neck, his fingers buried in my hair.

I pulled back, my emotions chaotic and my thoughts in a turmoil.

"I made a promise to Kade," Blane said, resting his forehead against mine. "When he was shot. I promised that if something happened to him, I'd take care of you. And I want to. God, I want to."

I jerked away, my eyes wide. "You made a *promise?*" I repeated in disbelief.

I stood and started pacing. "Don't you see how messed up this is?" I asked, an edge of hysteria in my voice. I gripped the sides of my head in frustration.

"Why is my making a promise so 'messed up'?" Blane had risen, and he approached me without making a sound.

"I don't believe you, Blane," I said baldly. "I *can't.*"

"You don't believe that I love you?" Blane's expression was forbidding, his jaw clenched tight. "You think I'd say that to just anyone?"

"Blane, your sense of duty, of honor, is such that I wonder if you even know if you really love me," I said sadly. "And I can't do this anymore, to either of us."

"What do you mean?" he rasped.

"I can't hurt you like this!" I cried, tears streaming unheeded from my eyes. "I'm in love with Kade. I'm having his baby. You don't deserve that! And my staying around is only going to hold you back."

He stiffened, his eyes narrowing. "What do you mean?"

The words were nearly impossible to get out. "I mean I've got to let you go."

Blane said nothing, but his face grew pale.

"It's not fair to you," I managed to say through my tears, "for me to keep holding on, keep needing you. You have to get on with your life." I swallowed. "And so do I."

I turned away, moving to grab my purse, but Blane was there in an instant, blocking me. His hands pressed against my cheeks, his fingers tangled in my hair as he forced me to look at him.

"Don't go," he said desperately. "Please—" His voice broke. "Kat, I've never begged a woman. Ever. But I'm begging you. Stay. For me. Please stay." Blane's eyes were a brilliant green.

"You're a good man, Blane Kirk," I whispered through my tears. "You mean so much to me. Which is why I can't." I placed my hand over his, turning my face to press my lips against his palm.

This time, he didn't try to stop me when I turned and walked out the door.

Driving away from Blane's house was the hardest thing I'd ever had to do, and tears I couldn't control blurred the streets as I drove. Everything in me screamed for me to turn around and go back to Blane, but I knew I couldn't.

Somehow, I made it home. I was fumbling with my keys to unlock my door when Alisha's door flew open.

"Kathleen! I've been so worried!" She launched herself at me, wrapping me in a huge hug.

"I'm sorry," I said, hugging her back. "I didn't mean to make you worry."

Letting me go, Alisha stepped back, scrutinizing me. "What else happened?" she asked.

I shook my head. "I've laid enough on you lately," I said. "I'm sure you're sick of hearing about it."

"Don't be ridiculous," she said with a snort, grabbing my arm and hauling me into her apartment. "Sit down and tell me all about it."

So I sat, and I told her what had happened. How I'd told Kade everything and how at first he'd reacted so great, but then he'd flipped out, or so I guessed, and left town. That Blane had taken me back to his place once they'd found me in Kade's apartment, ending with what Blane had offered tonight.

"But I can't do that," I finished with a sigh. "Marry Blane and have another man's child? That's insane."

Alisha didn't say anything, just kind of squirmed.

"Right?" I persisted.

"Well . . ." she hedged.

"You've got to be joking. You can't stand Blane. Now you think I should marry him?"

"It's just that he was so worried about you," she said plaintively. "He came by, told me how upset you were, and wanted me to go check on you in the morning. Then you didn't answer your door, or your phone, and finally, I didn't know what to do but call him. I think he was in court, because his secretary had to go to the courthouse to get him."

Oh no. Blane had left court because of my drama? Now I had guilt as well as embarrassment.

"He was frantic, Kathleen," she continued. "I know I haven't been Blane's biggest fan, but I thought he was going to tear this town apart, looking for you."

I didn't know what to say, which didn't matter because Alisha kept talking, now going on a rant about Kade.

". . . can't believe he'd be such a shit about it," she said, irritated. Getting up from the couch, she grabbed a cloth and started furiously dusting her already immaculate furniture. "Did he even have the decency to tell you to your face?"

I shook my head. "No."

Her rag moved faster. "Of course not! Men are such assholes," she groused. "I mean, don't you think that was a total asshole thing to do? And since when is he such a coward?"

I couldn't disagree.

"So what are you going to do?" she asked.

I folded my arms across my stomach. It was still hard for me to imagine, to wrap my head around that I was going to have a baby. I'd have someone of my very own to love and take care of. Would the baby be a girl with my color hair? Or a boy with eyes like his father's?

And it suddenly struck me: I wouldn't be alone anymore. I'd have a family.

And I knew what I had to do.

～

I was packed and loading my car by the time dawn rolled around. Alisha carried down Tigger in his pet carrier. He was none too happy, meowing pitifully the entire way. Bits followed her, whining as he tried to jump up on his little legs to help his friend.

"That's all of it," she said, setting Tigger in the passenger seat of my car. She closed the door on his complaining. "Are you sure you want to do this?" she asked.

We'd talked for hours last night, once I'd decided that I'd be leaving Indy. Alisha had thrown every argument she could think of at me, but in the end, she hadn't been able to dissuade me. We hovered at the door to my Toyota Corolla.

"I am," I said. "It's barely thirty miles from here. You can come see me anytime, and I'll come visit, too."

"What about your job?"

"I worked ten days straight. I'm off for the next four. Romeo should be able to find a replacement by then."

"And what are you going to do about money?" she persisted.

"I have the money Kade gave me for that job in Vegas," I said, pushing aside the thought of the millions he'd left for me in Grand Cayman as well. I wasn't touching that, not unless it was absolutely necessary. "And I'll get another job."

Alisha still looked worried, so I hugged her. "Thank you for being such a good friend," I said. Both of us were teary when I let go.

"I'll be back in a few weeks to get the rest of my things," I reminded her. "The lease on my apartment isn't up for another two months. I'll see you again soon." I slid behind the wheel and shut the door.

Alisha leaned through the open window. "And you're sure you don't want to tell Blane about this?"

My gut clenched at the mere mention of his name. I shook my head. "Not right now. I just need some time. Some space. If he asks, don't tell him where I've gone, okay? I'll get in touch with him at some point. The baby's related to him, after all."

Alisha didn't look happy, but she nodded in agreement. "I won't tell him."

We hugged through the open window one more time, then I started the car and backed up. Smiling, I waved at Alisha as I pulled out of the lot.

I heaved a sigh that felt like it came all the way from my toes as I drove down the highway. I was heading home.

KADE

CHAPTER SEVEN

The flight attendant handed Kade the vodka tonic he'd requested, a double, and moved on down the aisle to the rest of the customers in first class. Kade stared out the window, morosely drinking the cold liquor.

The seat beside him was empty, which suited him. He didn't want to talk, and if someone had tried to make chit-chat with him, he'd have been hard-pressed not to strangle them.

And with Kade Dennon, the threat wasn't an idle one.

It had been almost a month since he'd last seen her.

He closed his eyes, Kathleen's face immediately coming into focus in his mind. If he tried really hard, he could smell her scent, taste the salt of the sweat on her skin when he was buried inside her, feel the marks her nails left on his shoulders, hear her whimper and moan when he made her come.

And he'd almost made it happen. He'd almost gotten to keep her.

Almost.

The plan had seemed like a dream come true. He'd take Kathleen with him and they'd leave Indy, leave old memories behind and go make new ones. But a sense of foreboding had crept over Kade the moment Kathleen had left his apartment that fateful day—the day he'd had to give up everything he'd ever wanted.

He'd wanted to think it was just his cynicism overreacting, but listening to his gut had saved his life too many times for him to ignore the warning. Which was why he hadn't been surprised when his cell had rung only minutes after Kathleen had left to tell Blane the news. The call was from a blocked number.

"Yeah," he answered.

"Dennon," a male voice greeted him. "You're still alive."

"So it would seem," Kade replied. "Who's this?"

"Meet me tonight, under the Davidson Street bridge," the man said, ignoring Kade's question. "Nine o'clock."

"And why would I do that?"

"Do you think we don't know about the girl?" A pause. "See you tonight, Dennon."

The line went dead.

Kade slowly slid the phone back into the pocket of his jeans. He gazed out the window without seeing anything.

Kathleen.

He'd failed miserably at protecting her, saving her life several times by mere luck and chance. Kade put her into more danger just by being around her. And now she was having a baby. His baby.

The complete shock and happiness that knowledge had brought him earlier faded in light of reality. Who was he kidding? His past wasn't going away and the phone call was a reminder of that. Only months ago, Kade had killed a man who knew about Kathleen, wanted to use her as leverage on him. How much more would they target her now? And next time, he might be too late.

And what kind of father would he be? The only role model he'd ever had was Blane, for a while before Blane had left for the Navy, then Gerard. It wasn't like Kade was the kind of guy to coach Little League or soccer. His skills revolved around a computer and a gun.

Blane, however, would make the perfect dad. He already had a house and a steady career that didn't include dead bodies left in his wake. All he was missing was the pregnant girl—a girl he already loved, had wanted to marry, and no doubt still wanted to marry. All of Blane's dreams could have come true—if not for Kade.

Guilt hit Kade hard, sucking the breath from him.

How could he have done this to Blane? To his brother? To the only person who'd given a shit about him when he was nothing but a skinny delinquent, intent on ruining his own life and taking as many people down with him as he could.

He should've stayed away, far away from Kathleen. Kade had known instantly that she was his Kryptonite, yet he'd been drawn to her like the proverbial moth to a flame. Now Blane—the one who should be with her, the one who deserved her—had lost her.

And yet, what was he to do? Kade loved her. The rainbows-and-unicorns, worship-the-ground-she-walks-on, listen-to-bad-Taylor-Swift-songs kind of love. He'd do anything for her, but he was too selfish to give her up, not even for his brother.

Kade went to a closet in the far corner, pressing on a disguised latch to open the hidden panel in the back. Pressing his thumb to the scanner, he waited while it verified his identity, then opened. He pulled out a handgun and two clips, sliding one into the gun and the other into the pocket of his jeans before he closed the panel again.

Going into his office, Kade transferred money from his accounts in Grand Cayman to a new account in Kathleen's name. He then took the precaution of wiping the hard drive, starting a program that would reformat it and write data to all the sectors.

Kade didn't know what he'd be walking into tonight, but there was always the possibility that he wouldn't walk out.

In his bedroom, he pulled on a black T-shirt, throwing a black button-down shirt on over it that he left untucked to conceal the gun lodged in the waistband at his back. The wounds healing in his chest twinged when he moved a certain way, but Kade ignored the pain. There was nothing he could do about it, and besides, duty called.

Was he insane? Insane for wanting what seemed just within his grasp? Kathleen, a family, a life. A year ago, his sole focus had been surviving the next job, not that he'd cared much one way or the other. When your time was up, it was up—and all the wishing and hoping in the world couldn't change that.

But now, for the first time, he felt fear. He was afraid. Not just because he wanted to live—he did—but because he had someone to live *for*. He had to be there, had to protect her, because there was no one to do it if he wasn't around.

Kade wasn't a fool. He'd seen how Kathleen had rushed to leave the hospital every morning before Blane got there. He'd known that Blane had shut down on her, the way he always did when he wanted to stop feeling. Kade turned to anger when he wanted to escape; Blane turned to ice.

Grabbing his keys, Kade headed out the door. Twenty minutes later, he'd parked a couple of blocks away from where he was to meet the guy and started walking. His phone buzzed and he looked down at the screen.

Kathleen.

Kade hesitated, then hit the button to send the call to voice mail. He couldn't talk to her now. She'd want to know where he was and why. He'd have to lie, because if he told her the truth, she'd worry.

The weight of the gun at his back reassured Kade, as did the one strapped to his ankle. A knife was hidden under his other pants leg, though he hoped it didn't come to that. After two weeks in the hospital, his muscles felt stiff from disuse.

Kade melted from shadow to shadow, silently making his way to the bridge. Homeless people often camped around this area, but there didn't seem to be anyone around tonight. Sliding into the deep shadows under the bridge, Kade put his back to the concrete and waited.

He didn't have to wait long. A few minutes later, a dark sedan pulled up, its headlights flashing over Kade before they were extinguished. He watched as a man got out and began walking toward him. Kade recognized him as George Bradshaw, erstwhile campaign manager for Senator Keaston, now his chief of staff.

"Dennon," George said in acknowledgment when he was about ten feet away. He wore a suit and was maybe in his mid-thirties.

"George," Kade replied with mock cordiality.

"I believe we have a mutual friend," George said.

"I don't have any friends."

George laughed softly. "I suppose you're right. Friends of yours have a nasty habit of turning up dead, isn't that right?"

"So do people who piss me off and waste my time," Kade replied with a cold smile that disappeared immediately. "What do you want?"

"A man who likes to get down to business. I can appreciate that." George casually pushed his hands into his pockets as he walked closer to Kade, who stiffened, but the man didn't pull a weapon. "Your uncle sent me with a message."

Kade's expression didn't change. "I don't have an uncle."

"Of course you do," George said with a calculating look. "Do you think I wouldn't know every detail of Senator Keaston's life? And Blane Kirk's? You remember him, don't you? He is your brother, after all."

"You've been misinformed."

George shrugged. "I don't give a shit if you want to keep playing this game, because here's what you're going to do." He stepped closer to Kade. "You're going to ditch the girl and get your ass out of town."

"Fuck you."

"Kirk needs to get his shit together. He's not backing out of the race. And if this chick is what'll put his fucking head back on straight, then that's what he gets."

"You can tell Keaston to go fuck himself," Kade snarled. "No one pulls my strings, and no one is going to pull Blane's, either."

The two men stared at each other in a charged silence.

"Blane Kirk owes some very important people," George said. "This isn't the kind of game where you can just fold your cards and go home. You've fucked things up already. So hear this, Dennon."

George got in Kade's face, his finger poking hard at Kade's chest. "If you think you can just say 'Fuck you' and not do as we say? Then I swear to God, we'll kill them both."

"You're full of shit," Kade scoffed. "Keaston's not going to kill Blane."

"Blane is useless to us if he fucks over his career, and if he can't be controlled, he's a liability. Frankly, he'd be more use to us dead at this point."

Rage flashed through Kade, and he reacted without thought. In the sliver of time from one second to the next, he had George's hand in his and bent his fingers back. George yelled as three of his fingers snapped and Kade forced him to his knees.

When George looked up from where he'd landed on the ground, he was staring at the barrel of a gun pointed at the center of his forehead.

"What the fuck, Dennon?" George cried. "Do you have any fucking clue what you just did? I work for the senator, you dumb fuck!"

"You pissed me off," Kade gritted out. "Threatening the only two people on the fucking planet that I give a shit about. That was a bad idea. You and my uncle may think you can put me on a leash"—he leaned down to hiss in George's face— "but you can't."

For the first time, fear seemed to strike George. "You can't kill me," he babbled. "Keaston sent me. I'm just the messenger."

"And I'm sending a message."

Kade's gun barked once. George's body went limp and dropped to the ground, his eyes staring sightlessly upward.

Shoving his gun into his waistband at the small of his back, Kade searched George, taking his wallet and cell phone before heading back to his car. A few minutes later, he was speeding away into the night.

Kade's gut churned as he drove. Reaching into the glove box, he pulled out a burner phone. He bought a couple of new ones every few weeks. Being able to make untraceable calls came in handy. Dialing a number from memory, he waited while it rang. When a man answered, Kade got right to the point.

"Let me be the first to offer my condolences on the death of your chief of staff," he said coolly. "Good help's so hard to come by these days."

There was a pause. "Goddammit, Kade!" Senator Keaston exploded. "What the hell did you do?"

"Cut the bullshit," Kade snapped. "You should have known what was going to happen when you sent him. You're going to threaten me with killing Blane and Kathleen? Are you out of your fucking mind?"

"I'm through watching you screw up everything I've worked for," Keaston retorted. "If you don't do as you're told, I'll have no choice."

"You honestly expect me to believe you'd kill Blane—"

"I know about the baby," Keaston interrupted, making Kade's blood run cold. "Did you think I wouldn't find out she's carrying his child? Health records are the government's property now, and I am the government."

The words "It's my baby, not Blane's" were on the tip of Kade's tongue, but he forced himself to stay silent, waiting to see where Keaston would go with this.

"If you think I'm going to let some white-trash bartender run amok and go to the press in five years when Blane's running for president with some tragic tale of a love child, then you're dead wrong," Keaston said, his words laced with disgust.

"Since when do you give a shit about Blane's love life?" Kade scoffed.

"Blane's been out of his fucking mind the last few weeks, ever since you were shot," Keaston fumed. "He's lost all his ambition for office, as if he doesn't even care anymore. Then I find out why. That the little bitch is knocked up and *you* have swept in to fuck Blane over. Why am I not surprised? You always seem to screw up the best-laid plans."

"Maybe Blane's just realizing he's been following *your* ambitions, and not his own," Kade retorted. The guilt he'd felt earlier returned with a vengeance. Despite his words to Keaston, Kade knew Blane had worked with a single-minded focus on building a career destined for politics for as long as Kade could remember.

"Bullshit," Keaston spat. "He took you from nothing, from a fucking orphanage, and gave you everything! I never should have helped him find you, that was my second mistake. My first was not getting rid of your whore of a mother when I had the chance."

Cold shock poured through Kade. "What are you talking about?"

"Blane's father came to me when he found out your mother was pregnant. I thought about killing her then, but your father seemed convinced she was willing to take a pay-off and disappear. I should have gone with my instincts."

"What payoff? She didn't have any money," Kade argued.

"You think I was going to let John squander his money on some pregnant gold digger? I told her to never darken our door if she wanted to live, and if she breathed a word of who the baby's father was—who your father was—I'd take you from her and she'd never see you again."

Kade slammed on the brakes, the car fishtailing as it swerved on the empty road. "You sonofabitch—" he hissed.

"Shut up, Kade," Keaston broke in. "You listen to me and by God you listen good. You're going to go over to Blane's and convince him not to drop out of the race. Then you're going to tell him you want nothing to do with the girl and that she really loves him, she's just confused. He needs to stand by her side, marry her, give the child a name. Blane's all about honor. I'm sure you can convince him. Then you're going to leave and never, ever come back."

The words were like a poisoned blade, the way they sliced through Kade, leaving a burning agony in their wake. Kade swallowed. "And if I don't?"

"Then I will put down that girl like a fucking dog, you worthless piece of shit, and I'll enjoy doing it. The only thing saving her now is that she carries Blane's child and he still loves her. But that can change. Blane owes people—*I* owe people—people who do not take kindly to donating millions to a candidate who drops out of the fucking race because of a goddamn broken heart. I've put my ass on the line for him, but if he doesn't get his shit together, I'm not responsible for what happens to him."

"If anyone so much as *touches* my brother," Kade spat, "I will fucking drop you, old man."

"Do you think everything can be solved in that fashion?" Keaston asked, his voice rife with contempt. "Kill me and she dies, no question. I call it my Kade Dennon insurance policy."

Kade didn't see a way out. If he stayed, defied Keaston, Kathleen would die. If he tried to kill Keaston, Kathleen would still die. The only winning move was to take himself out of the equation. To do exactly as Keaston said.

Unless he confessed, told Keaston the baby was his, not Blane's.

And then what?

He and Kathleen would be constantly on the run, evading Keaston's reach, because Kade had no doubt that Keaston was crazy enough to try and kill them anyway, just because of Blane. Look what he'd done to Kade's mother. How much worse would he do to Kathleen? It was no way to live, no way to raise a child. Kade could protect them, yes, but it would only take a moment, one split-second of inattention, for them both to be gone.

Kade could see it now. Her body limp in his arms, a small hole in the center of her forehead as blood poured from the massive exit wound in the back of her head, streaking her blonde hair with crimson while her sightless blue eyes stared up at him.

Kathleen—dead. Blane would never forgive him. And he'd never forgive himself.

The only protection Kathleen really had was that Blane loved her, and that Keaston believe she carried Blane's child.

If Kade loved Kathleen, if he was serious when he told himself he'd do anything for her, he'd let Keaston have his way. If he really loved her, he'd want her to live, be happy. And Blane would be happy, too. Maybe Blane would forgive him and the guilt inside Kade would go away.

Kade would go to Blane's, convince him to get back in the race and that Kathleen loved him, not Kade. Blane would love her and the baby, would raise him as his own— Kade had no doubt about that. Kathleen still loved Blane, and she'd get over Kade. It was the best choice, the only choice, he had.

"Okay," Kade rasped. "You win. But hear this—if *anything* happens to either one of them, I will hunt you down and you won't even see me coming."

He ended the call. Helpless fury filled him, as well as an agony that was all consuming.

He'd been outplayed, outmaneuvered, and now he'd lose everything that meant anything to him.

~

Kade parked in front of Blane's house. For the last time, he suddenly realized. After tonight, he wouldn't be coming back, wouldn't be seeing his brother again. Perhaps ever.

Pain knifed through him, and he had to take a deep breath and close his eyes, leaning his head back against the seat. He had to bury it deep, in the place he kept all the things he didn't want to feel. The only thing that was going to see him through what he had to do was to shut it all down. Turning off emotions was what he had to do if he wanted to survive. Otherwise, the pain would destroy him.

The pain of leaving them. Blane. Kathleen. His unborn child.

Everything inside him rebelled at what he had to do, the things he had to say. The thought of seeing the trust on Blane's face turn to horror and dismay, and finally, loathing . . . If Blane knew all that Keaston had done—was doing—nothing would stop him from going after his uncle, a move that would ultimately destroy Blane. Kade wouldn't let that happen. It was the one thing Blane had always underestimated—Kade's unswerving loyalty.

All Kade could do was make a clean break from them both . . . and hope they put the pieces back together. Blane and Kathleen would cling to each other. Kade knew Blane loved her, and she loved him. They could forget about Kade and be happy, raise a family . . .

The thought made him want to eat a bullet.

Inside, it was dark save for a light burning in the library. Kade pushed open the door, unsurprised to see Blane sitting at the piano. He wasn't playing, though. He just sat, his body resting on his arms folded on top.

Kade committed the scene to memory, recalling the many times over the years that he'd sat listening to Blane play. It had always amazed him, the way Blane's fingers had flown over the keys, producing melodies that spoke of emotions too powerful for words.

Blane seemed to sense his presence, turning his body to face Kade, his expression blank rather than welcoming.

Well, what had he expected? Kathleen had been there. Kade should be glad. Blane's anger might make things easier. But he felt far from glad.

Glancing around, Kade realized the room was missing a lot of stuff. He frowned, seeing some broken glass on the floor, in one corner. Blane had cleaned up, but obviously hadn't gotten it all.

"I see you went all rock star on this place," Kade said. He'd only seen Blane do that once before. It had been a long time ago. "You missed the corner. Mona's going to be upset."

"What do you want, Kade?" Blane asked, ignoring his comment.

"I hear you're thinking of throwing in the towel on the whole governor thing," Kade said.

Blane stared at him, his face utterly expressionless. "*That's* why you're here?"

"All I've heard for years is how much you wanted it," Kade said. "Seems pretty stupid to give it up when you're so close."

Blane shrugged. "It doesn't matter anymore. Besides, my poll numbers have tanked since the arrest. I don't have a chance in hell of winning that race."

Kade cleared his throat. "That's easily fixed," he said. "People love a fucking wedding. Get married."

"Are you out of your mind?" Blane spat, anger flashing to the surface and obliterating the calm demeanor it seemed he'd only been pretending to have. "Or are you just here to rub it in? Kat told me you and she are leaving tomorrow."

"She's half right," Kade replied. "I'm leaving. Not her. And it's tonight."

Blane frowned. "What?"

Kade walked to the sideboard and poured himself an inch of the scotch that Blane always kept there, downing it in one swallow.

"I've changed my mind," he answered, keeping his gaze averted from Blane's.

"Changed your mind about what exactly?" Blane persisted, a note of warning in his voice.

Kade forced a laugh. "Do you really think I'm cut out for dirty diapers and a fucking minivan? Not to mention tying myself to one woman for the rest of my life. Please." He poured more scotch, using it to wash down the bitter taste of bile in his throat.

That statement seemed to ricochet around the room, fading into a charged silence.

"Are you fucking kidding me?" Blane ground out.

A fine tremor went through Kade's hand at the leashed fury in Blane's voice. He still didn't look at him, instead carefully setting down the crystal glass he held. The crystal had belonged to Blane's mother and Kade didn't want it broken.

"What the fuck would I do with a wife and kid," Kade said, his voice flat and cold. "Granted, she's an incredible lay, am I right? But there are plenty of those." His eyes slipped shut as agony seared his chest. The words felt like acid on his tongue. He braced himself for what he knew was coming, and he wasn't surprised when Blane suddenly hauled him around to face him, his grip like a vise on his arm.

"What the hell, Kade!" Blane hissed, his eyes flashing with fury. "You're *in love* with her. You told me. You told her. Now you've got her, she's yours, and you're tossing it away because she got pregnant?"

"I didn't sign up to be a dad," Kade snapped, jerking away. "And I'm not changing my entire life because some chick can't remember to take her fucking birth control pill."

"This isn't 'some chick'—it's Kathleen!" Blane yelled. He seemed to get himself under control with effort. "You took her away from me, got her to fall in love with you. You cannot just leave her. You know what Dad did to your mom. Why would you do the same to Kathleen?"

Kade's eyes narrowed. "I can do whatever the fuck I want," he said. "Maybe she's just not as interesting now that she's no longer a challenge. You love her so much, care about the brat she's carrying, then *you* marry her. That'll kill two birds with one stone, right? You're welcome."

Blane's face paled and it took everything Kade had not to crumple beneath the disgust and contempt in Blane's eyes.

He couldn't take any more. He had to get out of there.

Jerking out of Blane's grip, Kade walked to the door, careful to keep his steps unhurried. Digging in his pocket, he fished out a folded piece of paper and tossed it carelessly onto the coffee table.

"Here's an account with some money," he said. "She can use that to take care of herself and—" To his horror, his voice broke and he abruptly cut himself off. Thankfully, Blane didn't seem to notice. When Blane spoke again, his tone was low and threatening.

"You walk out that door—you leave her—and you're no longer my brother."

Kade's hand was on the knob but the words made him freeze. He couldn't stop himself from looking back at Blane. Their gazes met.

Words he shouldn't say fell out of Kade's mouth anyway. "Remember what you promised me," he said, his voice much too rough. Then he was out the door and in his car, Blane's house becoming a distant blur in the rearview mirror.

≈

The late-night breeze drifted past Kade as he stood in the shadows, watching Kathleen's window. He'd left Blane's house an hour ago, but hadn't been able to get farther than the city limits before turning back.

Placing a call to the woman he used as both maid and housekeeper, he gave her instructions on shutting down his apartment—what to put in storage, what to throw away. He didn't know when, or if, he'd ever be back.

His conscience, a part of him Kade had thought long since dead, was stirring, urging him to go up and knock on Kathleen's door. But what would he say? That he'd just come to say goodbye? Kade knew the truth—if he walked in her door, he wouldn't have the strength to leave, and so he'd be signing her death warrant.

A car drove up and Kade watched as Blane got out. He took the stairs two at a time, then stood outside her door, hesitating. Kade had left him with the shit job of telling Kathleen. Hopefully, making Blane the messenger would work to bring them back together. If there was one thing that was certain, it was that Blane deserved to get the girl—not Kade.

Finally, Blane knocked and a moment later, Kathleen answered.

Kade strained his neck, trying to see her around Blane's form blocking the doorway, but he didn't even get a glimpse of her. Blane entered the apartment, the door closing behind him.

And that was that.

Kade leaned against the tree behind him, the rough bark of the trunk abrading his back through the thin T-shirt he wore. He should leave. Blane was there and Kade didn't want or need to see Kathleen with him.

His mind told him this, but the masochist inside him wouldn't let him leave, forcing him to stay and watch. Would Blane stay the night? Would he sleep in her bed?

The idea of Kathleen making love with Blane had Kade shoving a hand through his hair, his skin practically itching with frustration, his muscles tensing as though preparing for a fight. He couldn't get the picture out of his head, his imagination painting Kathleen's naked body in vivid detail beneath Blane's. The sounds she made, the way her legs would wrap around his waist . . .

To his surprise, and shameful relief, Blane suddenly reappeared after only a few minutes. He went next door and spoke to the neighbor—Kade couldn't remember her name—then got in his car and drove away.

Kade wanted to both yell at Blane for leaving Kathleen alone, and thank him, for the same reason.

He needed to go. If he stuck around there like some love-smitten teenager hiding among the trees, the temptation to go see Kathleen would eventually become more than he could withstand. And she didn't need that. Kade needed to disappear from her life so she could get on with living it.

With Blane.

Kade stepped farther into the trees, preparing to go, then stopped when Kathleen's door opened again and she came flying out. His breath caught as pain pierced him, his eyes drinking in what he could see of her in the faint glow cast from the parking lot lights.

Hurrying down the steps, she got inside her car. Seconds later, she was pulling out of the lot.

Where was she going? If Kade had to guess, he assumed she was heading to Blane's. Maybe she'd turned him down and now realized that was a mistake. They were perfect for each other. The two of them together looked like each one had been made to complement the other. Kathleen was as pretty, innocent, and as girl-next-door as it was possible to be. Team that with Blane's all-American heartthrob good looks, and they made a formidable pair.

The cameras would love them.

Kade was standing in front of Kathleen's door without having consciously decided to move. Automatically picking the lock, he stepped inside.

What the hell am I doing? he thought. *Why can't I just leave? Why torture myself?*

But it seemed logic wasn't ruling his actions. Not tonight.

Kade drifted back to her bedroom. The sight of the half-packed suitcase sitting on the bed made his throat close up.

He was doing the right thing. He was. Maybe she didn't understand or wouldn't agree, but eventually she'd be glad he was gone. Both she and Blane would be.

A discarded T-shirt lay on the floor and Kade scooped it up, recognizing it as one of Kathleen's favorite sleep shirts. Though she had lingerie and pajamas, he'd most often found her sleeping in T-shirts.

A memory came to him, of when he'd once come to Kathleen's apartment looking for Blane. The Santinis had hired Kade to kill her. He had sat in a chair in a corner of her bedroom, watching her sleep as he'd contemplated what to do. If Kade hadn't found the photos they'd used to blackmail Blane—if he hadn't realized Blane had probably told them to go fuck themselves—he would've killed Kathleen without a second thought.

But Blane had disappeared, leaving Kade suspecting the Santinis of taking matters into their own hands.

She'd been wearing a little T-shirt then, the fabric riding up to her waist as she slept, teasing Kade with a view of the tiny pair of satin panties she wore. The virginal white fabric had nearly screamed "off limits" but that hadn't stopped him from wanting her. He'd briefly wondered what she'd do if she woke with his mouth on the paradise between her thighs . . .

Luckily, Kathleen had woken before Kade had done something stupid, her eyes frightened when she saw him, then filling with terror when she realized he was there to kill her.

In the end, he hadn't been able to do either of the two actions he'd considered—he couldn't kill her and he couldn't fuck her. Maybe it had been the innocence etched into every word she said, every move she made. Or perhaps it was the purity of her soul that shone in her clear blue eyes.

Kathleen was good, and even after all the darkness and evil that surrounded him and lived inside him, Kade had recognized it—and been unable to destroy something so precious and rare.

Of course, it hadn't hurt that she looked like a goddamn fairy-tale princess, her long hair lying in tousled waves over her shoulders and down her back. The shade of gold had a rose hue, as though the locks had been kissed by the sunrise. Her cheeks were ivory porcelain, a flush blooming in them when Kade had touched her, his hands slipping under her T-shirt because he hadn't been able to go a moment longer not knowing how the curve of her hip felt in his hand, or the exact dip of her waist.

Her eyes, still heavy with sleep, had held his gaze captive. The scent of her perfume drifted between them, reminding Kade of a time long ago—a time when he'd thought fate would be kind, that he'd paid enough in blood and tears for a lifetime.

He'd been wrong.

Holding the T-shirt to his face, Kade inhaled deeply. The fabric was drenched in Kathleen's scent. Not her perfume, but the scent of her skin and hair.

A wave of pure agony washed over him and Kade stumbled to the bed, sitting down heavily. Kathleen had only fitfully made the bed, her pillow still dented from the impression of her head, and he found himself resting his fingers on the hollow.

How quickly would she forget about him? Would she tell his baby about him, or would Blane's name only be spoken as the father?

Kade abruptly stood. Time to go.

Everything was blurred as he walked through the kitchen, and it wasn't until he was sitting inside his car that he realized he still clutched Kathleen's T-shirt in his hand.

Chapter Eight

It had been a fourteen-hour drive from Indy to Boston. Kade would have driven it without stopping, but his body wouldn't cooperate. He'd pulled off somewhere near Allentown, finding a dive of a motel and paying cash for a room.

After showering, he'd lain on the bed in his jeans, unable to sleep. He picked up his cell, a new burner phone he'd bought. His old phone lay at the bottom of the White River outside Indy, where he'd stopped to toss it after leaving Kathleen's apartment.

His fingers traced the numbers for Kathleen's cell, but he didn't dial. Kade had made it impossible for either Blane or Kathleen to reach him, which was best for them all. A clean break.

The T-shirt he'd taken from Kathleen's apartment lay on the bed beside him. Absently, Kade picked it up. The fabric was worn, soft, and still smelled of her. He wondered if she was with Blane, waking up in his arms this morning.

He fell asleep with her image behind his closed eyes. His dreams were filled with Kathleen in his bed, her eyes warm and soft as he kissed her, the feel of her nails digging into his back as he pushed deep inside her, her gasps and sighs echoing in his ears.

Waking to the reality he now faced from the peace and contentment of his dreams was like dying from a thousand cuts.

Kade arrived in Boston the next night. He drove straight to his office, pulling into the garage and parking. The garage was actually part of the space, his "office" being an old self-storage building. It was made of thick red brick, with a chain-link fence surrounding it to discourage any curiosity. If someone did get too close, the grounds were wired with numerous ways to scare them off.

Climbing a wrought-iron spiral staircase, Kade stepped into a loft that he'd converted to a living space. Unlike his apartment in Indy, it wasn't luxurious or even that comfortable. But it was functional, and that was all he really required.

The stark white, windowless walls were bare, and Kade pulled off his shirt, tossing it onto the bed as he headed to the kitchen area. Pulling open the fridge, he grabbed a bottle of water, twisted off the cap, and drank half the bottle in one long gulp. A moment later, he was heading back down the stairs to where he'd set up his computers.

Various green and blue lights glowed in the dark as Kade flipped on the overhead lights. A server rack was on his right, the computers it contained humming. The noise was familiar and comforting to Kade. At least he had control over this part of his life, considering the rest had gone to complete and utter shit.

Six computer monitors, stacked two tall, sat on a large table. Kade sank into the chair in front of the monitors, toggling a key on the lone keyboard. The screens flickered to life. Two of the monitors showed the black-and-white footage of surveillance cameras—some for here, others for his apartment in Indy. Glancing over the ones in Indy, he saw the housekeeper hadn't yet taken care of the place as he'd directed.

Kade's need to know about Kathleen ate at him, and it was only because of an iron grip on his self-control that he didn't try and call her. He briefly considered calling Blane, but knew he couldn't do that, either.

It was clear he should get to work. There were jobs waiting to be done, just sitting there on his desk. Jobs he'd taken when he'd thought going legit would solve all his problems. Now, he didn't give a shit.

The next night he sat in a bar, drink in hand. He'd lost track of how many he'd had. But still, no matter how much he drank, it didn't seem to numb the pain eating him from the inside out.

He'd been a fool to think somebody like him could have a happily-ever-after.

The joy and peace he'd felt when Kathleen had said she loved him, wanted to be with him, told him she was carrying their child—all of it had faded to ash. It had been so close . . .

Kade tipped the glass back, emptying the clear liquid in one swallow. He set it back down on the bar, caught the bartender's eye, and tapped it to signal a refill. Obligingly, the man came over, grabbing a bottle on the way, and poured another double for him.

"Everything all right there, buddy?" the bartender asked. "You wanna talk about it?"

Kade glanced up and frowned, pulled from his thoughts by the questions. The man was watching him with some concern, which just pissed Kade off. "What are you, a fucking bartender or a shrink? Fuck off."

Immediately dismissing the man from his attention, Kade returned to his thoughts. The bartender went away. He might've been pissed. Kade didn't care.

He left when the bar closed and the now not-so-friendly bartender kicked him out. Kade was unlocking his car when he heard the scuff of a shoe behind him and a voice say, "Give me your wallet, dickhead."

Kade sighed. He really didn't feel like this shit tonight. Turning around, he leaned back against the car, surveying the guy who was stupid enough to try and mug him.

He was about Kade's height, with a slightly heavier build. It was hard to tell his age in the dark, though there was no mistaking the knife in his hand.

"Listen," Kade said, his lips twisting into something resembling a smile, "you seem like a real nice guy, so I'm going to give you some advice. Go find someone else to play with tonight. I'm in a shitty mood."

"Shut up and give it to me, or I'll hand you your fucking spleen," the guy threatened.

Kade gave a mock frown. "Do you even know where the spleen *is?*" he asked. "Not that I'm doubting your sincerity, just your capability." This guy was starting to piss him off, the anger burning away both the alcohol and the pain.

Apparently, the guy didn't know where the spleen was located, because when he lunged, he was miles off. Kade reacted quickly, twisting to the side to avoid the clumsy knife thrust, then grabbing the guy's wrist.

Now they were in close quarters. Anger spiked hard in Kade. He jabbed his bent elbow up, catching the mugger on the soft spot underneath his chin. The guy faltered at the blow, his teeth clacking hard together. Kade bent the guy's wrist down and shoved, a crack letting him know he'd broken the joint. The guy cried out in pain, the knife dropping from his fingers, but Kade was too far gone to let things go with that.

His fist shot out in a crushing blow to the man's esophagus, then Kade's elbow caught him in the solar plexus. The guy went down, his good hand flying to his neck as he tried in vain to suck down air.

Kade watched for the one hundred and eighty seconds, thereabouts, it took for a man to suffocate. When the guy was still, Kade reached down and picked up the dropped knife. It wasn't a bad piece. Flipping the blade closed, he pocketed it and got in his car.

As he drove away, the anger and rage ebbed, replaced by the familiar tide of despair. It was an odd realization to come to and it only took Kade as long as the drive back to his office to figure it out. So long as he was inflicting pain and death, he didn't feel the pain of missing her. And it had felt good to not feel so fucking bad for even a little while.

Well. Problem solved. Because if there was one thing Kade could do, it was kill people. And as a bonus, it also paid well.

～

Once word got out that Kade Dennon had come out of retirement and was back in the field, business started booming.

Kade fell back into the routine almost too easily. Take a job. Study the target. Plan the mission. Execute it. Doing it kept his mind busy. You had to be cold on the inside to look someone in the eye—someone for whom you had no personal animus, no grudge or hatred—and kill them. And with each new contract he fulfilled, that coldness grew larger and even more frigid.

He took jobs no one else would, because in the end, there's nothing more deadly than an assassin with nothing to lose. Everything he'd almost had was already gone.

It was close to midnight in the part of the world he now inhabited, and the flat he was invading had a security system. *Had* being the operative word, as Kade had already disabled it.

In the past Kade had lived by a code of sorts, and it determined the contracts he'd taken. He'd choose only those jobs whose targets were already criminals, but for whom wealth or politics put them beyond the reach of traditional law enforcement.

Now he didn't particularly care what the job was. The more dangerous, the better. Some might say Kade had a death wish. He'd say he was already dead.

A guard stayed with his current target in his flat, and Kade stepped over the guard's now lifeless body while scanning the shadows for any further threats. The stairs were carpeted, which further muffled Kade's already silent footsteps. The study was down the hall and to the right, which was where—as the past three nights of surveillance had shown—the target always was at this hour.

Kade slowly approached the doorway, a sliver of light leaking through the open crack. Reaching out, he pushed the door open.

Only to be faced with a gun.

His target was standing in front of a desk, gun in hand, and pointing it directly at Kade.

"I've been expecting someone to come," he said.

"Well then, I'm glad I didn't disappoint you," Kade replied evenly.

"Toss your weapon on the floor," the target ordered. Kade complied. "Now put your hands behind your head."

Kade did as he was told while the man stepped back, carefully keeping an eye on Kade as he reached behind him for the phone on the desk. He dialed 999.

"You're calling the cops?" Kade asked in disbelief as the man held the receiver to his ear. He rolled his eyes. "You've got to be kidding me."

The guy ignored him, reporting a break-in and requesting someone to come arrest the intruder.

"Just shoot me already," Kade ordered in exasperation when the man hung up. "I am not going to fucking prison."

"I don't kill people if I don't have to," the man replied evenly.

Just then, a second guard came barreling down the hallway. He must've found his buddy's body, Kade mused. It was enough to send the guy into full alert mode, which turned out to be too bad for him when he ran through the doorway.

Kade was ready, turning and yanking the guy by his gun arm and jerking him off-balance. He stumbled and Kade pulled his body in front of his own, using him as a shield for when the target reflexively fired his gun. Two shots rang out before the target realized he was shooting his own guy, the body in front of Kade jerking from the impact. The target looked stunned as the blood began flowing. Kade grabbed the guard's hand, which still held a weapon, fitted his index finger over the one already on the trigger, raised the arm, and fired. The target went down. Kade dropped the guard's body.

The whole thing had taken less than five seconds.

Stepping over the body, Kade approached the man who he'd shot in the chest. He stood over him, trying to feel something as he watched the blood pulsing from the open wound in time with the man's heartbeat. All he could feel was a chilly detachment.

"Should've killed me when you had the chance," Kade mused. It was too bad, really. It could've been his body on the floor instead of the guard's.

The thought didn't cause so much as a flicker of concern or fear, only a somewhat tired resignation.

The man didn't respond, and a moment later, he couldn't. He was dead.

Police sirens wailed and Kade decided the window would have to do tonight. Luckily, the building connected to another, which led to a fire escape that took him back down to street level. Three hours later, he was on a plane and out of the country.

The next job took him to the West Coast and a home that overlooked the Pacific Ocean. The place had cost millions and had top-of-the-line security. It was a fool's mission to try an all-out assault on the place, which was guarded like a fortress. But Kade didn't try to get to the house. He only had to wait until the target came to him.

The target had a weakness: sailing. If weather conditions were just right, he'd drop everything on his schedule and take the small sailboat he owned out onto the water. Despite all his security, it seemed he liked being alone for this one activity. Which was perfect.

Kade penetrated the lax security on the sailboat and hid below deck. Then he waited. According to weather reports, tomorrow morning had an eighty-five percent chance of having ideal sailing weather.

Sleep wasn't an option, not while Kade was on a mission, so he didn't. Not that he was a big fan anymore of sleeping. It seemed he could control his waking thoughts much more than he could his subconscious. Nightmares plagued him, of Kathleen, of something happening to her, of what she'd say if she knew what he'd become. The look on her face as Kade confessed his countless sins. Horror, followed by disgust, then loathing.

In his nightmares, he begged her forgiveness, but before she could answer him, before she could absolve or condemn him, the blood began to flow. Wounds that had no source appeared on her flawless skin, slashes of crimson cutting her to shreds. Kade watched in helpless terror as Kathleen screamed, writhing in pain as blood seeped from her body, until the sounds she made faded into silence and her blue eyes stared into his, unseeing and lifeless. Only then did he see the knife in his hand, stained and warm with her blood, and realize . . . he had killed her. Horrified, he dropped the knife, only then seeing her blood coating his hands. Pulling his gun from its holster, he stuck the barrel in his mouth and pulled the trigger—

Kade woke with a start, a cold sweat sticky on his skin. He'd fallen asleep after all. Then he heard the sound that had woken him. Sounds above deck. The target was here. Fuck.

More rattled than he wanted to admit, Kade scrambled, grabbing the gun and silencer at his side and checking to make sure it was loaded and ready to fire. Getting to his feet, he crouched in the corner, behind the stairs that led up to the deck. All he had to do was wait until they were far enough from shore to prevent assistance and mask the gunshot, but not so far that he couldn't swim back.

It didn't take long, maybe twenty minutes, before the rocking of the boat signaled Kade they were well underway. He took a deep breath, finding it hard to remove Kathleen's image from behind his eyes every time he blinked.

A moment later, he was up the ladder, observing the shore and gauging the distance. He'd timed it just right. What he hadn't counted on was that the target would have chosen today, of all days, to bring along his daughter.

Kade stood, gun raised and aimed, as he watched the man and the girl freeze in place at the sight of him. Neither of them moved, shock and fear rooting them in place.

They were too close together, the girl and her father. He'd been showing her something, something to do with the workings of the boat. Kade didn't have a clear shot.

She was young, maybe nine years old, ten? Her hair was long and reddish-blonde, pulled back into a braid that hung far down her back. But it was her eyes that Kade couldn't look away from. They were as clear blue as a warm summer sky. The kind of blue he now only saw in his dreams.

After a charged moment in which Kade didn't speak or move, the father said, "Please. Just let her go down below." His throat moved as he swallowed. "Please."

The girl's eyes were filled with terror as she stared at Kade, her hands gripping her father's shirt in tight little fists.

Kade's voice wouldn't work, so he just gave a jerky nod.

"Sweetheart," the father said, keeping his eyes warily on Kade, "I need you to go down below for a while. And don't come up. No matter what you hear."

Tears welled in the girl's eyes and began pouring down her cheeks. "No, Daddy!" She clutched tighter at him.

Kade couldn't breathe.

The man began relentlessly removing her hands from him. "It's okay, sweetheart," he said, his voice almost preternaturally calm. "It'll be okay. Just do as I say."

The child threw her arms around the man's waist, burying her face against his shirt. "Please don't leave me!" she sobbed, her plaintive cry audible even over the wind.

Kade's hand began to shake.

The man, alarmed now, shifted the girl so she was behind him, moving his body to shield hers. "I don't want her to see," he choked out. "Please. I don't want her to see me die."

The girl peered around her dad. The wind had freed some of her hair from the tight braid and the loose strands whipped around her face. Her eyes were accusing as she stared at Kade, the man who would take her father from her.

Which left Kade only one choice. In a quick motion, he turned and dove into the crashing waves.

Kade lay gasping on the beach, wet sand coating his hands and wetsuit. He'd swum far and away from the boat, putting as much distance between him and them as possible, which had taken him into rougher waters. It had consumed all his energy just to drag himself onto this deserted shore.

He flopped over onto his back, staring up at the nearly clear sky dotted with puffy clouds.

Maybe he shouldn't have swum so hard. It would've been easy to just . . . stop, and let the ocean take him down to her depths. It was peaceful there, under the water. Peace, that elusive state of being that Kade had only experienced a handful of times.

He remembered the first time, in a fleabag motel room on the outskirts of Chicago, with a woman who seemed to want nothing from him—but to be safe.

Kathleen.

Kade had been alone for so long, worked alone for so long, that he'd forgotten what a woman's touch felt like when it wasn't all about sex. Kathleen had seemed to actually . . . care, which had shocked the hell out of him. When women saw him, they wanted one thing—a walk on the wild side, preferably naked. And that had been fine with Kade, for a really long time. And then it wasn't.

Kade closed his eyes, remembering how it had felt to rest his head in her soft lap, feel the slow slide of her fingers through his hair in a touch intended to comfort, not arouse.

Peace.

It had taken him a few moments to recognize the feeling, and when he had, he'd been bone-deep grateful for it.

Now it was gone, and Kade knew with a certainty beyond all doubt that he would never find it again. So that left one question.

What was the point?

He'd broken the heart of the woman he loved, left her to raise his child without him. Blane had been right. Kade was no better than the man who'd fathered him. He'd repaid

Blane's love and acceptance by stealing his girl, then dumped her back on him as if she were garbage.

No one hated Kade more than he hated himself. There was nothing redeeming about him, nothing good or decent in his character. And no one would miss him when he was gone.

Kade lifted his hand, the sun glinting off the metal of the gun he held. He watched his hand move as though it belonged to a different person. The cold barrel pressed against his temple. It would be so quick, take such little effort, to pull the trigger.

He couldn't do this anymore. He realized that now. The answer to the question was: *There was no fucking point.* Not without her. It was only a matter of time before he stopped swimming . . . and sank.

But before he did that, he wanted to see her—had to see her—just one more time.

Kade lowered his hand.

Now he had a purpose, and he automatically went through the motions of ditching his weapon and his wet clothes, removing all traces of his presence in California before heading to the airport. His flight to Boston would leave in thirty minutes. Instead of heading to the gate, he found a ticketing agent.

"Can I help you?" she asked, her tone contrasting sharply with her question. Then she looked up from the computer, surprise etching her features when she saw Kade. She smiled, her gaze taking him in. "What can I do for you?" This time, her question was far more friendly.

Kade paused, then asked, "When's your next flight to Indianapolis?" Which is how he found himself sitting in first class on a flight headed to the one place he shouldn't go.

With the takeoff came lucidity and rational thought.

What the hell was he doing?

He'd left. Left *her*. Now he was going to . . . what? Just show up? She was with Blane. He'd take care of her, protect her. Kade wasn't needed or wanted.

But he had to say goodbye.

He was sitting alone in first class, finishing his third drink, when the flight attendant came by to tell him they would be landing soon.

Excitement and dread churned along with the vodka in his stomach. Kade couldn't help the feeling of anticipation, of getting to see her again, but he also knew it was going to be like salt on an open wound. She'd be angry, he knew that, which would help. But leaving her this time would be permanent. Maybe she'd forgive him? He'd like to take that to his grave rather than her enmity and disgust.

It was late in the evening by the time Kade showed up at Kathleen's. He'd gone by his apartment first, replenishing his duffel bag with clothes and taking a final look at the place. He wouldn't be back.

Now he sat in the parking lot of Kathleen's run-down apartment building, staring up at her darkened windows. She wasn't home. Maybe she was working.

The thought made his gut tighten. He'd given her enough money, she shouldn't have to work, much less at a job that meant she had to be half naked and pour booze for too many ogling assholes.

He'd wait for her, Kade decided, finally getting out of the car. A quick goodbye at The Drop was not how he wanted her to remember him.

In a few moments, he was inside her apartment. He didn't turn on any lights, letting his eyes adjust to the dim glow of the streetlamps filtering in through the open blinds.

Instantly, he sensed something was off. The smell was slightly musty, like the windows hadn't been opened in a while and the AC was set too high to keep the air circulating. And where was Tigger? The cat had always hurried to greet him when he came through the door, acting more like a dog than a feline should. But there was no sign of him.

Kade moved with purpose now, heading back to the bedroom. He flicked on the light, then pulled open the closet door.

Most of her clothes were gone.

It was like a punch to the gut.

She'd gone, moved out. Most likely moved *in* with Blane.

Kade should be glad. His plan had worked. She'd be safe. Their child would be safe. So why did he feel like every breath he took was an effort, each heartbeat now counting against an imaginary clock inside his head?

He sucked in a lungful of air on a choked gasp, not realizing he'd been holding his breath. Backing away from the closet, he stood, staring at the empty space around him. He saw her personal things were gone, too. Pictures of her parents that had been displayed on her bureau, knickknacks she'd set on her bedside table, the books that had been stacked in the corner.

Kade's eyes stung. Holy shit, he would absolutely not cry. No fucking way. Kade Dennon did *not* fucking cry.

And yet his vision grew more blurry, until he couldn't swallow past the growing lump in his throat.

With a roar of pure rage, Kade turned and slammed his fist through the drywall, the thin Sheetrock crumbling at the unexpected onslaught. Pain exploded in his hand and coursed up his arm, but Kade didn't feel it. The anger burned away all other feelings, emotions he had no desire to deal with.

Pulling his hand from the hole in the wall—there went Kathleen's security deposit—Kade flexed his fingers, realizing with a distant surprise that he hadn't broken anything. The anger was leaching away, leaving a calm detachment in its wake. She was at Blane's. So that's where he'd go.

In the car on the way to Blane's, Kade tried not to think of how his last meeting with his brother had gone. Chances were pretty good that Blane wouldn't let him past the front door, much less in to say goodbye to Kathleen. Not after the things Kade had said last time . . .

Deciding not to give Blane the opportunity to refuse him admittance, Kade went around back. He was a little surprised that his key still worked. For some reason, he'd assumed Blane would have changed the locks by now, for precisely this reason.

The temptation to just head upstairs and see if he could catch Kathleen alone was strong, and Kade hesitated at the stairway. But it felt wrong to sneak behind Blane's back. She was his now, and despite the chilly reception Kade was sure to receive, he owed it to Blane to show his face.

Light shone around the doorway to the den, proof that Blane was inside and maybe Kathleen as well. Kade reached for the handle, noticing a fine tremor of his hand. Taking a deep breath, he slowly opened the door.

He'd been half right. Blane was in there, seated at his desk, but not Kathleen. A sharp sting of disappointment pricked Kade.

Blane looked up and his eyes narrowed as his gaze took in Kade, who hadn't moved from the doorway.

Neither spoke. After a moment, Blane pushed back his chair and came striding around the desk. Kade stiffened his spine, bracing himself for another tussle with his brother. Not that he wanted to fight back. Actually, Kade decided that if Blane wanted to beat the shit out of him, he wouldn't lift a finger to stop him.

Blane's face was unreadable as he approached, then to Kade's utter disbelief, his brother threw his arms around him, jerking him close and hugging him so tight it constricted the air in his lungs.

"Thank God," Blane murmured. "Thank God you're all right."

Shock left Kade speechless and he just stood there. Blane and he didn't hug. Ever. They just . . . didn't. Blane had learned early on that Kade was averse to close physical contact and he'd never forgotten it. But now, at this moment when Kade had expected the exact opposite response from Blane, he lifted his arms to hug Blane in return. His hand awkwardly gave a rough pat to Blane's back before he could no longer stop the compulsion to pull away. Blane released him, but seemed reluctant to do so.

Blane took a step back and Kade finally spoke. "I must say, that wasn't quite the welcome I expected." His voice was rougher than usual.

"I haven't been able to reach you since you left nearly a month ago," Blane said. "I've been going out of my mind with worry. Your phone's disconnected, you don't answer your e-mail. What the hell, Kade?"

"Had to go off the grid for a while," Kade said evasively.

"I'm hoping you've come to your senses and are done acting like a fucking prick," Blane said. "But for now, I'll just settle for the fact that you're alive and you're here."

"I thought I wasn't your brother anymore," Kade retorted, remembering just how deeply those words had cut.

"I was really pissed," Blane admitted. "Then I had some time to think about it and realized how freaked out you must've been. I know we don't spill our guts to each other, but I'd like to think the Kade I know wouldn't walk out on the woman he loves, especially not when she's carrying his child."

Shame crept through Kade, along with a burning desire to tell Blane the truth. But he couldn't, so he kept his mouth shut.

"Am I right? Please tell me that's why you're here."

Kade swallowed, then gave a minute shake of his head. "I came to say goodbye. Hoped you'd let me tell her goodbye."

Blane frowned. "What?"

"I didn't get to, and I'd like to. I'm . . . going away, and this time I won't be back."

"Going away? Where the hell are you going?"

Kade shrugged. Unable to meet Blane's eyes, he gazed instead over his brother's shoulder. "Just . . . away."

Blane's face paled as realization appeared to seep in. His jaw locked. "Oh no, you're not," he said. "I don't care if I have to lock you up in the goddamn basement, you're not leaving here. Not until you tell me what the fuck is going on."

"Where's Kathleen?" Kade asked instead. "Is she upstairs?" He glanced over his shoulder, already inching out the door. The burning need to see her had increased a hundredfold since he'd set foot in Indy.

"She's not here," Blane said, his voice stiff.

"Oh," Kade said, disappointed yet again. "Will she come here after work or will she go to her apartment?"

"She's not at work, either, Kade," Blane replied, tiredly shoving a hand through his hair. "I don't know where she is."

Now it was Kade's turn to be confused. "What are you talking about?"

"We're not together," Blane said baldly. "She loves you, not me, and nothing I said or did was enough to change her mind."

It was the second time that night that Kade had been struck speechless, which had to be a record.

"But . . . I saw you," he said at last. "That night. I saw you go to her apartment. Then she left, heading here."

Blane's eyes narrowed. "If I'd known you were hiding in the bushes like a fucking Peeping Tom, I'd have dragged your ass in there and made you break her heart yourself. She didn't come here, Kade. She went to your place that night."

"My place?"

"Yes, your place," Blane repeated, pushing a finger hard into Kade's chest. "Which is where I found her almost twenty-four hours later, practically catatonic."

The accusation in Blane's voice was hard to miss.

Now guilt warred with shame inside Kade, and under-neath that, a hint of relief. Kathleen hadn't forgotten about him. She hadn't just wanted to be with him because of the baby. She really did love him.

"Where is she now?" he managed to ask. He had to see her, touch her. Then he had to be an utter dick to her and make her hate him, convince her to go back to Blane. The thought was a shard of ice in his gut.

"That's what I'm trying to tell you," Blane said with exag-gerated patience. "I don't know. She left, over three weeks ago now, and didn't tell anyone where she was going. She just vanished one night. I've tried her phone—it's always turned off. I've left dozens of messages. I know she needed some space, but hell"—Blane shoved his hands in his pock-ets—"I hate not knowing where she is."

Kade had stopped listening after "just vanished one night." Panic struck, and struck hard.

"You let her go?" he asked, his voice loud.

Blane frowned. "I didn't *let* her do anything," he said. "She left, Kade. Short of keeping her a prisoner, what the hell was I supposed to do? I didn't even know she was think-ing of leaving. One day she was just . . . gone."

Adrenaline poured through Kade in a cold rush. Where could she have gone? And that was assuming she'd gone of her own free will. What if Keaston had found out that she'd left Blane? He could have had her killed, her body dumped somewhere no one would find it.

He grabbed the neck of Blane's shirt with both hands, the fabric crumpling in his fists as he hauled him close until they were nose to nose. "Did you tell Keaston?" he bit out, fury riding close on the heels of panic. "Did you?"

"I spoke to him yesterday," Blane said, jerking out of Kade's grip. "What's going on? Kade, tell me."

But Kade was already striding toward the front door, thinking. Keaston knew, but Kathleen had disappeared three weeks ago. The most important question was to make sure Kathleen had left of her own free will and hadn't been kidnapped. If she'd been taken—

Kade couldn't stand to finish that thought and he hit his car at a near run, vaulting behind the wheel and peeling out of the driveway in a squeal of tires and the smell of burning rubber. Glancing in the rearview mirror, he saw Blane standing in the driveway, watching.

It took thirty minutes to get from Blane's house to Kathleen's apartment. Kade made it in fifteen. He took the stairs two at a time. A frigid calm had settled over him in the wake of his earlier panic. He could find her. He would find her. It was what he did best, finding people who didn't want to be found. And he knew just where to start.

~

Light suddenly poured through Alisha's closed eyes, yanking her from a dead sleep, and she woke with a confused start. Her hand reached out to where Lewis was stretched beside her, also fast asleep, but he was no longer there.

"Looking for him?"

Alisha jerked around with a startled cry, automatically clutching the blankets to her chest. She was naked under the covers, but that was the furthest thought from her mind as she realized a man was standing in her bedroom.

His arm was around Lewis's neck, imprisoning him in a choke hold. Terror clawed at Alisha, making her hands shake as she stared openmouthed. Blood oozed from a cut on Lewis's cheek and his lower lip was split.

"What do you want?" Alisha asked. "I have money. I can get it for you. Just please, don't hurt him!" Lewis's eyes looked scared, and though he wasn't much smaller than the intruder, he couldn't escape his grip no matter how hard he struggled.

"I don't want your money," the guy said, causing Alisha to tear her gaze from Lewis and focus on him. "Where's Kathleen?"

And suddenly, it clicked. "Oh my God," Alisha breathed in shock. "It's you. Kade."

"Bingo," Kade said with a chilly smile. "Bet Kathleen never told you what I did for a living, did she."

Alisha felt the blood drain from her face. No, Kathleen hadn't. Looking at Kade now, it was pretty obvious what he did for a living. He wore black on black, a black shirt and black jeans. The ease with which he held Lewis immobile spoke of long practice.

Suddenly, he let Lewis go, only to spin him around and hit him with two punishing blows. The sound of flesh against bone was loud in the room. Lewis grunted in pain and Alisha screamed. Kade grabbed Lewis's shoulders, shoving him down just as his knee came up. Lewis's head snapped back at the impact, then Kade shoved and Lewis fell to the floor.

Alisha flew out of the bed, but froze at the sound of the slide being racked on a gun.

"I wouldn't move," Kade ordered. "Take one more step and you'll be looking for a new boyfriend."

Tears leaked from Alisha's eyes, but she did as he said. Looking up, she swallowed hard at the sight of the gun held steady in Kade's grip.

"I was on your side," she ground out through clenched teeth. "I've been telling Kathleen to ditch Blane for weeks, that *you* were the one she should be with, you sonofabitch!"

"Where is she?"

"You're insane if you think I'm going to tell you," she seethed.

"You're right there, sweetheart. Right now, I feel fucking insane. And if you don't tell me where Kathleen is, I've got no problem pulling this trigger."

Lewis looked up at her, pain creasing his features. Alisha looked back to Kade. He wasn't kidding. His eyes were like blue shards of ice, completely devoid of emotion. He held a man's life in his hands, yet could have been watching paint dry for as much as he seemed to care. The effect was chilling and sent another wave of fear through Alisha.

What would he do if he found Kathleen? Would he hurt her? She was pregnant—surely he wouldn't. And yet, from the looks of him just then, there was nothing to say that wasn't exactly what he'd do.

"I'm not telling you," she said, her voice shaking.

"Really?" Kade asked, cocking his head to the side as though she'd just said she preferred fish to chicken.

The gunshot was loud. Alisha screamed, falling to her knees next to Lewis.

"That was a shoulder. Easy in, easy out, no permanent damage done," Kade said. "I can't say the same for the next one. Now . . . tell me where she is!" His voice rose until he shouted the question at her.

Alisha was sobbing as she pulled Lewis's head onto her lap. Blood oozed from his shoulder, and he was passed out cold. Pressing her hand against the wound, she hissed through her tears, "Go to hell!" Expecting retaliation, she bent over Lewis, trying to shield him with her body the best she could.

"Kade!"

The voice was familiar and Alisha jerked around to see Blane enter the room.

"Kade, for God's sake!" Blane exclaimed, hurrying to where Alisha knelt beside Lewis. "What the hell are you doing?" he practically screamed at Kade.

Kade ignored Blane, his hard gaze focused on Alisha. "Where's Kathleen." It wasn't a question anymore. It was a statement of his intentions if she didn't answer.

"Kade, we'll find her," Blane interjected. "You don't have to do this."

"Tell me now," Kade said. "You have three seconds."

"I-I don't know. I swear I don't—" Alisha babbled, panic twisting inside her belly.

"Kade, stop!"

"One . . ."

"Please, no—"

Blane pulled a gun from the back of his jeans and pointed it at Kade.

"This has to stop. Kade—listen to me!"

"Two . . ."

Alisha couldn't breathe. "I don't know. I don't know! I—"

"Kade!"

But Kade didn't even look in Blane's direction, and his gun was steady and pointed at Lewis, who lay unconscious and bleeding on the floor, and Blane was going to shoot Kade, but Kade was going to shoot Lewis, and—

"She went home!" Alisha's scream cut through everything and silence fell.

Kade slowly lowered his gun.

"Sh-she went home," Alisha repeated, closing her eyes in dismay as she realized she'd just given up her best friend's whereabouts to a madman.

"Now that wasn't so hard, was it?" Kade said.

"I swear to God, Kade, I'm going to fucking kill you," Blane threatened. His gun was lowered, too, but his body language screamed anger.

"If I don't find her soon, she'll be dead when we do," Kade said, causing Alisha to jerk her head up in alarm.

"What? Who's after her? Kade, what's going on?" Blane's frustrated questions echoed in the room, but Kade was already turning to go.

"You shouldn't have let her leave," Kade said. "You were the only thing keeping her safe." Then he was gone.

"Goddammit!" Blane exploded.

Alisha could tell he really wanted to go after Kade, but he turned back to her instead. "I'll call 911," he said, guiding her hand to the wound in Lewis's shoulder. "Keep pressure on the wound. And, I'm really sorry about this, but we have to get our stories straight. My brother was never here, understood? It was an intruder, but it was dark and you didn't get a good look at him. He shot Lewis, but I was at Kathleen's and heard, so I came over and he took off. Got it?"

Her entire body was racked with tremors, and the relief Alisha had felt when Kade left faded. Blane's eyes held the same cold implacability she'd seen in Kade's. She realized she had no choice. She'd have to do what Blane said, say what he told her to say, because the price for not doing so would be one she wasn't willing to pay.

And Alisha finally saw the resemblance between the two men.

KATHLEEN

CHAPTER NINE

"Kathleen, can you get me another?"

I looked up from where I'd been crouched down loading bottles of beer into the fridge below the bar.

"Sure, Pete," I answered. Standing, I grabbed another frosty mug and filled it from the tap, tipping it to the side so the golden liquid hit the side of the glass rather than the bottom as it filled. The head wasn't quite as thick and you could get more beer in the glass if you poured it that way. When the white foam had reached the rim and spilled over just slightly, I set the mug in front of Pete. "Here you go."

"Thanks, sugar," he said, his worn, suntanned face creasing in a smile. I smiled back.

Pete used to work with my dad, once upon a time. He'd retired from the force a couple of years ago, and now spent his days outdoors, tending his extensive garden, lawn, and flowerbeds. It seemed he had a habit of stopping by the one and only local pub for a beer around midday. If the Cubs were playing, he'd stay and watch the game on one of the televisions in the bar, though I teased him that rooting for the Cubs was bound to end in disappointment.

"I'm a perennial optimist," he'd reply. "Sooner or later it's bound to pay off."

I'd been back home now for almost a month, and in some ways it seemed like I'd never left. Although technically I didn't need the money since what Kade had left was more than adequate for my needs, I'd wanted a job so I had something to do. Sitting around feeling miserable and sorry for myself wasn't an option.

Once I'd had time to recover from the shock of Kade's "parting gift," I saw the logic in what Blane had said. If it was just me, I wouldn't have touched a dime of that money. But it wasn't just me. I had our baby to consider. I had to buy things—things a baby needed—and eventually there'd be braces to pay for, and college, maybe a wedding if the baby was a girl. It would be foolish of me not to use the money, so I set aside my pride and did what I needed to do.

I'd returned to my old job at O'Sullivan's, an Irish pub where I'd worked when my mom had been sick. The owner, Charlie, was a wizened older man of indeterminate age who had owned the place for as long as I could remember. He'd been glad to see me. I think. It was kind of hard to tell with Charlie, but he'd sort of smiled and then asked when I could start. I'd put on an apron the next day.

The sounds of the pub were familiar and comforting to me as I worked—the televisions broadcasting the baseball game, the clink of dishes and the sizzle of the grill from the back, the low rumble of conversation from the dozen or so patrons in the middle of the afternoon.

I'd been lucky when I'd shown up in town. One of the first people I'd run into when I stopped in the little café on the town square for lunch had been Jan, an old friend from high school.

"Oh my God, is that you, Kathleen?" she'd exclaimed, wrapping me in a hug. A cloud of perfume descended. "Are you back or just visiting?"

When I'd confirmed I was, indeed, back in town, she'd wasted no time in telling me everything going on with her, ordering a cup of coffee, and sitting with me while I ate my chicken salad sandwich and chips.

"So I'm a Realtor now," she said, after a monologue about how she'd married Brian, a guy I vaguely remembered from high school who now sold insurance. She waved a manicured hand as if it was nothing, but I could tell she was real proud of her new job. "I can help you find a place to stay, if you're looking to stick around." Her shiny platinum blonde hair bounced around her shoulders as she spoke.

"I am," I said, and her eyes had lit up like fireflies.

"Wonderful! I know just the place for you! The owner is a widow who's moved to Florida in one of those, you know, retirement communities. Anyway, she's looking to sell her house. It's out by the old Miller place, remember?"

And I did. Jan had taken me to see it right then and I knew instantly that it was perfect. About three or four miles out of the town proper, it was in the country and the last place on a long gravel road. The nearest neighbors, the Millers, weren't within shouting distance but were within walking distance.

An older home that had been built in the forties, it was a two-story white house with a deep porch that spanned the front, complete with a swing. In the back, another porch was screened in and overlooked a vast yard dotted with big oak trees. Roses climbed a trellis, their blooms perfuming the air, and it seemed they'd been allowed to grow a bit wild and hadn't been trimmed back in a while.

The downstairs had a living room, kitchen, bath, and bedroom. Upstairs were another two bedrooms and a bath. The place was even furnished, and though the pieces were older, they looked like they'd been well cared for.

I bought it immediately and closed within ten days. It was amazing how fast things could be done when you paid with cash, and thanks to Jan, I'd been allowed to start staying in the house right away, so I hadn't even had to spend one night at the old Covered Bridge Motel on the outskirts of town. Jan was so pleased and excited with the sale, I thought her perfectly applied cosmetics might crack with the huge smile she sported whenever I saw her in town.

I hadn't yet gone back to Indy for the rest of my things, and thought I might just get a company to move the stuff into storage for me. Kade had bought all the furniture when he'd had my apartment redone after the fire, and I wasn't sure I needed the reminder. My personal things I'd brought with me, so the only real reason for me to return was to visit Alisha.

I needed to call her, I decided as I cleared the empty glasses on the bar left by two customers. I hadn't talked to her in a couple of weeks, not since I'd told her about the house and reassured her that I was doing okay.

And I was. Mostly.

Rushville was a small town and everyone had known me and my family. People I'd grown up around greeted me with open arms, genuinely glad to see me back. Old Mrs. Johnson had even stopped by my place to bring me a casserole she'd made and welcome me home.

No one asked why I was back or inquired too deeply as to what I'd been up to while I was gone. My family was part of the town's tragedy—my dad's death hitting the community hard when it had happened nearly ten years ago now, then everyone had known about my mom's battle with the cancer that had eventually taken her life. No one had batted an eye when I'd moved away. I think most people understood that I'd needed time and space, but they also knew that there was no place like home, so it hadn't seemed a bit strange when I'd turned up out of the blue.

"Think we'll be busy tonight?"

I glanced up at Michelle, the waitress. I'd gone to high school with her, too, but she'd been a couple of years older than me and we hadn't known each other real well. We'd chatted a bit since I'd returned, since we were often on the same shifts, and I liked her.

Her parents were farmers and Michelle had been a bit of a wild child, the youngest of four. Pregnant at seventeen, she'd married the baby's daddy, but that hadn't worked out. He'd up and left them when baby number two was on the way, and she'd been on her own ever since.

Michelle worked hard and had a little place of her own. Her mom often helped out, watching John, who was now ten, and little Maddie, just turned four.

"I hope so," I said, knowing that slow business meant fewer tips. "There's a doubleheader Little League game tonight, someone said, so we'll probably get people once that's over."

Rushville was small enough that the ebb and flow of town life affected most everyone. If there was a game, chances were you knew somebody who'd be there. Either because their kid was playing, or they were going to support a friend whose kid was playing.

"Is Carol coming in later, do you know?" Michelle asked, sliding onto a barstool.

"Yeah, I think she's on at six?" I answered, trying to recall the schedule in my head. "Then it's just the three of us on the floor until close." Of course, closing time in Rushville was way earlier than in Indy. Here, if no one was in the bar at eleven thirty or even eleven, we closed. Technically, we closed at midnight, but usually the pub stayed open that late only on the weekends.

Carol was a bit over thirty and new to town, having moved here only six months ago. She was single, didn't have any kids, and I wasn't sure what had brought her to Rushville but hadn't pried. She kept to herself and seemed nice enough.

Michelle and I chatted while it was slow, then things started picking up for the dinner rush. There were two other restaurants in town, but one was the café that only served breakfast and lunch. The other was a chain all-you-can-eat buffet place where a lot of families with kids ate. The result was that though O'Sullivan's was a pub, people came to eat as well as drink there.

The main cook was a guy named Danny, who had an overabundance of personality and was impossible not to like. He was black and about six feet tall, but skinny as a post. Danny fancied himself an undiscovered singer of some talent, so he was often belting out tunes while he worked the grill. In his early twenties, he said he was saving money to head to California, and that he'd made it to the final rounds of callbacks for one of those talent shows on TV that held auditions all around the country.

I hadn't told anyone that I was pregnant. First, it wasn't really anyone's business, and second, I wasn't ready to answer questions. Although I was pretty universally liked, there were still a lot of eyebrows that would go up when my "condition" became common knowledge. I didn't think anyone would be outright mean to me—times were a lot different from twenty years ago—but I wanted more time to settle in. I'd barely grown accustomed to the idea myself. I wasn't yet ready to spread my future status as a single mom around town.

The usual dinner rush was delayed because, as I'd predicted, everyone went to the game, which meant that business started hopping around nine thirty. Carol, Michelle, and I didn't have time to spare as we hustled food and drinks. A lot of people liked to sit at the bar to eat, so I was going nonstop. After the initial rush, moms started departing with tired kids in tow. Some of the men stayed put to have another drink or two as they recounted the game. The Colts had a preseason game coming up on the weekend, so conversation also revolved around the team and their chances for the year.

I filled a pitcher of beer and headed to a table of seven guys. Several of them I knew from high school and they were regulars, often stopping by in either twos or threes or sometimes all together, like tonight. They were all buddies, though two were unmarried. The rest were in various stages of early marriage, some with babies on the way or young children.

"Hey, Kathleen, how're you doing tonight?" one of them asked. His name was Matt and he'd been two years ahead of me in school. He was nice and good-looking, with blue eyes and light brown hair. Matt's dad was a pig farmer and now that he was getting up there in age, Matt mostly ran the rather affluent family business. In school, he hadn't paid me a bit of mind, but it seemed he was looking to settle down and he'd been real friendly to me since I'd got back. We'd had several conversations and I enjoyed seeing him come in, which he'd been doing more often lately.

"I'm good, Matt," I said with a smile. "How was the game tonight?" Matt had a buddy, Steve, who was several years older and had two kids, twin boys, on the team. Matt helped coach. He was a big guy, over six feet, with broad shoulders and lean hips. He had the perfect athletic physique, honed by years of working on a farm.

"It was fun, the kids did great," he replied, his enthusiasm contagious.

I smiled and turned to go, but he stopped me with a hand on my arm. I turned back, raising my eyebrows. "Did you need something else?" I asked.

Matt's ears turned a little pink as he tugged me closer, as though he wanted to say something quietly so that the guys he was with wouldn't hear. They didn't seem to be paying attention, instead arguing over the relative strengths and weaknesses of the Colts' offensive line.

"Um, Kathleen," he said in an undertone. I leaned down a little to hear him. "I was just wondering if you'd want to have dinner with me Saturday, if you're not working. Or Friday. Or, just, whenever you're off."

It was real sweet, how nervous he seemed, which took me by surprise. I hadn't garnered much attention in high school from boys, but it seemed age and time had turned me into a girl they now noticed. I'd caught a few glances my way during the past few weeks, but Matt was the first to actually ask me out.

Of course, I had no idea what to say. I wasn't ready to go out on a date with someone, not when I still lay awake nights staring at the ceiling and seeing Kade's face every time I closed my eyes. And what was the proper protocol for telling anyone I might get serious with that, oh, by the way, I was having another man's child in a little over seven months?

"Thanks, Matt," I said finally, "but I . . . can't right now. Ask me again sometime, will you?" I smiled, hoping to soften the rejection, and it seemed to work because the initial disappointment on his face was followed by a grin.

"I sure will," he said.

I headed back to the bar, breathing a quiet sigh. Things were complicated enough in my life without involving another man in the picture. But I also counted my blessings. Things could be worse, that's for sure. I had my own place, and didn't have to worry about money. I was close enough to Indy to still keep in touch with Blane once the baby was born. I was sure Mona and Gerard would want to be involved in the baby's life, too, as well as his Uncle Blane. At least, I hoped so.

Though I hadn't yet broken the news to Chance, which I was dreading, I thought I could count on Lucy to support me. She knew what being a single mom was like and I didn't think she'd let Chance rant for too long about Kade, which he was sure to do once he found out Kade was no longer in the picture.

The evenings were getting cooler now that September was just days away, and people lingered tonight. I didn't mind. There wasn't much to go home to and I enjoyed listening to people talk. Michelle left, so it was just me, Carol, and Danny by the time eleven thirty rolled around.

The group of seven guys had dwindled to four and I hovered by their table as I delivered another pitcher. They were feeling good but weren't drunk, and were trying to get me to solve a friendly disagreement. I laughed at their jokes and teasing, then made my excuses and headed back to the bar to continue my prep work for the next day. It felt good to be home. The people here were just different than city people. More relaxed, more friendly. It was nice to be where I had a history and with people who not only knew me but had known my parents, too.

I was singing along softly to the music playing over the sound system when the door opened. I glanced up, then promptly dropped the empty mug I'd been holding.

Kade had walked into the bar.

I stared at him in openmouthed shock, whereas he looked wholly unsurprised to see me.

He wore a black button-down shirt and black jeans. The shirt was untucked, which I knew meant his gun was lodged in his jeans at the small of his back. His hair was exactly as I remembered, inky black and slightly tousled, the strands long and brushing his forehead. The blue of his eyes pierced me despite the distance between us, and it was like someone had shoved their fist into my gut.

I realized then that the bar had gone quiet, the only sound that of the music playing, as the customers who remained turned to get a look at the newcomer who was very obviously not from around here.

He'd changed, in just the month since I'd last seen him. Not physically, but in his demeanor. The planes of his face were as smooth and unreadable as granite, his eyes as hard and cold as I'd ever seen them. He radiated menace and danger, his palpable presence seeming to proclaim "Don't fuck with me." And only a fool would.

Kade finally broke our staring contest, his gaze taking a quick catalog of the bar and people, then he headed toward me. Conversation resumed and the moment was over.

Jerking myself out of my shock-induced stupor, I dropped down to pick up the mug with shaking hands. It hadn't shattered, thank goodness. The thick rubber pads I stood on behind the bar had cushioned the fall. I stood again, putting the mug with the other dirty dishes that Danny would pick up shortly and take back to load in the washer.

I ignored Kade as he rounded the bar, sliding onto a stool that faced the door and let him keep his back to the wall.

My pulse was racing and I broke out in a cold sweat. I was nearing panic as I struggled to figure out what I was supposed to do. He'd left me, left *us*, without even a goodbye. Why was he back? To torment me? I didn't know, couldn't understand it. What I did know was that I didn't have it in me to watch him leave again. If I let him in even an inch, allowed my feelings to break free from the cage in which

I'd imprisoned them, this time when he left, I would shatter permanently.

"You just going to ignore me?" Kade asked, his tone dry.

I cleared my throat and answered without looking at him. "Pretty much."

Two older men were also sitting at the bar, nursing the last of their beers, and I noticed they were unabashedly watching the exchange between Kade and me.

"Last call," I said to them, forcing my lips to curve into something resembling a smile. I walked out from behind the bar to let the two remaining tables know, too, that it was last call. Usually, I'd just holler it out from the bar, but I felt a pressing need to put some space between me and Kade.

When I returned, Kade hadn't moved.

"Aren't you going to ask me if I'd like a drink?" he asked.

"We're closing," I replied curtly, grabbing the rack of dirty dishes myself to haul to the back. Maybe I could hide back there for a few minutes and Kade would leave. But just as I turned, Danny was there beside me.

"Don't be trying to lift that yourself, Kathleen," he chided me. "I bet it weighs more than you do." He chortled, his smile blinding as he teased me.

"Thanks," I said, letting him take the heavy rack. He started humming a tune as he walked away, and let loose with a full-throated verse and chorus by the time he reached the swinging door into the kitchen. Danny had a great voice, and on any other night, I'd have encouraged him to sing a little for me. But not tonight.

"You can ignore me all you want—it won't make a fucking bit of difference."

Kade's words ricocheted through my head, sending me into a new state of apprehension and panic.

It seemed the guys at the bar took exception to Kade, because one of them piped up, "I don't know where you're from, Mister," he said gruffly, "but round here we watch our mouths in front of a lady."

I looked up now, suddenly hyperaware of what was happening. Kade didn't take kindly to people telling him what to do, and tonight was no exception.

Catching his gaze, I saw an eyebrow lift in sardonic amusement. "A *lady*, is it?" he sneered. "My mistake." The look in his eyes made me shiver, and not in a good way. "Do excuse me," he said. The words were a humble gesture, but the way in which he said them was not.

It seemed the man who'd spoken to Kade thought the same way I did, because I saw his jaw harden and he pushed his stool back from the bar. I hurried over before he could get up, forcing my lips into a smile.

"It's okay," I said, trying to forestall him. "Really. It's not a problem. Did you need to settle up your tab?"

The man, I thought his name was Wade, seemed reluctant to let it go, but I guess he also didn't want to make trouble for me, because he gave a curt nod and tossed some money down on the counter.

"I'll just get you some change," I said, but he shook his head.

"Keep it." He gave me a fatherly smile and a pat on the arm from his work-roughened hand. "You be careful gettin' home tonight, you hear?" He gave Kade a hard glare.

"I will, thanks," I said, slipping the change from his tab into my pocket. He left and his friend finished off his beer and left, too.

Carol brought over the tabs for the remaining two tables and I ran them through the register. The one table left and two of the guys from the other as well, but Matt and his buddy Steve remained. I noticed them talking quietly to each other and casting glances at Kade, then me.

I could see where this was going. Shit.

I hurried behind the bar as Carol brought back a tray of empty glasses from the two tables. She, too, eyed Kade sitting behind me.

"What's with him?" she asked in an undertone. "He looks like bad news. Really bad news. Want me to go call Roger?" Roger was a deputy on the town's small police force. He ate lunch here all the time and I'd noticed had taken more than a passing interest in Carol. It didn't surprise me that she would have his number.

"It's okay," I said, though I wondered if I believed that myself. "I . . . know him."

Her eyes widened to the size of proverbial saucers. "You *know* him?"

I nodded. "He can be a bit of an asshole," I said, which was a massive understatement. "I'll get rid of him. It's fine."

She looked skeptical but nodded. "Okay. If you're sure. I'm going to head home, okay? My prep's done for the night and my feet are killing me."

I could certainly relate to that. I'd pulled a nine-hour shift with two half-hour breaks and the dogs were barkin'.

"Yeah, no problem. See you tomorrow."

I turned around as she left and wanted to groan with dismay. While I'd been busy talking to Carol, Matt and Steve had approached Kade, each taking a stool on either side of him.

"It's closing time, buddy," Matt said to Kade. "Way past time for you to go."

He could have been a breeze blowing for as much attention Kade paid to him. Instead, his eyes were locked to mine.

Matt and Steve exchanged glances and silent communication.

"We don't want any trouble," Steve added. "Come on outside with us and leave the girl alone."

Kade rested an elbow on the counter and crooked his finger, beckoning me.

I swallowed, taking hesitant steps forward until I stood directly in front of him. He crooked his finger again and I leaned toward him, my ponytail swinging forward over my shoulder.

Kade caught my hair between his fingers, tugging lightly until my stomach was pressed against the curve at the edge of the bar. Then I felt his lips near my ear, his fingers trailing down my jaw in the lightest of touches, though it felt like an electric current. A shiver danced down my spine. Then he whispered to me.

"I've killed ten men over the last few weeks. Do you want me to make it an even dozen?"

The warmth of his breath against my skin was in stark contrast to the ice that froze my veins as the meaning of his words sank in. In stunned horror, I jerked backward, my shocked gaze again meeting his. The corner of his lips lifted in a chilling smirk.

"Matt, Steve," I said, my voice sounding strangled, "it's okay. Come on, I'll walk you out."

Matt looked at me like I'd lost my mind.

"No way, Kathleen," he said with a disgusted snort. "We'll stick around until you're done."

"You've been busy," Kade said conspiratorially to me.

My jaw fell open in shock at his insinuation.

Kade turned to Matt. "Let me guess, the quarterback? Captain of the football team?"

My cheeks burned because, yes, that had been Matt exactly in high school, right down to captain of the Rushville High School Lions football team. Which was, coincidentally, one of the reasons he'd never noticed me. Girls had trailed after him like they were kitties and he was catnip. Why he wasn't married yet, I had no idea. I hadn't asked and he hadn't said.

"What's it to you?" Matt retorted.

Kade shot me a sideways look. "Knew it," he said in an aside.

"Matt, really, you and Steve should just go," I pleaded. I still had prep work to do, but I'd forgo it and pay the consequences tomorrow if I could just get Steve and Matt to leave. I pushed back from the bar, intending to round it and physically walk them outside, when Matt grabbed my arm, pulling me to a halt.

"What's going on?" Matt asked, his brows creasing in confusion.

But I was no longer looking at Matt. I was looking at Kade, whose gaze was fixed on Matt's hand wrapped around my wrist. Kade's body tensed and a dangerous light came into his eyes. Alarm shot through me. I jerked my arm out of Matt's grip and hurried out from behind the bar.

"Please, just do what I say," I said, taking Matt by the hand. "It's okay. I know him and it'll be fine."

Matt let me tug him to his feet and Steve reluctantly followed. I led them out the door and into the parking lot.

"You know that guy?" Matt asked, his disbelief evident.

I nodded. "Yeah. I used to . . . work for him." What else was I supposed to say? How to explain? *I was engaged to his brother, but then I fell in love with him, then I got pregnant and told him I loved him. Then he left me.* Yeah, not even I wanted to try and make sense of that pathetic story.

"What's he doing here?"

Good question.

"I don't know," I said, "but I'm sure it's nothing. He can just be a jerk, that's all. I'll be fine."

"Are you positive?" Matt asked. "Because I don't mind waiting. I'll follow you home, make sure everything's all right."

"I'm sure. It'll be all right. I promise." I smiled. "But thanks so much for wanting to stay and help." Because it *was* nice of him. Matt was a nice guy, a good guy, and I didn't take that for granted. Impulsively, I gave him a hug. He was hard and solid in my arms, hugging me back in the slightly awkward way of a big guy who was aware of his size and didn't want to unthinkingly crush something much smaller than him.

I stepped back and Matt considered for a moment, studying me, then gave a reluctant nod. "Okay. If you say it's all right, then I guess it is."

"It is," I reiterated.

Steve waved at me and I thanked him, too, watching as they got in their separate trucks and left.

I pondered just walking to my car and driving home, but that would only be delaying the inevitable. Best to see what Kade wanted and send him on his way. Then at least I'd get a decent night's sleep.

Fat chance of that happening, I thought with a sigh, heading back inside.

Kade had moved to the windows of the pub, startling me as I opened the door to go back inside.

"Were you watching me?" I asked sharply, my eyes narrowing.

"No," he said flatly. "I was watching the quarterback."

Before I could retort, the music suddenly got louder.

"What the hell is that?" Kade asked over the strains of Florence and the Machine.

I sighed. "Danny likes to turn up the music after closing and sing while he cleans the kitchen."

Kade's eyebrows flew up. "He sings this?"

I laughed unexpectedly at the look on Kade's face. "No. He likes me to sing, too." It had become our little ritual, Danny and me. Once he'd heard me singing to myself, he decided that belting tunes out after closing was a great way to "clean out the old pipes," as he put it. Once everyone was gone, he'd put on different music and turn it up. It was fun and helped pass the time while I finished my work. Sometimes he came out and we'd sing something together before we locked up.

Kade didn't say anything to that, his eyes searching mine. I liked the song playing, had once listened to it all the time, but now it made me think of Kade, which just tore me to pieces.

I sighed, exhaustion overtaking me. It had been a long day.

"Why are you here?" I asked, passing a hand tiredly across my eyes. "What do you want?"

He didn't answer immediately, and when I finally glanced up, he was frowning, his brows drawn sharply together.

"I could ask you the same thing," he said. "Why are you here? You're supposed to be with Blane."

If he'd said he wanted me to dye my hair purple and dance the hula, I couldn't have been more surprised. My mouth hung open until I finally closed it with a snap.

"I'm what?" I hissed, feeling the anger rising inside me. Had I heard him correctly?

"You're supposed to be with Blane," he repeated.

"I'm *supposed* to be with *Blane?* Are you kidding me?" I was fuming now. Deciding I'd better do something else before I flew at Kade in a rage, I spun on my heel and started stacking chairs on tables. The morning crew did the sweeping, so the night crew just had to get things ready.

"No, I'm not kidding you," he retorted. "Blane—"

I whirled, cutting him off. "If you say that again, so help me God, I'm going to throw this chair at your head."

The idea that I might actually hurt Kade was laughable, but he shut up, his lips pressing into a thin line as his eyes narrowed.

I turned away and resumed my task. After a moment, I saw Kade in my peripheral vision, copying my movements and stacking chairs on tables. Sooner than it would have taken me to do alone, it was done.

The lights went out, leaving just the ones by the bar lit. I figured Danny must be about done in the kitchen. Sure enough, I'd just gone to get my purse from under the bar when he poked his head out.

"I'm finished back here!" he called. "See you tomorrow."

"Bye, Danny!" I hollered back. He went out the back way and locked up, while I took care of the front. Kade followed in silence.

I walked stiffly to my car, drawing from my energy reserves, which were dangerously low. Gravel crunched under our feet, ratcheting up the tension lodged between my shoulder blades. When I got to my car, I took a deep breath before I turned around to face him.

"Listen, Kade," I said, "you made it damn clear that you want nothing to do with me, or the baby. So you should just leave. You're pretty good at that." And if my voice held more than a trace of bitterness, I thought it was my due.

Kade's face was stark in the harsh light of the streetlamp in the lot. If I hadn't known him and had happened to bump into him like this, I'd have turned and run in the opposite direction. The hard edge to him that had been so prominent when we'd first met was back with a vengeance, a malevolence that made a chill creep down my spine.

He took a step closer, but I stood my ground. I'd never let Kade intimidate me into backing down before, and I sure as hell wasn't about to do it now. He was so close, I could feel the heat from his body, though we didn't touch.

"I'm here to do something else I'm pretty good at," he said roughly, the deep blue of his eyes seeming unfathomable.

I swallowed. Hard. I wasn't proud of the images that flashed through my mind then or the way my body was exulting in how close he was. The slight breeze stirred, sending a waft of his scent my way. A shaft of pain flashed through me even as a shiver of arousal whispered across my skin. I bit my lip against the moan that wanted to crawl from my throat.

"And what's that?" I managed to ask, my voice mortifyingly breathless.

"Keeping you alive."

CHAPTER TEN

K ade followed me home, something I didn't really have a choice in. I hadn't asked what he'd meant by his reference to keeping me alive, and didn't want to know. I'd had enough worrying about those who were intent on physically hurting me. At the moment, I was much more concerned about my emotional well-being.

The gravel road was long and dark, the beams from my headlights cutting through the blackness. I'd left my porch light on, though, so I didn't have to find my way to the front door in the dark.

I didn't look around when I unlocked the door. The crunch of Kade's boots as he walked through the gravel made it impossible to miss his approach. My hands trembled and I had to fuss with the key more than usual before it finally turned in the lock.

I walked through the living room, pausing to flip on a light once I reached the kitchen. It was a country kitchen, homey with lots of light oak cabinets and trim, and I liked it a lot. I dropped my purse on the counter and went to the little laundry room down the short hallway that led to the garage to shuck my shoes. I took off my apron and socks, too, then tossed them into the washing machine for later. When I returned to the kitchen, I saw Kade taking everything in.

"It's late and the motel's at the other end of town," I said stiffly. "You can sleep here for tonight, then go in the morning." I'd shut off the upstairs vents to save on the AC bill—old habits die hard—but figured Kade could just open a window. Besides, it wasn't that hot up there now that the nights were cool.

Kade didn't say anything, the tension between us thick, so I just said, "C'mon." Turning, I headed up the narrow staircase, the old wooden steps creaking beneath my feet. I heard pretty quickly when he started following me.

I led Kade to the smaller of the two bedrooms, grateful that I'd shut the door on the other one earlier in the day. There was a twin bed in this one that would work for the night.

"Here you go," I said. "Bathroom's across the hall. Night." I turned to leave, but he caught my arm. Of course he did. Should've known it wouldn't be that easy.

"Where do you sleep?" he asked.

"My room's downstairs," I replied.

"Then I'll sleep on the couch."

I stared at him in confusion but was too tired to argue. "Whatever," I said, pulling away and retreating back down the stairs. He followed me again, which was starting to make me feel like a pied piper, as I grabbed sheets and a blanket from the linen closet. I set them on a chair in the living room, then picked up a sheet to begin making up the couch.

"I'll do it," Kade said roughly, taking the sheet from me. "Go to bed. You look like you're about to drop."

"Gee, thanks," I retorted, but there wasn't much heat behind it. I was just too tired.

I showered because I couldn't climb into bed with nine hours of french fries and beer aroma wafting from me, but it was a quick one. I resisted the urge to peek into the living room to see how Kade was settling in before I climbed into bed, though it was tough.

Only when I was at last in my T-shirt and curled under the blankets on my bed did I allow myself the pleasure and pain of thinking about Kade and how close he was, and of how I'd thought I'd never see him again—and how, after tomorrow, I likely never would.

~

I woke earlier than I'd intended, then found I couldn't go back to sleep. My stomach was still queasy in the mornings, which made my trip to the bathroom more urgent now than before I'd gotten pregnant. Afterward, I brushed my teeth and washed my face. I brushed my hair until it gleamed, then pulled it up into a high ponytail. I'd planned on doing more painting today, so I dressed in an old, faded pair of cutoffs and an even older T-shirt. I abruptly realized that the shorts were too tight to fasten, right where the waistband went beneath my navel.

I lifted my shirt and turned sideways, studying my reflection. Yes, there was a small but definite bump that I hadn't noticed before.

I stood there too long, a little awestruck, a lot afraid. Each day that passed seemed to increasingly bring home the reality that I was having a baby. It felt strange to be both excited and terrified. So far this hadn't been at all what I'd pictured when I was younger and imagined having a child.

I'd thought I'd be married, of course, and that my husband would be just as thrilled as I was. We'd paint the baby's room together, argue over names, shop for tiny little baby clothes in tiny little sizes . . .

And just like that, I was a sobbing mess.

Dammit! The hormone changes that now seemed to rule my emotions with an iron fist showed no mercy, and I was often left reeling between being overjoyed one moment and sobbing in self-pitying misery the next.

The crying jag lasted several minutes before I could pull myself together and wash my face again. My eyes were puffy, my cheeks red and blotchy, and my shorts didn't fit.

My eyes swam with tears again. I took a deep breath, swallowing them down. One emotional breakdown was enough before I had my coffee. Thank God the morning sickness didn't include coffee in the list of things that suddenly made me ill.

When I entered the kitchen, wearing a pair of knit shorts with a stretchy waistband, I saw that Kade was already up as well.

And that's as far as my thought process got.

He'd used my shower, apparently, but as usual, had dressed in just jeans. He stood at the kitchen counter with his back to me, pouring a cup of coffee. His hair was still damp and curled slightly at the ends. The muscles in his back flexed and rippled as he moved, the scars less visible in the soft glow of morning light filtering through the windows.

It seemed pregnancy also had an effect on my libido, because I had to curl my hands into fists, my nails digging into my palms, to keep from licking Kade like an ice-cream cone.

He turned around and I was treated to the lovely view of Kade's chest. The long scar that ran diagonally across his chest was overshadowed by two new scars, the ones from the bullets that had nearly killed him.

My hormones fled at the reminder and a wave of sadness combined with thankfulness washed over me. Even if we weren't together, I was so grateful Kade was alive.

Kade took a sip of his coffee as he watched me. He didn't seem startled that I was there and I thought he must have heard me retching in the bathroom. It was kind of hard to miss.

"Feel better?" he asked.

"I'm fine," I said automatically.

Just then, the doorbell rang, which was odd. It wasn't like I got company, other than when Mrs. Johnson had brought over the casserole.

The reaction in Kade was immediate. He had set down the coffee and had his gun in his hand before I'd even turned to start toward the door.

"I'll get it," he said, wrapping a hand around my arm.

I rolled my eyes. "It's not like a killer is going to ring the doorbell before he shoots me," I said.

"Yes, that's exactly what he'd do," Kade shot back. "For precisely that reason. You're not expecting it."

I swallowed. Okay, he had a point, and really, he would know. While I hadn't cared too much last night about whatever trouble had brought Kade to my door, this morning I was acutely aware that I wasn't just protecting myself but also the little bump that made my shorts too tight.

I watched as Kade moved silently to the door, gun held at the ready, then he peered ever so slightly through the window. The tension in his body eased and I relaxed, releasing the breath I'd been holding.

Kade turned, an eyebrow raised sardonically as he mockingly called, "Honey! It's for you."

Frowning, I headed for the door, just as Kade opened it on a very surprised Matt.

"It's the quarterback," Kade said with a sneer. "And I'm sure he's not here to see me." He moved out of the way as I came to the door.

"Matt," I greeted him, feeling my face get hot at what I was sure he had assumed, especially with Kade only half dressed. "I . . . I wasn't expecting anyone."

Matt's jaw was locked tight and his gaze was still on Kade, who I could feel behind me. He'd retreated, but not far, and I could imagine the look he was giving Matt.

"After last night, I was worried about you," Matt said stiffly. "Thought I'd drop by this morning, make sure you were okay."

"That's so sweet," I said, forcing a smile. "I appreciate you checking on me, but I'm fine." My embarrassment was making a flush crawl up my neck. "Was there anything else?" I asked, trying to be polite despite wanting the floor to open and swallow me whole.

"I guess not," Matt said, shoving his hands into his pockets. "Just . . . be careful." Matt's gaze stared daggers at Kade behind me and I noticed his eyes dropping to the scars decorating Kade's chest. His Adam's apple moved as he swallowed and I guessed he was rethinking the wisdom of getting into a confrontation with Kade.

"I will," I said. "Thanks again."

Matt gave a curt nod, then headed back to his truck. I shut the door with a sigh. Not exactly the impression I'd wanted to give Matt, but it couldn't be helped. Now to deal with Kade.

I decided I needed coffee before I took on the task of dislodging Kade from my home, and bypassed him as I moved into the kitchen and filled a mug for myself.

"Did you sleep all right?" I asked, thinking how weird it was to be making small talk with Kade and trying not to stare at his bare chest. My hormones started jumping up and down again when I caught a whiff of his aftershave.

"Sure," Kade replied, his tone noncommittal.

And that was it for small talk. Deciding I needed some fresh air, I grabbed a blanket off the couch and went out onto the back porch. I loved sitting out there in the mornings. It was quiet and I could be outside without having to deal with the bugs. I sat down on the wicker couch, which had seen better days, tucking my feet beneath me and covering my legs with the blanket. The morning was a little chilly.

To my surprise, Kade stepped out, too, pulling a gray Henley over his head. I watched the muscles in his chest move as he dressed, briefly mourning the loss of the view, then he was taking the seat beside me. I inhaled deeply, but tried not to make it too obvious that I was smelling him, which would just be mortifying if he knew.

"Are you hungry?" he asked.

I shook my head, blowing on my coffee to cool it before I took a sip. "Not right now. I'll make something in a little while, if you want."

Two squirrels were gathering nuts in the yard, chattering away at one another as they scampered up one of the trees. Birds were twittering overhead and a slight breeze made the leaves rustle. It was a beautiful, peaceful country morning, and I was acutely aware of Kade sitting so close that my arm brushed his when I raised my mug to my lips.

"Why did you come here?" Kade asked.

I watched the squirrels as I answered. "It seemed like the right thing to do. If I'd stayed in Indy, it wouldn't have been fair to Blane. Both of us needed to move on. I know people here, have a history here. I thought it'd be a good place to raise—" The words *our baby* stuck in my throat. I swallowed, then took another sip of coffee.

"So let me ask you now," I said after a moment. "Why did *you* come here?"

Kade breathed a sigh, reaching an arm back to rest on the back of the couch. His sleeve brushed the back of my neck, causing the hairs there to stand on end. I was so acutely aware of him, it was almost painful.

"To talk you into marrying Blane."

Well, at least he was being honest, though I couldn't pretend those words didn't bring a lump to my throat. He'd rather me marry Blane, have our child raised by his brother, than be with me himself?

When I knew I could talk without my voice breaking, I said, "So is that why you were being such an asshole to me last night in the bar?" Kade didn't respond, which I took to mean I'd guessed correctly. I should've known. He'd always been nastiest to me when he was trying to push me away. I gave a weary sigh. "There's nothing you can say."

"How about if I told you that Keaston's likely to kill you if you don't?"

Senator Keaston. I should've known I hadn't heard the last of him.

"He should be happy," I said. "I'm out of Blane's life for good. You'd think he'd be ecstatic."

"Not if he thinks you're carrying Blane's child."

That made me jerk my head around to look at Kade. His gaze met mine, with his black lashes so thick and his eyes such a beautiful blue, it made me want to drown in them. I pushed the thought aside.

"And why would he think that?" I asked.

Kade just looked at me.

"But it's been months since Blane and I . . . I mean, you and me happened after . . ." This was getting awkward. "Did you tell him the truth?" I asked instead.

"Nope."

"Why in the world not?"

"Because you and me should never have happened," Kade said firmly. "It was a mistake."

I felt the blood drain from my face. If Kade had slapped me, it would've hurt less. The look on my face must have betrayed my dismay, because Kade cursed. I barely noticed as he took the coffee cup from my trembling hand and set it aside.

"How can you say that?" I managed, my voice a near whisper.

"Because I am the absolute worst thing for you," Kade replied. His voice was harsh with bitterness and anger, but it wasn't directed at me. "I'm the stuff nightmares are made of, princess. I'm not the kind of man who gets the girl. We both know that."

Of course. Kade and his damn inferiority complex when it came to him and Blane.

"I'm not a machine," I said. "You can't just tell me how to feel and expect me to obey. I'm not going back to Blane. It's not fair to him, or to me, or to *our* child." I got to my feet. "So you're wasting your time. You can stay for breakfast, if you want, or leave now if you'd rather. But I'm not going anywhere, no matter what Keaston does. I have a gun, and I know how to use it, so he'd better think twice before sending someone after me. This is my home and if he wants me dead, he'll have to come do it himself."

I didn't give Kade a chance to respond, just walked past him into the house. My stomach was growling and based on the limited experience I'd had so far, I needed to eat right away while I was hungry.

Grabbing eggs and a packet of bacon from the fridge, I loaded some bacon on a cookie sheet into the cold oven, then turned it on. While that started cooking, I scrambled several eggs in a bowl, adding a little half-and-half to make them creamier.

Kade walked in while the frying pan was heating, so I decided to treat him the way I would any other friend by asking him to hand me the loaf of bread from the cabinet.

I poured another cup of coffee and sipped it while I slowly stirred the eggs in the hot pan. Kade put a few pieces of bread in the toaster and searched the cabinets for plates. We didn't speak as the food cooked, but it wasn't uncomfortable. I was trying real hard not to think about him leaving, or what he'd said to me. I'd wait until later to dwell on it and have another crying jag.

The aroma of bacon filled the kitchen as I pulled the cookie sheet from the oven. I scooped the scrambled eggs onto two plates, added liberal portions of bacon, and snagged the toast when it popped up. I set the plates and a couple of napkins on the table, then grabbed two forks.

Some things just taste better when you're pregnant, I'd realized, and bacon was one of them. I'd taken to buying it in bulk, since it was a protein my stomach didn't seem to mind. Whereas beef was a definite no-go.

With food in front of me, my hormones took a backseat, and I made short work of the meal. I was buttering my toast when Kade caught my eye. He was watching me.

"What?" I asked, immediately self-conscious. "Do I have something on my face?" I picked up my napkin and wiped my mouth again, just to be sure there weren't some lingering crumbs.

Kade shook his head. "It's good to see you eating again—that's all."

I didn't know what to say to that, so I just finished off my toast. He must've been hungry, too, because his plate was also clear.

He helped me clean up, bringing dishes to me to load into the dishwasher. It was too quick, and then breakfast was over.

I stood, my back pressed against the counter, twisting a dish towel in my hands. I was determined not to cry. This was what he wanted and there was nothing I could do or say to change it, just as there was nothing he could do or say to make me marry Blane.

It was a sad way to end things. No one, except maybe Kade, had gotten what they wanted. There was no happily-ever-after, for any of us. Kade had been right after all.

"There's no such thing as a happy ending."

Kade walked over to me, not stopping until we were inches apart. I couldn't hold his gaze, was afraid I'd start crying, so I looked down at the towel.

"Stop fidgeting," he murmured, placing a hand over mine.

It was the first he'd touched me and I felt it to the tips of my toes.

We didn't move, both of us breathing the same air, and my pulse kicked into overdrive. His thumb lightly brushed the top of my hand, the caress as soft as a butterfly's wings against my skin.

My eyes slid shut, and it took all my willpower not to lean forward and press my body against his. I wanted him with an intensity that frightened me. Not just sexually, though that was high on the list. I wanted him to stay with me, be with me, build a life together. And more than anything, I wanted him to want that, too.

Kade's other hand lifted to settle under my chin, his fingers gently turning my face up. I opened my heavy-lidded eyes and our gazes collided.

Pain and desire warred in his eyes, his brow creasing as he seemed to drink me in. My gaze dropped to his mouth. I wanted him to kiss me, could almost taste him already. My tongue darted out to wet my lips.

Suddenly, Kade pulled back, taking several steps and turning away from me. He shoved a hand roughly through his hair.

I let out a little sigh of disappointment. If he'd wanted to drop down on the kitchen floor and do it right there, I would have been an enthusiastic participant, judging by how damp my panties were. Nice. Real classy.

I took a deep, shuddering breath. Manual labor seemed the way to go to work out the sexual frustration I was feeling.

"Listen," I said, my voice throatier than usual, "I have stuff I need to get done today, so are you leaving? Or are you staying?" I held my breath, waiting for his response.

Kade glanced back at me. "It seems I don't have much of a choice now, does it," he said wryly.

Did I mention that besides the crying jags and emotional roller coaster I was on, it also meant my temper could be on a hair trigger and send me from zero to flaming superbitch inside of three seconds?

I was supremely pissed off in the time it took to draw another breath. Grabbing my empty coffee mug from the counter, I sent it hurtling toward Kade's head. He ducked, depriving me of the satisfaction of seeing the heavy ceramic crack against his even thicker skull.

"Fuck you, Kade!" I yelled. "You want to leave? Then don't let the door hit you on the ass on the way out."

My hands were shaking, I was so angry, yet tears also stung my eyes. I turned and ran up the stairs. Even though I was pissed off enough to want to yank Kade's hair out, I wasn't so far gone that I thought I could handle watching him walk out that door.

I burst into the bedroom that I hadn't shown Kade last night. Standing in the middle of the room, I took several deep breaths, trying to calm down. The anger was ebbing now, leaving an overwhelming pit of despair and loneliness in its wake.

Robotically, I began setting things out to continue painting. This was going to be the baby's room, and though I didn't know if it was a boy or a girl, I'd decided on a shade of blue that was precisely the color of Kade's eyes. Tears rolled down my cheeks as I remembered standing in the paint store, scrutinizing and debating the color swatches. I'd started crying then, too, and the salesclerk had looked almost panicked. He'd been very happy to sell me the paint and send me on my way.

The crib was in a huge box that I'd wrestled up the stairs and then to one corner, where it waited for me to put it together. I'd also bought a mobile, with little stars and moons, that played "Twinkle, Twinkle, Little Star" when it turned.

I plopped down on the floor with a sigh, the paint forgotten. I cranked the mobile, holding it and watching it turn as the music played.

Was I going to be enough for this baby? I'd loved my dad, had spent a lot of time with him growing up. It hurt that my baby wouldn't have that same relationship with its dad. What was I going to say when he or she was old enough to ask where Daddy was? How could I possibly explain that Daddy had chosen to leave us? When would it not hurt anymore to say that?

Kade suddenly stood in the doorway, making me start in surprise. How the heck had he gotten up the stairs without me hearing him?

I quickly swiped at my wet cheeks and set aside the mobile. "You don't have to stay," I said, my voice flat, resigned. "If something happens, it's all on me. I get it."

But Kade wasn't paying any attention to me. He was taking in the room, the look on his face one of stunned shock. As if he'd been pretending this wasn't real, that I wasn't really pregnant. And maybe he had been.

After a minute or two, he focused on me, sitting on the floor. He seemed to recover his poise and stepped forward, crouching down next to me. Reaching out, he wiped away a stray tear track. Our eyes met.

"Don't cry, princess," he said softly. "It kills me when you cry."

He was so close to me. I couldn't help leaning forward just slightly, and it was enough for me to rest my forehead against his chest. I let out a trembling sigh, my eyes slipping shut. Yes, I knew that if I had to, I could do this by myself, could raise our child by myself.

But I didn't want to.

I had no way of convincing Kade that my need of him outweighed all the reasons he thought we shouldn't be together. If he believed I was better off without him, nothing I said would convince him otherwise. He had to believe it for himself, or he would always have doubts, would always wonder if he should leave me.

But it felt so good to lean on his strength, even if it was only temporary.

Kade lifted a hand, settling it gently on the back of my head. It was not quite an embrace, but I figured I'd take what I could get.

"So are we painting today?" Kade asked.

I pulled back, not meeting his eyes, and nodded.

"Okay then," he said, getting to his feet. He reached down, offering his hand, which I took and then stood as well.

I'd already painted one wall and had started on another. Kade stirred the paint and poured some into the pan, grabbed a roller, and began painting. I only had one roller, so I picked up a brush and started on the smaller areas around light switches and outlets.

We painted in companionable silence for a while, Kade being much quicker with the roller than I had been. At the rate he was going, we'd be done in an hour or so.

"Did you buy this place?" he asked.

"Yeah," I said, "with some of the money you left." A sore spot with me, but I didn't want to argue.

"Do you have enough?"

"Enough what?" I asked in confusion. "Money?"

"Yeah. Because I have more. If you need it."

I was on all fours, but stopped painting and turned to stare at him over my shoulder. "You're joking, right? Kade, I couldn't spend all that money in my lifetime, much less in a month." I rolled my eyes, then a thought struck me and I sat back on my haunches.

"Kade," I said.

"What?" he asked. When I didn't answer, he paused from painting to glance at me, his brows raised in a question.

"Please tell me you were making a bad joke last night when you said you'd killed ten men."

Our eyes locked for a moment, then Kade turned back, dipping the roller into the pan of paint. "When have I ever joked about shit like that," he said, and it wasn't a question, because the answer was—never. Kade had always been perfectly serious and matter-of-fact about what he did.

Oh my God. Ten people. Kade had killed ten people. That was more than a baseball team. He'd killed a baseball team. Why-why-why?

My thoughts were slightly hysterical and I was reeling from the actual number. And in so little time? How many people had he killed overall? And still the question: Why?

"Take it easy. Just breathe."

Kade was crouching next to me again, and I realized I was breathing in choked gasps.

Ten people.

"Why?" I managed, looking up at him. "Why would you do that?"

"It's who I am," he said.

I shook my head, adamant. "No, it's not. That is *not* who you are. You're a good man—"

"Will you stop?" he cried, jumping to his feet and pacing away from me. "I am not a 'good man'! I never have been and I never will be, Kathleen!"

I got to my feet, angry now. "That's not true! I know you believe it, but you're wrong. What, did you kill those people just to prove to me how horrible you are?"

His eyes flashed blue fire as he glared at me. "I'm not explaining myself to anyone. Not even you."

"You don't have to," I shot back. "You think I don't know you? That I don't know that all of this"—I waved my hand to indicate me and him—"and shoving me away and pushing me at Blane, that all of it is because you think you're some kind of horrible person who doesn't deserve to be happy?" I used quotey fingers for "deserve." "Because you're wrong—"

"I killed those people so I wouldn't have to feel anymore!"

Kade's shouting interrupted my tirade. His hands were in fists, his jaw clenched as he stared at me.

"I don't understand—"

"I couldn't handle the pain of giving you up," he said, his voice much quieter. "And I didn't want to be the person that I am without you. So I came back to Indy to say good-bye. That's when Blane told me you'd disappeared."

There was a lot of information in those few sentences and I struggled to process it.

Kade turned away, using the roller to cover the last few inches of the wall that needed paint, then he turned again and picked up the pan.

"I'm going to wash these out," he said, brushing past me and out the door.

"Giving you up."

Those words gave me hope. So he had wanted me. Kade hadn't been lying when he'd said we'd go away together. Now just to figure out a way to convince him we could be together. He didn't have to say goodbye to anyone, least of all me.

That thought snapped me out of my shock-induced stupor, and I hurried down the stairs, the steps creaking like crazy beneath me.

Rounding the corner, I glimpsed Kade through the window, using the hose out back to clean the brushes. I took a step forward, then was yanked backward.

I spun around in surprise, only to see a strange man in my house. He smiled.

"Oy there, lovey," he said. "Be still now and this'll be quick."

CHAPTER ELEVEN

I screamed. His hand went to my throat, grabbing me and lifting me to my toes. I didn't bother trying to pull his arm away—I knew I wouldn't be able to. His hand squeezed.

My hands were free, so I cupped both my palms and slammed them over his ears. I got him good and he howled in pain, releasing me. I dropped back down to my feet and stumbled. I scrambled, turning to run, but he grabbed the neck of my shirt and yanked me off my feet. I landed hard on my back on the floor and the force of it knocked the wind out of me.

He must've decided he didn't care about the noise a gunshot would make, because that's when he pulled out a gun. He pointed it right at me and I froze, terror icing my veins. There was nowhere I could go, nothing I could do—

Kade came out of nowhere, hurtling into the guy, and they both crashed to the floor. I watched in horror as they grappled. The gun went skittering across the floor and I crawled to it, then picked it up. I pointed it but couldn't fire. I wasn't a good enough shot that I was sure I wouldn't hit Kade.

They fought dirty and I saw up close and personal how deadly Kade could be. His face was terrifying, cold fury blazing in his eyes. The guy didn't have a chance, something that became immediately apparent. I heard the crack of breaking bone and the guy cried out, then Kade's knife was in his hand. A split second later, Kade had slit his throat.

I was still on my ass on the floor, my eyes wide as I tried to breathe. Kade was straddling the now motionless body and he glanced my way, getting to his feet and moving toward me.

The gun I held shook like a leaf in my hands, my eyes glued to the blood seeping from the man's sliced throat onto my wooden floor.

"Hey," Kade said softly, crouching down. He reached out and slowly wrapped his hand around the barrel of the gun. "It's okay now. Give me the gun, sweetheart." But my fingers wouldn't move, as though they'd been dipped in ice. Kade gently pried my hand loose and took the gun from me, tucking it in the back of his jeans.

"He's . . . dead," I croaked.

"Yes, and you aren't," Kade said.

I broke my stare and turned to Kade. He pulled me into his arms, holding me tight against his chest. My fingers clutched at his shirt, but my eyes were dry. It seemed I had no tears to shed for people who tried to kill me and ended up dead instead.

If Kade hadn't been there, I'd be dead now and so would our baby. A shudder went through me.

"It's all right. I've got you," he murmured soothingly in my ear.

After a few minutes, I felt strong enough to pull away and stand. I looked at the dead man on the floor.

"Now what?" I asked.

"Now you find me an old sheet that you don't want to see again, and a trash bag."

I left, returning quickly with the items he'd requested. Kade wrapped the head and throat in the sheet, then tied the trash bag around that. Pulling the dead man by the arms, he hoisted the body in a fireman's carry.

"Grab a shovel and follow me," he said.

I ran to the garage and found an old shovel, then followed Kade as he trekked into the woods. We went some distance, then Kade dropped the body and held a hand out for the shovel.

"At least there's a bright side to you living in the middle of fucking nowhere," he said. "Plenty of places to bury a body."

It took a while for Kade to dig a hole deep enough, but finally the body was buried and the dirt replaced. Kade was drenched in sweat and had discarded his shirt some time ago, but hadn't shown any sign of fatigue until he was through. He leaned on the shovel for a few minutes. I stayed quiet and watched him.

After we got back to the house, he had me get a bottle of bleach and we cleaned the blood off the floor. Well, Kade did. I started dry heaving, so he ordered me into the kitchen to wait until he was done.

I had time to think while I waited, which probably wasn't a good thing. Keaston had sent someone after me, just like Kade had said he would. What was I going to do? Just wait for the next killer? I'd be a sitting duck.

Kade came back into the kitchen carrying another garbage bag. "We'll burn this one," he said, heading to the sink. "No one's going to come looking for that guy anyway. It's the nature of the business."

As he washed the dirt and blood from his hands, sweat still shone on his skin from the hard work he'd done digging in the warm sunshine. I'd need to wash his jeans. They were dirty from the digging.

"Thank you," I said. "For being here. If you hadn't—"

"Let's not discuss what might've happened," Kade interrupted, drying his hands on a dish towel. "I'm going to take a shower."

I nodded, glancing at the clock. "Okay. My shift starts soon."

"You're going into work?" Kade asked.

I looked at him strangely. "Yeah. Why wouldn't I?"

"I would think being attacked and having to bury a body might make you see sense," Kade retorted. "The sooner you hightail it back to Blane's the safer you'll be."

"The only place I'm going is into work," I shot back. It stung every time he brought up the idea of me going to Blane, as if I were a burden to be shoved off onto somebody else.

Turning away, I headed upstairs, leaving him to fend for himself.

Going to my bedside table, I retrieved my gun from the top drawer. I checked to make sure it was loaded, then set it by the door so I wouldn't forget to put it in my purse.

The uniforms at O'Sullivan's were a lot less revealing than the ones at The Drop, just jeans and a T-shirt with the pub's logo printed across the chest. The shirts came in black, white, and green, and tonight I put on a green one before doing my makeup. At least my jeans still fit, though they were more snug than I was used to. I heard the shower start in the bathroom across the hall.

I sat on my bed, thinking. I wanted two things—for me and my baby to be safe, and I wanted Kade. Now I just had to figure out the best way to go about getting them.

After a few minutes, I grabbed the gun and opened my bedroom door just as Kade came out of the bathroom.

I froze. Kade was naked save for a white towel wrapped low around his hips. He had another towel he was using to dry his hair, so he hadn't seen me yet. My gaze drank in his damp chest, following the thin line of hair that started below his navel and disappeared beneath the towel. My hands itched to reach forward. It would just take a little tug to pull the towel loose. It would drop to the floor and I would drop to my knees—

I think I made a little sound, kind of like a whimper, because Kade suddenly stopped drying his hair. He may have looked at me—I didn't know. I was still eyeing the towel and trying to figure out if I could grab it faster than he could stop me.

"Kathleen?"

"Mmm?" Maybe if I took off my shirt, distracted him—

"Everything all right? You okay?"

I sighed a little, making my eyes lift to his. "Fine. It's just that being pregnant . . . Well, let's just say I haven't been this horny since . . ." I thought about it. "Ever." Huh.

Kade's face looked pained. "I don't think sleeping together would be a good idea."

"Really?" I asked. It sounded pretty damn good to me. "I didn't realize you'd taken up chastity." I sidled a little closer. Men were all the same. I could probably change his mind if I could get my hands on his—

But Kade caught my wrist just as I reached out to snag the towel. He yanked me forward and my breasts brushed his chest. I bit back a moan at the contact.

He was so close, his mouth inches away.

"I just killed a man," Kade said in disbelief. "In your living room. And you want to have sex with me?"

Well, when he put it like that . . . Nope, still didn't kill my mood.

A droplet of water trailed from the ends of his hair down his neck and over his collarbone, then started a slow path down his chest. It tantalized me, practically screaming "Lick me! Lick me!" so I obligingly leaned forward . . . only to have Kade jerk back, out of my reach.

I frowned at him. This was getting irritating. "You're playing awfully hard to get," I complained.

"It's for your own good."

Now *that* killed my mood. I stepped closer, getting in his face.

"You're starting to sound a lot like Blane," I hissed. I jerked my wrist out of his grip, turned around, and flounced downstairs. I knew I was in a snit, but I just didn't care.

There was a knock on the front door and I froze. Carefully, I checked my gun to make sure the safety was off before I went to the door. I peeked out the side window . . . and my jaw gaped.

Pulling open the door, I said, "What in the world are you doing here?"

Blane reached up and took off his sunglasses, eyeing me. "Hello to you, too," he said wryly.

"I'm sorry," I said, "I'm just . . . surprised. Come in." I stepped aside so Blane could enter. He was dressed casually in jeans and a white button-down shirt he wore untucked, the cuffs turned back several times.

Blane glanced around the house with interest, taking in the bedding on the couch where Kade had slept before his gaze landed on me again.

"I'm glad to see you're all right," he said roughly, hooking his sunglasses on his shirt. "A phone call would've been nice."

"I'm sorry," I apologized again. "I just thought . . . you and me . . . we needed some time."

"How're you feeling?" he asked.

I shrugged. "Okay." It was super awkward to talk about being pregnant with Blane, so I moved on pretty quick. "How about you?"

His lips twitched. "I'm fine, but I'm not the one who's having a baby."

So much for not talking about it. "So, uh, how'd you find me?"

"I called him," Kade said.

He had come downstairs, again without making a sound. I was really going to have to make him show me how he did that. Then I processed what he'd said.

"*You* called him?" I asked, facing off with Kade. I could feel my temper flaring.

"Don't get upset," he warned.

"Then don't do things that *make* me upset," I ground out.

"Thought you might want to know how Lewis was doing," Blane interrupted.

I glanced around to him, confused. "Lewis? Alisha's Lewis?" At his nod, I asked, "What's wrong with him?"

"Kade shot him."

I whipped my head back toward Kade, who was glaring at Blane. "What?" I screeched. "You *shot* him? What the hell for?"

"Really?" Kade said to Blane. "I tell you where she is and *that's* the bomb you wanna drop? Asshole."

"I'm not the asshole in this situation, and Lewis is fine, thanks for asking," Blane said.

"I already knew he was fine," Kade retorted in disgust. "I know where I shot him."

"So you did shoot him?" I asked, interrupting their argument.

Kade's gaze swiveled to mine. "Alisha wouldn't tell me where you'd gone," he said simply, as though that was justification enough for shooting Lewis.

"Oh my God," I moaned, grasping the sides of my head. "Alisha's going to hate me! And poor Lewis!" It's not like being shot was any fun. Even if he was going to be all right, it wasn't okay that Kade had done that.

"Alisha's not going to hate you," Kade said.

I jerked my head up and got in Kade's space. "You're right," I said. "She'll hate you!" I poked his chest hard to emphasize my point.

Kade's eyes narrowed. "May I remind you of what would've happened this morning if I *hadn't* been here?"

I swallowed, some of my anger leaching away.

"What happened this morning?" Blane broke in.

"Do you want to tell him about the body now buried in your backyard or shall I?" Kade asked.

"A body?"

I ignored Blane. "You didn't have to threaten Alisha," I argued. "I'm sure she would have said where I was if she knew I was in danger. You could've just told her that. You certainly didn't have to shoot Lewis!"

"I'll keep that in mind for the next time you disappear and someone has a contract out to kill you," Kade sneered, not at all apologetic.

"Let's talk about that," Blane interrupted again. "Kade, what's going on? Who's after Kathleen? And what body's in the backyard? And last but not least"—he held his arms out, palms up—"why am I here?"

"Yeah, I'll let you two figure it out," I groused. "I've got to get to work."

"You're not going to work," Kade said.

"Watch me." I grabbed my purse, stuffed my gun into it, and headed outside.

"Come on," I heard Kade say to Blane, and I'll be damned if I didn't have both Blane and Kade following me in their separate cars into town.

I parked and got out, glancing around to see both Kade and Blane mirroring my actions. In a moment, they were trailing two or three steps behind me as I headed into the pub.

Yeah, this isn't conspicuous or anything, I thought grumpily. So much for blending back into my hometown. Blane and Kade stuck out like they'd been dropped from another planet into Smalltown, Middle America—their planet being one filled with designer clothes, cars that cost six figures, and a surplus of incredibly hot men who accessorized with deadly weapons.

I went in back to clock in, grabbing a black apron to tie around my waist. The morning cook, Randy, was finishing up and he waved hello as I walked by. Danny would be in any minute. Carol was clocking in, too.

"Glad to see you survived your midnight visitor last night," she said, falling into step with me as we headed out the kitchen door.

I sighed. "Survived, but didn't ditch. He's still here." I nodded to where Blane and Kade now sat side by side at the bar. Sal, the other bartender, was just setting two bottles of beer in front of them.

"Wow," Carol said. "Who's the new guy?"

"My ex." And I left it at that.

Carol looked at me, her eyebrows raised, but she didn't ask anything further. Since she was someone who seemed to keep her business private, I appreciated that she didn't want to pry into mine. I wouldn't have known how to explain anyway.

I relieved Sal, a guy in his late fifties who poured drinks at the same speed he moved—turtle slow. He was fine during the early part of the day, but I was glad I didn't have to work with him in the evenings. It would have driven me nuts.

There was barely a handful of customers, since it was still before the dinner rush, so it didn't take me long to put the bar in order and make sure everything was set the way I liked it. When I was through, I walked over to Blane and Kade.

"So you two are just going to sit here all evening?" I asked.

"I'm not too thrilled with someone trying to kill you in your living room," Blane replied.

"Then call your uncle and take care of it," I retorted. "Hasn't he done enough now? You know he was behind Summers taking me, that he tried to have Kade killed. I'm just trying to figure out why you're sitting here instead of taking this right to his front door."

"It's not that easy," Kade broke in.

"What would you have me do, Kat?" Blane asked. "Go kill my uncle?"

"So you'd rather he kill me?" I asked.

"No, of course not—" Blane replied angrily.

"Well, then you two better figure something out," I interrupted, "because I'm not living this way, looking over my shoulder all the time and being afraid. Something's gotta give." I stalked away.

We got busier soon after that, and it was a while before I returned to Blane and Kade.

"You two want something to eat?" I asked, handing them each a menu. I waited while they looked it over. I couldn't help it—even with what had happened this morning and the awkwardness of being with both of them, I was happier for their presence.

They both ordered the exact same thing, big surprise, and declined more beer. Instead, I gave Blane water and Kade a Coke.

"So did you come up with a plan?" I asked as I slid two plates of double cheeseburgers and waffle fries in front of them.

"Aren't you going to eat?" Kade asked.

"Hello—I'm working," I said in an isn't-it-obvious tone, resting my elbows on the bar, chin in hand, and eyeing his fries.

Kade must've read my mind, because he picked one up and offered it to me as he said to Blane, "Keaston's gotten out of hand."

I leaned forward and snagged the fry from his fingers with my teeth. Yum. Still hot and crispy.

"You said you'd found something linking him to Sheffield and the Waters trial," Blane said, taking a bite of his cheeseburger. "What about that?"

Kade shook his head, chewing a fry before offering another to me. I let him feed me that one, too. "Won't hold up," he said. "A witness would be better. Someone who knows all Robert's dirty little secrets."

Blane chewed thoughtfully. "What about George?" he asked. "He's his chief of staff. He'd know everything. Maybe he'd help us in return for something."

Kade took a bite of cheeseburger, dutifully holding up another fry for me to eat. He swallowed, then said, "Yeah, George is dead."

Blane paused mid-chew to glance at Kade, then rolled his eyes. "Let me guess," he said, his irritation obvious. "He met up with you in a dark alley."

"Mugging gone bad," Kade replied. "Don't you read the papers?" He shot Blane a look and I wasn't sure who to believe, not that I cared much. My hatred for Keaston seemed to overshadow any qualms or ethics I had.

"Are you going to eat your pickle?" I interrupted, eyeing said pickle on Kade's plate.

Kade looked at me with a raised eyebrow. "Really? Pickles?"

I ignored his sarcasm. "Are you or not?"

Kade picked up the pickle spear and handed it to me. "You're such a cliché," he said, but he said it in a fond sort of way and the corner of his mouth twitched upward, so I didn't think he really minded.

I chewed on the pickle while they talked.

"If not George, then I don't know who," Blane said. He finished off his burger. "It's not like Robert lets anyone else get close enough."

They both fell silent, thinking. I finished off the pickle, which had made me thirsty, so I copped a sip of Kade's Coke.

"What about the wife?" I asked.

They both looked at me.

"Whose wife?" Kade asked.

"George's," I explained. "If Keaston had George into all kinds of bad stuff, which ended up getting him killed, she's going to be angry. Resentful. And chances are she knows what's up with Keaston, or could point us in the direction of where to look."

"Us?" Blane asked.

I raised my eyebrows. "Surely you don't think you two can go after Keaston and leave me behind?"

"Thought we could stash her with Mona," Kade said to Blane. "Or maybe Clarice."

"Clarice might be better," Blane replied. "There's no tie between the two of them anymore. They won't think to look there."

"Huh-uh, no way," I interrupted. They both turned to look at me. "I am not going to sit this one out, nor am I going to bring danger to a friend's doorstep. I either stay in my home, by myself, or I'm coming with you."

Neither man looked pleased by my assertion, but I didn't care. I wasn't going to be sidelined.

"If she comes, we gotta drive," Kade said to Blane. "The flight lists will be tagged to alert for her name."

"Could you please stop talking about me as though I weren't standing right here?" I said, irritated. I went to take their plates away, but saw Blane hadn't eaten his pickle. I hesitated, then snagged it, holding it in my teeth while I carried the plates away. A ghost of a smile flitted across Blane's lips.

Kade and Blane's continued presence didn't go unnoticed. More than a few glances were sent their way as the evening progressed, though the brothers didn't seem to notice or care. Or if they did, I couldn't tell. They were deep in conversation while I worked, and it made me feel warm and fuzzy inside, especially since they didn't seem to be arguing. I even caught Blane laughing once or twice and Kade grinned.

"Hey, Kathleen."

I recognized Matt's voice and turned to see that he and Steve had popped in and taken seats at the bar.

"Hey, guys," I said with a warm smile. "No practice tonight?"

"Got rained out," Steve said, jerking a thumb toward the windows. Sure enough, it was pouring outside.

I got them both draft beers, catching Matt looking across the bar at Kade and Blane.

"You going to tell us who the guys are?" Matt asked me.

I hesitated, but it wasn't like it was a secret. "I met them in Indy," I said. "Just some friends of mine. Thought they'd drop in for a visit, that's all."

"That one looks familiar," Steve said, his face creasing in a frown. "Yeah, I know. He's that guy running for governor, right? The one who dropped out?"

"Um, yeah, that's him," I confirmed, unsure what else to say.

"And you're friends with him?" Steve asked, a bit of admiration creeping into his voice. "Wow. That's cool."

If Matt had been cranky before due to the presence of Blane and Kade, he was downright surly now. He finished his beer quickly and ordered another. As I delivered it, he started chatting with me.

"Remember old Mr. Tyler?" he asked.

"The basketball coach?"

"Yeah, that's him. Well, he retired, but his son's the coach now, you know Andy. And he married Betty McCarthy. They have two kids."

"Really?" I said. "How 'bout that." I was pulled down memory lane as Matt started reeling off names I knew and telling me what had happened to various high school friends. Even while I'd still lived in town when my mom was sick, I'd been so focused on paying the bills and caring for her that my social life had been nonexistent. I'd fallen out of touch with so many people.

The dinner rush was over, so I stood in front of Matt for a while as he continued to bring me up to speed on old friends and where-were-they-now. He had me laughing at a tale of how the geekiest kid had hit it big, and as a result, married the homecoming queen and moved to LA.

"And don't get me started on Theresa Honeycutt," Matt said with a laugh.

"What did she do?" I asked, grinning. Even I knew that Theresa had been dubbed Tiny Tits Theresa in high school.

"She decided she wanted a boob job," Matt said, "so she went someplace in Indy, came back, I shit you not, like a double F or some shit like that. I thought Sal's eyes were gonna pop right out when he saw her."

"Oh my God!" I giggled, shaking my head. Theresa had always struck me as having more ambition than sense. Why someone would want boobs that big was beyond me. I was pushing a C cup and definitely wouldn't want to be any bigger.

Steve had been laughing with us, but suddenly stopped. He took a nervous swig of his beer, then said, "Kathleen, I think your, uh, friends need a refill . . . or something."

I glanced over my shoulder to Blane and Kade, then sucked in a breath.

Blane had always been on the possessive side, so it shouldn't have surprised me to see the hard glare he was sending Matt's way. But considering our new "friends" status, I wasn't expecting him to still display that streak toward me, yet that's exactly what he appeared to be doing. And as for Kade . . . Well, he'd apparently left the notion of possessive way behind, and by the look in his eyes, had already moved on to contemplating Matt's untimely demise.

"Um, yeah, I'd better go see what they want," I said uneasily.

"And they're just friends?" Matt scoffed, bitterness edging his words.

I cleared my throat. "Maybe a little more than friends," I admitted.

I thought Steve's eyes were going to bug out of his head. "Both of them?" he asked.

My face felt on fire at the look Matt gave me. I didn't bother answering Steve—it wasn't any of their business anyway—and I scurried back to Blane and Kade.

"Will you two stop with the glaring at Matt?" I hissed at them. "Now he thinks I'm sleeping with both of you!"

Kade just raised an eyebrow and smirked.

"At the same time," I clarified, my embarrassment reaching new heights, or lows, depending on how you looked at it.

Kade's smirk got bigger. "That would be—"

"Awkward," Blane cut him off.

I covered my burning face with my hands, moaning, "Oh my God . . ."

"Yeah, on that note, I'm gonna bug out," Blane said, getting to his feet.

I dropped my hands. "Wait, where are you going?"

"Since it looks like we're driving to DC, he's heading home to pack a bag," Kade answered.

I let out a breath, not sure why I was relieved. "Oh. Okay then."

"I'll grab Tigger and see if Mona will watch him," Blane said. "I'm sure she will."

My hand rested on the bar and Blane reached out, giving it a light squeeze. "I'll be back in the morning," he said reassuringly, then he clapped a hard hand to Kade's shoulder. "Kade'll pick up my tab, won't you, Kade."

Kade grimaced. "Why do I think I'll be picking up your tab for the foreseeable future?"

"You got that right," Blane said, then headed out the door. I watched it swing shut behind him.

"So we're taking a road trip?" I asked. "Just the three of us? To DC?" Talk about epic proportions of awkward.

"Looks like it," Kade said.

Hmm.

It was just after ten when the place had cleared out, and I thought we'd get to close early tonight, which would be nice. Matt and Steve had left shortly after Blane. Matt hadn't said much to me, but Steve had given me a friendly smile on his way out.

Carol offered to close and since I was too tired to argue, I took her up on it. Kade followed me home and it felt good to kick off my shoes. I headed up to shower, trying not to think of how Kade had been the last one to stand under the water and how he must've looked while doing it . . .

My eyes suddenly popped open. Wait a second. Who said I had to wait for Kade to make the first move? If nothing else, the past few months had shown me that he wasn't immune to the chemistry between us. If I could manage to get him back into my bed, that should put the kibosh on him shoving me at Blane. Surely not even Kade would think that I would sleep with him one moment, then get back together with Blane the next.

Excited and a little nervous, I hurried to dry my hair. Too impatient to get it fully dry, I settled on damp. Crossing the hall to my room, I dug through my closet. Surely I had some kind of sexy nightgown I could put on.

Okay, well, maybe not. I settled on the skimpiest, laciest black thong I owned. My little bump showed, but there wasn't a thing I could do about that. I dug an old satin robe from a drawer. It was for looks only and I never wore it. It came just to the top of my thighs and was also black. I belted it around my waist, then for the final touch, I added the champagne-colored stilettos I'd gotten when Kade and I were in Vegas.

Looking in the mirror, I used my fingers to fluff my hair, then added a spray of perfume and a touch of lipstick. My intent was ever so obvious, but I didn't care. If Kade was going to persist in being a stubborn ass, then it would take drastic measures to make him see the error of his ways.

I turned down the covers on my bed, wondering if I was being too optimistic. Well, I'd find out in a few minutes.

Taking a deep breath, I headed down the hall to the living room. I could hear Kade moving around as he settled into his makeshift bed on the couch. My heels clacked on the floor and I winced, now wishing I hadn't worn them. Stupid stupid.

My pulse was hammering from nerves and my palms were clammy with sweat. If this didn't work, I was going to feel like a complete and utter idiot.

I tried not to focus on that.

My steps slowed as I rounded the corner. I stopped, leaning sideways against the wall, which probably looked like I was posing, but really I needed the support so my trembling knees wouldn't give out.

A lamp was lit, providing a soft glow in the room, and Kade glanced my way from where he lay on the couch. His entire body went still.

"I thought I'd check on you," I said, my voice a little too high. "See if you needed, or wanted, anything." I cringed inside. That was the best I could do? Yeah, there went my career as a telephone sex operator.

Deciding that actions spoke louder than words, I fiddled with the tie on my robe. The satin was slippery and it loosened and fell away almost immediately.

Even from the distance between us, I saw Kade's throat move as he swallowed.

"What're you doing, princess?" he asked, his voice soft and nearly like a touch.

"It's obvious, isn't it?" I replied. I trailed the tips of my fingers from my throat down between my breasts, the satin robe parting, just catching on my nipples. My palm splayed across my stomach, then down farther to my panties. Kade's eyes were riveted to the path my hand took, which made my nervousness fade to nothing. When he looked at me like that, I felt beautiful, desirable. Wanted.

I took two slow, sultry steps toward him, watching as he sat up on the couch. His shirt was off and the sight of him made my mouth water. A slight shrug and the robe spilled from my shoulders, sliding down and off my arms to drop to the floor in a soft whisper of silk.

Kade groaned, a low, pained noise coming from deep in his throat.

I couldn't help my satisfied smile. When I reached him, I didn't hesitate. Settling my knees on either side of his hips, I straddled him. The tips of my breasts brushed his chest and I swear he ground his teeth. His hands automatically gripped my hips.

I leaned forward and tilted my head, allowing my hair to fall to the side and brush his arm as I whispered in his ear.

"What was it about this that was such a bad idea?" I teased. My lips brushed the shell of his ear and I could feel the shudder that went through him.

"I can't fucking remember," he rasped. His hand slid from my hip up to tangle in my hair. He closed his hand into a fist, the long strands wrapped around his fingers, which sent a sharp tug to my scalp, pulling my head back.

My pulse was racing as arousal shivered through my veins. His warm skin was against mine, my fingers tracing the contour of muscles in his shoulders. Our eyes locked, his pupils dark and dilated and surrounded by pure blue. His head bent toward me, his lips millimeters away—

A loud knock on the front door startled a shriek from me.

Kade swiftly and unceremoniously dumped me off his lap and onto the couch. Sliding his hand beneath the pillow, he pulled out his gun.

"It's me!" called a voice through the door.

Blane.

I was cussing a blue streak inside my head as I scrambled to wrap a sheet around me before Kade pulled open the door.

"I thought you weren't coming back until morning," Kade said by way of greeting, and I was gratified by his tone that it wasn't just me who wanted to scream in frustration at the interruption.

"Had a friend of yours show up at my house," Blane said, stepping inside. "She insisted on coming along."

I glanced up from where I was trying to cover my exposed thighs and my jaw fell open.

Branna was there.

CHAPTER TWELVE

Branna launched herself at Kade, throwing her arms around his neck and planting her lips on his.

Blane and I watched as the kiss went on for entirely too long, in my opinion. Branna finally pulled back, then shocked me again by taking a step back and giving Kade a sound slap on his cheek.

"You're such a bastard," she groused in her lilting Irish accent. "You fall off the grid and don't even tell me where you're going. Bloody hell."

Kade didn't seem a bit surprised by her actions. "What the hell are you doing here?" he asked.

"That's a fine way to greet me," she retorted. "I've been worried sick and here you've been"— she glanced around, zeroing in on me sitting on the couch, and it didn't take a psychic to see the utter contempt in her eyes—"screwing the bartender in the Middle-of-Nowhere, Fucking-Indiana."

That got my dander up pretty darn quick. "Listen, you—"

"Yeah, we gotta talk," Kade said, cutting me off. Grabbing Branna's arm, he hauled her toward the kitchen and out of earshot.

Blane sat down next to me on the couch. "I take it you know her?" he asked.

I glanced at him, noticed his gaze was traveling from where I clutched the sheet to my naked breasts and down to where way too much of my thighs was showing. "Um, yeah. We've met," I replied. My mom had always taught me: *If you can't say anything nice, don't say anything at all.* So that's where I left it.

"Nice shoes."

Shit. This had turned from a good idea into a mortifying disaster. I stood, wanting to make a quick exit, but was caught up short by the rest of the sheet trapped underneath Blane.

"Um, you're on my sheet," I said, blushing furiously.

Blane looked singularly unrepentant. Grasping the fabric in one hand, he stood and slowly wrapped the sheet around me, getting way too close to do so and tucking the tail in the valley between my breasts.

"Looks like our arrival interrupted something," he said softly. "Can't say I'm sorry about that."

I swallowed. Nice. Branna was kissing Kade while Blane was touching me way too intimately and bragging about cock-blocking Kade. Well, this had all turned to shit pretty damn fast. Yeah, let's all three of us go on a road trip! Whose fucktastic idea had *that* been?

My ears were straining to listen to Branna and Kade in the kitchen, but I didn't hear anything. Were they kissing again?

"I'd better go get some clothes on," I said, avoiding Blane's eyes. He didn't try to stop me as I hurried down the hall, my ridiculous high heels *click-clack*ing on the floor.

Once I got to my bedroom, I hurriedly dropped the sheet, then bent to undo the stilettos strapped to my feet.

"You forgot this."

I let out a startled cry, spinning around to see Blane standing in the doorway, my black robe in his outstretched hand. His eyes burned a path down my body.

"Blane!" I cried, making a grab for the discarded sheet and holding it in front of me. "You could've knocked!"

"Then I'd have missed the view," he said, a wicked gleam in his eyes and a tilt to his lips. Before I could retort, he was gone, closing the door behind him.

I sat heavily on the edge of the bed, wondering how things had gotten so complicated so fast.

Grabbing a pair of yoga pants, I pulled them on then yanked a T-shirt over my head. In moments, I was back down the hall and found all three of them together again in the living room.

Branna was glaring at me as though she wanted to slap me the way she had Kade, or even harder. I returned the sentiment.

"We all need to get some sleep before we leave in the morning," Kade said.

"Wait," I interrupted. "Who's 'we'?" If he so much as hinted that Branna was coming along—

"All four of us," he replied evenly.

"Oh no," I said, shaking my head. "She is definitely *not* coming along."

"Afraid I'll kick your ass again, sweetie?" Branna asked, venom coating her words.

My anger wasn't far under the surface and it sprang to life, fueled in no small part by jealousy. I shot her a glare. "Just try it, you little Irish bitch," I hissed.

"With pleasure, hillbilly whore."

Branna came at me and I eagerly went for her, my fingers curling into claws. I couldn't wait to inflict some damage on her perfect, sneering face . . .

"Whoa there!" Kade said.

Blane grabbed me just as Kade wrapped an arm around Branna, the two of them stopping us from tearing into each other. She twisted and struggled in Kade's grip, as I did in Blane's, but neither of us could break free, which just pissed me off even more.

"Let me go!"

"I don't think so," Blane replied. He sounded a bit surprised by my behavior, not that I cared. I was still fuming that the best-possible outlet for my pent-up fury had been suddenly derailed.

"You two, play nice," Kade ordered.

"I. Hate. Her," I seethed, glaring at the object of my intense dislike.

"The feeling is mutual," Branna spat.

"Well, this should be fun," Blane deadpanned, looking over at Kade.

"Enough!" Kade said. "I don't care if you two aren't going to be besties, but you have to get along."

"Tell *her* that," I gritted out. "She's the one who has problems following directions, right, Branna?" She'd been supposed to "train" me in hand-to-hand combat, the only time Kade had asked for her assistance, but instead she had used the opportunity to beat me up. Kade had been pissed.

"I don't like to piss away opportunities handed to me on a silver platter," she retorted.

I'd stopped struggling against Blane, my temper temporarily under control, but his arms were still locked around me. "Let me go," I said. "I'll play nice if she will." For now.

Blane slowly released me, as though he didn't quite believe me and wanted to be able to grab me again should I launch myself at Branna. Kade similarly released Branna, who didn't cease glaring at me.

I caught Blane and Kade glancing uneasily at each other and a slight embarrassment crept over me for my fit of temper, but I was still too consumed with dislike and jealousy to be really embarrassed.

"I only have two beds," I said. "Mine, and the twin one upstairs. Branna will have to sleep on the floor." I smiled coldly at her.

"She can have the bed," Blane said. "I'll take the floor."

Of course. Blane's chivalry would extend to Branna, I thought irritably.

"Fine," I said. "I'll get you some blankets."

I glared again at Branna as I passed, brushing my shoulder hard against her. She stumbled back, then took a step toward me, fire flashing in her eyes. But Kade grabbed her arm, stopping her. I smiled sweetly.

When I returned, I handed Blane some bedding and a pillow. Kade and Branna were gone, but I could hear them walking around upstairs. Kade must have taken her to the bedroom. Good thing, too, because if I had, she might've suffered an "accident" on the stairs.

"Sorry I don't have a place for you to sleep," I said. I felt bad that Blane would have to sleep on the cold, hard floor. "You and Kade can take my bed," I offered. "I can sleep on the couch."

"The day I take a pregnant woman's bed and make her sleep on the couch is the day I give up my man card," Blane joked.

"Not to mention that sleeping with another guy is just weird," Kade added, stepping into the room. He was alone. "Even if we're related."

I smiled at that, Kade's easy manner making the tension in my shoulders relax. Then I remembered Branna and stiffened again.

"So will you two tell me how Branna is in my house and why she's coming with us?" I asked.

"She showed up at the house," Blane said, turning to Kade. "Had a fine time kicking my ass before demanding to know where you were."

"She attacked you?" I asked, anger rising again. My hands clenched into fists. Yet another reason to hate Branna, as if I didn't have plenty already.

Blane seemed to read my mind, his eyes flashing to mine. "I'm fine, Kat," he said.

"It's not like she's going to hurt him," Kade interjected, scoffing.

I got in his face. "I don't like her trying to hurt him," I argued. "Any more than I like her kissing you." I poked his chest for emphasis.

"She can help us," Kade insisted. "So she's coming along whether you like it or not."

A little part inside me curled up into a pain-stricken ball at those words, but I kept my face carefully impassive.

"Have you told her who we are?" Blane asked. "You and me?"

Kade tore his gaze from mine to look at Blane. "No. I just told her to come to you if she ever needed me and couldn't find me. That you'd know where I was. But she doesn't know we're brothers. "

"And who is she to you, exactly?" Blane persisted. "You've never mentioned her."

Kade hesitated and I knew why. He and Branna had been in the same foster home as children for a short while. He'd saved her from being molested, enduring beatings and abuse for his interference. And I knew he wanted to tell Blane none of that.

"We met a long time ago," Kade hedged. "We've done some work together. I've never mentioned her, the same way I never mention any of my work to you. You know I keep that shit separate."

"Except when that shit turns up on my doorstep and I have no fucking clue what's going on," Blane said. "And why am I not surprised that a 'friend' of yours would be deadly? Not to mention that I really don't like that at some point you let her beat up Kathleen."

Kade winced at that. "That may have been a slight error in judgment," he admitted. "But she can still help us."

"You really think that's a good idea?" Blane asked, tipping his head ever so slightly toward me.

Kade's eyes met mine. "You know Branna and I have a history," he said.

I wondered just what that history included. I'd known for a while that Branna was in love with him. Had they slept together? Were they lovers? Maybe friends with benefits? Kade had never said and I hadn't asked. I wasn't about to humiliate myself by doing so now.

"Yeah, I know you have a history," I said stiffly. "I was wondering more about the present."

I turned away and headed back to my bedroom. I hadn't forgotten how Kade had said us getting together had been a mistake. Now, with Branna by his side for the immediate future, I wondered if my chances to convince him otherwise had just gone up in smoke.

~

The now usual morning routine of retching before my shower had me feeling more depressed and tired than usual. I wandered into the kitchen once I was dressed, trying to think of something that sounded good despite my temperamental tummy.

Blane was already in there, leaning against the counter and sipping a cup of coffee.

"How are you feeling?" he asked.

I opened the refrigerator, morosely eyeing the contents. "Tired," I said glumly. "Where's Kade?" I'd noticed his absence when I'd passed by the living room. *Maybe he'd decided to share Branna's bed,* I thought bitchily.

"He went to pick up some supplies for the trip," Blane replied. "Branna went with him."

Of course she had. I closed the refrigerator door, any desire to try and eat something now completely gone.

"I like your house," Blane said, changing the subject. He handed me a cup of coffee. "It's very . . . you."

That made me smile a little. "Thanks." The coffee smelled good and I took a cautious sip. I wanted to sit outside, craving the peaceful feeling it gave me. "Want to sit on the porch with me?"

Blane smiled. "Sure."

He followed me outside and sat down next to me on the wicker couch. The blanket I'd left was still there and he tucked it around me against the early morning chill. We sat in companionable silence and I let out a deep sigh.

"I'm worried about you," Blane said after a while.

I had finished the last of my coffee and was setting aside the mug when he spoke. I glanced up at him, frowning. "Why? I'm fine."

"I'm really proud of you, that you moved back home, bought this house, and seem bound and determined to have this baby alone," he said. "But I know you need more than money and a house." His brushed my hair back with his hand. "You need Kade."

I looked away, unsure what to say.

"I was so pissed at him," Blane continued. "When he came by the house, told me he was leaving. I was still reeling and wasn't thinking straight, or I'd have known right away he was full of shit, the things he said."

"What did he say?" I asked.

But Blane shook his head. "You don't want to know. Robert has played me for a fool before and I should've realized he'd have found another way, through Kade."

"Kade said Keaston's worried I'm going to come out of the woodwork in ten years with your love child or something," I said. "And even when I asked him why he didn't just tell him the baby's not yours, he said it had been a mistake, me and him." Repeating Kade's words made my stomach twist.

Blane sighed. "He needs you, whether he wants to admit it or not." He lifted my chin in his hand and our eyes met. "If you don't fight for him, if you just let him go, then he won't survive. I saw it in his eyes. He came back to Indy to say goodbye to me, to you, and I'm sure whatever job he took next, it would have been his last."

I stared at Blane in shock. "I—I . . . he told me he wanted to say goodbye," I stammered, "but I didn't think he meant . . ." I couldn't finish the sentence.

"I think Kade is hanging by a very thin thread," Blane continued. "We'll go to DC. I'll have it out with my uncle. And you have to convince Kade you need him more than he hates himself."

I swallowed. This had to be hard for Blane. "I'm sorry," I said, "about you and me—"

"This isn't about me or the past," he interrupted gently. "This is about you, Kade, and the baby. I'll be fine." He smiled, but it didn't reach his eyes. "I want my brother alive, Kat. And you're the only one who can convince him he's worth saving. Not even I can do that."

Tears swam in my eyes. I didn't deserve how nice Blane was being to me, didn't deserve him still caring about me after all we'd been through. But I was grateful for it.

I leaned into him, wrapping my arms around his waist in a hug. He hugged me back and I felt his lips brush the top of my head.

Kade suddenly stepped outside. When he saw me in Blane's arms, his eyes turned cold and hard. "So sorry to interrupt a tender moment, but we need to get going."

"You're right," Blane said, releasing me and getting to his feet. "Kathleen's been sick and hasn't eaten, but we can just grab her something on the road, right?"

I frowned. That didn't sound like Blane, but he was already heading inside.

Kade's head swiveled back, his gaze pinning me. "You were sick again today?"

"I'm sick every day," I corrected him. "The nausea wears off after a while, then I can eat."

Kade frowned. "But you can drink coffee?"

I shrugged. "I didn't say it made sense."

"I don't want to leave until you get something to eat," he said. "What sounds good? I'll go get it."

I was taken aback by Kade's concern, then abruptly realized what Blane had done. Kade had always taken care of me when I'd needed someone to, so Blane was playing off that now.

"Gosh, I don't know," I said. I stood, then faked a little stumble. Kade was there instantly, an arm around my waist. "Wow, I guess I didn't realize my blood sugar was so low," I said. Good gravy, I really sucked at this, but Kade seemed to buy it. I leaned on him, wrapping an arm around his neck. He'd showered and smelled really good.

"You didn't eat anything but fries and pickles last night— no wonder you're weak," he groused, but concern laced his words. "Come on. Sit inside where it's warm and I'll make you some eggs."

"Eggs sound good. And bacon," I said, smiling a little to myself. I let him help me inside and he sat me at the kitchen table. I watched while he scrambled some eggs and cooked them, openly admiring the way his body moved. Dressed in a T-shirt and jeans, his gun stuffed in the small of his back, it was an incongruous sight to see—an admitted assassin making me breakfast in my country kitchen filled with rooster decor and homespun appliance cozies.

"Here you go," he said, sliding some eggs and bacon onto a plate in front of me. Just then, Branna walked in.

"I thought we were going," she said.

"We are," Kade said. "Getting something to eat first."

Branna frowned. "But we already ate."

Oh, they had, had they? The eggs suddenly didn't taste as good.

"Kathleen hasn't," Kade said, a note of warning in his voice.

"Well, she might want to skip a meal or two," Branna said breezily. "These jeans I borrowed are about to fall off me, they're so big."

And that's when I noticed she was wearing my clothes. My fork clattered to the plate and I shoved back my chair as I stood, the legs scraping against the wooden floor.

"Why are you wearing my clothes?" I asked, my supposed low blood sugar forgotten as my temper began to heat up.

"I needed something to wear," she said, sending me a you're-an-idiot look.

"And who said you could steal my clothes?" I bit out.

"Borrow," she corrected me. "Trust me, I'd rather burn them than keep them."

"Branna, dial back the bitchy," Kade interrupted, his brows furrowed in irritation.

"I don't think she can," I sneered. "It just comes too natural." I spun around and hurried down the hall. I could feel tears threatening and the last thing I wanted was for Branna to see me cry.

Damn! These stupid hormones! I slammed my bedroom door behind me and blinked back the tears, taking deep breaths. I was so sick of crying at the drop of a hat.

Okay, I had to pack. I pulled my little suitcase out of my closet and started throwing things in, Branna's words echoing in my head. I had no idea what we'd be doing in DC, but I wasn't going to look like a country bumpkin next to her.

I tossed in the flimsiest underwear and bras I had, then added the evening gown I'd bought in Vegas but never worn. After a moment's hesitation, I tucked my peacock-blue stilettos in as well, then added more sensible things like jeans and shorts. A couple of summer dresses, my Vegas bikini, makeup, and I was set.

I was wearing yoga pants and a T-shirt, mainly because the pants were nice and stretchy and felt good on my slightly expanded tummy. Branna's bitchy comment about my jeans being too big for her had me digging through my closet for my skinny jeans. I shucked the yoga pants, then thought twice and tossed them into the suitcase before pulling on the jeans.

Oh. Wow. Okay, this was going to be difficult. I jumped several times, finally managing to hoist them up over my hips and ass, but then I couldn't zip them.

I muttered curses as I tried to get the zipper up but couldn't. Finally, I lay down flat on the bed, sucked in my tummy, and held my breath. When I did that, I could get them zipped and buttoned, but only just.

Standing up, I winced. Yeah, this should be okay, so long as I didn't sit. Or breathe. No problem.

I grabbed a different shirt from my closet, yanking off the T-shirt I was wearing and putting on the new top. Made of a thin, pale pink material, it was sleeveless and buttoned up the front. I left three buttons undone. My ass might be too big, but my boobs weren't, even though they'd gotten a little fuller in the past couple of weeks. Hopefully the ample cleavage on display would distract someone from noticing that my jeans were too tight. And by *someone* I meant Kade.

I slipped on a pair of flat sandals and rolled my suitcase down the hall. Kade was waiting for me.

"Did you get enough to eat?" he asked. "You didn't finish your eggs."

My cheeks burned. I didn't want to discuss food with him, not when I'd been so embarrassed by the things Branna had said. I didn't think I was the kind of woman who obsessed over my weight, but what would Kade think in three months when I would be six months pregnant? Would he be disgusted, think I was fat? I refused to consider the possibility that he wouldn't be around in three months.

I avoided Kade's eyes, fussing with my suitcase instead. "Yeah, I'm fine. Ready to go."

He took the suitcase from me, moving in to stand close.

"Hey," he said, making me look up at him. "I'm sorry about Branna. She's always been . . ." He hesitated.

"A bitch?" I offered, making him smile slightly.

"Possessive," he countered.

I stiffened. "I didn't realize you and she were . . . involved." My heart sank. I'd been hoping Kade hadn't had that kind of relationship with Branna.

"It was a long time ago and very short-lived," Kade explained. "We're friends now, colleagues, nothing more."

"Does she know that?" I said bitterly.

Kade regarded me seriously. "I told her then that she and I weren't going to happen again, but I don't know if she ever really believed me."

"She's in love with you," I said, my voice flat. Kade winced. "If you aren't in love with her, too, then you're being cruel not to tell her." And I could've been speaking for myself as well as Branna.

Kade's eyes searched mine, then he gave a curt nod.

"Let's go," he said, and I followed him out the door, locking the house up tight behind me.

Branna and Blane were standing outside, talking, but I couldn't hear what they were saying. Kade put my suitcase in the trunk of his Mercedes. I really, really hoped we were taking two cars, because if I had to be in the same car with Branna for nine hours, I just might kill her. To my relief, both Blane and Kade had their keys out.

I stepped up to Kade's passenger door at the same time Branna did.

"Excuse me, but I believe you have the wrong car," Branna said, her eyes challenging me.

There was one thing I absolutely would not do, and that was lower myself to fighting over a man. I hated Branna for how she treated me, and yes, I was jealous, too. But I would not stand there and bicker over who got to ride with Kade like we were two sixteen-year-old twits.

"Fine," I said with a thin-lipped smile. I turned away.

"Kathleen rides with me," Kade said, stopping me in my tracks. "Branna, you ride with Blane."

Branna's fair skin turned pink, but she didn't say anything, brushing by me to get in the front seat of Blane's

Jaguar. Kade got into his car and I slid into the front seat as well.

The miles flew by and Kade turned on satellite radio. I was really regretting the jeans choice. It felt like I was being cut in two and my stomach was aching. Clearly, vanity had gotten in the way of my common sense.

Being locked in a car with Kade for nine-plus hours, though, was a prime opportunity that I couldn't pass up. After debating several different openings, I at last picked one and cleared my throat.

"So . . ." I said brightly, glancing over at him. His sunglasses concealed his eyes from me. "I was thinking I really like the name Miranda. Or maybe Luke, if it's a boy. What do you think?" Nothing like jumping right off that conversational cliff.

Kade's hands tightly gripped the wheel, but he didn't say anything. I tried again.

"Or maybe, if it's a girl, we could name her after your mother," I said. "What was her name?"

This time I waited, letting the silence between us get thick and uncomfortable. Eventually, Kade answered.

"Shouldn't you be naming it after a famous Turner?" he asked briskly.

My stomach dropped. He meant that I'd have no choice but to use my last name, because he wouldn't be offering his. I should look on the bright side—at least it seemed he'd acknowledged that I wasn't going back to Blane. While that should have been consoling, it wasn't, and I turned to stare sightlessly out the window.

Nausea began curdling inside my stomach about an hour later, and I leaned my forehead against the cool glass of the window. If I took deep breaths and focused, maybe I wouldn't get sick. Between not eating enough earlier when I was hungry and the tension between Kade and me, plus the jeans from hell, I wasn't doing so great.

A few bumps in the road later, and I knew I wasn't going to make it much longer.

"Can we stop somewhere for a minute?" I asked, my voice weak. I didn't turn my head, too focused on not puking to look at Kade.

"Yeah, sure."

To my relief, we were near an exit and minutes later he was pulling into a gas station. I barely waited for the car to stop before I was out and hurrying inside. And not a moment too soon. I'd barely locked the bathroom door before I was heaving.

When it was over, I washed out my mouth and splashed some water on my face. I thought the nausea had gotten better, but my body didn't seem to like my empty stomach or riding in a car. Even a Mercedes. The thought of food made me want to retch again, so I didn't buy anything to eat before heading back outside.

Kade was leaning against his Mercedes, waiting for me. When I emerged, he pushed himself away from the car and approached me.

"Are you all right?" he asked.

I nodded, giving him a wan smile. "Fine." So much for trying to look sexy. Knowing I'd just thrown up in a gas station bathroom was enough to put any man off.

It seemed everything I tried to say or do to bring Kade closer to me was backfiring. All the misguided effort was depressing and demoralizing. And if I thought the day couldn't get any worse, I was way wrong.

Even though I had nothing in my stomach, I had to ask Kade to stop four more times before we finally hit the outskirts of DC. We'd gone through a drive-thru somewhere in Ohio around midday, but the smell of grease had been enough to send me hurtling from the car. Fortunately, Kade had made short work of his meal by the time I returned. He'd tried to get me to eat, but just the thought of trying to get something down had turned my stomach.

I was miserable and weak by the time Kade pulled into a motel parking lot. It was one of those places I always teased him about, though that was the last thing I felt like doing at the moment. I just wanted to lie down on something stationary, like a bed, and take off the damn jeans, which I'd decided I would burn at the earliest opportunity.

I waited in the car for Kade to rent a room, my head lolling against the headrest. I dozed, jerking awake when he opened the car door. He drove across the lot to one of the rooms and parked again. I saw Blane park a space or two down from us.

Kade got out of the car, then met Blane and handed him a key. I couldn't hear what they were saying, but Kade was there at the car door as I opened it. I slung my purse over my shoulder. My hands were shaking and it took a lot of effort just to stand. But I was highly motivated. A bed was mere yards away. I just had to make it inside, then I could collapse.

I took a step, only to have Kade sweep me up in his arms.

"I've got you," he said softly, and I was too tired to argue. I rested my head against his shoulder as he walked to the motel room door, which Blane was holding open. A moment later, Kade deposited me on one of the two beds. Slipping its strap from my shoulder, he set my purse aside, then took off my sandals.

"I'm sorry," I said. "I didn't realize I'd get carsick."

"Don't apologize," he said, his fingers brushing my cheek. "Blane went to get some things for you. Just rest."

I closed my eyes, his touch comforting me, and soon I was asleep.

~

When I woke, night had fallen, and I felt a little better, albeit weak and thirsty. I sat up, glancing around.

Kade stood from where he'd been lying on the other bed and sat down next to me.

"Feel any better?" he asked.

I nodded. "What time is it?"

"Elevenish," he replied. He grabbed a bottled sports drink from the table between the two beds and twisted the cap off. "Here. Can you drink this?"

I nodded, taking it from him. It tasted good and I emptied the bottle in a few big gulps. The gnawing pit in my stomach eased a bit.

"Where are Blane and Branna?" I asked.

"Next door."

I wondered how *that* was going.

"I've got to get out of these jeans," I muttered. I lay back on the bed and undid the button and zipper. My stomach immediately felt ten times better. Okay, lesson learned.

I peeled the denim down over my hips and slid the fabric lower, off my legs, then kicked the hated jeans onto the floor.

"Christ, Kathleen!" Kade exclaimed, pushing me onto my back and yanking up my shirt.

I glanced down and winced. Yeah, the jeans had left red marks and indentations. Nice.

"What the fuck did you wear those for if they're too tight?" Kade asked. "Is that why you've been puking all day?"

Face flaming, I pushed his hands away and let my shirt drop, covering my abdomen. "She said I was fat, okay?" I retorted. Yes, I knew I'd been stupid. I didn't need Kade to point it out. "And she's right, because my shorts didn't fit yesterday and I used to be able to zip these jeans, but now I just want my stretchy pants . . ." Suddenly, I was bawling.

Kade looked at me like I was crazy, which didn't help. I turned away from him, but he reached out and rolled me back.

"You're insane," he said, brushing tears from my cheeks, "and if I'd known those ridiculous jeans were doing this to you all day, I'd have taken them off you myself."

My tears dried up as quickly as they'd come. God, the mood swings were killing me. But we were in a motel, just me and Kade, and maybe I could work this to my advantage.

"I'd love to brush my teeth and have a shower," I said hopefully.

Kade took the bait immediately. "I can help with that," he said. He gathered some things from my suitcase and helped me into the bathroom.

I brushed my teeth and hair, stripped, and stepped under the hot spray of water. After washing, I called out for Kade, who was instantly at the door.

"What's wrong?" he asked.

I poked my wet head out from behind the limp shower curtain. "I'm feeling really weak," I said, which wasn't too far from the truth. "Will you help me? I don't want to fall."

Kade's eyes narrowed, but I just gazed innocently back at him. Finally, he took three steps forward until he was right there in front of me.

Steam from the shower billowed around us. Feeling brave, I pushed the curtain aside. Kade's gaze immediately dropped, skating down my body.

"You'll get your clothes wet," I said, tugging his shirt free of his jeans and pulling it off over his head. My hands settled on his chest, reaching up to curl around his shoulders. To my instant gratification, his palms lifted to cup my breasts, the calloused pads of his thumbs brushing the tips.

"You really think I don't know what you're doing?" his voice rasped gently in my ear.

I was working on his belt and since my brain had decided it could really only concentrate on one thing at a time, my "Hmm?" reply was a bit lackluster. His hands felt amazing on me, my breasts hypersensitive to the slightest touch.

Kade's lips grazed my neck and I gasped, a moan clawing its way up my throat.

"Having sex isn't going to convince me to stick around, princess," Kade said against my skin. "I'm like poison to you. A death trap."

"Not true," I managed, burying my fingers in his inky-black hair. His mouth closed over a nipple and I promptly lost my train of thought. Kade was my fallen angel, had always been. My protector. My dark knight in black armor. I just had to convince him.

"I need you," I breathed. "Don't you see that?"

A loud knock on the motel door startled me. It seemed that answering it was the last thing Kade wanted to do, and whoever it was had to knock hard again before he reluctantly pulled away from me. His hair and chest were damp from my hands and the shower mist, and he didn't bother putting his shirt back on as he left the bathroom.

I hurriedly turned off the water and grabbed one of the thin towels, wrapping it around me before cracking the bathroom door and peeking through.

Blane and Branna stood in the room. Peachy. All three glanced my way.

"Blane and I need to go check out George's residence," Kade said, buttoning a fresh shirt he'd put on. "Branna's going to stay with you."

"No way," I said. "I'm going, too. You are not leaving me here with her like some sort of babysitter." I didn't even bother looking Branna's way.

"Afraid, sweetie?" Branna piped in. The three of us ignored her.

Kade considered me for a moment, then gave a little nod. "Fine. Get dressed."

All three went out the door and I set a new record for how fast I got dressed. My hair was wet, so I left it loose, hoping it would dry on the way to dead George's former home. Soon, I was outside, too.

"Let's go," Kade said, leading me to his car. He got in the front seat while Blane held the passenger seat forward for

Branna to slide into the backseat. Blane looked at me and I took the hint, stepping past him to climb in the back next to Branna, leaving the front passenger seat for Blane. As soon as the door shut, Kade pulled out of the lot.

CHAPTER THIRTEEN

"Well, isn't this cozy?" Branna said in the silence. No one replied. She turned to me and I stiffened. "So tell me, sweetie, do you plan on playing the damsel in distress indefinitely?"

"Excuse me?" I asked, my eyes narrowing.

"Surely the two of them must tire of it," she kept going. "It seems Blane already has. Kade surely isn't far behind. Do you have any other tricks up your sleeve?"

"Why? Need some tips?" I asked, white-hot anger singeing my veins, even as I wondered how she'd found out about Blane and me.

Kade interrupted our bitch match. "Ladies, for fuck's sake. Give it a rest."

I bit my tongue to keep from saying, "She started it."

After a few minutes of silence, Branna spoke up again. This time, thankfully, her words weren't directed at me.

"What's the plan tonight?" she asked Kade.

"We're going to check things out," Kade replied. "Try the nice approach first, see if it works."

"And if it doesn't?" I asked.

His eyes met mine in the rearview mirror. "Then tomorrow night we'll do the not-so-nice approach."

I looked away as Blane said, "Sarah doesn't need to be harmed for us to get what we want, Kade."

"How do you two know each other again?" Branna interrupted. "Kade, how in the hell did you hook up with a slimy politician? Or is it the fabulous vagina sitting next to me that brought you two together?"

"You mean he never told you?" I asked, feigning shock. "Wow. I thought you two were . . . closer than that." I smiled and shrugged. "Guess not."

That pushed some buttons.

"What the fuck, Kade—" she spluttered.

"Oh my God, he's my brother, Branna," Kade said in exasperation. "I'm about to dump both your asses on the sidewalk and let you fight it out."

But the revelation that Kade had a brother was enough to silence Branna. Her expression looked stunned, hurt. Then she turned and gazed out the window and didn't say another word.

I almost felt bad for her.

We approached a two-story brick mansion in a neighborhood filled with them. Lights glowed in some of the windows. Kade pulled up alongside the curb in front of the house and parked.

"I think it'd be best if Kat and I go talk to her," Blane said, surprising me. "She knows me and she's met Kat. A woman there might make her feel more like opening up. And Kat's good at getting people to talk and trust her." The last was said matter-of-factly. I thought it was the first time Blane had ever said something like that about me.

Kade glanced back at me, then nodded. "You have your gun?" he asked Blane.

"Always."

With that, Blane and I got out of the car and I followed him up the long walk to the colonial-style front door. Reaching out, he took my hand, threading our fingers together. I nervously combed a hand through my hair, now nearly dry.

"Branna's a lot like Kade," Blane said out of the blue. I glanced up at him and our eyes caught. "Damaged. I'm guessing she's been through some of the same shit he has."

"It's not my story to tell," I replied. "You'd have to ask her, but yeah, I think so."

Blane gave a curt nod but said nothing more as we stepped up onto the porch. Reaching out, he rang the doorbell. Though it was nearing ten o'clock, the door swung open quickly, revealing a butler.

"May I help you?" he asked.

Blane told him his name and asked to see Sarah. We were led into a sitting room that looked like no one ever really sat in it. I perched gingerly on the edge of an antique couch, glancing around at the decor, which seemed straight out of a European magazine. Blane remained standing, energy and purpose seeming to radiate from him as he paced.

"Blane? Blane Kirk?"

I glanced up to see Sarah Bradshaw entering the room, her brows furrowed in confusion as she inspected Blane.

"What on earth are you doing here? And at this hour?"

Blane smiled softly, taking both of her hands in his and pressing a kiss to her cheek. "Good to see you, Sarah."

I got to my feet too as Blane gestured my way. "You remember Kathleen, don't you?"

Good manners bred into her had Sarah sending an artificial smile my way and reaching out to clasp hands with me. "Of course," she said, which may or may not have been the truth. We'd met very briefly at a victory dinner for Senator Keaston, and she'd barely spared me a glance then.

"Please, sit down," Sarah said, gracefully sinking into a Queen Anne–style chair opposite the couch. Blane took a seat on the couch next to me.

"I heard about George," he said, leaning forward, elbows braced on his knees. "And I'm sorry for your loss."

Sarah's smile was tinged with bitterness. "Thank you, Blane, but you and I both know George wasn't a good man. He did a lot of things to a lot of people. It was bound to catch up to him."

I was surprised at how matter-of-fact she was, but I guess you couldn't live long in Washington without being disillusioned.

"Speaking of which," Blane said, "it's late, so I'll get to the point of our visit."

"I would appreciate that," Sarah said.

"George worked for Robert for a long time," Blane said. "Lately, Robert's gotten . . . a little out of hand—"

"He's a megalomaniac," Sarah interrupted.

"Yes," Blane confirmed. "He's come after me, after Kathleen. She was nearly killed, twice, because of Robert." Sarah's eyes flicked toward me, then back to Blane. "I need something I can use, something that'll keep him in line, and I thought you might know if George had anything like that. Maybe told you anything that might help me."

"Why should I tell you that?" Sarah asked. "If Robert finds out I helped you, I'll be dead. And how can I trust you? You're related to him. For all I know, this is some test to make sure I'll keep his secrets as well as my husband did."

"This isn't a test," Blane said.

"And how do I know that?"

I figured it was my turn to chime in. "Mrs. Bradshaw," I said, drawing her attention toward me, "a few months ago, Senator Keaston had me taken. Taken by people whose job it was to make sure I was never seen or heard from again. Not to be killed, but to be sold into human slavery, into sex trafficking. My crime? Falling in love with Blane. If not for Blane . . ." I turned to look at him, my hand reaching out. He clasped my hand in both of his. "If not for Blane," I continued, looking back to Sarah, "I wouldn't be here now. This isn't a test. This is Blane asking you for help in taking down a very dangerous man."

Sarah seemed to weigh my words, meeting my eyes steadily. I didn't say anything more, just waited. After a moment, she spoke.

"There's a man," she said, "someone new. I could tell George wanted to be real hush-hush about it, but I know he was getting money from him. I don't know how or why, just that the campaign coffers have received huge influxes in the past six months."

"Do you know anything about this man?" Blane asked.

Sarah shrugged. "Very little. He came by the house one night, which made George angry. From then on, they met outside the house. I followed George once. I was worried about him, wondering what he'd gotten himself mixed up in. He went to this house, here." She got up and went to one of the tables, pulling paper and a pen out of a drawer, then jotting something down and handing the paper to Blane.

"Here's the address. The man, he was tall, over six feet, and broad, with dark hair, a goatee, and dark eyes. He spoke with a Russian accent."

"You're sure?" Blane asked.

Sarah nodded. "I only caught part of a name, and I don't know if it's his first or last."

"What is it?"

"Lazaroff."

～

"Well, at least we have a name," Kade said, taking a drink of the coffee the waitress had just poured for him.

We were in a late-night diner in a part of DC that had me questioning the wisdom of us stopping for dinner, no matter how hungry I was.

I sat across from Kade in the booth, Blane by my side. I toyed with the Pepsi I'd ordered.

"Yeah, but does it strike any bells?" Blane replied.

"This address," Branna interrupted. "I've heard of it. Russians run an illegal gambling joint there and a brothel. Strictly high rollers only."

"In the heart of DC?" Kade asked, raising an eyebrow.

"Some kind of deal with the Russian consulate," Branna replied with a shrug. "Cops look the other way. The Russians get a taste of the homeland when they want to and occasionally a piece of a US politician."

"You think George gambled?" I asked Blane. "Or Robert?"

Blane shook his head. "Maybe this was just Lazaroff's home base. I don't see Robert being stupid enough to indebt himself in gambling. He's smarter than that."

"We need to get in there tomorrow night and find this guy," Kade said just as the waitress reappeared with our meals.

I dug into the blueberry pancakes I'd ordered, ignoring the fact that Branna had gotten a salad. It seemed everyone was hungry and conversation ceased

"I can find out more about Lazaroff," Branna said after a few minutes. "I have someone I can call tomorrow. They might meet with me."

"Might?" Blane asked.

Branna shrugged. "I shot him the last time I saw him, but it was just a flesh wound. I'm sure he'll have gotten over it by now."

Blane stopped chewing for a moment, then glanced at Kade, who hadn't batted an eye at this information.

"You're just going to let her go see some guy she shot who may or may not want revenge?" Blane asked.

Kade looked up from the Denver omelet he was eating just as Branna spoke.

"Excuse me, did you say 'let her'?" Branna said, her tone making it clear exactly what she thought of that. "Need I remind you that I handed you your ass just twenty-four hours ago? I can take care of myself."

"No, Blane's right," Kade said, wiping his mouth with a napkin. "We shouldn't split up, even if it's just for intel. I'll go with you."

"You need to stay with Kathleen," Blane said. "I'll go with Branna."

"Why does he have to stay with her?" Branna asked, sending a glare my way. "If someone's watching my back, I'd prefer he not be troubled by things like morals and ethics."

"I'm a lawyer," Blane retorted. "Morals and ethics aren't a problem."

I watched the two of them continue to spar as I finished my pancakes. My brow furrowed, as it seemed they were only aware of each other. Surely, Blane wasn't . . . attracted to Branna? The thought tumbled through my mind like a stray paper caught in the wind.

We were walking to the car when Branna suddenly asked me, "You're not going to puke all over the backseat, are you?"

"No," I said shortly. "But if I do, I'll be sure to aim it your direction."

"Don't even breathe on me," she scoffed. "I certainly don't want what you have."

I stopped at the car, turning to look at her incredulously. I grabbed Kade's sleeve. "You didn't tell her?" I was hurt. What the hell had he told her last night in my kitchen if not that I was carrying his baby?

Kade frowned, huffing out a breath as he studied me.

"Didn't tell me what?" Branna asked.

My eyes were locked with Kade's. "Are you just going to leave and pretend this never happened?" My words were quiet, but I couldn't keep the pain and accusation out of them.

I could feel myself on the verge of breaking down, so I quickly turned away, jerking open the car door and climbing inside. I could still hear Branna.

"What is it?" she asked again. "Kade, tell me what's going on. What's wrong with—"

"Kathleen's pregnant," he interrupted her.

Branna was silent for a moment. "I take it congratulations are in order," she said stiffly.

I couldn't hear if Kade said anything, because the next thing I knew, she was climbing in beside me. Blane had already taken the front seat and Kade got behind the wheel without a word.

To say that the drive to the motel was awkward would be an understatement. Kade tried to meet my eyes in the rearview mirror numerous times, but I avoided looking at it.

I was out of the car as soon as possible when we were back at the motel, and I stood outside the door to our room, waiting stiffly for Kade to unlock it.

Movement caught my eye and I saw Blane looking at me before he opened the door and let Branna in ahead of him. Branna looked upset, and well she should have been. Kade and she were supposed to be close, yet not only had he never told her about Blane, he hadn't even told her I was having his child.

I'd be pretty upset, too, if I was her. I wondered if Blane would comfort her, and then I wondered how I felt about that.

Kade unlocked our door and I hurried inside, not looking at him. I brushed my teeth in the bathroom, then took off my jeans and headed for one of the beds, all without speaking to him.

"Kathleen . . ." he began.

I ignored him, jerking the bedcovers down, then slipping off my bra and putting it in my suitcase. The T-shirt I wore was fine to sleep in.

"Kathleen," he tried again, taking hold of my arm. "Could you stop and just listen to me?"

"What should I listen to, Kade?" I snapped. "The sound of you *not* telling Branna about us?" I jerked my arm away just as Kade released me and I stumbled backward, falling flat on my ass on the floor.

"Dammit!" Tears threatened, but I blinked them back, pulling my feet under me to stand. That's when I felt it.

Kade shoved his hand through his hair in frustration, then leaned down to help me up.

"Wait," I said urgently. My hands dropped to my bump as another cramp knifed through my abdomen. "Oh God," I gasped, the blood leaving my face in a rush.

"What's wrong?" Kade dropped into a crouch next to me.

"I don't know," I breathed. "It hurts—" Another cramp cut me off as I sucked in a breath.

In a flash, Kade had me in his arms and was hurrying out the door.

"What are you doing?" I asked, cringing. I didn't even have pants on. But Kade was kicking on the door to Blane's room.

"Something's wrong with Kathleen," he blurted when Blane opened the door. "I'm taking her to the hospital."

"You're what?" I squeaked. "I'm fine!"

"You're not fine," Kade said to me. "Get the car door for me," he ordered Blane, who rushed to open it.

"Kade, will you just stop for a second?" Another cramp seized me and Kade saw my hands go to my abdomen.

"Nope," he said, slamming the door and hurrying to slide behind the wheel. Seconds later, he was burning rubber as we sped out of the lot.

I tried to reason with him all the way to the hospital, but it was like talking to a brick wall. No matter how many times I tried to tell him that cramping sometimes was normal and that we should just go back to the motel, he ignored me.

I wanted to sink under the seat when Kade pulled to a shuddering stop at the ER entrance, grabbing his keys and rushing around the car to pick me up and carry me inside.

"You can't just leave your car there!" I protested.

"Fuck the car," he growled.

"You're making a scene," I hissed, my face burning as people turned to look at us.

"I don't give a shit."

There was no stopping him from bullying the admittance people, and soon I was ensconced in a bed in the ER, clad in a gown and awaiting a doctor.

"I can't believe you did this," I muttered. "I'm fine. The cramping has stopped. It was probably nothing."

"Maybe it was," he said. "But won't you feel better to find out for sure?"

He was right, so I didn't say anything.

The doctor and a nurse came in shortly after that and asked me a bunch of questions. No, I hadn't had this happen before. No, I wasn't spotting. No, I wasn't cramping right then.

"Let's take a look," the doctor said with a kind smile while he snapped on a pair of latex gloves. He glanced at Kade. "Does Dad want to stay for this or wait outside?"

The look on Kade's face was unreadable. "I'm staying," he said, coming to stand by me. He took my hand.

"Everything looks all right," the doctor said a few minutes later, discarding his gloves and lowering the sheet to cover me. "But let's get a sonogram, just to be sure."

He stepped out of the cubicle and didn't return for several minutes, but Kade didn't release my hand. When the doctor came back, a technician followed him with a machine in tow.

Baring my stomach, the doctor squirted some gel on my skin, then placed the sonogram device on me, moving it around. A fast, whooshing beat immediately came through the speakers.

"What's that?" Kade asked.

"That's the baby's heartbeat, of course," the doctor replied, watching the screen. He pointed. "There he is. Or she." There was a white blob that squirmed.

My eyes burned with tears as I stared at our baby. Kade's hand was like a vise, crushing mine, but I didn't care.

"It looks like it was just one of those scares they like to do," the doctor said, giving the tech the wand and grabbing some paper towels to wipe the gel off my stomach. "Get used to it. They only come up with more ways to make you worry about them." He smiled, then discreetly handed me a tissue to wipe my eyes.

"Thank you," I managed, swallowing the lump in my throat.

"You're welcome. Take care of yourself, now." He left, pulling the curtain shut behind him and leaving Kade and me alone.

I chanced a glance at Kade. He was staring at me. His gaze dropped to my mouth and he leaned down, pressing a warm, soft kiss to my lips. He cupped my jaw, his fingers sliding into my hair. I lifted my hand to lightly grasp his arm. When he pulled back, he rested his forehead against mine.

"We made that," he said, his voice hardly above a whisper.

My smile was a little watery. "Yes, we did."

"We're having a baby."

"Yes, we are."

Kade pressed a kiss to my forehead and helped me dress. He called Blane on the way back to the motel to let him know I was okay, and soon we were back inside the run-down room.

I got into the bed and he pulled the covers up over me. I turned, my back toward Kade, and I felt the bed dip as he lay behind me, his body stretched alongside mine. His hand brushed the hair back from my face.

"I didn't tell Branna because I was trying to take your advice," he said, his lips grazing my ear. His fingertips gently traced the curve of my cheek and jaw. "I just hadn't had the chance yet to tell her that she and I aren't ever going to be what she wants. That I'm in love with someone else. That I'm in love with you. And no matter how many times I tell myself that you and the baby are better off without me, I can't stop wanting you."

I turned to look at him, almost afraid to hope. "Do you mean that?"

He nodded, still tenderly smoothing stray hairs back from my face. "I left, but that never meant I didn't love you. You own me, body and soul. From the moment I first laid eyes on you in the courthouse."

"Then why, Kade?" I asked. "Why would you lie to me, pretend everything was going to be okay, that we'd be together, and then just leave me without a word?"

"I'm so sorry, princess," Kade said, the anguish in his voice painful to hear. He gazed down into my eyes. "My staying would've put you in danger, and I couldn't even say goodbye because I knew if I did, I wouldn't be able to walk away from you. I wanted you to be safe, needed you to be safe. And I knew I couldn't do it, but Blane could."

I took his face in my hands, the shadow on his cheeks a soft abrasion against my palms. His eyes were beautiful pools of a blue so deep, I never wanted to stop gazing into them. "It's you . . . or it's no one," I said simply.

Kade studied me intently, and I prayed he was finally hearing me, finally understanding that there was no one else for me—just him.

His gaze dropped and he slowly lowered his head. My breath caught. His lips brushed mine once, twice, then settled softly in a gentle caress. My fingers slid into his hair and it seemed my chest cracked wide open as Kade kissed me. All the longing and heartbreak of being apart was poured from me into him and back. Kade pressed kisses to my cheeks, my eyes, my jaw, then returned to my lips, the warm slide of his tongue against mine spreading heat through my body. I felt cherished as he held me, loved.

Yet a whisper of caution made me pull away. "Wait," I said, my voice breathless from his kisses. Kade's mouth moved to my neck and I had to tug on his hair to get his attention. "Wait," I said again.

"What?" he asked. His lips were red and a little swollen, the slight sheen to them making me want to swallow what I

294

was about to say and dive back into kissing him. I shoved the thought aside.

"I have to know," I said. "Is this temporary? Are you going to leave me again?"

Kade's expression turned solemn. "I swear to you," he said. "I will never leave you again."

My eyes stung, but I didn't want to cry. I pulled his head down, kissing him with everything I felt, sure that if I didn't find an outlet, the overwhelming love and joy and tenderness flooding through me would explode.

Kade kissed me back with the same desperation. I locked my arms around his neck, climbing out from underneath the covers until I was kneeling between his legs as he sat back on his haunches. His hands settled on my waist, my T-shirt riding up, and I impatiently pulled it up over my head and off.

Kade groaned, a sound that brought a smile to my lips, then my breath was torn from me when his mouth closed over a nipple. Pregnancy had increased the already acute sensitivity of my breasts, and Kade seemed to have figured that out pretty darn fast. His mouth and hands paid lavish attention to my breasts until all I could hear was a nonstop litany of whimpers and pleas falling from my lips. And all I could think about was the feel of his tongue, flicking against me before he sucked the flesh into his mouth. The insides of my thighs were coated with my arousal and I remained upright only because his hands were holding me up.

"Can we do this?" Kade asked, his lips moving against my skin. "I don't want to hurt the baby."

"I'm fine," I managed to gasp. "The baby's fine. Sex is fine, won't hurt the baby. Don't stop." If he didn't make love to me right then, he was going to be on the business end of one hell of a hissy fit.

Kade's hand slipped underneath the elastic waistband of my panties, the heat of his palm branding my rear as he tugged the fabric down my thighs. The next thing I knew, his fingers were pushing into me from behind. I choked on a cry, a keening sound coming from my throat as he teased me, thrusting his long fingers inside me, then spreading my arousal to my clit, coating the flesh with moisture until I couldn't breathe. Then he'd do it again, leisurely fucking me with two fingers, and all while his mouth, tongue, and teeth played relentlessly with my breasts.

I was hovering on the edge, each touch making me whimper and moan and beg until I couldn't think, couldn't process anything but what Kade was doing to me. I knew at some point I was mindlessly begging, each teasing brush of his fingers against my clit making my thighs tremble. I was so wet, I knew I should probably be embarrassed at the moisture dripping down my thighs, but was too far gone to care.

Kade suddenly withdrew his fingers and I moaned with disappointment. My eyes were closed but I felt his lips whisper against the skin of my neck, "Don't worry, princess. I won't leave you hanging."

Carefully turning me, Kade laid me across the bed on top of the covers, tugging my panties farther down my legs and off. I was beyond coherent thought, my fingers scrabbling at the shirt he wore. I wanted to feel his skin, wanted his body inside mine. Kade pulled his shirt over his head and tossed it. A moment later, his jeans were kicked aside as well. The sight of his straining erection had me lifting to my elbows to see more, but then he lay between my legs.

Bracing his weight on his arms, Kade gazed into my eyes. "Tell me if I hurt you," he said softly.

I was more than ready, and the head of his cock slipped easily inside me. I bent my knees, lifting my hips to eagerly take in more of him. Kade pushed forward, sheathing himself inside me, and I gasped. There was the tiniest twinge as my body accommodated his, then it was as though we'd never been apart.

Kade retreated then thrust hard into me, once, twice. That was all it took to send me splintering into a thousand pieces. He stilled inside me as my body gripped his, my orgasm rippling through me as though it were drawn from my toes. Dimly, I heard Kade groan at the sensation. I cried out, tears slipping from the corners of my eyes.

Kade started moving again before I'd even caught my breath. Our eyes locked and I couldn't look away. I wrapped my legs around his hips as the pressure built inside me once again. I lifted my hips to meet his thrusts, the hard length of him stroking me in just the right spot, as he moved faster. I couldn't help my eyes slipping shut as I moaned, repeating his name over and over like a litany, until I couldn't keep up with him. His hands dug into my hips and sweat dripped from his brow. He grew thicker inside me, moved faster, harder, until I couldn't hold out any longer.

Stars exploded behind my eyes as Kade's body jerked into mine, guttural moans and gasps filling the space between us. His mouth suddenly covered mine, his tongue sliding inside my mouth the way his cock was deep inside my body, and I clutched him to me as aftershocks rippled through us.

Kade tore his mouth away, gasping for breath as he settled heavily on top of me. He tried to roll away, but I tightened my arms and legs, holding him in place.

"I'm too heavy," he murmured in my ear.

"I like it," I whispered back.

He buried his face between my shoulder and neck,
kissing me there, his lips moving up to my jaw and cheek.
Tightening his arms around my waist, he rolled us over,
taking me with him so I lay on top of him. My legs settled
between his as I rested on his chest, the feel of his heartbeat
strong against the rhythm of mine. His lips brushed the top
of my head.

"I don't know how I thought I could live without you,"
he whispered.

I squeezed my eyes shut, gripping him tightly. "You
can't," I said before glancing up at him. "And don't you forget it."

His smile was crooked, and one hand brushed my hair
back from my face and over my shoulder. "I won't."

I was cold, so Kade rearranged us underneath the covers, my bare bottom nestled against his hips as he cuddled
me spoon style. His arm lay in the dip of my waist, his palm
pressed to my stomach. That made me self-conscious, thinking of the new bump protruding from my abdomen, and I
tried to unobtrusively move his hand higher.

"What's the matter?" he asked, the low timbre of his
voice in my ear sending a delicious shiver through me.

"Nothing," I hedged, "just adjusting, that's all." I laced
my fingers through his, drawing his hand upward.

"But I like it down here," he said, slipping his hand free
so it curved over my lower abdomen. "Please tell me you're

not going to get all weird and start thinking you're fat just because you're pregnant, are you?"

My cheeks flamed and I didn't answer because, well, when he put it like that, yeah, it sounded pretty dumb.

Kade suddenly loomed over me. "You know Branna was just being a bitch," he said. "Hey, look at me." His fingers tipped my chin up so our eyes met. "You're beautiful, and your body is gorgeous. You're creating a whole new life inside you, and there isn't a damn thing about it that doesn't amaze me."

Who would have thought Kade would know just the thing to say to ease all my worries and fears?

I reached up and pulled him down for a kiss, and this time when he pulled me back against his chest and his hand settled on the little bump we'd made, I didn't move away.

~

I woke to the sound of the door closing and sat up with a start.

Kade had just walked in and I guess I must have missed his departure, because he was fully dressed and setting two steaming cups and a paper bag down on the wood laminate table in the corner.

"Rise and shine," he said, hooking his sunglasses on his shirt. "I've got coffee."

It smelled wonderful, but I made myself go into the bathroom first. After brushing my teeth and showering, I came back out.

With one of the thin motel towels wrapped around me, I scurried over to the table for a cup of coffee. Kade had dug out his laptop and was sitting in front of it, a cup at his elbow. He glanced up, eyeing me with a predatory look in his eye.

"You'd better get some clothes on," he said. "Blane's on his way over and it'd be real awkward for him to walk in on me eating you for breakfast."

I think even my ears turned red at that, and I wasted no time grabbing my clothes and hustling back into the bathroom, Kade's soft laugh following me.

When I emerged again, both Branna and Blane were there. I was about to say something when I was startled by the sound of two people arguing in the room on the other side of us. My eyebrows shot up at some of the expletives hurled back and forth.

"Yeah, walls are pretty thin," Blane said, turning my attention back to him. "You can hear just about . . . everything."

Oh God.

Kade ignored him, with his and Branna's attention focused on the laptop, but I caught the message loud and clear. I swallowed hard, feeling the color leave my face. Blane's eyes were on mine, but I couldn't read his expression. While I knew he had come to grips with the fact that I was with Kade, I never intended to throw it in his face as blatantly as it seemed we'd done last night. I wasn't quiet during sex, never had been. It used to be one of the things Blane had really liked about me. Somehow I doubted he liked it much anymore.

"So go buy some fucking earplugs," Kade suddenly piped up, swinging around to look at Blane, a hint of challenge in his tone.

"Can we get back on task, please?" Branna broke in. "Lazaroff is definitely a regular member here, and judging by the people going in and out, I'd say he uses it as a base."

"Then we need to get in there tonight and see what he's got," Kade said.

"I think the easiest way is to just walk in the front door," Branna replied. "Pose as a player, flash some cash, we're in."

"Sounds good," Kade said. "We need to run by the electronics store, pick up a few things—"

"Hold on, wait a second," Blane interrupted. "You and Branna are just going to go after this guy and, what, leave me and Kathleen here to watch the walls? I don't think so."

I was surprised he'd included me, but hey, I wasn't going to complain.

"Suddenly you want to put Kathleen in harm's way?" Kade asked in mock disbelief. "That's not like you." His derision had Blane's jaw tightening.

"If you're implying that I wouldn't want to keep her safe just because she's with you now, then you can go to hell," Blane bit out. "I just know her well enough to get that she's not going to stay behind while the three of us go to this place."

Damn straight.

Kade's eyes narrowed. "Fine. We'll *all* go. Happy?"

Of course, I hadn't realized that apparently the role Branna and I would be filling was as arm candy for Blane and Kade. Well, she obviously had more to offer, given her training and technical skills. I was solely decoration, it seemed.

Blane and Kade had left, returning later with clothes for all of us. Suits for them, dresses for me and Branna. Of course, arm candy couldn't wear normal dresses.

Branna and I wore identical skintight sheaths that left our shoulders bare and ended right above mid-thigh. Mine was gold, hers silver. The guys had even managed to find matching designer stilettos. I did my hair and makeup to match, then eyed myself critically in the mirror. I looked pretty good, I guess, for what the purpose was tonight. I felt like I was showing way too much skin, but if I pulled the dress up to try and cover more of my boobs, then it just showed more thigh. Another couple of tugs and my vagina would be showing.

I exited the bathroom and struck a playful pose. "How do I look?" I asked.

"It's about time," Kade said, tucking his gun into his holster before glancing up. I did a little twirl for him, gratified when his eyes widened slightly.

"Holy shit," he breathed.

"I'll take that as a compliment," I teased, giving him a similar once-over. He'd opted for black on black, big surprise, and looked so good I wondered exactly how much time we had before we had to leave . . .

Kade approached me, taking my hand and leading me to the table. "Let's try and fit one more thing into that dress," he said. "Put your foot on the chair."

Wondering what exactly he could be doing, I obeyed, lifting my foot to the seat of the chair. Kade reached behind him, then inched my skirt even farther up my leg and fastened a thin knife sheath to the top of my thigh. His cologne drifted to me and I inhaled greedily.

"The knife isn't big, but it's sharp and it'll do some damage," he said, tightening the strap. I tried to focus on what he was saying and not on the feel of his hands touching me. His face was mere inches away and my eyes dropped to his mouth as he spoke. I must not have been that successful in concealing what I was really thinking, because he suddenly asked, "Are you even listening to me?"

I quickly nodded. "Of course," I said. "Small but sharp. Got it."

Kade's lips twisted in a smirk as he gazed intently into my eyes. "Somehow I think your mind's on . . . other things." His fingers drifted farther up my thigh to lightly touch between my legs. I sucked in a breath, my nails digging into his biceps.

He leaned forward, putting his lips to my ear. "You look like you want to be fucked," he murmured, sending my pulse into overdrive. He easily pushed aside the scrap of lace that covered me. I bit back a moan as a long finger pushed inside me.

"So wet," he whispered against the skin of my neck. "Tell me you only get that way for me."

But I couldn't speak, my whole attention focused on the slow slide of his finger inside me.

"Tell me," he repeated, withdrawing his finger. He brushed my clit, then circled the entrance to my body, teasing me. "Tell me you only want me."

"Just you," I managed to gasp. "I only want you."

"Tell me no one gets you dripping wet like I do," he said, his words a low growl in my ear. His finger slid inside me again and I clung to him, trying to stay on my feet.

I pried open my eyes to see Kade watching me. The expression on his face was fierce, his blue eyes blazing.

"No one makes me wet like you do," I repeated, my voice breathless. "Only you can do this to me." It felt freeing to say what he'd ordered me to say, as strange a dichotomy as that sounded. The words seemed to have an effect on Kade, too, because before I knew it, my panties were gone and he was unzipping his pants. A moment later, my dress was hiked to my waist and my back was pressed against the wall as Kade buried himself inside me.

It was hard and fast, and Kade's tongue in my mouth kept my noises to a minimum. I came in a shuddering climax only seconds before Kade, then we were both panting for breath as he kissed his way down my neck. My legs were hooked around his waist and when I let my feet slip back to the ground, my knees trembled under my weight.

I heard the sound of Kade's zipper as he put himself to rights and I tugged my dress back down.

"Gimme a minute," I said against his mouth, his lingering kisses making me regret pulling away. I returned to the bathroom to clean up and put my underwear back on. My eyes were bright and my cheeks flushed, but I couldn't make myself regret the immensely satisfying interlude with Kade. My body was humming with pleasure and I couldn't help a satisfied smile as I reapplied my lipstick. It was good to know Kade was as susceptible to me as I was to him.

The plan seemed solid. Find this guy Lazaroff, figure out what he had on Keaston, confront Keaston, then Kade and I live happily ever after without having to look over our shoulders, and Blane is at last free from his uncle's machinations and able to live his own life.

Of course, everyone knows what they say about the best-laid plans.

They always get shot to hell.

CHAPTER FOURTEEN

The four of us checked out of the motel, then drove both cars to the location, what with Blane and Kade wanting to cover all the bases, and we met up on the sidewalk in front of the place.

Blane and Kade were dressed in suits that I knew cost thousands of dollars each. Kade wore entirely black—black slacks, black silk shirt, black jacket. Blane wore deep charcoal gray with an identical black shirt. Side by side, Kade with his inky-black hair and Blane with his dark blond, they looked mouthwatering, two sides of the same dangerous coin. The expensive fabric of their suits enhanced the hard edge of their collective presence, making them appear formidable and deadly.

Branna looked gorgeous in her silver dress and I noticed with more than a little envy that her waist was narrower than mine. She carried a small clutch bag and I wondered if she had a knife strapped to her thigh like I did.

Although the three of them had spent the afternoon planning, trying to think up all contingencies, the extent of my role seemed to be "stick close and don't get hurt." I hoped that would be as easy as it sounded.

"Ready or not," Kade said in a little singsong voice, his lips twisting as he looked to Blane, who gave a curt nod, his expression much more grim than Kade's.

The entrance was guarded by two huge guys, twins by the look of them. I ignored them as I hung on to Kade, his arm wrapped around my waist. Branna was similarly draped on Blane. Money changed hands and we were allowed to pass. We followed a third guy into an elevator with red fabric covering the walls. He didn't speak and let us out on an indeterminate floor.

The hallway was shadowed, dark wood paneling the walls. Heavy, antique brass sconces glowed on the walls, lighting the way to a set of double doors with long, twisted wood handles. The carpet was thick and red, an oriental style that seemed vaguely out of place. It felt like we were going into a place run by vampires who took Hollywood stereotypes way too seriously.

Kade clasped my hand as he opened the door. I took a deep breath, trying to calm my racing heart, and sent up a prayer that we'd all be okay by the time tonight was said and done.

The room was full of people, the noise hitting us as we walked in. They surrounded what I could see were gaming tables. Not like in Vegas, with flashing lights and bells, but serious card tables that were for serious players. A few of the patrons looked our way when we entered, most taking a quick glimpse of Blane and Kade before returning their attention to whatever they'd been doing.

I could pick out the security guys immediately, especially since they didn't seem to try and hide their presence. Big men, the guns attached to their hips visible, though all were dressed well, which seemed to be a theme. If I'd been worried we might be overdressed, that fear was immediately put to rest. The men were dressed in suits, and the women— a minority of probably one to ten among the men—were wearing dresses as slinky as mine or even more so.

I had a sneaking suspicion that most of those women were actually prostitutes. Nice.

Blane and Kade leisurely circled the room. I kept my eye out, counting the security guys and seeing if I could find any exits other than the doors through which we'd entered. A table with two empty seats sat in one corner and Kade headed toward it.

"Mind if we join you?" Kade asked those seated at the table in general, his smile thin, his eyes calculating. None of the men objected, so the dealer gestured for Blane and Kade to sit. Several pairs of eyes took in the cut of Blane's and Kade's suits, the Rolex on Blane's wrist, the flash of metal at Kade's side.

I took up a position mirroring Branna, who stood next to but slightly behind Blane. Kade drew my arm over his shoulder while the dealer dealt the cards.

I knew nothing about poker other than what could be gleaned from watching television and movies, and it became rapidly apparent that whatever game they were playing was far beyond my level of understanding.

A man came by to exchange the large wads of cash Blane and Kade gave him for chips. My eyes widened at the stacks in front of them, and as they began to grow with each successive hand.

I immediately realized they must have passed hours playing poker when they were younger, because each of them seemed to almost instinctively know if the other one held a winning or losing hand. Soon the only question at the table was who would win—Blane or Kade. The pile of chips grew taller and wider, and I could sense the growing disgruntlement and suspicion from the other players.

My feet grew tired as time passed and I shifted my weight, trying to ease the ache in my lower back. Branna caught my eye and frowned. I resisted the urge to stick my tongue out at her. I guess being uncomfortable wasn't sexy.

Two of the men at the table began conversing in Russian, it sounded like, and it didn't take a genius to realize they were discussing Blane and Kade. To my shock, Kade opened his mouth and spoke as well. In Russian.

Of course I couldn't understand a word he said, save one. *Lazaroff.*

The men eyed him, then one of them raised his hand and crooked a finger, signaling someone behind us. I turned just as whomever he must have called over stepped up behind us.

"If you'll come with me," the man said in heavily accented English.

Kade and Blane stood. "You'll cash these in for us, right?" Kade asked the guy, gesturing to the pile of chips. I could tell by the sarcasm in his voice that we'd never see any of that money again and a little part of me sighed at the loss. Such a waste.

"The women stay," the man said, gesturing for a security dude to block me and Branna from following. "Just you two."

Alarm shot through me and I thought fast. "Back off," I snapped at the security guy. "You may do your job just for fun, but I get paid to do mine and he's my paycheck."

"Find another john," he said, dismissing me with a hard shove. I stumbled back and Branna caught me. I righted myself quickly.

Blane didn't look like he was going to go, but Kade grabbed his arm, shooting Branna a look. A moment later, they were taken through a dark doorway and disappeared from view.

Branna grabbed my hand. "Let's go," she said, pulling me through the room.

Shocked, I stumbled after her and then managed to jerk back, stopping us. "What are you doing?" I hissed, trying to keep my voice down. "We can't just leave them."

"Kade was very clear on what I was to do if we got separated and that was to get *you* out of here," she said. Branna didn't look at me as she said this, her eyes scanning the room.

"What are you talking about?" I asked. "And since when do you give a shit about what happens to me?"

Her green eyes met mine. "Since Kade is in love with you and you're carrying his child." Her gaze flitted over me. "I suppose we can't help who we fall in love with," she muttered.

"I'm not just going to leave when God knows what could be happening back there," I said. "And as much as you care about Kade, I'm surprised you'd want to, no matter what he told you to do."

Branna huffed a frustrated breath. "Fine," she said. "But just remember that you're the liability here. Frankly, I'd have been happier if we'd left you behind."

That's the thing about Branna—it wasn't exactly a mystery where you stood with her.

"Follow me," she said.

We made our way through the crowded room, keeping close to the walls. I could see where she was heading, a dark door near where we had entered. We were almost there when I was brought up short by a hard grip on my arm.

"Where are you going?" One of the security guys had hold of me, his eyes narrowing in suspicion as he looked at me.

"I-I, um . . ." I stammered, completely at a loss as to what to say.

"Viktor told us he had a special client," Branna suddenly piped up next to me. "We're freshening up first."

I held my breath as the guard seemed to consider that, then he nodded. "Hurry up then," he growled, giving me a shove as he released me.

A moment later, we were through the door and I breathed a sigh of relief. "Who's Viktor?" I asked.

Branna shrugged. "It was a guess. They're Russians. Gotta be a Viktor here somewhere."

I swallowed. Quick thinking, I supposed, but I shuddered at what might have happened if there hadn't been a Viktor.

We were in a short hallway with two doors to the left.

"Which one?" I asked.

Branna didn't say anything, but she hesitated before reaching for a handle and I figured she probably didn't know any more than I did.

She pulled open the door, and my heart dropped to my feet.

There was an entire table of men playing cards, all guards by the look of them, and every one of them turned toward us.

"We were just looking for Viktor," Branna said. "Sorry to interrupt."

One of the men, bigger than the others, pushed himself back from the table and stood. "I'm Viktor," he said. "Who are you?"

Oh shit.

Branna slammed the door shut without a word and I opened the second door without being asked. I could hear men shouting and the scrape of chairs as we burst through the second door into a long narrow hallway.

"Run!" Branna said, kicking off her shoes. I wasted no time in copying her, the Jimmy Choos another casualty of the evening as we both sprinted down the hall.

I heard the door slam against the wall as the men came through, yelling at us. We threw ourselves through a door at the other end, which happened to open to a stairwell.

"Up!" Branna said, which was the exact opposite direction I'd intended. I obeyed, though, hightailing it upstairs. We hit the top landing just as the stairwell filled with the sound of the men. Branna clapped her hand over my mouth and hers, stifling our breathing.

We waited as the men spoke tersely in Russian, then listened as they hurried down the stairs, disappearing into each floor. When I thought they were all gone, Branna carefully removed her hand from my mouth, then placed a finger over her lips. I nodded to show I understood.

Since we couldn't go down, it looked like we were stuck with entering the top floor. The doorknob turned easily in my hand and I closed my eyes, sending up a quick prayer.

The hallway was empty, thank God. I let out a relieved breath.

"Now what?" I asked in a low voice.

"Now you come with me."

I squeaked and spun around in alarm. Viktor stood there with a gun pointed at us, and now I saw the camera mounted in the ceiling, facing the stairwell door.

"Okay," I managed, raising my hands in a gesture of surrender. Branna did the same.

Viktor made us walk in front of him into an opulent office. The carpet was the same thick and red oriental style, the furniture dark, heavy wood. A computer sat on a desk and the window overlooked the city lights.

"Over there," he said.

I complied but Branna hesitated. He prodded her in the back with the gun. "Move."

Branna suddenly turned and knocked the gun from his hand, then they were fighting. I watched in stunned amazement as Branna held her own, but it soon became obvious that she was tiring and unable to get the upper hand on the huge Russian.

I winced when he knocked her down, then Viktor had Branna by the throat and slammed her against the wall. She whimpered at the pain. He spoke in Russian and though I couldn't understand what he was saying, I could tell by the way he said it that it wasn't good.

Reaching under my dress, I pulled out the knife Kade had given me. My palms were slick with sweat and I wasn't sure I'd be able to do what I had to do. I didn't want to use his gun, afraid the noise would bring more of them. But knives were an up close and personal kind of weapon. Viktor was choking Branna, her feet dangling and not even touching the floor, and hesitating was no longer an option.

Moving stealthily forward, I gripped the knife tight, then lunged.

Viktor roared in pain and rage, releasing Branna to try and twist to grab the knife out of his back. When that didn't work, he focused on me, a fist flying and catching me on the temple, the force of the blow knocking me aside.

A gunshot sounded and I flinched, but it was Viktor who staggered, then fell. I scrambled out of the way as his body toppled heavily to the floor.

Branna stood behind him, gun in her hand. That must've been what she'd been carrying in her purse. I guess she wasn't worried about the noise.

My head throbbed from where he'd hit me and both of us were breathing hard. Branna had livid marks around her neck from where he'd choked her.

"Thanks," she said, her voice too rough. "I didn't expect that from you."

I frowned. "I know I can't do what you can, but I wasn't going to let him kill you. Not if I could help it."

Branna's laugh was bitter and hoarse. "I've beat the shit out of you, said horrible things to you, made it very clear I hate you. I would've let me die."

I swallowed. "No, you wouldn't have," I said.

Her gaze swung from Viktor's body to meet mine. "You might've let me die if you knew I slept with Blane last night."

I gaped at her in shock, anger and hurt flooding through me. Blane and Branna had had sex? A day after they met? Blane knew Branna hated me, had hurt me, yet he'd still slept with her?

Branna must have read the look on my face, because her expression hardened. "Kade was everything to me," she said. "I love him, and you took him."

"I took nothing," I retorted, my fists clenching in anger. "Kade loves you, but he's never been *in* love with you, Branna. And I'm sorry you've never faced it, but that's not my fault." I took a breath, trying to calm my fury. "So you slept with Blane to get back at me?"

"You and Kade were fucking like rabbits next door," she sneered, "a really lovely thing to do to your former fiancé, by the way. Blane and I were both hurting. Did you expect we weren't the kind of people to take comfort where it can be found?"

Well, that took some of the heat from my anger, and I couldn't think of a thing to say.

Branna retrieved Viktor's gun from where it had fallen onto the floor, then handed it to me. "I'll trust you not to put a bullet in my back," she said. "Watch the door." She hurried behind the desk to the computer.

I held the gun steady in my hands and trained it on the one door. My nerves were strung tight, my heart pounding so hard from the adrenaline in my veins that it felt like I'd been injected with ice water. We were surrounded by bad guys and I had no idea how we were going to get out. And on top of that, my nemesis had slept with my ex while I slept with his brother. God, this was so messed up.

It seemed like Branna was taking forever. "What are you doing?" I asked, keeping my eyes on the door. "We need to get out of here."

"It'd be pretty pointless to get this far and not see if there's anything on their system that we can use," Branna said dryly.

"Then hurry it up," I snapped. "If you do find something, it'll be pretty pointless if we're dead."

"I'm trying," she ground out, "but they have advanced encryption. I need Kade."

Suddenly, the door swung open. I sucked in a breath, my finger tightening on the trigger, and I only just stopped myself from firing in time.

Blane and Kade stepped inside, each of them holding a gun. Blane looked surprised to see us; Kade just looked pissed.

"What the hell, Branna?" Kade barked. "I thought I was pretty fucking clear on what your instructions were."

"Shut up and get over here and help me," she retorted.

I noticed both Blane and Kade didn't look as put together as they had before. Their clothes were slightly askew, and now I could see cuts and bruises on their faces and hands. They'd been fighting, maybe with the same guys who'd come after us.

"I thought they were taking you to see Lazaroff?" I asked.

"Point that somewhere else, Kat," Blane said, motioning to the gun I held. Embarrassed, I lowered my arm. I hadn't even realized I was still pointing it at them. Then the first thing that flew through my head was an image of Blane and Branna having sex.

"Are you all right?" Blane asked, moving over to stand next to me while Kade headed for Branna. His eyes examined me.

It was only by mustering a great deal of self-control that I didn't say what was on the tip of my tongue. I'd ended it with Blane, and if he wanted to sleep with the goddamn Rockettes, then that was his prerogative.

"I'm just fine," I said stiffly. Our eyes met. His lips thinned.

"She told you," he said quietly.

"Was it a secret?" I asked, trying and failing to keep a lid on my anger.

"What, am I supposed to apologize to you now?" Blane asked, his words bitter.

I stepped closer. "You once told me I'd gotten my revenge," I hissed. "So congratulations. You have, too."

"Whatever drama you two have playing out over there, can we save it for later?" Kade interrupted. "Blane, you need to see this."

Blane broke our staring contest, heading over behind the desk. I remained where I was. Whatever was on the computer, I doubted I'd be able to make heads or tails of it.

"I didn't realize Keaston had such ties to the Department of Energy," Kade said.

Blane's voice was grim when he replied. "It certainly looks like it pays well. Are you getting this?"

Kade hit a few more keys. "Uploading now. It'll be safe on my server."

A smell suddenly hit my nostrils, sickly sweet and thick, just as I heard a thin, hissing sound behind me. I turned around.

"Does anyone else smell—" And then I couldn't breathe, choking and gasping on the cloud of white coming from the vent in the wall in front of me and aimed right at my face.

"Tear gas!" Blane said. "They know we're in here. Get Kat!"

I dropped the gun, my hands covering my nose and mouth while my eyes streamed, the burning sensation nearly unbearable. I couldn't see anything and I stumbled back, trying to get away from the vapor inching its way through the room.

Arms closed around me and I was lifted bodily. I could feel us moving, then we were out of the room, the fog gone.

But I'd been too close to it, breathed too much in, and still coughed and choked. I was blind, my eyes burning so badly I'd be crying even if water wasn't already streaming from my eyes.

Kade, I think, had his arm wrapped around me and I clung to him, trying to stay on my feet.

"Gentlemen," someone said, "I was told you wanted to see me."

Kade pressed some fabric into my hand, his pocket square, maybe, and I used it to wipe my face.

"You were told wrong," Kade said. "We were just on our way out, but if you'd validate our parking, that'd be a big help."

The man laughed and now I could sort of see him, at least the outline of him. He was tall and broad, and there were a half dozen men surrounding us, all pointing what I assumed were guns.

"You were in my office, accessing my files," Lazaroff said. "The only part of a car you're going to see is the inside of a trunk." His voice hardened. "Now drop your weapons."

"Not a big chance of that happening," Kade replied.

"You're surrounded. One word from me and you're dead. Drop your weapons."

Kade glanced at Blane, who gave a curt nod. I heard the dull thud as Blane, Kade, and Branna dropped their guns.

"I have a . . . gift, you might say," Lazaroff continued, "for finding the weakest link. It's come in helpful over the years." He paused. "Two men invade my place of business, hack my computer system, and overall seem quite competent. So why bring along two females?"

This didn't look to be going anywhere good. I squinted, my cheeks still wet from my teary eyes, and saw his head turn my way.

"Bring me that one," Lazaroff said, pointing at me. Two men immediately closed in.

Kade's arm tightened, yanking me closer. "I don't think so," he said, his voice like ice.

I panicked, knowing that resisting could very well get Kade hurt, maybe killed. "No, don't!" I said, pushing against him to free myself. "You'll just get hurt." Kade made a grab for me, but I backed away just as the two guys got between us.

I stumbled back but caught myself, blinking fast to try and clear my vision. I wasn't thrilled with being called the "weakest link," but considering the four of us, I couldn't disagree.

Warily, I approached Lazaroff, stopping when I was just out of reach, but it didn't matter because a guard grabbed my arm and yanked me right up to him.

"What's your name, *milaya moya?*"

I didn't know what to say. Should I tell him the truth? The guard twisted my arm hard, up behind my back, and I cried out.

"Name," Lazaroff repeated.

"Kathleen," I gasped. "Kathleen Turner."

"And why are all of you here, Kathleen?"

Well, I certainly couldn't tell him that. I pressed my lips closed because I knew what was coming wouldn't be pleasant.

"We'll tell you," Blane said. "You don't have to hurt the girl."

Glad to know he still cared.

"Ah, but what if I want to hurt the girl?" Lazaroff replied. "By the looks of you two, hurting you might prove somewhat arduous. Whereas hurting the girl"—he reached out and gripped my jaw—"is much easier, and highly effective." He hit me without any warning, the flat of his palm striking my face with enough force to knock me down had the guard not been holding me up. As it was, my knees buckled, which put more pressure on my shoulder, with my arm still twisted up behind me, and a whimper escaped as I tried to regain my shaky footing.

It was immediately apparent that Lazaroff's actions had provoked a response, because I could hear Blane and Kade yelling and cursing. I shook my head to clear it, only to have Lazaroff grab my jaw again.

Then I hauled off and kneed him in the nuts.

Smart idea? Probably not, but I wasn't about to be a punching bag just to torment Blane and Kade. I'd been hit twice tonight, and I thought I'd better not start keeping count or things were going to get really depressing, really fast.

Everything seemed to stop as the guards looked in horror at what I'd done. Lazaroff was bent over, his hands cupping his abused crotch.

Then all hell broke loose.

CHAPTER FIFTEEN

I heard gunshots and the man holding me suddenly let go. I fell to the floor, my arms instinctively coming up to cover my head. I couldn't make sense of the forms swirling around me—they were moving too fast and my vision was still too blurred by the tear gas. I prayed while I made myself as small as possible on the floor, then realized that Lazaroff was lying next to me . . . and that he was dead.

It was all over in a few minutes and I lay amid the carnage of dead men. Someone's hands landed on me and I cringed in terror.

"It's me, baby," Kade said. "It's okay."

I threw my arms around his neck and clung to him. His hands settled on my waist as he lifted me to my feet.

"Is everyone okay?" I asked. "Blane and Branna, are they hurt?"

"We're fine, Kat," Blane said from behind me. Kade released me and Blane pulled me close, his lips brushing my forehead. "Jesus, Kat," he said. "I think I lost a few years off my life when you kneed him like that."

"She gave us the opportunity we needed," Branna defended me.

I blinked blearily, wishing I could see properly to make out their faces. As it was, everything was a blur.

Kade pulled me back from Blane, an arm resting protectively behind my back.

"Let's get out of here before more of them come," Kade said.

I wasn't sure how they knew the way out, but they did, finding a stairwell behind a door that dumped us into a dark alley. I half walked and was half carried by Kade.

"Follow me," Blane said. "I'm not staying in some flea-bag dive tonight, and neither is Kat."

Kade didn't argue. He had me buckled inside his Mercedes in a flash and we were driving down the street.

I closed my burning eyes, settling back against the leather seat with a deep sigh. Kade found my hand resting between us and laced our fingers together.

We pulled up to a hotel whose sign I couldn't quite make out, but I could tell the place was expensive. The lobby seemed deserted at this hour and I was glad for that, since I for one looked a mess.

The four of us had adjoining rooms, and the first thing Kade did once the heavy door swung shut behind him and me was take me into the bathroom and sit me down on the closed toilet. He then doused a washcloth and patted gently at my eyes.

"How are you feeling?" he asked.

"I'll be okay," I said. The water felt heavenly.

After a few minutes, I felt well enough to wash my eyes out in the sink. Ten minutes after that, I could actually see again, but then I wished I couldn't.

The skin around my eyes looked like I'd been burned. My eyes were bloodshot worse than the most awful hangover I'd ever had. My face was blotchy and I had an angry red welt on one cheek from Lazaroff.

I came out of the bathroom, toweling my face dry, then stopped short in shock.

Kade had been beat up, with blood from his nose and his mouth now dried on his face. The skin across the bridge of his nose had been sliced, more blood oozing from it, and there was a long cut by his eye.

He'd broken open the minibar and was drinking whiskey straight from the bottle.

"Oh my God," I breathed, hurrying to him. "They did this to you?"

He caught my hand in his as I reached to touch his face. "It's okay, princess. I just didn't take too well to Lazaroff hitting you. Neither did Blane."

I knew then that he and Blane must've gone for broke to get us out of that mess, and that it had been a near thing.

Going back into the bathroom, I got a fresh washcloth and wet it. Making Kade sit on the bed, I knelt next to him and tried as carefully as I could to clean him up. There was a lot of blood, more than the last time I'd cleaned him up so long ago at The Drop.

"Did we get what we needed?" I asked. Was what we'd gone through worth it?

Kade nodded. "Yeah, we did."

I gave a sigh of relief. "Let me rinse this out," I said. "You've got a lot of blood on you." I moved to get up, but Kade grabbed me, his mouth settling on mine in a fierce kiss.

I dropped the washcloth as Kade's hand cradled the back of my head. His tongue stroked mine, the slight tang of blood reminding me of how close a call we'd had, and suddenly I was kissing him back just as hard.

My fingers tore at his shirt, his jacket already discarded, and in moments I had it off him. He pushed the top of my dress down to my stomach, freeing my breasts. I climbed onto his lap, pushing him down onto his back. In seconds, I had his belt and pants undone, and his hard cock in my hand.

He groaned, tugging the bottom of my dress up until it was around my waist. I shoved my panties down and settled atop him, his erection pushing inside me in one smooth thrust.

I bit my lip at the sensation, my eyes sliding shut. His hands settled on my hips and instinct took over as well as a little madness. We both could've been killed tonight, and somehow that fact made it more urgent, more desperate.

I couldn't live without him.

Kade's hips rose in counterpoint to mine, our bodies slamming together, making my breasts bounce, not that I cared. If the things Kade was saying were any indication, he seemed to enjoy the view, and as some of his words penetrated the haze engulfing my mind, my cheeks flamed. Yet I grew even wetter until, if I'd been in my right mind, I would have been embarrassed at the wet noises his cock made sliding in and out of me.

Pressing his hands on my back, Kade forced me down, his palm cradling my head again as we kissed, our tongues and teeth clashing with little finesse. His other arm curved over my lower back, stilling my movements as he jackknifed hard into me. He held me immobile, his tongue and cock fucking me, and I whimpered, allowing him to claim me even as it seemed I was in the dominant position. Heat exploded between my legs as I came, Kade swallowing my cries. Then he was pulsing inside me, holding me so tightly to him that the jerking of his cock made another orgasm crash over me.

I collapsed against his chest, the pounding of Kade's heart loud in my ear. I knew I'd never tire of hearing that sound, not after the many times he could've been taken from me.

I was exhausted and could have just rolled over and slept, but Kade ran a bath and soon had both of us in the steaming water, my back to his front as I sat between his spread legs. It was a really nice hotel, with the kind of bath-tub I'd never even realized they put in hotels.

He had one of those big natural sponges, squeezing warm water over my shoulders and chest as we relaxed.

"Your eyes look better," he said.

"Yeah, they feel better. Not an experience I'd like to re-peat, though." That tear gas had hurt. "Was Branna okay?" I couldn't stop thinking about her. Had she gotten beat up, too? I knew she could fight, but she was so little . . .

"Yeah," Kade replied. "She's fast. It's hard to lay a hand on her."

I debated saying something more, took a breath and then let it out.

Kade stilled. "What?" he asked.

I shook my head. "It's nothing. None of my business."

"Tell me," Kade said in my ear, "or I'll be forced to use dire measures." His fingers trailed a path down my side and I giggled, arching away.

"It's nothing, really, I guess . . ." I decided to just say it. "Branna and Blane had sex."

Kade said nothing for a moment, then resumed trickling water on me. "How do you know?"

"Branna told me."

He sighed. "So how do you feel about this unexpected development, Kathleen?" His voice held a trace of mockery. I turned to look up at him and he shrugged, raising an eyebrow. "I can't pretend I'm glad that you're concerned about who Blane sleeps with."

I frowned. "It has nothing to do with you," I said. "It's just . . . he barely knows her. What he does know of her is that she hates me."

"There's more to Branna than her hating you," Kade said. "Do you think I'd have stuck with her if she wasn't someone worth caring about?"

Now I felt guilty and embarrassed. I didn't answer.

"Hey," Kade said, lightly grasping my chin and making me turn to face him, "I understand. I do. But you've got to let it go." He paused. "Unless you're regretting the choice you made?"

"No," I said immediately. "I love you. It's just harder than I thought . . . letting go."

Kade's brows were drawn together as he studied me, and he gave a short nod. "Time. Space. That's what we need," he said.

I agreed. I lay against his chest, wrapping my arms around his waist. He trickled water on my back and we sat in silence for a while as the water cooled. Finally, I said, "Is it weird?"

"Is what weird?" Kade asked. He'd stopped trickling water and now his fingers drew wet patterns on my back.

"You and Blane. Me and Branna. Both of you have slept with the same two women. Isn't that . . . weird?" I said "weird," though other adjectives came to mind.

Kade laughed, taking me by surprise. I sat back, looking up at him in confusion. I certainly hadn't been thinking "funny."

"Princess, look at me," Kade said, his lips twisting in a half smile. "I've got gunshot scars, knife scars, and scars I don't even want to remember how I got from a life I didn't give a shit about living until I met you. The last thing I'm going to worry about or dwell on is your past lovers, even if I share a bloodline with one of them."

What could I possibly say to that? He loved me, didn't care about my past, and wanted to be with me. He was right. I needed to let it go. Blane and Branna didn't concern me anymore. Kade and our unborn child were my world now.

I wrapped my arms around his neck and kissed him the best I knew how. He held me close and it seemed the past finally slid off my shoulders.

∾

I eyed my reflection, nerves making me bit my lip. I was dressed in a somber black-and-white dress that hit just below the knees. A thin belt circled my waist and I wore sensible black heels.

"I feel like we're going to a funeral," I said to Kade, glancing over my shoulder to see he was tying his tie. He was also dressed formally, in a black suit, white shirt, and black tie. I moved in front of him and brushed his hands aside as they fiddled with the tie.

"Now I know why you never wear a tie," I teased, undoing the uneven knot and starting over.

"We *are* going to a funeral," Kade replied, allowing me to fix the silk. "Figuratively, anyway. Time to put a nail in the coffin of Uncle Robert."

"Is Blane going to be able to do that?" I asked. I knew how much Robert meant to Blane, and I'd yet to ask him how he really felt since he'd realized all his great-uncle had done to control him—to the point of putting Kade and me in mortal danger.

"He has to," Kade said grimly. "If he doesn't, I will—only my solution will be much more permanent." His smile was thin and cold.

"I thought we couldn't just kill him," I said.

"Blane can't," Kade replied. "But I can."

I grabbed his arm. "No, you can't," I said. "I need you. The baby needs you. You can't throw yourself in harm's way anymore. Not even for Blane."

Kade's eyes narrowed.

"Promise me," I said, taking his face in my palms. "Don't do something that could leave me to raise this baby alone."

His piercing blue eyes searched mine. "I promise," he said finally.

We met Blane and Branna in the lobby, where Blane was checking all of us out of the hotel. Branna was the only one not dressed up, instead wearing jeans and a shirt. She gave us a nod as we approached her, taking a sip of coffee from the paper cup she held.

I sucked in a breath when Blane joined us, the marks on his face mirroring Kade's. He glanced at me, then slid his sunglasses on.

"Your eyes look better," he remarked. "No other ill effects from the tear gas, I hope?"

I shook my head. "I'm fine."

We headed outside and that's when I realized we were within walking distance of the Capitol building, which is precisely where we headed. Except for Branna. She branched off toward where we'd parked last night.

"Isn't she coming with us?" I asked.

"Thought we might need a quick exit," Blane explained, "so she's going to be nearby with the car."

"So why am I coming along? I'm not exactly family." And it wasn't like I trusted myself to be in the same room with Senator Keaston without trying to hurt him.

"Aren't you?" Blane asked. I glanced up at him. A soft smile played at the edges of his lips.

Reaching down, he took my hand, and that was how we walked up the Capitol steps and into the building—Kade on one side of me, my hand firmly clasped in his, and Blane on the other. I hoped I was able to give something to them in the same way they both gave strength and courage to me.

We went through security, Blane showing them a special ID he took from his wallet, then we were allowed to pass.

There were throngs of people everywhere, but Blane seemed to know where he was going. Before long we stood in front of a large wooden door with a bronze placard, emblazoned with *Senator Robert W. Keaston*, on the wall next to it. Underneath his name was *MASSACHUSETTS*. Blane rapped twice on the door, then walked in.

An older woman sat behind a large desk made from cherry wood. Two flags stood in a corner of the room, one an American flag, the other the state flag of Massachusetts, I assumed. The woman glanced up.

"Mr. Kirk," she said with a smile. "It's been a while since you've been up to see the senator."

"Hi, Jackie. Been a while since I've been to Washington," Blane replied, his easy smile making the dimple appear in his cheek. "Is he in?"

"He's in a meeting at the moment," Jackie said, "but you're welcome to wait in his office."

"Thank you," Blane replied. He held open another door, allowing me and Kade to step inside the senator's office. Jackie eyed me curiously but didn't ask any questions. Blane softly closed the door behind him.

The office wasn't terribly large, but then again, I thought space was probably at a premium in this building. There was a gray marble fireplace situated between two windows. Another cherry wood desk took up a good amount of space along one wall and a thick oriental-style rug covered the floor. A large portrait painting of John Adams hung behind the desk.

Two leather armchairs flanked an antique table along the wall opposite the desk and that's where Kade sat. He slid his sunglasses into the inside pocket of his suit coat and crossed an ankle over the other knee. Taking a small device from another pocket, he flicked a tiny switch.

"That should take care of any listening devices within a twenty-foot radius," he said, sliding it back into his pocket.

Blane nodded. He seemed restless, moving around the room, stopping to gaze out the window. My heart hurt for him. The look on his face was stark, grim. I went up to him, resting my hand on his arm. He glanced down at me and it seemed I didn't have to say anything. He read my face, then lifted a hand to cup my cheek, his thumb brushing gently across my skin. Sliding his hand underneath my hair to the back of my neck, he drew me closer, brushing a kiss to my forehead.

"Don't worry," he said softly.

The door opened and the man I hated walked in.

Senator Keaston looked like any other powerful politician, and his expression said that while he wasn't surprised to see us, he wasn't happy about it, either.

"Did I miss the memo on a family meeting?" The senator's words were chiding, but his gaze was calculating as he took in Kade, me, and Blane. He settled into the chair behind the desk.

"I prefer not to claim you," Kade said, his lips twisting into a chilly smirk.

The senator glared at him. "Likewise, boy," he said, his voice rife with contempt. He turned and gazed my way. "And I see you've brought the trash in with you."

Blane stiffened and Kade's eyes narrowed dangerously. I tightened my grip on Blane's arm, but he didn't make a move toward Keaston. Instead, he turned to me, solicitously taking my hand and drawing me across the room to sit in the chair next to Kade. My knees were shaking, so sitting down seemed like a great idea. After I sank into the seat, Blane's hand brushed my hair back before he turned again to face Keaston.

"I think it's time you and I had a talk, Uncle," Blane said, approaching the desk. He leaned one shoulder against the fireplace and crossed his arms over his chest. "You've lied to me, manipulated me, tried to hurt the people I love. Why?"

"It sounds like you've been listening a bit too much to Kade," Keaston replied, raising an eyebrow.

"Matt Summers confessed," Blane said. "He said you were behind Kathleen being taken. You know, by the sex traffickers who would have sold her to the highest bidder for a life of misery, for however long she lasted?" His voice was hard. "And before you start saying he was lying, Matt had a gun to his head, so I think he was pretty intent on telling me the truth."

Now I knew that Blane hadn't been the one to pull the trigger on Matt and that Matt had actually confessed to me and Lucy, though I'd been too drugged to remember it. But I wasn't about to contradict Blane's story.

Unbelievably, Keaston smiled. "Well, it all worked out, didn't it? She's sitting right there, healthy as can be. Now, when can I expect the wedding bells?"

"Kathleen and I aren't getting married, Robert," Blane said. "You helped see to that. And I'm through with politics. The games you've been playing with my life have . . . Well, let's just say it's all left a bad taste in my mouth.

"You've had your fingers in some pretty nasty pies, Robert," Blane continued. "All the way back to the TecSol case, only you weren't the one rigging the election, but the one helping to sell access to China—and using a teenager and her captive parents to do it."

My eyes widened. I'd had no idea Keaston had had anything to do with imprisoning CJ's parents or her subsequent blackmailing.

"You worked with Matt Summers to try and intimidate me into losing the Waters case, threatening Kathleen, hurting her. You sent someone to try and kill Kade, my *brother*, then lied to me about my *fiancée!*" Blane's voice had risen, fury filling each syllable, until he stood in a towering rage that made me shrink back in my chair.

None of this seemed to have the least effect on Keaston. "Are you through having a temper tantrum?" he barked. "You're a soldier. You know that sometimes you have to do things you don't want to do in order to achieve an end result. The end justifies the means, and I am not going to explain myself to you."

Blane shoved a hand through his hair, turning away to press both hands on the mantel, leaning on the fireplace as though for the support and strength to be calm.

"How far back does it go, Robert?" he asked, not looking at him. "Did my dad decide Kade couldn't come live with us, or did you decide for him?"

"Your brother's been a liability since the day he was born," Keaston scoffed. "I never should have helped you find him when William died. That was a mistake. He should've disappeared when his mother died."

I jumped when Blane suddenly swept an arm across the top of the fireplace, sending everything on it—picture frames, figurines, candlesticks—smashing into the wall and onto the floor in a cacophony of breaking glass. I was reminded of when I'd told him I was pregnant and he had destroyed the den. Blane's rage was terrifying. I'd never seen him so angry before. I started shaking and Kade took my hand, folding it reassuringly into his.

That was the moment I saw a visible reaction from Keaston. His eyes widened slightly and his throat moved as he swallowed, but in seconds he'd regained his composure.

Blane faced him. "Do you have any idea the hell Kade would have been spared if he'd been allowed to come live with us?" he rasped, the words edged in bitterness and guilt.

"Kade was not my concern," Keaston said. "You were. Everything I've done, I've done to help pave the path for you, your career."

"Bullshit," Blane spat. "Everything you've done has been for you, not me."

Keaston rubbed a hand across his forehead and sighed. "We could argue semantics all day, Blane, but frankly I don't have the time. You're here, Kade's here. Why? What do you want? Or are we done?"

"We're not done," Kade replied, "but *you* are."

"Haven't we already had this conversation about threats, Kade?" Keaston retorted. "I was very clear, was I not?"

"You were very clear that, should I not make Kathleen go back to Blane, you would kill her, yes," Kade said matter-of-factly.

I gulped. To hear it spelled out so plainly, my life or death dependent entirely on my relationship with Blane, was sobering. I'd known Keaston was crazy—he had to be to have done some of the things he had—but the reality of it was still sad and unnerving.

"Is that what you told Kade?" Blane asked.

"She's carrying your child," Keaston said in a reasonable tone. "Don't you think you ought to marry her? You go on and on about Kade and his childhood. Are you going to let your child grow up fatherless as well?"

Kade stood, approaching Keaston until he mirrored Blane, flanking the other side of the senator's desk. "Kathleen is pregnant with *my* baby, Uncle Robert, not Blane's." His lips twisted. "Bet you didn't see that one coming."

"Is that what she told you?" Keaston asked, his eyes swiveling to meet mine. He leaned forward, his arms crossed and flat on the desk. "She slept with both of you and you believe her? She's a white-trash whore, gentlemen."

I didn't flinch from his gaze. I'd been called worse.

"She'll tell you whatever she thinks will get her the best deal," he continued. "I should know. I've dealt with women like her before." He glanced at Kade and I sucked in a breath, realizing he meant Kade's mother.

"That's rich, accusing her of lying," Kade said. "Coming from you."

"We know about Lazaroff," Blane said, "and the money he was funneling to you."

Keaston went still at those words.

"I hear it's real hard to get a fracking permit through the Department of Energy," Kade said. "What with all the environmental groups so opposed to it. Those groups do seem so well funded, don't they? Getting the word out, staging protests, making movies about how dangerous it is."

"Of course the primary export of Russia is natural gas," Blane said. "They stand to lose a lot of revenue if the US started expanding our own production, reducing the need to buy foreign natural gas. If I were them, I'd be doing everything I could to scare people away from fracking, right, Robert?"

"You wouldn't happen to know anything about that?" Kade asked. "Except, we know you do, because we have every record of every transaction Lazaroff made to you."

"Your career is over," Blane said. "Ties to Russia and China? Not even your buddies in the media can whitewash that for you."

Keaston sat back in his chair. Tense silence reigned. I held my breath, wondering if even this would be enough to take him down. Then he smiled.

"Well, you two think you've got it all figured out, don't you," he said, looking from Blane to Kade and back.

Kade shrugged. "I think we've got all the bases covered, yeah."

"Resign," Blane said. "Say it's your health, say it's Vivian's health—I don't care. I'll let you 'retire' with dignity."

"And if I don't?"

"If you don't, then you leave us no choice," Blane replied. "We'll release it all and you'll lose everything."

"I would think Lazaroff would have something to say about your plans to out our arrangement to the public."

"Lazaroff's dead," Kade retorted. His smile was cold. "I saw to it myself."

Keaston calmly opened the drawer in his desk . . . and pulled out a gun.

My breath caught on a gasp, my fingers digging into the arms of the chair where I sat. I knew neither Blane nor Kade were armed. They wouldn't have gotten through security if they'd brought their guns with them.

It seemed the same thoughts went through Blane and Kade's heads, because they both stiffened.

"I always knew it was a careful balance," Keaston said, "having two men such as yourselves close to me. Blane, you may not believe me, but I have only ever wanted the best for you, for your career, and have worked tirelessly to achieve those ends." He turned to Kade, pointing the gun in his direction. "You, however, have been nothing but a grave disappointment."

"I'm all broken up about that," Kade sneered, but his hands were clenched in fists at his sides.

Keaston ignored him, straightening to face me instead. "But you," he said, leveling the gun at me. "You've been a pain in my side since you screwed up the TecSol project. Then you wrapped those legs around Blane, got inside his head, and he hasn't been the same since. In actuality, I can blame all of this"—he gestured to encompass all four of us—"on you."

"What are you doing?" Blane asked, his tone calm and reasonable. "You can't fire a gun in here, kill Kathleen. Security would be on you in minutes. You want to go to prison for killing a pregnant woman? They'll call you a monster."

"You say I have to retire or you'll destroy my reputation anyway, probably sending me to prison as well," Keaston said. "Why not hurt both of you with one shot and have my revenge? It appears I have nothing to lose anymore."

Blane took a step to his left, trying to block me, I thought, and Kade mirrored him, moving to his right, but Keaston stopped them.

"Make another move, either of you, and she's dead," he threatened.

338

I couldn't breathe as I stared down the barrel of the gun. He was going to shoot me. I could see it in his eyes. After everything, all I'd been through, I was going to die right there in Keaston's office, by his own hand.

Well, I guess I had said he'd have to kill me himself if he wanted me dead. I just hadn't expected that to come true. How ironic.

And I was suddenly incredibly furious.

I stood, my body no longer trembling, and took a step toward the senator.

"The only thing that I can be blamed for? Is wasting even one thought for the things you've said to me," I bit out. "There was a time when I wanted your approval, wanted you to be happy for what Blane and I had. I didn't see until too late how warped you are. Your love for Blane is twisted and perverted. You've done all this to help him? You've hurt him more than anyone else." I was seething now, moving closer to the desk, my entire focus on Keaston.

"Kat—" Blane said, a note of warning in his voice, but I ignored him. This was between me and Keaston.

"Blane and Kade have more honor, integrity, and love for each other than you can possibly comprehend," I continued. "You could've been a part of that. Instead, your own greed and ambition has poisoned you, turning you into someone to be despised."

Keaston's face was flushed with rage as he stared at me. I was almost at the desk now. I could sense the tension in Kade's and Blane's bodies as they watched me, but I knew neither of them dared move.

"You presume to take *me* to task?" Keaston hissed. "You know nothing."

"I know that you are a lying hypocrite," I spat. "You've lied to *everyone*, including Blane, and destroyed the family you'd been given. You think Blane or Kade will let you live if you kill me? I'm a part of their family now, not you." I paused, taking a deep breath. "You pull that trigger and the only question will be which one gets to you first."

"You make the mistake of thinking you're not replaceable," Keaston said. "I assure you, you are."

"No, she's not," Blane interrupted. "Not to us."

Blane's words seemed to be a catalyst, because Blane lunged toward Keaston just as I was suddenly shoved to the ground, Kade's body covering mine. The scream in my throat was cut off, the air was pushed from my lungs by Kade's weight. A gunshot shattered the silence, then there was nothing.

I couldn't move. I couldn't breathe. Oh God, Blane . . .

I shoved at Kade, trying to get up, to suck in a lungful of air.

"Blane," I gasped, terrified Keaston had shot him. "Blane!"

"I'm okay," Blane said, crouching down in front of me. Kade rolled off me and I threw myself at Blane, our arms wrapping tightly around each other. "I'm okay, Kat."

I started crying, the terror I'd felt now ebbing as relief that he was okay flooded over me. I was practically strangling him with the tight grip I had around his neck, but I couldn't make my arms let him go.

"Shhh, I'm fine," Blane soothed me.

The door flew open, startling me, and Jackie stood there. Her eyes lit on the senator and she screamed, her hand flying up to cover her mouth.

"Call 911!" Blane barked.

Jackie didn't move.

"Go!" Blane said even more loudly.

Jackie spun around and ran to her desk, the door swinging closed behind her.

Blane stood, taking me with him, and I turned . . . then stared in openmouthed shock at what remained of Keaston. His eyes were still open, but the back of his head was splattered against the wall in a gory mixture of blood, tissue, and brain matter.

"I don't . . . what . . . Oh my God." My knees gave out and I would have fallen if Blane hadn't had hold of me. I had no idea what had happened. Blane couldn't have killed Keaston. He'd told me flat out that he wouldn't kill him, his only blood relative other than Kade.

"You were right, Kat. It was either him, or you," Blane said, turning my chin so I again faced him. "And I chose you."

I stared at him in stunned disbelief, knowing I should feel guilty for being part of what had brought Blane and Keaston to this point, but I couldn't. Keaston had been a horrible, evil man who'd hurt us all. Blane had made a decision that spoke unequivocally about what I meant to him.

"I'm so sorry," I whispered. "I never meant—"

"Shhh, stop," Blane said. "This is not your fault. None of it was. I swear to you."

I couldn't look away from Blane, his face blurring slightly in my vision, and I saw in his eyes the things he could no longer say aloud. He tenderly brushed my wet cheeks before again tucking me tightly against him.

"Security will be here in seconds," he said, speaking over my head to Kade. "Let me do the talking."

The next few hours were a blur. Police came and men with military uniforms, with rifles and guns and so many questions. I saw the paramedics remove the senator's body and then watched as the police took photos and we were ushered out of the office. I was separated from Kade and Blane and asked question after question about what had happened, but I'd heard Blane's voice above the hubbub and repeated his story.

The senator had quarreled with Blane over Blane's decision to leave the governor's race. He'd become agitated and had pulled a gun. Blane had tried to talk to him, take the gun away, but the senator had committed suicide before we'd even had a chance to call for help.

I was a friend of Blane's, his ex-fiancée, and had come along to support him. Kade was a friend as well. Yes, Blane had mentioned his concern to me about his uncle's mental state, given his age, but I hadn't realized it was so bad and neither had Blane. No, there was no warning that the senator would become violent. No, there was nothing we could've done to stop him.

Over and over and over, I was asked the same questions a dozen different ways, but I stuck to the story and didn't deviate. Eventually, I was able to plead shock and exhaustion and the paramedics intervened. I wasn't faking. My hands shook and I felt too close to passing out, my emotions swinging crazily between despair for what had just happened, to relief that the senator was finally out of our lives, to guilt for feeling relieved.

Evening was closing in by the time we were allowed to leave the Capitol and I leaned heavily on Kade as the three of us walked out a back entrance, away from the press swarming the front. When we were far enough away from the building to not garner any attention, we paused underneath a tree and Kade called Branna to come pick us up.

Blane heaved a sigh. He looked exhausted but resolute, and I worried that the coming days would take a toll on him. He'd have to speak to Vivian, arrange the funeral, and handle a thousand other things as his uncle's relative and heir.

I reached out and grasped his hand. First glancing at me in surprise, he hesitated, then tugged me close for a hug. I inhaled the scent of him, my arms wrapped tight around his waist. After several long moments, he released me and I stepped back. Kade took my hand.

"Well, I can't say I'm not glad he's gone," Kade said. "But that leaves us with another problem."

"What's that?" Blane asked.

Kade sighed. "He told me he had a 'Kade Dennon insurance policy.' If something happened to him, there's a contract on Kathleen."

Nice. I inched closer to Kade.

Blane seemed to take that information in stride, giving a curt nod and glancing away. His eyes squinted against the rays of the sunset.

"I'll dig through his stuff, see what I can find," Blane said. "If it was Lazaroff, we might already be covered. If it was someone else he hired, I'll find out." He looked at Kade. "Go. Take her. Keep her safe."

Kade gave a curt nod, his expression grim.

And it suddenly struck me that . . . this was it. Kade and I were leaving, who knew for how long? For however long it took Blane to clear whatever machinations had been set in motion by Keaston's death, I supposed. It might be a very long time indeed until I saw Blane again. And I started to cry.

"So this is goodbye?" I managed to ask through my tears.

Blane muttered a curse and reached for me. Kade let me go and I was again in Blane's arms.

"Just for now," he said, cradling me to his chest. His chin rested on top of my head. "It's for the best. You know that." And I knew he didn't just mean because of any danger I might be in, but also for everything else between us.

I nodded, my throat too full for me to speak. I knew he was right, but it was so hard to leave him.

"Everything will be okay," Blane said, and his voice was thick. "You and Kade will be safe. I promise. The baby, too." His hand gently stroked my hair.

"What about you?" I asked, tears pouring down my cheeks.

Blane pulled back slightly and I looked up at him. "I'll be fine," he said, smiling softly. Tears shone brightly in his eyes. "I have many regrets, but loving you isn't one of them." He leaned down, kissing me lightly on the lips. "You showed me what love can truly be, Kat," he whispered. "I'll always thank you for that."

Then he kissed me again, a long, tender kiss that was achingly bittersweet in that I knew it was goodbye.

When he released me, he handed me carefully over to Kade as though I were made of the finest porcelain.

"You're the only one I trust to keep her safe," Blane said. "Take care of her. Take care of you." He swallowed heavily. "I love you both."

Kade's eyes were shining, their blue depths bright. His expression was stark as he looked at Blane. "Ditto, brother," he said, his voice a low rasp. "Don't worry. I'll protect her."

Blane nodded, blinking rapidly as he glanced away from us. "Then go on," he said roughly. "Get out of here. Branna can take me where I need to go." He seemed close to losing his composure, and I think Kade sensed it as well, because he said nothing more, just tightened his grip on my hand and led me away.

My last glimpse of Blane was his back as he stood on the grass, the Capitol building framed to his left and his body silhouetted against the setting sun.

KADE & KATHLEEN

CHAPTER SIXTEEN

Kade collected our luggage from the hotel and put it in the trunk of his Mercedes, then he took me to a quiet restaurant on the outskirts of DC and fed me. Not that I was in the mood to eat, but my body was complaining very loudly of an empty stomach, leaving me little choice in the matter.

Still, I picked at my food, pushing it around my plate as I worried about Blane. Kade was outside making a phone call and I finally gave up, setting aside my fork with a sigh.

The image of Keaston's blood on the wall, the back of his head blown away, kept replaying in my mind. I struggled with how I should have felt versus how I really felt. I'd never thought of myself as the kind of person who would be . . . glad about someone's death. And yet the only thing I was sorry about was the effect killing his own uncle had had on Blane. What did that say about me as a person? I wasn't sure I wanted to know.

"Not hungry?" Kade asked, sliding back into the booth across from me.

"I ate some," I said with a weak smile. "What was your phone call about?"

"Needed to arrange some paperwork for you," he replied. "We'll pick it up in New York."

"What kind of paperwork?"

"A passport."

My eyebrows flew up. "Are we going somewhere?" I'd never been out of the country before.

Kade lips twisted in a half smile. "Maybe," he teased, which made me smile, too. "It's a surprise."

"Will Blane be all right?" I asked, my smile fading. Kade's grin also melted away.

"He'll be fine, princess," Kade said, reaching to take my hand in his.

"Shouldn't we stay? Help with the funeral? Something?" I hated leaving Blane to deal with that alone.

"If we stay, it'll just make him worry about you," Kade said reasonably. "He'll be better knowing you're out of town and safe."

I nodded, knowing he was right.

The waiter came and Kade paid the bill, then we were back in the car and heading out of town.

"Try to get some sleep," Kade said. "It's a four-hour drive to New York."

He was right. I was exhausted. The emotional turmoil of the day had taken a toll. I slipped off my shoes and curled up in the seat, turning my body toward Kade. The glow from the dash softly lit his face, easing the hard edges and planes. I knew he was trying to keep things light, but I could also tell he was worried. Whether he was worried about Blane, me, or all of the above, I didn't know.

But I wasn't worried about my safety. Kade would protect me.

I reached up, my fingers brushing his cheek, and he glanced my way. One corner of his mouth lifted in a soft smile as he took my hand and pressed a kiss to my knuckles before resting our joined hands between us.

The warm feel of his palm against mine, the strength of his presence beside me, comforted and soothed me. Eventually, the gentle motion of the car lulled me to sleep.

~

The slowing and then stopping of the car woke me. I sat up from where I'd been slumped and glanced around.

"Are we there?" I asked Kade sleepily.

"Close enough."

It was after midnight. Kade got out of the car and I heard the trunk open. Climbing out, I realized we were in the parking lot of a motel that was more the usual for Kade than the posh one we'd stayed at last night. I heaved an inner sigh. I'd known it was too good to last.

Kade had a duffel bag on his shoulder and was carrying my suitcase.

"Come on," he said, taking my hand in his. "And I know what you're thinking."

"I don't know about that," I replied with a snort.

"This'll be the last dump you have to stay in, okay?"

I shot him a look and he rolled his eyes. "Old habits die hard," he said. "I'll just feel better if we don't leave a name behind. Cash only. Easy in, easy out."

Well, it wasn't like I could argue with that.

He rented us a room and I collapsed onto a bed, eyeing the thin bedspread with distaste. I watched with interest as he changed out of his suit and into his usual jeans and T-shirt, throwing his leather jacket on over that. He tucked his gun into the back of his jeans and added his knife to the holster at his ankle.

"I've got to go out," he said, sitting next to me. He handed me the smaller of the two guns he usually carried. "I won't be gone long, but just in case."

I nodded, not liking the idea of him leaving at all. "Can't I come?" I asked.

"Not where I'm going," Kade replied. "I'll be back soon." He tipped my chin up and gave me a light kiss, then he was gone.

I knew I wouldn't be able to sleep until Kade returned, so I took a shower and slipped on a T-shirt, sliding under the covers and flipping channels on the television. An hour went by, then another. I worried and was starting to panic when I finally heard the lock turn and Kade walked in.

I flew at him, my arms wrapping around his neck while his went around my waist.

"You were gone a long time," I complained.

"Sorry about that," he said. "We had a . . . disagreement on price."

I decided I really didn't want to know how Kade had solved the "disagreement," I was just relieved he was back and in one piece.

"Brought you something," he said.

His hands had dropped from my waist to my satin-covered rear, bared by the little T-shirt, and my thoughts were drifting elsewhere. "Hmm?" I asked.

Kade reached into his jacket pocket, pulling out a small container and holding it up for me to see.

My eyes lit up. "You got me rocky road ice cream?"

"Is there any other kind?"

I laughed in delight, snatching the ice cream and sitting cross-legged on the bed to tear open the lid.

"You might need this," Kade said, handing me a plastic-wrapped spoon.

The ice cream was the perfect temperature between frozen solid and melty, and I wasted no time digging in. Kade discarded his jacket and weapons while I ate, then settled onto his stomach beside me.

"Wanna bite?" I mumbled through a mouthful of ice cream

He opened his mouth and I fed him a spoonful.

"How're you doing?" he asked.

I shrugged. "I said horrible things to Keaston, pushing him and Blane into a confrontation where Blane had to pick his uncle or me. I should feel bad, but I don't, which pretty much says I'm a terrible person."

"You're not a terrible person," Kade chided me. "Keaston tried to kill both of us, numerous times. You're human. I'd be worried if you were all broken up about him dying."

He had a point.

Kade poked me. "Don't I get another bite? I did have to go to three places before I found rocky road."

I frowned. "I'm feeling a little selfish with my ice cream," I said archly. "You did buy it for *me*, you know." My spoon scraped at the bottom and I shoved the last bite in my mouth, choking on a laugh as Kade made a grab for the container. It fell to the floor and Kade had me on my back, his fingers beneath my shirt and tickling my ribs.

A sudden noise outside made my laughter die. "Was that gunshots?" I asked worriedly, glancing at the window. A neon sign across the street blinked. Dogs started barking and I heard the distant sound of sirens. "Maybe we could find a bad motel in a slightly better neighborhood?"

Kade rested on his elbows, his body above mine, one knee insinuated between my legs. "We're fine," he assured me, leaning down to press a kiss to the underside of my jaw. My eyes slipped closed. His lips moved against the tender skin of my neck as he spoke. "The most dangerous thing around here," he murmured, "is me."

Then he started whispering in my ear, his dark voice telling me exactly what he planned to do with his mouth and tongue while his hands tugged my panties down and off my legs, and I forgot all about the noises outside.

∼

The surprise destination wasn't another country, but it was very far away.

"Hawaii?" I squeaked, looking at the departures board for our flight. I remembered when we were in Vegas and how Kade had told me about when he'd been to Hawaii and how he thought I'd like it.

"Just sunshine, beaches, palm trees, and miles of nothing but ocean," Kade replied, wrapping his arms around my waist and pulling me back against him. His lips nuzzled my ear. "A trip to paradise sound good to you?"

My smile was so wide I thought my face might crack. "It sounds amazing," I said, turning in his arms. "Thank you." Just Kade and me, together in one of the most beautiful places on the planet? It sounded like heaven.

The flight was really long, though Kade had gotten us first-class seats, so it wasn't as bad as it could've been. When we landed in Honolulu, it was nighttime.

I was busy looking all around, taking in the airport, which was smaller than I'd thought it would be. Kade bought a lei with beautiful, bright pink flowers and placed it around my neck. The petals were soft and cold against my skin, the scent drifting up to me.

"Aloha," he said, kissing me lightly. "Welcome to Hawaii, princess."

We took a cab and Kade told the driver our destination. Twenty minutes later, he was paying the cabbie and getting our luggage from the trunk.

"This way," he said.

I followed him, glancing around. The ocean breeze gently whipped the long skirt I wore around my legs. It seemed like we were at some sort of marina. I could hear the ocean lapping at the boats. Not that *boats* was really an appropriate word. My jaw fell open as Kade and I walked down a long pier. Yacht after huge yacht was berthed there, and I nearly tripped, I was so busy trying to see them all.

"Where are we going?" I asked.

"Right here."

Kade stopped in front of a yacht that looked different from the others we'd passed. It had rigging for sails and was longer.

"Here?" I asked in disbelief.

Kade's lips twitched. "Yes, here." He climbed aboard, set down the luggage, then reached out to help me.

I stood on the deck, looking around in amazement. It was beautiful, opulent. And big.

Kade moved suddenly and I gasped as he swung me up in his arms. Turning, he walked across the deck, stepping down into a room. I wasn't paying attention to where he was taking me— I was too busy studying the curve of his jaw and line of his throat.

"Don't take this the wrong way," Kade said suddenly, "but I'd rather not knock you unconscious."

"Wha—" was all I had time to say before Kade had slung me up and over his shoulder.

"I want to carry you, but the stairway's too tight. So next best thing," he explained.

"Please tell me you're joking," I said, bracing my hands against his back. Everything was upside down, though I did have a nice view of Kade's ass. And what a fine ass it was . . .

"Duck!" Kade called out, and I squeaked as I narrowly missed cracking my skull. He carried me down a spiral staircase that just wouldn't have worked had he been carrying me the other way.

The incongruity of the situation tickled my funny bone and I laughed. Even I could appreciate the ignominious entrance I was making to a multimillion-dollar yacht—ass first.

Kade stopped and swung me down into his arms again.

"There," he said with a small smile. "That's better."

I smiled back, reaching up to curve my hand around the back of his neck and pulling him down to kiss me.

Kade lowered me to what I belatedly realized was a bed. We didn't stop kissing. He lay between my legs, the denim of his jeans abrading the tender skin on the inside of my thighs as Kade inched the hem of my skirt up to my waist.

"Wait," I said, worry crowding through the fog in my head. "What if Blane can't call off the contract? Will they be able to find me here?" I couldn't handle it if Kade was hurt again, and I knew he'd throw himself in harm's way to protect me, which could get him killed. It had taken years off my life when he'd been shot. One too many close calls and eventually even his luck would run out.

Kade must have heard the worry in my voice, because he glanced down at me, his brow furrowing. "If they do, I'll take care of it. No one's going to hurt you. Not while I'm around."

That's what I was afraid of.

We christened the bed and several other places on the yacht that night, and when the sun peeked over the edge of the horizon, we were on the top deck, a sheet wrapped around us as I sat cuddled in Kade's lap.

I watched the sky turn a faint turquoise, then rose, and finally the sun came up, a huge ball of red rising from the ocean.

"Wow," I breathed. "It's beautiful." But Kade wasn't looking at the sun, he was studying me, the backs of his fingers lightly brushing my cheek, then drifting to twine gently through my hair. I turned my face toward his, smiling. "You're not even looking," I accused.

He raised his head, his gaze serious. I lifted my hand to cup his cheek, the soft stubble a gentle abrasion against my skin. Kade closed his eyes, turning his face to kiss the center of my palm, then his eyes met mine again.

"I need to ask you something," he said.

The seriousness of his tone struck a note of panic in me. What was wrong now?

Kade's smile faded as he spoke. "I once told you that you made me want impossible things, and I was right. I never allowed myself to hope that the life I wanted would ever be in my reach. I'm a bad man, and I've done bad things, most without an inch of remorse. But I love you, and I love our baby."

Tears began to leak from my eyes. Kade brushed away the tracks with his thumbs.

"I don't deserve you," he said, his voice a hoarse rasp. "I'm the absolute worst thing for you. My name isn't honorable and I can't change the selfish bastard that I am. But I want you, and I don't ever want to be without you."

I couldn't speak, couldn't look away from his eyes, so blue and so intense, his soul shining in them. A beautiful soul, no matter what he said.

"Marry me, princess?"

CHAPTER SEVENTEEN

Tears blurred my vision, my throat too clogged with emotion for me to answer, so I just gave a vigorous nod as a sob built in my chest.

Kade hugged me so tight I could barely breathe. He rained kisses on my face—my forehead, cheeks, eyes, lips. He kissed me until I was breathless. When he finally lifted his head, his smile was blinding.

"I have something for you," he said.

Before I could reply, he'd set me aside and jumped up with all the excitement of a kid at Christmas. He bent to grab his discarded jeans off the floor while I admired the view, then he was back and holding a small box.

I recognized the Tiffany blue immediately as he took my hand and set the box in my palm.

"I bought this when we were in Vegas," he said. "I was out of my mind to even buy it—one hell of an impulse buy."

My hands trembled as I opened the box. A ring was nestled inside, the stone reflecting the light in brilliant glimmers.

I started crying again as Kade took the ring out and picked up my left hand.

"It's a princess cut diamond, of course," he said, his lips twisting in a grin as he slipped the ring onto my finger, "and they don't make them any bigger than this."

I laughed through my tears, reaching up to pull him down for a watery kiss.

"Thank you," I said, looking up at him. "It's beautiful."

Kade's grin widened. "I done good," he said smugly.

I rolled my eyes. His arrogance knew no bounds, but in this, he was correct. The ring was exquisite, diamonds embedded into the platinum band on either side of the stone.

"I love you, Kade, even if you hadn't 'done good,'" I said, then raised an eyebrow. "But if you ever even *think* of leaving me again, I will kick your ass."

His face turned serious in an instant. Taking my hand, he placed it on his chest, directly over his heart.

"I won't. I swear it. I'll never leave you."

Then the moment was broken when his lips twisted and he said, "But I would like to see you try to kick my ass." His eyebrows waggled suggestively.

I pinched him.

"Ouch," he said with feigned hurt. "I didn't know you liked to play dirty."

I could feel my face heating and couldn't smother my grin. "There's more where that came from, pretty boy," I warned him.

"I certainly hope so."

I squealed in surprise when he tossed me down on my back, then he was scooting down my body until I felt the warmth of his breath against my inner thighs.

I started to protest. I hadn't showered after our last bout of lovemaking and was immediately self-conscious. But then his mouth was on me, his hands pressing my legs farther apart as he slowly licked me. The feeling was torturous, the warm heat of his tongue dipping inside me then sliding to my clit, wiping every objection from my mind.

It seemed Kade didn't mind dirty at all.

～

Later, I woke alone. We'd gone back down to the bed, jet lag catching up to us. Confused, I sat up, trying to get my bearings. The yacht was moving, I could tell that, then I heard water running in the shower.

Getting out of bed, I stretched, smiling a bit at the little aches that came with a vigorous night of sex with Kade. He'd seemed insatiable, wringing orgasms from me even after I would have sworn I didn't have the energy for it.

I glanced down at my hand, the ring sparkling. Kade had proposed. I was going to marry Kade. It seemed unreal. Untouchable, harder-than-nails Kade Dennon was marrying me.

Deciding to wait until Kade finished in the shower, I wandered naked to the windows, which were at eye level, and looked out. The sea was moving past, waves crashing against the sides of the yacht as it made its way through the water. The sun should have been blinding against the ocean, but the windows were tinted. I sighed, crossing my arms along the sill and resting my chin on them.

I heard the water shut off but didn't turn. A few minutes later, I felt Kade at my back.

"Now this is a sight I could definitely get used to," he said, his lips by my ear. His hands caressed my bare bottom before settling on my hips. I could feel the denim from his jeans against the backs of my thighs.

"Well, you'd better get used to it," I said, turning to face him. "Because I'm not going anywhere."

Kade's expression was one I hadn't seen before. A small smile played about his lips and his eyes were soft as they studied me.

"What?" I asked, smiling back. "What's this face?"

"I'm happy," Kade said simply. "You've made me happy." He shrugged. "It's a new feeling."

My heart hurt a little at that and I stretched up on my toes to loop my arms around his neck. "And you've made me happy," I said. "It goes both ways."

Then my stomach decided to remind me that no matter how happy I was, morning sickness waits for no one.

"What's wrong?" Kade asked, frowning at the sudden change in me.

"Bathroom!" I gasped, pushing past him. I made it in time and had the sense to lock the door before heaving into the toilet.

"Kathleen!" Kade called, twisting the knob. "Unlock this door and let me in," he demanded.

I heaved again, though there was nothing in my stomach. God, I really hated it. I hated that nauseous feeling and the way my stomach twisted sometimes at just the wrong smell. Morning sickness sucked.

"Kathleen! Open this door or I will break it."

I flushed the toilet and grabbed a towel to cover myself. A wet washcloth was on the edge of the tub so I grabbed it and wiped my mouth. Shakily, I leaned against the wall.

"I'm fine," I called out, my voice weak. "Just—give me a minute, okay?" The last thing I wanted was Kade to see me sick . . . again. I'd just take a shower, brush my teeth, then I'd be more presentable. My current condition wasn't so great.

There was a crack and a splintering sound, then the door flew open. Kade stood there, anger mixed with worry on his face.

"No, that is not okay," he said flatly.

"Kade," I whined, covering my face with my hands, "I didn't want you to see me like this." If I'd had the energy, I would've been pissed, but lack of sleep and the boisterous vomiting had taken it all out of me. And here I'd thought this part of pregnancy was finally over.

"Too bad," he said, crouching down by me. He pulled my hands away from my face. "I do believe it's 'in sickness, and in health,' right?"

"We're not married yet," I said. "And this is gross." I wrinkled my nose.

The corner of his mouth lifted in a smirk. "I'll decide what's gross," he said, "and my bride, who carries our unborn child, is most decidedly *not* gross. Even when she's puking her guts out."

Kade helped me off the floor and started the shower for me. "Do you need help showering?" he asked. "Because I can wash your back. And your front." His lips curved in another smirk.

I gave a huff of laughter and pushed him away. "I do not feel sexy at the moment. It'll have to wait."

"Fine," he groused. "I'll wait."

I felt much better after the shower and wrapped myself in a towel before I emerged. Kade was checking his phone.

"Are you hungry now?" he asked.

I considered. "Yeah. I think the nausea's passed."

"Then let's feed you," he said. "Come topside when you're dressed."

He curved a hand around the back of my neck to pull me close enough for him to brush a kiss to my forehead before he disappeared up the stairs. I gave a contented sigh. I would never have guessed Kade to be the doting type, but I wasn't complaining.

Something Alisha had said came to mind then. She'd been telling me how comfortable she was with her new boyfriend, Lewis, and how she'd never felt that way before.

"It's like, you know how you're with a guy and he's driving you home or something, and you need to pass gas? Well, you hold it, right?" she'd said, all matter-of-fact. "Even if it gives you a stomachache. And it's nice to date those kind of guys, but I'd rather find the kind of guy who'd just laugh and roll the window down. If I found a guy who made me feel like that, I'd marry him."

I'd laughed at the ridiculous analogy, though I could admit she had a point. It struck me that morning sickness and pregnancy and all the things that came with that, all the changes my body was going to go through, none of it seemed embarrassing or beyond Kade's ability to take it in stride. He'd seen me sick several times now, had stood by my side unflinchingly when the doctor had examined me, and hadn't batted an eye or made me feel like I needed to hide anything from him.

Going to my suitcase, I pulled out a sundress and flat sandals, finding my brush, too. My hair would dry quickly in the breeze and I dug out my sunglasses and then headed up to find Kade.

To my surprise, a man was bustling around a table for eight that was set for two. He wore white pants and a white shirt. Catching sight of me, he smiled. "Good morning," he said. "I'm Andrew, the chef. You must be Kathleen."

My eyebrows climbed. Chef? "Um, hi," I said, shaking his hand.

"Kade said you were hungry," Andrew continued. "I have some fruit for you, but if you want to tell me what you'd like, I can prepare it."

I felt a little out of my depth as Andrew clasped his hands behind his back and seemed to be waiting for my request. I scrambled to think of something that wouldn't sound too demanding.

"Breakfast?" I tentatively asked, even though it was midday.

Andrew smiled. "No problem," he said. "There's coffee, if you'd like some. I'll be back shortly."

"Thanks," I said. "Do you know where Kade is?"

"Sure, he's on the upper deck." Andrew pointed to a set of stairs leading up.

I looked around a bit before going to the stairs. The yacht was long, not like the typical white luxury yachts I'd seen in pictures. It had to be over half the length of a football field, the long honey-colored deck gorgeous in the sunshine.

I climbed to the top deck. The wind whipped my hair and I caught sight of Kade sitting on the couch where we'd watched the sunrise. I made my way toward him. He had his sunglasses on, shorts, and a white shirt, most of the buttons undone. His arms were stretched along the back of the couch, one ankle resting on the opposite knee as he leaned back, his face tipped up to the sun.

"So what's the story with the yacht?" I asked, sitting down beside him. I kicked off my sandals and tucked my feet up underneath me.

Kade's lips twisted as he lifted an eyebrow. "You like?"

I laughed. "What's not to like? It's amazing. I've never seen anything like it." Three huge sails billowed in the wind and I tipped my head back, shading my eyes with a hand, to gaze up at them. The couch we were sitting on was ivory. The whole decor downstairs, up here, and in the bedroom was in whites and ivories. "Another loaner from 'a friend'?" Kade had access to odd things—nice things—from people he called friends, but who I suspected were really clients.

"It's mine, actually," he said.

I jerked my head back around, my mouth dropping open in astonishment. "Are you serious?" I asked.

"Got it for a song from a guy desperate to sell," Kade smirked.

Alarm bells went off in my head. "And *why* was he desperate to sell?" I asked.

"He pissed me off, so I may have intimated that it would be . . . healthier for him to stick to land for a while."

I shook my head, not in the least bit surprised, though I couldn't help the smile that tugged at my lips. Incorrigible. Spontaneous. Unstoppable. Together, they equaled Kade.

"So where are we going?" I asked.

"Just out for a day cruise," Kade replied. "Thought we'd find a good place to see the sunset tonight."

"That sounds lovely," I said. It seemed dreams really did come true. Kade and I were going to be together.

Kade reached for me, pulling me onto his lap. I hooked an arm around his neck.

"What do you say to marrying me today?" he asked. "When the sun sets?"

My heart leapt. "Really?"

"Really."

"How?"

"The captain used to be a Navy chaplain," Kade said, combing back my unruly hair with his fingers. "I'll introduce you later. He said he'd marry us. I had some connections get us a license, and there's no waiting period in Hawaii."

We could get married today. By the time the sun set tonight, it would be official. Suddenly, I wanted that. I wanted it more than anything. Maybe I was gun-shy because Blane had broken our engagement, or maybe it was because even though Kade had promised to not leave me again, a little part of me was still unsure. Whatever it was, I felt a measure of relief to think it would be a done deal by the time the day was through.

Reaching up, I carefully removed Kade's sunglasses. I wanted to see his eyes, their clear blue rivaling that of the sky above us. "Yes," I said. "Yes, I want that."

Kade had my hair clasped in a loose ponytail, his hand holding the wayward strands over my shoulder. He gently tugged, pulling me toward him for a kiss. I melted into him.

"Ahem."

I pulled back, turning to see Andrew standing a few feet away.

"Breakfast is ready," he said with a smile.

"Thank you, Andrew," Kade said, taking his sunglasses from my fingers and sliding them back on.

Andrew had made French toast, the warm maple syrup soaking into the thick slices of bread. I ate until I was nearly groaning, I was so full.

"So where'd you find these people to work here?" I asked.

Kade helped himself to a slice of pineapple. "They came with the boat," he said with a shrug.

After we ate, Kade had us change into swimsuits, then he introduced me to Captain Hugh, a nice man who looked to be in his mid to late fifties. His skin was tanned a deep brown, his face creased with crow's-feet from many hours in the sun. He was friendly and easygoing, and I liked him right away.

A woman was aboard, too, the only female member of the crew, and her name was Jennifer. Kade introduced me to her and said she was the first mate. The last member of the crew was Taylor, the butler. He arranged two deck chairs for Kade and me, and he gave me a friendly smile before disappearing below deck.

I was wearing the white bikini Kade had bought for me in Las Vegas. I caught Kade blatantly staring as I settled myself on one of the chairs.

"See something you like?" I teased, preening just a bit under his appreciative gaze.

"See something I adore," Kade frankly replied.

Ah, the things Kade said sometimes. My face almost hurt from smiling so much, even as tears pricked my eyes. I was so happy and yet, deep down I was terrified. I'd been happy before and look how that had ended. Surely this couldn't be real. I should enjoy it while it lasted because who knew when it would end?

"What happened to your job in Boston?" I asked, reminded of what felt like ages ago when Kade had said we'd be traveling there. I wondered if the security job had been sidelined when he'd gone back to his old occupation while we'd been apart.

Kade shrugged, lying back in the other chair with his arms bent behind his head. "I decided to take a vacation," he said noncommittally.

I let it go at that. I didn't want to argue and there would be plenty of time to discuss the future. I really wanted to enjoy the here and now. My stomach was full and I wasn't feeling sick, despite the rocking of the boat. I was on an amazing yacht in the middle of the ocean, enjoying a gorgeous, sunny day with the man I loved. Nothing got better than this.

Of course, Kade wasn't one to lie around doing nothing for a long period of time, so pretty soon he was wandering, digging up a radio and fiddling with it until music drifted from the speakers. Then he got thirsty and had Andrew make five different types of smoothies, both of us trying each one and choosing a favorite. After that, he dug up fingernail polish from somewhere—I didn't ask where—and proceeded to drag me back to the couch so he could paint my toes a candy apple red.

"You just can't stand sitting still, can you?" I asked with amusement as Kade carefully painted the last two toes.

"I get antsy on a boat," he said.

I looked quizzically at him.

"No escape route," he clarified.

I snorted. "Then why did you buy a yacht?"

He shrugged, blowing a little on my nails to dry the polish. "Thought you'd like it."

My eyebrows climbed. "Kade," I said carefully, a suspicion forming in my mind, "how long have you owned this yacht?"

He didn't answer right away. Testing the dryness of my nails, he seemed satisfied, resting my feet in his lap as he leaned back on the couch.

"Since Christmas."

I was speechless for a moment, the implications of that statement sinking in. When I spoke, my voice was quiet. "You've known for that long?"

"I knew the moment I first laid eyes on you," Kade said, matter-of-fact.

I remembered that day in the courthouse. Me, still reeling from being attacked and held as a hostage. Kade, stopping to make sure I was all right. Now looking back on it, I realized it had been out of character for him to do so. Kade wasn't known for his compassion toward strangers.

"You were like a princess out of a fairy tale," Kade said, his hands caressing my legs as he spoke. "I still remember my first glimpse of you, standing in line at security. Your hair was the color of the sunset."

I couldn't help my smile. "I didn't know you'd noticed me," I said, "at least, not before that guy held me hostage."

"You saved his life that day," Kade said, surprising me again. "If you hadn't done what you did, I was about two seconds from blowing his brains out."

"How did you have a gun inside the courthouse?" I asked, bewildered. Kade just smirked and I rolled my eyes. Of course *he* would have found a way around that.

"Though it did give me a chance to talk to you," Kade continued. "But you weren't real talkative."

"I was in shock," I defended myself, though my cheeks heated. The real reason I hadn't said much was because I'd been blown away that a man who looked like Kade did had stopped to talk to me.

"And here I thought it was my stunning good looks that had your tongue all tied up," he teased.

Even though Kade's ego needed no stroking, I 'fessed up. "Yeah, that too."

Kade's laugh was a soft rasp that made my face even warmer, but I was still smiling. It was good to see him so happy and relaxed.

"So why didn't you ask me out?"

Kade's smile faded and he cocked an eyebrow at me. "What would I have said to you? *Hey, I kill people for a living, but I'm really great in bed.*" He shook his head. "There was nothing about me that was worthy of you. You were innocent, sweet. It would've been a fucking crime for me to ask you out."

There were so many things wrong with that statement, it was hard to know where to start. "I was not innocent, or sweet," I argued. "And you know I hate it when you say stuff like that about yourself."

"Yeah, well, it doesn't matter anyway," Kade dismissed. "I'm not exactly known for my self-restraint, which is how we find ourselves sitting here." He indicated the yacht.

I thought for a moment. "Kade," I began carefully, "would you have ever said anything to me if Blane hadn't made you play bodyguard when he was working that case?"

Kade didn't answer for a moment. "I wanted to stay away, not come back to Indy. Being around you while you were with Blane was torture."

"Is that why you were so mean to me?"

His smile was bitter. "It was easier if I could make you hate me. But then you had to go and almost get yourself killed . . . and I couldn't make myself be cruel to you. Not after that."

I pulled my feet away, crawling over to settle on my knees next to him. I looped my arms around his neck and smiled. "I'm glad," I said, pressing my lips to his.

"Mmm," Kade murmured. "You smell like coconut."

He still wore the white shirt, only now no buttons were fastened. His chest was warm from the sun, our bodies touching and sliding from my suntan oil.

I abruptly sat back. "Coconut," I said. "That sounds good. Do you think Andrew has any?"

Kade slid his sunglasses down to peer at me over the top. "You want coconut? Just coconut?"

I nodded. "Yeah." My stomach growled.

Kade grinned. "I'm on it."

He returned shortly with a bowl of shredded coconut and insisted on feeding it to me. I didn't mind. My head in Kade's lap while he teased me and fed me coconut was the stuff dreams are made of—my dreams at least.

A few hours later, I was standing in our bedroom, surveying myself in the mirror, dressed in what would become my wedding gown.

I'd never gotten to wear the dress I'd bought in Vegas, instead stashing it in the back of my closet when I'd gotten home. It happened to be made of a floaty white chiffon, with little straps that went over my shoulders, then crossed and tied behind my back. The sweetheart neckline dipped low between my breasts, meeting an empire waistband of rhinestones and crystals that wrapped around me to another deep V in the back. The chiffon skirt fell all the way to the floor. The dress wouldn't have worked for a regular wedding, but for this setting, it was perfect. And it seemed fitting that Kade had unknowingly ended up buying my wedding gown.

My peacock-blue stilettos winked at me from my suitcase. I slipped them on. That took care of my "something blue." I added the diamond bracelet Kade had given me in Vegas. It was a few months old, I supposed. As for "borrowed"—well, I guess I'd just have to go without.

There was a knock at the door.

"Come in," I said.

Jennifer stepped inside. "I hope you don't mind my intruding," she said with a smile, "but Mr. Dennon had mentioned you might want to borrow these." She held out her hand. Two diamond stud earrings lay in her palm.

"That's perfect!" I exclaimed in delight. "Thank you so much! I was just thinking how I didn't have the 'something borrowed.'"

"Glad to help," she said with a twinkle in her eye. "This is for you, too." This time she gave me a small bouquet of deep purple flowers, then she left, closing the door softly behind her.

It seemed Kade had thought of everything.

I put in the earrings and studied my reflection. My hair was in waves down my back, the way Kade liked it. We'd docked on the far westward side of Oahu, and it was a lot less windy there than on the open sea, so I thought my hair-style would be okay. My tan had deepened today and the white dress was a really nice contrast against my bronzed skin.

My wedding dress. Tears stung my eyes and I had to hurriedly blink them back, not wanting my mascara to run. I held the bouquet in front of me, the diamonds at my wrist, ears, and finger sparkling in the mirror.

I was getting married.

There was a deep pang inside. I was sad that my parents weren't here, to see me happy and marrying the man I loved. But it seemed like I could feel them, looking down on me. I closed my eyes.

"I miss you so much," I whispered. "But I'm happy, and loved, and I know that's all you wanted for me." A sense of peace came over me, soothing the lingering melancholy, and my heart lifted.

It was time.

When I appeared on the deck, I gasped in surprise and delight. It appeared the crew had been hard at work while I was getting ready. Flowers that matched my bouquet were everywhere, wrapped around lines that stretched overhead, covering the rails at the edge of the deck. Everything was lit by strings of lights, their soft glow intermixed with the flowers twined among them. I caught sight of Taylor adding a final few blooms to a railing.

Music floated softly through the air. Someone must have found the yacht's sound system. It was lovely, but I couldn't place the tune.

Then my gaze landed on Kade.

He stood at the far end of the bow, the setting sun a blazing shimmer of red and orange behind him, making him a stark figure limned in gold. He was speaking to Captain Hugh and laughed at something Hugh said. Glancing up, he caught sight of me, and his whole body went still.

At that moment, everything faded away and it seemed it was just him and me. I was only aware of Kade, our gazes locked together.

He began walking toward me, his steps sure and unhurried. I couldn't move, my heart so full of emotion it seemed incomprehensible that I could feel so much for this man. Surely my body couldn't contain all the love inside.

Kade stopped in front of me and I knew I would remember the look in his eyes for the rest of my life.

"My bride," he murmured, his voice edged in awe. His hands drifted lightly down my arms. "You're the most beautiful thing I've ever seen."

My face split into a smile. "Likewise," I said, my voice a bit breathless. The way he looked was enough to take my breath away. Now that he was close, I could see the tuxedo he was wearing. The lines were classic, the fabric expensive and tailored to fit him perfectly. The white of his shirt was blinding, a stark contrast to the deep black of the jacket. He'd even tied the bow tie.

"What's this?" I teased, reaching up to tug a bit at the tie. "Another attempt at a tie?"

"Well, I went all out," he said with a shrug, the corner of his lips tipping up. "Took me forever to get it right, and if Taylor says he had to help me, he's lying."

I laughed. "You look amazing, but it's not . . . you." I tugged on the tie until it came loose, then undid the top two buttons of his shirt. "That's you," I said with satisfaction, pressing the silken tie flat as it dangled on either side of his collar.

Kade wasn't even looking at what I'd done. His gaze was fixed on my face, a small smile playing about his lips.

Taking my right hand, he threaded it through his bent elbow, resting my palm on his left arm.

"Ready?" he asked.

I nodded. I was more than ready.

Glancing up, Kade gave Taylor a nod. The crew assembled near the bow, Captain Hugh at the head and all of them facing us. They looked glad to be there. It seemed everyone really did love a wedding.

Kade walked me slowly toward the bow and the setting sun, the music drifting around us. I could smell the heavy perfume of the flowers mixed with the salt of the ocean. The lights above us danced in the breeze and gave everything a fairy-tale quality.

"You wore the shoes," Kade said softly as we walked.

I glanced down. The toes of my blue shoes peeped from underneath my gown with each step I took.

"They're my 'something blue,'" I replied, glancing up at him with a twinkle in my eye. "Plus, I seem to remember you telling me a while back what I *wouldn't* be wearing the next time you saw me in them."

Kade gave a low groan. "I love you."

I grinned. "I know."

It seemed like I shouldn't be smiling so much for such a solemn occasion as my own wedding, but I couldn't help it. Kade had always made me smile, no matter the circumstances.

Kade didn't look away from me as we made our way across the deck, his gaze seeming to drink me in. I kept an eye on the deck, which rolled a bit with the waves. I didn't want to end up falling on my ass, but Kade's presence at my side was strong and steady. I glanced up at him every few steps, feeling a little shy at the adoration in his eyes.

We drew to a halt in front of Captain Hugh, who was waiting with an indulgent smile on his face. Kade took my bouquet from me and gave it to Jennifer to hold as he clasped my hands in his.

Kade's eyes captivated me and I barely heard Hugh begin the ceremony. The bottom of the sun had just hit the ocean's edge and the burnished golden rays bathed us in a warm glow. The cry of a seagull resonated through the baritone rumble of Hugh's voice, the pulse of the waves a steady undercurrent.

The breeze gently tousled Kade's hair, as if touched by loving fingers. His hands were warm and reassuring as they covered mine, his thumbs tenderly brushing my knuckles.

"I have," Kade said, answering a question I hadn't heard. I glanced questioningly at Hugh then back at Kade. "He asked if we had written our own vows," he said. "I have."

I was surprised. This was unexpected. But then again, when had Kade ever done what I'd expected?

"From the moment I saw you, I was lost," Kade began, moving a little closer to me. "You hold my heart and my soul. I promise to be with you, to be your friend and your lover. I'll be your strength when you're weak, your comfort when you're sad. You are the best part of me, and the best thing that's ever happened to me. I will love you, for always."

His beloved face was a blur, tears welling and spilling down my cheeks. Reaching into his breast pocket, Kade took out the white linen square and softly brushed my tears. Leaning down, he pressed his lips to my cheek.

I blinked rapidly, taking the handkerchief and quickly dabbing my eyes. I replayed his words through my mind, memorizing them and the cadence of his voice as he'd spoken the vows so I would always remember this moment.

I looked at him, the love shining in his eyes, and I spoke from the heart.

"Kade," I said, my voice thick with tears, "I looked in your eyes and saw my perfect match. You're every good thing I've ever dreamed my husband would be. I never knew who and what I could be, until I met you. You see the very heart of me. It beats only for you, and always will."

Kade's eyes were very bright, the blue so clear it seemed I'd get lost in their depths.

"I'm going to need that pocket square back," he deadpanned, drawing a little laugh from me. The slow smile on his face was entrancing.

"The ring," Hugh said, handing it to Kade. "Repeat after me."

Taking my left hand, Kade slipped off my engagement ring to slide a platinum band with more diamonds embedded in it onto my finger, then replaced the engagement ring, repeating "With this ring, I thee wed, and with all that I am and all that I have, I honor you."

Hugh handed me a thick plain platinum band. My hands shook as I took Kade's left hand in mine. Everything blurred again as I pushed the band over his knuckle and into place. I wished I could stop time, freeze this moment for just a little while longer.

"With this ring, I thee wed, and with all that I am and all that I have, I honor you," I vowed, my voice barely above a whisper.

"I now pronounce you husband and wife. You may kiss the bride."

Kade cupped my face in his hands, leaning down to kiss me. His lips were soft as they moved over mine. His tongue was a gentle brush before he lifted his head. Distantly, I heard the crew applauding, then Kade had wrapped his arms around my waist and lifted me in his arm. I twined my arms around his neck, holding on as he swung me around in a dizzying circle. He laughed and I kissed the joy from his lips.

No longer was I Kathleen Turner. I was Kathleen Dennon.

Our kiss deepened and Kade let me slide down until my feet touched the deck once again. He pulled back and I abruptly realized the crew had melted away and that the music playing had changed.

"Hope you don't mind that I picked the first dance," Kade said. "It seemed fitting."

The strains of a song I recognized washed over me. It was "Kiss Me."

"I wouldn't have pegged you for an Ed Sheeran fan," I teased. My hands moved to his shoulders as Kade began to slowly turn me in time to the melody.

"I'm not usually," he said, "but heard this, and thought of you. When I missed you, I'd listen to it, and dream."

I had no words, but we didn't need any.

And we danced.

Chapter Eighteen

K ade took me to a hotel on Oahu for our wedding night. At least it was supposed to be a hotel, even though it seemed like another part of the fairy tale to me. We ended up being shown to our own little bungalow right on the beach. The bedroom had an entire wall that could be opened to the outdoors, giving us a spectacular view of the ocean.

"I can't believe this," I said, staring at the waves glistening in the moonlight.

"Can't believe what?" Kade murmured. He stood behind me, his arms sliding around my waist as his lips brushed the skin of my shoulder.

I still wore my wedding gown. When we'd arrived, there had been a private candlelit dinner arranged for Kade and me, and I'd had lobster for the first time ever.

"Can't believe we're here, in this place," I said, then turned in his arms. "Can't believe we're married."

"Believe it," Kade said, and I felt a tug on the tie at the back of my dress. "You're mine."

The tie fell loose and the straps drooped. A shrug of my shoulders, and the white chiffon was lying in a puddle at my feet. All I wore now was my jewelry and my blue stilettos.

"I believe this is what you requested," I teased, reminding him of when he'd told me: *The next time I see you wearing those shoes, they'll be the only thing you're wearing.*

Kade was silent, his gaze slowly traveling down my body and back up. He was still dressed, though he'd discarded his jacket and rolled back the cuffs of his sleeves.

"I wish you could see yourself," he said, his voice low and rough. "The moonlight makes your skin shine and your hair and eyes turn silver. Like a mermaid. My mermaid."

He reached out a hand, trailing his fingers up my stomach to my breast, barely brushing a nipple, then up to my collarbone, and finally lightly clasping my neck.

The waves crashed and pounded on the shore, but I could barely hear them over the beating of my heart. Even though we'd made love many times, this was different. This would be the first time I'd make love with . . . my husband.

I reached up, slipping the buttons of his shirt free, then tugged the shirt from his pants and pushed it over his shoulders and down his arms. There was a soft rustle as the cotton dropped to the floor to join my dress.

Kade kissed me, taking his time to tease my lips before slipping his tongue inside to tangle with mine. He tasted of the champagne we'd drunk with dessert. My hands rested on the warm skin of his chest, the firm planes underneath my fingers reminding me of his strength. I could feel the hard length of him pressing against my stomach and an answering ache bloomed between my legs.

It was a matter of a few quick tugs for me to undo his pants. I pulled back slightly, moving my lips to his chest. His skin was soft beneath my tongue and I could feel the beat of his heart under my fingertips. My tongue grazed his nipple and I heard his sharp intake of breath.

I lowered the zipper of his pants, pushing them down as I dropped to my knees. I wanted to show him how much I loved him, pay homage to his amazing body.

His erection stood proud and long, jutting out from his body. Glancing up, I saw Kade avidly watching me. I held his gaze as I slowly licked him from root to tip, swirling my tongue around the head before taking him in my mouth.

Kade groaned, his eyes drifting shut. His hands tangled in my hair as I lightly sucked. The taste of him, the feeling I got when I watched his face transform into one of pained ecstasy, was like a drug. Moisture dripped from me, coating my inner thighs as I slid him in and out of my mouth, my hands cupping his amazing ass. Soon, he forgot himself, his hips thrusting his heavy cock in my mouth. I was so aroused, I thought I might come from just watching him, knowing I could do this to him. Kade panted, his chest glistening with a light sheen of sweat, moans and gasps falling from his lips. I couldn't stand it anymore and I lowered a hand to ease the ache between my thighs.

"No," Kade gasped, abruptly pulling away. "Want to be inside you."

He'd scooped me up off the floor before I'd even processed what he'd said, then we were on the bed, my legs wrapped around his waist.

Grasping my hands, Kade interlocked our fingers and stretched my arms over my head before burying his cock inside me.

I was so aroused, it didn't take long before I was coming, my cries cut off by his mouth on mine. Kade moved hard and fast, prolonging my orgasm. He came seconds later, tearing his mouth from mine as he cried out, his body shuddering, the thick length of him pulsing deep inside me.

I was breathing hard and it was difficult to tell whose heartbeat I felt, his or mine. Kade's head was buried in my neck, then he was kissing me again, a long, lazy kiss that made my toes curl.

"You're so fucking amazing," he murmured against my lips. "God, I love you."

"Ditto," I managed to reply. "On both counts."

We lay there like that for a while, both of us getting our breath back, before Kade moved to lie beside me. I turned to face him.

Rays of moonlight scattered across the room and the bed as we each looked into the other's eyes.

"Thank you," I said softly.

"I know I'm good, but there's no need to thank me," he said, his lips quirking up at the corners.

I laughed, punching him lightly on the arm. "Not for that," I said. "For today. It was beautiful. Perfect. I couldn't be happier. Thank you for that."

Kade reached an arm around my waist, pulling me close to the cradle of his body. "I would do anything for you," he said simply.

I nestled against him and heaved a deep, contented sigh, the soothing sound of the ocean lulling me to sleep.

～

Kade woke me during the night. I'd turned in my sleep, my back to his chest spoon style. Now my leg rested on top of his as his cock moved inside me. His thrusts were slow and deep, his fingers slipping between my legs to tease my clit. His lips were pressed against my neck, the touch of his tongue sending a shiver through me. I turned my head and he kissed me. My body felt like molten heat, the fire he was building spreading through me. Soon I was panting, begging for him to move faster, harder, but he wouldn't, and I didn't even see my orgasm coming until it overwhelmed me. I splintered apart under the force of it, stars exploding behind my eyes.

Kade groaned at the feel of my body gripping his straining cock, his fingers digging into my hip. Then he was moving me to my stomach. My body felt boneless as he pushed my knees underneath me, lifting my backside up, then I cried out again when he pushed inside me, my flesh overly sensitive.

This position let me feel every inch of him as he pounded into me. Kade losing control was something I couldn't resist and soon I felt my body tensing again. His hands held my hips steady, and the sound of our bodies coming together and our combined moans and gasps filled my ears. This time when I came, I took Kade with me, both of us flying over the edge together.

~

Kade was still asleep when morning came, whereas I was wide awake. I grabbed the tuxedo shirt he'd shed the night before and pulled it on. There was a small television in the living room, so I closed the French doors to the bedroom and made a pot of coffee, then turned on the TV. Hawaii was five hours behind the time back home, so even though it was early on Oahu, it was a fine time to call Alisha.

I switched on my phone for the first time in over a week, unsurprised to see a ton of voice mails, all from Alisha. I cringed as I listened to them. Kade had some serious apologizing to do to Alisha and Lewis. After I'd listened to the last one, I dialed her number.

"Oh my God, I thought you were dead!" were the first words out of her mouth.

"I'm not," I assured her. "Though I could very well have been if Kade hadn't shown up." I thought I'd better start greasing the wheels immediately for her to forgive him.

"What happened?" she asked. "Did you get my messages? Did Kade tell you what he did? He is such a bastard, Kathleen!"

Okay, it might take more than grease. Kade might have to send Alisha and Lewis a couple of first-class tickets to Hawaii, too.

"I'm so sorry about that," I said. "Is Lewis okay?"

Alisha spent the next several minutes telling me how he was doing, and it seemed he was healing nicely—and from the sound of it, he was also enjoying the resulting attention Alisha was lavishing on him maybe a little too much.

"But don't think for a second that I've forgiven Kade," she said. "And why didn't you ever tell me he could be so . . . so . . ."

"Scary?" I provided.

"Among other things," Alisha said. "The way he just stood there and pulled the trigger so easily. It scared the shit out of me, Kathleen."

"I'm really sorry," I said. "He's not like that. I mean, he is, but he's not. Not really. I'm just . . . I'm sorry."

Alisha gave a huge sigh. "It's okay. Lewis is okay. And thank goodness you're okay. You are, right? He didn't hurt you or anything?"

"Of course not," I said. "I'm doing good. I'm in Hawaii. And . . . I'm married."

That took a moment to sink in and then my ear was splitting. "You're *married?*" Alisha shrieked.

I grinned. "Yeah. Last night. Kade and I got married. I guess I'm on my honeymoon now."

"Oh my God, Kathleen, that's wonderful!" Alisha squealed, her earlier animosity toward Kade apparently forgotten. "I'm so happy for you! And in Hawaii? How romantic! Tell me everything!"

So I told her pretty much everything, the Reader's Digest Condensed version, right up through the purple flowers and sunset wedding.

"I heard about the senator," Alisha said when I was through. "It's been all over the news. That's the guy who threatened you if you didn't break up with Blane, right?"

"Yeah, that was him," I confirmed.

"Blane's been on the news, too," she said hesitantly.

"Is he okay?" I asked, suddenly worried.

"He seems fine. He's been doing the press thing about his uncle. I think the funeral is tomorrow, maybe?"

My eyes slipped closed and I rubbed my forehead. I ached to talk to him, know how he was doing, and I wished there was a way I could still be someone who provided comfort to him, though I knew that wasn't possible right now.

"You know there's talk of the Massachusetts governor appointing Blane to the empty seat, right?" Alisha asked.

My eyes flew open. "What? No, I didn't."

"Yeah. There's been a lot of coverage about Blane, including that thing where they arrested him for Kandi's murder when someone else really killed her—and lots of people like him. I guess there's just under two years left of that senator's term, so they're saying since Blane was his great-nephew and only heir, the governor might appoint him. You know, kind of like a Kennedy."

"Wow," I breathed. Blane, a United States senator. That would be something.

"I know, right?" Alisha said.

We went on to talk about other things and I told her a little bit about Hawaii, but my mind was stuck on what she'd said about Blane. I wondered if he'd want a position like that, then chastised myself. Why wouldn't he? He'd been running for governor. Why wouldn't he jump at the chance to be a senator?

After a while and several promises from me to call again soon, we hung up. I was sitting on the couch, watching the waves crash along the shore, when Kade came out of the bedroom. He was drying his hair with a towel, another wrapped around his waist.

"Who was that?" he asked.

"Alisha," I replied. "You're in such deep shit with her."

Kade raised an eyebrow at me, and I could tell he really didn't care. I sighed. Looked like it'd be up to me to make things right with her and Lewis.

"So what do you want to do today?" he asked. "We can swim in the pool, sit on the beach, go sightseeing . . ."

I pushed him down on his back against the couch and gave a sharp tug on the towel around his waist. It fell aside.

"Or we could stay here for a while," he added hoarsely as I took him in my mouth. Then he stopped talking altogether.

～

We spent three weeks in Hawaii, touring Oahu, Maui, and the Big Island. Sometimes we stayed in a hotel, sometimes on the yacht. The days were perfect and blended together into one long memory of blissful happiness. My morning sickness had at last passed and I felt great. Kade taught me to snorkel, which was really cool, until I came face-to-face with a fish as large as I was.

I screamed through my snorkel, immediately getting a noseful of water, and Kade had to help me back onto the yacht, giving me a hard time the entire way.

"He was big enough to eat me for dinner!" I complained as Kade took off my flippers.

"He was not," he chided me, sliding his sunglasses back on and running his fingers through his wet hair. "He was just coming closer to get a good look at you." Kade smirked at me, the sun making his hair shine like a raven's wing. Leaning toward me, he said, "Though *I'd* be happy to eat you for dinner."

I smacked him lightly on the chest. "You're insatiable," I complained, but I was smiling. My bump seemed to be getting larger by the day, and I would've been self-conscious about it, except that every morning Kade would lay me on my back and scoot down my body to kiss my abdomen and croon, "Good morning, baby." The first time he'd done it, I'd laughed.

"What the heck are you doing?" I'd asked.

"He gets to hear your voice all the time," Kade had explained. "I want him to know my voice, too."

It'd been such a sweet sentiment, I couldn't stop the big, stupid grin on my face. "How do you know it's a *he?*" I'd asked.

Kade had looked up at me as though I'd asked him what color the sky was. "Because I know."

Of course he did. I'd rolled my eyes and left it at that.

That night, Kade took me to dinner at a beautiful restaurant right on the beach. The meal was five courses, and Kade had poured more Perrier in my glass as he told me about the time he'd gotten snagged at customs when he'd been entering Russia. I was completely enthralled with his story as I listened to him talk about how he'd ended up spending three months in a Russian prison, which was how he'd learned the language.

"How did you get out?" I asked.

"Luck and circumstance," Kade said evasively. "The guy I was there for was actually another prisoner, so once it was done, I managed to get out. Rusty was helping me on that job." He laughed. "Man, he hated being there. Said the food sucked and that the only decent thing the Russians made was vodka."

My eyes were wide. "Yeah, but . . . a Russian prison? For three months? Wasn't it . . . dangerous?" Which was probably a stupid question. Kade's entire life had been dangerous.

He shrugged, finishing off the wine in his glass. "A couple new scars for mementos. Not a big deal. People learned quick enough to leave me alone if they valued staying ambulatory."

A shiver went through me and Kade frowned, reaching for my hand.

"Should I not have told you?" he asked.

I shook my head. "No, it's not that." I wanted to hear what Kade would tell me about his past, though I knew a lot of it was sanitized—and there were some things he'd never tell me. My face heated and I looked away from him, embarrassed. "It's just that sometimes, when you talk like that, it's . . ." I couldn't say it, so I just shook my head.

"It's what?"

I didn't answer. Instead, I raised my gaze to meet his. His brow was furrowed as he tried to puzzle out what I had been unable to say, then understanding dawned and he laughed softly.

"You, my dear, are a cliché," he teased, leaning toward me. His hand traced a length of my hair, wrapping the long curl around his finger as he spoke into my ear. "And here I thought my being such a sexy badass had no effect on you."

The warm touch of his breath sent another shiver through me even as my cheeks flushed hotter. Maybe I was a cliché, but I didn't care. The fact that Kade was more than capable of taking care of himself and me was a turn-on. I'd own it.

"Admit it," he whispered. "You love it when I go all Batman."

I giggled at his teasing, but before I could reply, his cell phone rang.

Kade heaved a sigh, then reached into his pocket for it, glancing at the display.

"Probably should take this, princess," he said soberly. "It's Blane."

My stomach dropped. I quickly nodded and Kade hit the button to take the call.

"Yeah," he said. He listened for a minute. "Are you sure?" He was silent for a few moments, listening, then glanced at me. "She's fine. She's here with me."

I chewed on a fingernail, wondering what Blane had said.

"When?" Kade asked, then glanced at his watch. "No, you couldn't get here in time." Silence again as he listened, his brows furrowing in irritation. "Because he's already here."

My breath caught at that, my eyes wide.

"Trust me," Kade said. "I know." He listened some more, his eyes glancing at me, and when he spoke again, his voice was softer. "You know I'd die before I let anything happen to her."

That certainly wasn't what I wanted to hear just then.

Kade ended the call and signaled the waiter to bring the bill.

"What's going on?" I asked after he handed his credit card to the waiter. "What did Blane find out?"

"He found out which assassin Keaston hired, then called to say Interpol had spotted him entering the US."

The waiter returned and Kade quickly signed the bill and pocketed his card.

"He could be anywhere," I said. "Do we need to worry?"

Kade stood and took my hand, his eyes scanning the restaurant and the darkness of the beach. "He entered the US through Honolulu," Kade said.

Ice flooded my veins. "But how?" I asked, panic creeping into my voice. "How did he find me?"

But Kade was already hustling me toward the entrance and flagged down a cab, shielding me with his body as he helped me into the backseat. When he slid into the cab beside me, I saw his gun was in his hand. He gave the driver the hotel address rather than the marina, then flashed a hundred-dollar bill.

"This is yours if you can get us back inside of ten minutes," he said.

The cabbie laughed, then floored it, flattening me against the back of the seat.

"We're not going to the boat?" I asked. Getting off the island sounded like a pretty good idea to me.

Kade was looking behind us when he answered. "Nope. No escape route. Remember?"

His body was tense, the gun sitting easily in his grip.

"Get down," he said, suddenly clutching my shoulder and pulling me down into his lap.

I obeyed, though fear clogged my throat. "Do you see something?" I asked. "What's happening?"

"Relax," Kade replied evenly. "Just a precaution." He glanced down at me, a tiny smirk on his face. "I thought you like it when I go all Batman," he teased.

"Yeah, well, all Batman's girlfriends die," I retorted.

"You watch too many movies."

Moments later, the cabbie was pulling up to the hotel. Kade tossed the money at him and had me out the door faster than I would have thought possible. The path to our bungalow was through dense foliage and skirted small ponds filled with koi. Kade had his arm so tight around my waist, it seemed I could barely breathe as he half carried me.

"If he's already here, then what are we doing?" I asked. "Shouldn't we be leaving? Finding somewhere to hide? What if he knows we're staying here?" The questions came pouring out in a torrent of fear and panic.

Kade suddenly stopped, hauling me close and taking my face in his hands. The cold metal of his gun pressed against my cheek.

"Listen to me," he said, his voice low and intent. "I know you're scared, but you have to trust me. I know this guy. I know what he'll do. You're going to be okay. Do you believe that?"

I gazed into his eyes, staring so fixedly into mine, and nodded. How could I explain that it wasn't me I was worried about? If someone was trying to kill me, it only made sense that they'd try to first take out whoever was trying to protect me.

"Good," he said. "Because I really need you to *be quiet.*"

I bit my lip, my gaze dropping in embarrassment as I nodded again.

Kade pressed a kiss to my forehead, then we were moving. Moments later, we were outside our bungalow.

The lights were on inside and Kade pulled me behind him as he silently turned the knob and pushed the door open.

It was quiet inside but although the silence had been peaceful before, it now seemed ominous.

A sudden movement in the bedroom startled me and Kade whipped his gun around, pointing at the maid, who let out a frightened cry.

"Turndown service," I said quickly, relieved.

"Out," Kade ordered, and the maid nodded, scurrying past us out the door.

I stood and watched as Kade turned off all the lights, stashing me in a corner without a direct line of sight to me from any window or door.

"You said you knew him," I said quietly. "Is that true?"

Kade took a bowlful of tiny decorative seashells and began scattering them on the wooden floor in front of the open doors to the beach.

"I killed people for a living, princess," he said. "It's a small world."

"Is he . . . good?" I couldn't think of another term, though the adjective seemed inappropriate given the profession.

"He's called the Krait," Kade said, "after one of the deadliest snakes in the world. It hunts at night, and its bite is almost always fatal."

Yeah, that wasn't exactly comforting.

"What's his real name?" I asked.

"No one knows," he replied. "Well, I know it, but I doubt many other people do. His name's John."

John. A somewhat pedestrian name for a notorious assassin. The stress and tension was getting to me and my bladder decided it needed a timeout. I headed for the bathroom.

"Whoa, wait," Kade said, stepping in front of me. "Where are you going?"

"I have to use the bathroom," I said. "Too much water at dinner." I eyed him. "Is that allowed?" I asked.

"I'll come with you."

My mouth dropped open. "Oh no, you won't!" Yes, Kade was my husband, but I believed there were some things in marriage that should remain a mystery. How I looked while peeing was one of them. "I'll be quick, I swear," I promised.

Kade watched as I walked down the hall and into the bathroom. I shut the door behind me and breathed out a sigh. I got that he was trying to protect me, but my nerves were shot and I didn't know how long it would be like this. Would the guy come tonight?

I flipped on the light just as a hand came down tight over my mouth, stifling my instinctive scream. I was brought back hard against a man's chest, his arms like iron wrapped around me.

The mirror in front of me reflected the man who held me captive, not dressed as I'd expect in all black but in island garb of khaki pants and a silk aloha shirt. He had a knife to my throat and I could immediately tell by the way he held me that getting away from him wouldn't be as easy as the move I'd made so long ago in the courthouse.

He was attractive, with sandy-brown hair and blue eyes, but his eyes were cold and emotionless. If I hadn't known better, I'd have said he was bored, which sent a chill through me.

"Knew you'd come in here eventually," he said in my ear. I couldn't place his accent, which caressed the words spoken so calmly. "If you're quiet and do what I tell you, only you will die tonight. Make a noise, cry for help, and I'll make sure your boyfriend out there dies, too."

I was breathing hard, not getting enough air with his hand covering my mouth and nose so tightly, and I gave a jerky nod. Slowly, he removed his hand and I sucked in a lungful of air. I was trembling all over, the knife in his hand glinting in the light, but I didn't make a sound.

"Good girl," he said. "Now we're going to exit through the window. And don't try running, because I'll throw this knife and you won't get five steps, understand?"

I nodded again, tears I refused to let fall filling my eyes. I didn't want to die, not like this. But I was too afraid to call out for Kade. I was sure I'd be dead in seconds if I did, then would he kill Kade? I couldn't take that chance.

It took us only a moment to climb outside, then he had hold of my arm and was leading me down the beach, away from the bungalow and hotel. I swallowed, trying to think.

"Where are you taking me?" I asked.

"Somewhere your body will be easily disposed of," he said. "I just need a finger to prove your identity to my employer. But don't worry, I'll wait until you're dead to take it."

He spoke so matter-of-factly, reassuring me as to when he'd cut off my finger, it made me want to vomit. It took me a minute or two to fight back the panic and despair.

"You . . . you must be John," I finally said.

That got a reaction. His head whipped around and he jerked me to a stop.

"What did you just say?" he hissed.

"I . . . I said you must be John," I repeated, wondering if I'd just made a colossal mistake.

He jerked me closer. "Who told you that name?" he snarled. When I didn't immediately reply, he shook me. "Tell me now or I swear to God, I'll slit your throat right here."

"John, you always were so overly dramatic," Kade said.

Both of us whirled around in the direction of the voice and I rejoiced even as I panicked. John pulled me in front of him as a shield, the knife pressing into the skin under my right ear. I tried to tip my head up, but the knife stayed steady. If I so much as breathed too hard, it would slice right through me. John wasn't an amateur at this.

John squinted into the darkness. "Dennon?"

I saw Kade step closer until he was about ten feet away, then he stopped.

"What the hell are you doing here?" John asked. "Don't tell me we both got sent on the same contract." Now he sounded irritated. "Bloody hell."

"Sorry, man," Kade said with a shrug. "But I was here first."

John seemed to think about that. "I'll split it with you," he offered.

"You can have all of it," Kade said, taking a few steps closer. "I'm getting paid in a slightly different way." His eyes traveled down my body and back up, the look in them predatory.

John laughed. "Ah yes, I'd forgotten. You like to play with them first. We have a deal, my friend. I just need a finger, then you can have her." The knife left my throat and he grabbed my hand.

"I want her intact," Kade said, his voice colder now. "She's not much good for fucking if she's writhing in pain and bleeding all over me."

John hesitated. "The employer wants proof," he said with a shrug, and the affability in his voice was gone now, too.

"Since when is the word of the Krait not good enough?" Kade scoffed. "I'd tell him to go fuck himself if I were you."

John considered and I held my breath, waiting. "You're right," he said at last. "I have your word then? She'll be dead when you're . . . finished?"

"Since when is *my* word questioned, either?" Kade growled, menace dripping from the words.

"Sorry, you're right," John said. He gave me a shove toward Kade, who wrapped an arm around my waist, dragging me to his side. I tried not to look relieved, which wasn't hard since I was still terrified.

"See you around," John said. He turned to walk away and only then did I let out the breath I'd been holding.

Kade didn't speak for a moment and we both watched the darkness consume John. Finally, he looked down at me, turning my head so he could see the small cut on my neck from where the knife had pressed too hard.

"The thing is—"

I choked on a gasp, clutching at Kade. John had returned without a sound and he was staring shrewdly at us.

"The thing is," he continued, "she knew my name." His head tipped to one side. "How would she know that?"

Time seemed to stop as horrified realization set in. No one moved. John stared at Kade and Kade stared back.

"You should've kept walking," Kade said, and his voice was as cold as an arctic wind.

John moved suddenly, as did Kade. I saw a knife flying through the air toward us, then I was on the ground, Kade crouching over me. A scream climbed up my throat as I saw the knife embedded in the back of Kade's left shoulder. He jerked it out by the hilt, flipped it to grab the blade, and sent it flying through the night. It happened so fast, everything was a blur.

The blade sank into John's throat. His eyes went wide and his hands clutched at his neck, pulling out the knife, but blood was flowing and he couldn't breathe. He staggered, collapsing to his knees. I watched in horror as he fell face-first onto the sand.

Kade got up and walked to the body. Taking the knife from where it had fallen, he went to where the surf was flowing up the sand with the waves and washed it. Then he carefully wiped it off before tossing it back to the ground.

When he reached me, he took my hand and helped me to my feet. I was still shaking and now I could see blood staining the back of his shirt from the wound in his shoulder.

"You're hurt," I said stupidly. Hello, obvious. I'd seen him pull the damn knife out.

"I'll be fine," he said. "Are you okay?"

I nodded, a sob of relief building in my chest. "Is it over?" I managed to ask. "Is it finally over?"

"Yeah, it's over."

I threw my arms around him, burying my face in his neck as I cried. His arms circled my waist, holding me close. One hand rose to cradle the back of my head.

"I was s-so afraid he was going to h-hurt you," I blubbered through my tears.

"Shhh. I'm fine. Let's get out of here."

Kade packed us up and we left the posh hotel right then. And when he had the cabdriver drop us off at a run-down motel far from the beach, I didn't complain.

"Old habits die hard," he said with a half smile as he unlocked the door to our room.

We showered together and I took great pains to clean the wound in the back of his shoulder. I knew he wouldn't get stitches, which meant he'd have another scar. He didn't seem to mind, though, his hands drifting over any part of me he could reach as if he was reassuring himself that I was okay.

Butterfly bandages we'd bought at an all-night drugstore kept his wound closed and I used lots of them, not wanting Kade to be in pain from the skin tearing apart more.

We were both solemn as we climbed into bed. I hadn't dressed and neither had Kade, though sex wasn't on either of our minds. Instead, Kade nestled me against him spoon style, his hips cradling my backside while his arm draped over my waist, his large palm resting on the bump of my abdomen.

"How'd you know where he'd taken me?" I asked, my voice quiet in the dark.

"I knew what I'd do, if I was him," Kade replied. "The bungalow presented limited options."

I was silent as I digested that, then said, "Thanks for going all Batman and saving me."

Kade chuckled at that and I smiled. I thought of something and turned in his arms so I could see him.

"So if John was called the Krait, did you have a code name, too?"

Kade's lips twisted in a smirk. "Yep."

"Well? What was it?"

Leaning down, he whispered in my ear.

I looked at him and grinned. "Okay, that might be hot."

"Might be?" he asked, rubbing his nose alongside mine.

"Okay. Definitely," I amended. "Definitely hot."

Kade chuckled softly. "You're such a cliché," he said, his lips a hair's breadth from mine.

Then he kissed me and I had to amend my earlier thought that neither of us had sex on the brain tonight.

CHAPTER NINETEEN

Mona and Gerard were overjoyed to see Kade and me once we returned to Indy. Blane was in Washington, and it seemed Alisha had been right—word all over the news was that he was a shoo-in for the senate appointment. Kade and I told Mona and Gerard about the baby, and Mona got tears in her eyes, hugging me so tight and so long she nearly brought me to tears, too. They insisted on us staying for dinner, which was why we were still at Blane's house late into the evening.

"We should probably go," I said, turning to look up at Kade from where I lay on the couch, my head in his lap. Tigger readjusted his position lying across my legs. "Mona and Gerard left a while ago." He took another drink of the scotch in the glass he held, his other hand resting on my stomach. I smothered a yawn.

"My place is still shut down," he said. "I need to get the utilities turned back on. We can stay here or get a hotel, if you'd rather."

I grimaced. "You really think I trust you to pick a hotel that won't give me hives?"

Kade shook his head. "Such a princess," he said, trying to hide a smile.

"You know," I said, a sudden thought occurring to me, "you've never actually shown me your room here." I'd seen him disappear into it many times, but I'd never been inside. "Does it still have all your high school stuff?" I'd pay serious cash to go through Kade Dennon's yearbooks.

"All that crap is buried in a box somewhere in the closet," he said, finishing his drink.

I climbed off his lap and stood. Tigger jumped to the floor, disgruntled. "I wanna see," I said. "Show me?"

Kade cocked an eyebrow at me, but he stood and took my hand. He led me upstairs, only this time I didn't go to my room, nor did I head for Blane's at the end of the hall. Kade stopped in front of the door to his room and opened it.

I followed him inside, curiosity raging. I wanted to know more about who Kade was, what he'd been like when he was young.

Kade stood to the side, watching me as I looked around. The room was larger than mine, though not as big as Blane's. Like in mine, the walls were painted in a mural, only the theme was . . .

"Cowboys and Indians?" I asked.

"Frederic Remington," Kade clarified. "Famous American painter. He specialized in depictions of the Old West. I think Blane told me his mother hired someone to duplicate a few of his pieces as a mural in here."

It was beautifully done, the figures of men on horses captured in such a way that they appeared to be moving. The landscape showed both the beauty and desolation of the American West. I spent several minutes moving around the room, inching along the walls to see the entire mural.

When I turned back to Kade, he was still watching me. He wore his typical dark jeans and black button-down shirt, left untucked and with one too many buttons undone in the front. He was the only man I'd ever seen who could get away with that and not look sleazy. His hair was black as night, a lock falling over his forehead, and his eyes were piercing blue beneath thick, dark lashes. His cuffs were turned back several times and my eyes caught on his hands—large, strong, capable. His forearms were marked by the trace of veins just under the skin, evidence of hours pumping iron.

"I love when you look at me like that," Kade said, his voice a low murmur.

Startled, I jerked my gaze back up to his face. "Like what?" I asked innocently.

Kade moved closer. "Like you want to rip my clothes off and have your way with me," he teased, reaching out to wrap a lock of my hair around his finger.

"Your ego is imagining things," I said loftily, moving out of his reach. "And I'm still exploring."

"Can you explore naked?" Kade asked, settling onto the bed. He leaned against the headboard and bent his arms to lock his hands behind his head, his legs crossed negligently at the ankles.

I gave him a look but he just smirked, completely unrepentant.

The bed was similar to the one in his apartment only not as big, queen-size rather than a king, the frame a heavy, dark oak. There was a matching desk in the corner with computer equipment on it, which even to a nontechie like me had to be at least a decade old. It must have been what Kade had used in high school or college and I found myself drifting toward it. The keyboard was so well used that the letters were nearly worn off. My fingers traced the keys as I pictured Kade sitting there years ago, typing.

"So . . ." I said slowly as I explored, "tell me about the first time you . . . you know." I deliberately didn't look at him. I was embarrassed but too curious not to ask.

"The first time I what?" Kade asked.

"The first time you . . . you know . . . your first time," I tried to clarify, glancing over at him now.

His eyebrows climbed. "You want to hear about the first time I had sex?"

My cheeks were burning, but I nodded. "I'm curious," I said defensively.

Kade shook his head. "You know these conversations never end well."

"Tell me," I insisted.

He shrugged. "It wasn't a big deal. I was fifteen. She was my fifth-period algebra teacher."

My jaw dropped. "You're joking," I said in disbelief. Kade just smirked at me. "You had sex with your *teacher*?"

"Ms. Thompson," he said. "And before you go thinking it was a long-term thing, it wasn't. She had a thing for me and I took advantage of that." He waggled his eyebrows.

Wow. I didn't even know what to say. I shook my head and went back to exploring the room.

Two framed photos peeked out from a couple of shelves, likely put there by Mona, I figured. Both were of Blane and Kade together. One looked to have been taken when Kade was really young. I picked up the photo to examine it more closely. Kade looked thin, almost scrawny, in clothes that were too big. He wasn't smiling as he and Blane posed for the picture, his lips twisted in the poor parody of a smile I'd seen on him too many times. Though he and Blane stood close, they did not touch.

"When was this taken?" I asked, moving to sit next to him on the bed. Kade glanced at the photo.

"About a month after Blane assumed guardianship of me," he replied. "I wasn't exactly warm and fuzzy."

"What was it like?" I asked. "When Blane came for you and you first started getting to know each other. Was it hard?"

Kade hesitated. "I didn't know what his agenda was," he said. "Why he'd take me to live with him. In walks this guy who looks like he just stepped off the pages of *GQ* and he tells me we're brothers and he's taking me home." He paused. "It was too much for me to believe it was real, and it took a long time and a lot of patience and persistence on Blane's part for me to trust him."

"So what made you decide to trust him?" I asked. "Did it just take time or did something happen?"

"He almost got himself killed because of me," Kade answered, "and he didn't have to. He could've just let it go, let me go, but he didn't."

Kade didn't offer any more to the story and I didn't ask, only nodded. I wasn't surprised. Blane was a good man. I looked back down at the picture. "So why don't you two hug more?" I asked idly, my thoughts still dwelling on what Blane had gone through to reach Kade.

"I don't like guys touching me."

Kade's answer surprised me, as was the vehemence with which he'd said it, and I glanced up at him. His expression was utterly blank.

"It's creepy," he added with a dismissive shrug.

And I suddenly realized what Kade would probably never tell me, what had most likely happened to him when he was young that had made him so averse to men touching him.

I felt the blood leave my face and I looked away, hurriedly standing to replace the picture on the shelf, my hands trembling slightly. Tears blurred my vision and I quickly blinked them back. I knew Kade. Any sign of pity would not be welcome, nor would he want to know that I'd guessed what he hadn't said.

I bought some time to regain my composure by drifting around the room some more, studying knickknacks here and there, probably placed by Mona, and a stack of magazines. I smiled a little. Some men might have a pile of *Playboys*; Kade had a hoard of techie publications.

"I'm hungry," Kade said, getting up. "You want anything?"

I shook my head. "No, I'm good. I think I'll just take a shower."

Kade nodded and headed out the door. I walked into the bathroom attached to his bedroom and stripped.

I took my time, trying not to think about Kade as a little kid because when I did, I started crying. Breathing deeply, I pushed away the images my mind drew, instead focusing on the present. I was Kade's future, as was the baby I carried. The past was the past and there was nothing I could do to change it. All I could do was love Kade and build a life for us together.

When I emerged from the bathroom, Kade still hadn't returned. I tightened the towel around me, wondering if our conversation had upset him more than he'd let on. I opened the bedroom door and stepped into the darkened hallway.

"There you are."

I spun around, a startled cry on my lips, and I recognized the man who stood there immediately.

James.

He thrust his hand at me, something hard in his grip, and pain arced through my body. Then I knew nothing.

~

My eyes fluttered open, a headache pounding in my skull. I slowly became aware that I couldn't move my arms or legs.

"Waking up, I see."

I focused my eyes with effort. James stood over me looking more unkempt than I'd ever seen him. Two days of beard growth shadowed his jaw, and he wore a wrinkled shirt and slacks. His hair was rumpled and he looked like he hadn't slept in a while.

"What are you doing?" I asked. I raised my head and saw that I was naked, my towel gone, and that James had tied me spread-eagled to Blane's bed. The sharp tang of fear rose in the back of my throat.

"Did you think I was gone for good?" James asked, his calm voice belying the wild look in his eyes. "Or were you too busy fucking Dennon while Kirk's out of town to bother thinking about me?"

That's when I caught sight of Kade and my breath left me in a rush. James had duct-taped him to a chair. He was unconscious, his head lolling on his chest, a gag in his mouth. At least, I prayed he was unconscious. If he was dead, I reasoned, James wouldn't have bothered restraining him.

"I've lost everything," James continued. "But you know that, don't you. Now that Kirk's going to slide into a senate seat, everyone's scrutinizing how I pushed for his arrest in Kandi's murder." He swallowed. "I've been forced to resign. My career's over."

"I didn't have anything to do with that," I said, desperately trying to reason with him. "Why are you doing this to me?"

James started unbuttoning his shirt. "You could say I've had an epiphany," he said, his gaze unblinking as he stared at me. "Ever since I met you, my life has gone to shit." He tugged the shirt off and dropped it to the floor.

I shook my head. "I didn't do anything to you, James."

"And I realized," he continued as though he hadn't even heard me, "that all this time, you were trying to keep me from a dark path, the path I was on. Only I was too stupid to see it. Just like Dennon. That's why he keeps you with him. To save himself from the demons inside his head. The same demons inside me."

A noise made me jerk my head toward Kade and I saw with a sinking knot in my gut that he was awake. His eyes blazed with rage as he stared at James, every muscle in his body straining against the bonds that held him. But even as I prayed he'd be able to save me, I knew that there was no way Kade would be able to break free. No one could.

James was looking at Kade, too, then to my horror, walked over and punched him. Kade's head snapped back from the force of the blow, but his eyes were no less filled with fury as he looked back at James. James hauled back and hit him again and blood spurted from Kade's nose.

"Stop! James, please!" I cried out. I couldn't stand watching him hurt Kade.

James turned to look at me.

"Please," I begged. "Don't hurt him any more."

He seemed to consider this, then glanced back at Kade. "He killed my father," he said. "He should be punished for that." His fist clenched like he was going to hit Kade again.

"Your father tried to kill me," I said quickly. "He wasn't a good man, James."

After a moment and to my relief, James turned away from Kade and walked back over to me. "You're right," he said. "I should listen to you." He reached out and I flinched as he drew his fingers through my damp hair.

"How could I not have known?" James said, his words so quiet it seemed he was talking to himself more than me. "You're beautiful, an angel. How could I not have seen that you were sent to save me, just like you saved Kirk?"

His words were crazy, as was the way he was looking at me, his gaze drifting from my face down my body. Fear sent a dose of cold adrenaline through my veins.

James unbuttoned his pants, then continued shedding his clothes until he was naked. I dared not look at Kade again and tears leaked from my eyes to trail down the sides of my face, wetting the bedding underneath my head. Was James going to rape me? Kill me? All while Kade watched?

The horror of it made me nearly pass out, which I knew wouldn't help me at all. I squeezed my eyes shut and took a deep, shuddering breath. I would survive. I had to. For Kade's and the baby's sakes. I had no doubt that if James killed me, Kade would be utterly lost to the darkness inside him.

When I opened my eyes, James was naked and holding a revolver.

"Put the gun away, James," I said, my eyes wide. "I'll do whatever you want. Just put the gun down."

He ignored me, emptying the chamber of bullets. I watched in confusion and saw him put one bullet back in, then spin the chamber and lock it in place.

"Me and you," he said, kneeling next to me on the bed. "We kept coming together like magnets. You see the scar you gave me?" He indicated the long white line on his chest. "It's your brand on my skin, forever marking me as yours."

James reached out, his touch almost reverent as his fingers trailed from my cheek and down my neck to between my breasts.

"I still see the mark I gave you," he mused, tracing the faint outline of the *J* he'd carved into my skin. "See? We're tied together in blood." He flattened his palm over the mark.

I swallowed. "What are you doing, James?"

Reaching for the table, James picked up a knife he must've placed there. My heart rate must have tripled, but he didn't turn the knife on me. Instead, he held up his arm and drew a long cut from his wrist to his elbow. Blood began flowing and he held the cut over me. The thick, warm fluid dripped onto my stomach and chest. James was saying something, murmuring words I couldn't hear or understand, and his eyes drifted out of focus.

"I don't understand what you're doing," I said help-lessly, trying to stay calm, which was becoming more and more difficult.

James brandished the gun. "One bullet. Fate determines who dies."

Noise erupted again from Kade's chair as he fought the bonds and gag. James jerked toward him, his eyes narrowing dangerously, and I panicked.

"James," I said, then had to repeat, "*James,* look at me." I had to keep his attention from Kade, which wouldn't be easy if Kade kept it up. "James!"

He finally looked down at me.

"Dennon first," he said, and before I could say anything to stop him, he pointed the gun at Kade and pulled the trigger.

"No!" I screamed, but the click of the hammer falling on an empty chamber chased my cry.

Kade's face was like granite as he stared at James, his eyes promising death.

Relief that James hadn't killed Kade was followed by more fear as he turned the gun on me.

"Your turn," he said.

Kade was yelling around the gag, but James ignored him, his entire focus on me. He placed the barrel of the gun between my breasts, then drew it down through the blood he'd spilled on my skin.

"Don't do this, James," I said. "You don't want to hurt me. I'm your angel, remember?" I was babbling, trying to figure out anything I could say that would end this night-mare.

James's finger tightened on the trigger and my muscles tensed, as though I was bracing myself. I squeezed my eyes shut.

Another click of an empty chamber.

My breath let out in a loud gasp and I snapped my eyes open. James looked pleased.

He reached out again, and I had to steel my resolve as he began to touch me, his hand painting blood over my breasts and stomach. Bile rose in my throat and each second that passed felt like an eternity.

"You should untie me," I managed to choke out. "So I can . . . touch you, too."

But James just shook his head. "You're an angel," he murmured. "You'll disappear if I untie you." His words were nonsensical and I began to fear that he was on some kind of drug, which meant reasoning with him was going to be impossible.

"The last test," he murmured.

My arms strained at the ties holding me as James reached for the knife again. To my surprise, he sliced through the bonds holding my wrists, then carelessly tossed the knife away. Grabbing the back of my neck, he pulled me up so our chests were pressed together. He placed his head alongside mine and held the muzzle of the gun to my ear.

"Decide our fate, angel," he said. "I'll pull the trigger and we'll see if we die together, or not at all."

The blood slickened our bodies and my ankles were still tied, preventing me from getting away. My hands were free now, but his hold was too tight, the muzzle of the gun pressed painfully hard against my head.

"Decide our fate," he repeated. "Decide . . ."

He had already pulled the trigger twice. With a six-round chamber, my chances didn't look good.

I didn't want to die.

The sharp click of the hammer falling made me flinch, a whimper escaping from between my lips. Three pulls. Three empty chambers.

I had no idea why James had decided to free my arms, but now that I could move, a blood lust like I'd never felt before rose in me. He'd pulled that trigger one too many times. A haze of red filled my eyes as rage consumed me—and if I'd never before slept in Blane's bed, I wouldn't have known how to save myself.

Blane was an extremely cautious man who'd spent too much time in a war zone, sleeping in places that could go from relatively safe to highly dangerous in minutes. It was the ingrained SEAL in him that had made him hide a knife behind the center of the headboard. The first time I'd spotted it, he'd been up-front and unapologetic about why it was there, acknowledging that while it didn't make a lot of sense outside a war zone, it helped him sleep better at night.

I reached up, my hand unerringly finding the knife and pulling it from its sheath. I didn't hesitate, despite the gun still held to my head, and put all my strength into driving the blade down, straight into James's chest.

James froze. His face was creased in lines of pain as he looked down at the knife protruding from his chest. His fingers seemed to go numb, the gun falling from his hand. I grabbed it, pointing it at him.

As he looked at me, his face cleared. "How can I hate you and love you at the same time?" he asked.

"You don't love me," I hissed. "You're a monster. You don't know what love is."

Suddenly, Kade was there, beside me. I had no idea how he'd gotten free, but his hand settled over mine.

"Don't kill him," Kade said. "You can't take something like that back. I'll do it."

"No," I said, pushing his hand away. "He would've killed you, me, and our baby. He deserves to die." Hatred coursed through my veins and I didn't take my eyes off James.

"Yes, he does, but you don't need to be the one to do it," Kade insisted.

"In this case, yes, I do."

James closed his eyes, raising his face heavenward. "I'm ready. Kill me, my angel."

"Go to hell." I pulled the trigger, the report of the one bullet left in the chamber reverberating through the room. The aim couldn't be off, not this close, and the wound was dead center in his chest.

James's body collapsed.

Kade lifted me bodily from the bed, holding me so tight I could barely breathe, but I didn't mind. Shock was setting in and my skin felt ice-cold.

"How did you get free?" I asked, twisting to look at the chair he'd been taped to.

"James tossed that knife and it landed near me," Kade said. "He hadn't taped my legs, so I got bendy and managed to get the knife up to my hand."

"I want the blood off," I said.

It took three washings before I felt clean, Kade grabbing Blane's robe and wrapping me in its depths once I was through.

"Come on," he said, helping me from the room.

My gaze caught on James's body lying on Blane's bed, blood pooling underneath him, his sightless eyes staring. Never again would he be able to terrorize me or the ones I loved. I didn't have an ounce of regret for killing him.

From the den, Kade called Chance. It took him less than fifteen minutes to get there, and he brought Lucy, too.

Lucy sat with me on the couch, holding my hand, while Kade took Chance upstairs and explained what had happened. The kitchen door had been the one James had broken in through, then hitting Kade with a stun gun before searching the house for me.

It took a couple of hours for Chance to call it in, the ME to come collect the body, and for Kade and me to give our statements. Chance looked grim as he took my statement, giving me a long hug when I was through.

"I'm glad you're okay," he said roughly, his eyes wet.

"Me too."

Mona and Gerard came to see what the fuss was about, alarmed that the police had come to the house in the middle of the night. I kept things vague. No need for Mona to know the details of what had transpired in Blane's bedroom. She made me a cup of tea, which helped warm me up.

I refused to go to the hospital. I was all right. Nothing damaged that wouldn't heal. I just wanted to be alone with Kade. I kept looking at him as he handled the police and the questions and the paramedics.

James could so easily have killed Kade. I knew that if he had, I wouldn't have been able to fight James off. I'd have made him keep pulling that trigger until both of us had a hole in our heads.

Finally, Kade was bundling me into his car. I think we both knew we didn't want to stay at the house tonight. He drove us to a hotel, and not one that rented rooms by the hour.

The guy at the desk didn't bat an eye at the robe I was wearing, and soon Kade had whisked me up the elevator. I wanted another shower—I still felt like James's blood was on me. Kade set me gently on the bed in the suite before running a bath. He helped me into the steaming water, then sank to his knees on the floor next to the tub. His hands dipped into the water as he tenderly washed me, his touch so careful, as though he thought I would break apart.

Afterward, he lifted me from the tub, the water soaking his shirt, then patted my skin dry with a towel and wrapped a hotel robe around me. He carried me to the bed and tucked me against him as he sat with his back to the headboard. I noticed that his free hand, resting on the mattress, held a gun.

"Put that away," I said quietly. "Rest with me."

"I let down my guard once and look what happened," Kade rasped. "I won't let anything happen to you. I swear it."

"It's not your fault," I said, twisting to look up at him. He glanced down at me and the pain and guilt I saw in his eyes made my heart hurt. "You couldn't have known what James was going to do," I continued. "He had a crazy fixation on me. You can't predict crazy."

"If he hadn't emptied the gun of five bullets, you'd be dead right now."

I sat up and took Kade's face in my hands. "I refuse to let what happened tonight poison our lives," I said. "James has taken away my peace of mind before, has hurt me before.

None of it was your fault or your responsibility to prevent. He's dead now. It's over. Now I just want to forget.

"Only you can help me do that," I said. "So stop blaming yourself. Put away the gun and hold me. I love you. You're safe. I'm safe. The baby's safe. That's all I want to think about."

To my relief, Kade reluctantly set aside the gun and wrapped both arms around me. It seemed we couldn't get close enough, and even though I knew Kade would probably lie awake all night, I heaved a sigh of contentment and drifted to sleep almost immediately.

～

Morning had sunshine streaming in through the windows and I woke with a stretch. Amazingly enough, I wasn't very sore. My ankles and wrists hurt, but other than that my body was okay. Surprisingly, I hadn't had any nightmares. Maybe that had been because my subconscious knew James was dead and therefore no longer presented a threat, or maybe it was because I'd been with Kade, or maybe both, but my sleep had been peaceful.

I heard the low rumble of Kade's voice and got out of bed. He'd nearly closed the French doors dividing the sitting room from the bedroom, leaving them open a scant inch. I realized he was talking to someone on the phone.

I brushed my teeth and used the bathroom, using my fingers to try and tame my hair, before I emerged from the bedroom. Kade glanced up from where he sat in an armchair, but kept talking.

"Yeah. It was close," he said. "Too close. And you're going to want to burn that bed. I never want to lay eyes on it again."

I grimaced, then spotted the pot of coffee Kade must have ordered from room service. I poured myself a cup and listened to him talk.

"Chance took care of it," Kade said. "And Gerard's planning on fixing the door today." He paused, listening. "Yeah, she's right here. Hold on." He held his cell phone out to me. "Blane wants to talk to you."

I was suddenly nervous as I took the phone from him. Did Blane know everything that had happened the past few weeks? Had Kade told him we were married now?

"Hey," I said softly.

"Kat," Blane said, releasing a sigh, "Kade told me what happened. Jesus. I'm so sorry, Kat."

"It's not your fault," I said. "Just like I told Kade. No one could have predicted he'd go so far off the deep end. I just want to forget it and move on."

Blane was quiet for a moment. "Then I won't mention it again, okay?"

"I'd appreciate that," I replied. James was part of the past now.

Blane cleared his throat. "I hear congratulations are in order," he said. "Kade told me you two made it official. Mrs. Kade Dennon."

Hello, awkward. My stomach felt like I'd swallowed a ten-pound rock. "Um, yeah," I said. "I . . . yeah, we did."

"I'm really happy for you, Kat," Blane said, and if I hadn't known him so well, he might've fooled me.

"It's okay not to be. You don't have to lie," I said, drifting to look out the window. "I understand." *After all, if things had worked out differently, I'd be Mrs. Blane Kirk instead.* It was unspoken, but I could hear his thought as though he'd said it aloud.

We were both quiet for a moment.

"I, um, I hear you'll probably replace the senator," I said, changing the subject. "That's really something. Congratulations."

"Yes. Unexpected, but I think if it happens, I'll accept the appointment."

I wondered if he would have accepted it if he and I had still been together. "So you'll be in Washington from now on," I said, my heart sinking. "Not Indy."

"For a while," Blane said. "The session's already begun, so it'll probably be a few months before I make it home."

"So by Christmas, you think?" I asked.

"Maybe," he hedged. I didn't push.

More silence, but I was loath to say goodbye. Finally, Blane spoke again.

"I love you," he said, his voice roughened, "and I'm glad you're okay, all three of you."

"Me too," I replied, my own voice hardly above a whisper.

Blane cleared his throat again. "Okay, well, tell Kade I'll talk to him later."

"Okay."

"Take care of yourself. Take care of Kade."

"I will. I promise."

"Goodbye, Kat."

"Bye, Blane."

Then he was gone, the call ended. I stared blindly out the window and blinked back the tears.

CHAPTER TWENTY

"I don't even want to know how much you paid for these tickets," I said.

Kade just winked at me. "It's the least I could do. Especially since I'm the reason you missed your pop princess in Indy."

We were in the front row of the Sprint Center in Kansas City, waiting for Britney to come onstage. The tickets and backstage passes Blane had given me last Christmas had been for her show in Indy, but Kade had gotten shot and I'd been at the hospital constantly, thus missing the concert. I hadn't said anything at the time—as much as I loved Britney, Kade nearly dying had consumed all my thoughts and attention—but Kade had eventually figured it out.

So now, two months later, we were in Kansas City for her show and somehow Kade had scored front row center seats. He'd begged me to wear my Britney costume from last Halloween, but I'd put my foot down. Skimpy Catholic schoolgirl outfit would normally be sexy; *pregnant* Catholic schoolgirl was just not, no matter what Kade insisted to the contrary.

I was too excited to sit, so I stood, leaning against the tall fence that separated the front row from the stage. The show should start any minute now. The opening act had finished and the stage looked nearly set up for Britney.

The past couple of months had been a whirlwind. Kade and I had bought a house and begun, again, to decorate a room for the baby. I didn't want to sell the house I'd bought in Rushville, though. That house had been something I'd done on my own when I'd realized I was strong enough to do what needed to be done to raise our child by myself. We still went there occasionally for the weekend.

Charlie hadn't seemed to mind that I'd had to quit my job so quickly after I'd started, citing how I was pregnant and married and lived in Indy, but then again, it was hard to tell with him. I thought I'd seen him crack a tiny smile before he turned away.

Kade didn't exactly love visiting Rushville, but he humored my desire to keep ties to my hometown. Though people were slow to warm up to him, eventually they seemed to accept his presence by my side.

My lease was up on my old apartment and I'd been a little sad to move out. So much had happened there, good and bad. The afterimage of Blane and our time together seemed to be burned into the place and that made my chest hurt if I thought about it, so I didn't.

Lewis had proposed, and he and Alisha were getting married at Christmas. I was thrilled for her. As a gift, and an apology, I'd made Kade buy them tickets to Hawaii and he was also footing the bill for their honeymoon there. I felt it was the least he could do after shooting Lewis. But the wound had healed and there was no lasting damage, thank goodness, so I thought all was okay between the four of us. Though I didn't think either of them would probably ever look at Kade the same way again.

Blane had gotten that senate appointment, to the surprise of no one. Kade and I had watched on television as he'd been sworn into office. *Blane Kirk* was now a name that was nationally recognized, and his handsome face had graced the covers of several news magazines. The press seemed to love him, though I was sure that wouldn't last. The gossip pages once again had photos of Blane with beautiful women on his arm, though the same one never seemed to appear twice.

Blane had escorted Vivian to Keaston's funeral. The story that had been circulated was that the senator had suffered from terminal cancer and had decided to spare himself and his family the pain of a long, drawn-out illness. I didn't care what story was put out to explain his death. I was just glad he was out of all our lives, permanently.

Kade and I had gone to James's sparsely attended funeral. We'd stood at the graveside and I'd sprinkled a handful of dirt over the coffin. Closure. It was good for my mental health.

Clarice had been dumbfounded to hear about Kade and me, but she'd recovered quickly, wishing us happiness. I thought she was hiding disappointment that Blane and I hadn't worked out, which I understood. She was loyal to both Blane and Kade, but I knew she held a special place in her heart for Blane and wanted to see him happy. So did I.

Chance wasn't nearly as quick to let the past go and I made sure it was just him and me when I told him the news. He'd been stunned.

"You're married?" he'd asked, his eyes wide with disbelief. "To *Kade Dennon*, an assassin?" The utter outrage in his voice had made me cringe.

I didn't know if Chance would ever believe that Kade had left his old life behind, so we just took it day by day. I had to hope that, eventually, he would see the good in Kade the same way I had.

Kade treated me like gold, and he had been true to his word about leaving his old career behind and focusing on work that was legal and had zero chance of him ending up either dead or in prison. Initially, I'd been somewhat worried that his old life might cause problems, but it seemed that being an assassin was a lonely and secretive profession. He'd asked Branna to help him put out some rumors that he'd been killed on a job and it seemed he was right—no one came seeking the truth.

"So how about Aidan?" he asked in my ear, his arms wrapping around me from behind.

I leaned my head back against his chest, turning my head to look up at him. I made a face. He rolled his eyes.

"You don't know it's going to be a boy," I said. We'd decided not to find out the sex of the baby and picking a name was an ongoing discussion, especially since Kade was convinced it was a boy.

"Yes, I do," he said. "Trust me. I know things."

It always made me smile when he said stuff like that and I laced my fingers through his as they rested on my abdomen.

"How about Tripp?" he asked.

I didn't even bother responding to that one. "If you're so sure it's a boy," I said, "that means I'll have two of you to handle, so I think I should get to name him."

Kade looked at me skeptically. "I don't know. I wouldn't want my son to end up with some name that could be a girl or a boy, like Jordan or Tory."

"You don't trust me?" I asked, raising an eyebrow.

"Ooh, now you're reaching for the big guns," he teased, making me laugh. "All right, fine. If we have a boy, like I know we will, then you get naming rights."

"Deal."

We sealed it with a kiss and I was just getting into it when the lights went out. I jerked my mouth away.

"It's time!" I said excitedly.

"You know, most women would rather kiss me than watch Britney Spears," Kade chided me.

"I'll make it up to you later," I promised with a laugh.

"I'll hold you to it," Kade said, "because I also got you this." He held something up in front of me as the stage lights came on and the music started.

"Backstage passes?" I cried. I turned and threw my arms around his neck. "You're amazing!" I pressed a hard kiss to his mouth.

When I pulled back, Kade's expression was soft, his eyes tender as he looked at me.

"No," he said, "you are."

EPILOGUE

The pains began in the morning while I was drinking my coffee. Starting in my lower back and expanding around my abdomen, flaring in intensity, then fading. I knew what it was immediately and glanced at the clock. Another one came in ten minutes. I waited it out, breathing through my mouth and gripping the counter.

Once it passed, I took a shower. Kade was already in his office working and I knew he'd go apeshit the second I told him. He'd practically refused to leave the house the past couple of weeks, saying he just knew that the moment he left was when the baby would decide to come. The second I told him it was time, he'd have me hustled into the car and to the hospital. Well, I wanted to shower first and shave my legs.

I sat on the shower seat when another pain came, breathing through it, then finished rinsing my hair. I dressed in comfy clothes and blew my hair dry before pulling it back in a French braid. When I deemed myself ready and the contractions were about seven minutes apart, I went to find Kade.

He was typing away at the computer and the windows in the office were open, the warm spring air drifting in along with the scent of the daffodils and lilacs blooming outside.

The first thing he'd done when we'd arrived back in Indy from our honeymoon was to buy me a beautiful two-story brick home surrounded by an expansive lawn dotted with trees. We weren't in the country, like my little house in Rushville was, but there was enough space between us and neighbors that I didn't feel boxed in.

"Good morning," I said, sliding my arm across his shoulders.

Kade glanced up and smiled, turning his chair and tugging me down onto his lap. I wasn't as dainty as I used to be, not with a nine-month pregnant tummy, but Kade seemed to love everything about it. His hand rested on top of my stomach. "'Morning, princess," he said, giving me a kiss. "How are you feeling today? Is the baby awake?"

I grinned. "Not only is the baby awake," I teased, "but it's time."

It took a second for Kade to catch on, then his eyes went wide. "Now?"

I laughed. "Well, not right now, but hopefully by tonight it'll all be over."

That put Kade into high gear, as I'd known it would. In minutes he'd closed up the house, gotten my suitcase, called Mona, and was trying to hustle me to the car.

"Wait," I said, "did you eat breakfast?"

He looked at me like I was insane. "You're seriously not asking me if I've eaten, right?" he asked incredulously.

"Well, the hospital food is awful," I said, thinking I was being perfectly reasonable and he was the one reacting all out of proportion. "You should eat something before we go."

"Oh my God, Kathleen, just get in the car," he moaned. "Please. Before I stuff you in it myself."

"Will you relax?" I said in exasperation. "You act like we haven't done this twice before." Still, I got in the car before his face got any redder.

"If you think that makes it easier, it doesn't," he said firmly, sliding behind the wheel.

"Are the boys all right at Mona's?" I asked.

"They're fine," Kade assured me, one corner of his mouth tipping up. "I told them their mommy and I were going to bring home their little sister and they were quite excited."

"Nice that they were already there spending the night," I said, then another pain hit and I gripped the door, breathing until it passed. I noticed Kade's speed had increased while I'd been quiet.

"I'm fine," I said, reaching for his hand. "Slow down. There's plenty of time."

Kade, for all his coolness under pressure, proved to be the typical husband when it came time for me to give birth. I thought that was because it was something out of his control, which he hated.

It took a little while to get me admitted and situated in a room, then all the equipment hooked up to me, the IV put in, yadda yadda. The pains were closer together now and I hoped that after having two babies, the third would arrive quickly.

It took a couple of hours, then the nurse proclaimed I was dilated enough for an epidural, and I heaved a sigh of relief. I knew lots of women did childbirth the natural way, but I was fine with the label of wimp. I wasn't a fan of pain and if modern medicine had a way for me to avoid it, I was all about it.

Kade hated watching, though, his fear of needles making him extremely uncomfortable seeing one go into my spine. Of course he said he wasn't afraid of needles, he just didn't "like them," though he'd never told me why.

I felt much better after the epidural and the next few hours passed relatively easily.

"Did you call Blane?" I asked Kade at one point.

"Yeah," he said. "He was in a meeting, but I left him a voice mail."

I nodded, a little disappointed, though I knew Blane was a very busy man. Blane was a US senator in his own right. After being appointed to fill the remainder of his great-uncle's term, he'd run for election and won the seat. He'd inherited Keaston's estate, which not only included the house in Georgetown but also his family home in Cambridge, where Vivian still lived, and a vacation home on Nantucket. Now Blane divided his time between DC and Nantucket with occasional visits to Indy. Congressional recess was coming, though, and he usually came back for a visit before taking our boys with him to Nantucket for two weeks every summer.

By late afternoon I was pushing and by dinner, Kade and I were holding the newest member of our family.

"You're going to be insufferable now," I teased Kade as he held our seven-pound, two-ounce little girl.

"I can't help it if I was right," he said, arching an eyebrow. "I told you. I know things."

I just smiled. I was tired, though it had been an easy delivery. At least, easier than the first time I'd done this. That had taken hours and I'd thought Kade was going to kill someone when the epidural had worn off too soon and I'd felt every bit of the final stages of labor and delivery.

"She's beautiful," Kade said softly, rubbing a finger over one tiny cheek. "But not as beautiful as her momma." His free hand reached for mine and he slotted our fingers together.

"Now there are two princesses," I said, but he shook his head.

"You've just been promoted to queen."

I laughed lightly. "My turn to hold her," I said. Kade placed her carefully in my arms. Her hair wasn't the usual newborn black but a shock of reddish gold that was just a shade lighter than mine. Her eyes were a beautiful, deep blue, though she was sleeping at the moment.

Flowers came, a huge display of two dozen pink roses that the nurse set on a table where I could see them.

"'Congratulations on the latest set of tiny, pattering feet,'" Kade read. "'Love, Blane.'"

"That's nice," I said with a smile. The smell of roses drifted through the room.

It was close to ten when I let them take my baby girl back to the nursery. The nurses always offered to let the baby stay, but I knew better. This would be one of the last decent night's sleep I'd get for a few months.

"Go home and get some sleep," I told Kade. "Bring the boys in the morning."

Kade leaned down and kissed me, his hand cupping my cheek. It was a lingering kiss and when he pulled back, he gazed into my eyes.

"You're amazing," he said softly, "and I love you. You know that, right?"

"Of course I do," I replied. "I love you, too."

"Are you happy?" he asked, his brows drawing together as he frowned slightly.

"Incredibly so." I smiled. "You make me happy, Kade. You always have."

Kade's frown melted away and he kissed me again in a way that made me wish I hadn't just given birth, but then again, he could always make me feel that way.

After he left, I didn't fall asleep as quickly as I thought I would. It had been a recurring question from Kade over the years: Was I happy? It seemed Kade still had trouble sometimes believing all this—the house, the kids, our marriage. He'd told me once that he was so happy and content that it terrified him—it could so quickly be gone.

There wasn't anything I could say to alleviate his fears, so when he got that way, I'd just hold him, tell him I loved him, then kiss him until he made love to me. He'd made all my dreams come true and I cherished each day because it was true—you never knew what the future held, but neither could you let the fear of it hold you captive.

~

Something woke me and I glanced around, figuring a nurse had come in, but it was a man's silhouette that stood at the window.

I must've made a noise of alarm, because he turned and a shaft of light fell across his face. I breathed a relieved sigh.

"Blane," I said, "you scared me to death."

He walked to the bed and took my hand. "Sorry about that. And I'm sorry I couldn't get here earlier."

"It's fine," I said. "You're here now. What time is it?"

"About three thirty," he said.

"When did you get here?" I rubbed my eyes, glad the room was dark, because it wasn't like I looked my best.

"About an hour ago."

I pushed the button on my bed to move me to an upright position. "You didn't have to come tonight," I gently chided him. "You could've come in the morning."

"Wanted to make sure you were all right," he said, sitting down on the bed beside me. "And the baby."

"Did Kade send you pictures?" I asked.

"He did."

"Isn't she beautiful," I said with a smile. I leaned my head back on the pillow. The pain medicine was making me sleepy.

"She most certainly is," Blane agreed, his lips turning up at the corners. His hold tightened on my hand. "I'm glad everyone's healthy."

"You're an uncle again," I said. "But I don't think this one's going to be as into fishing as the boys are."

"Then I'll have to find something else she'll like just as much," Blane said, reaching to tuck a lock of hair behind my ear.

My eyelids drooped. "I don't know what we'd do without you," I murmured.

Blane didn't answer. The bed creaked and I felt his lips press against my forehead.

"Do you need anything?" he asked quietly. "Can I get you something?"

I pried open my eyes and shook my head. "No, I'm fine." I smothered a yawn behind my hand.

"You should get some sleep," Blane said, smoothing a few stray hairs back from my forehead.

I was pretty tired. "Okay. Will you be back in the morning?"

"I'll stay," Blane said. "I know how much you hate the hospital."

I smiled. "That's sweet of you," I mumbled, my eyes slipping shut again. It was just way too hard to keep them open.

Blane tucked the blanket closer around me and lowered the bed again. I forced my mouth to move.

"I'm glad you're here," I murmured.

"Me too," he said, the words so low I barely heard them, then I was out.

~

"Mommy!"

I looked toward the door as my youngest boy came hurtling toward me, only to get swept off his feet by Blane hoisting him in the air.

"Easy, buddy," Blane said. "Your mommy's a little fragile and so's your new sister." Blane gently sat him next to me on the bed.

"How's Mommy's Teddy Bear?" I asked him, leaning down and puckering up for a wet kiss.

"Good," he piped up. Theodore was his full name, after my dad, but we called him Teddy. His hair was golden blond, his angelic looks a contradiction to his mischievous ways. "Dad got us doughnuts."

"He did?" I said, glancing up at Kade, who'd followed Teddy through the door. "Did he bring me any?"

"Here you go," my oldest said, handing me a paper bag. My hands were full, so Blane took it and set it aside.

"Kane, you want to meet your new sister?" I asked as he moved closer, eyeing the pink bundle in my arms a little skeptically. Kane was the spitting image of his father, right down to the unruly lock of hair that always fell in his eyes. Though he was only six, he'd been born with an old soul, it seemed, always the one to observe and take measure of things before committing himself.

"Boys, meet the newest member of the family," I said, pulling the blanket aside a little so they could see her face. "Lana." They both peered down at her.

"That's kind of a weird name," Kane said.

"It was your grandmother's name," I said, glancing at Kade. "She died a long time ago, but I think she would've liked your sister."

Lana opened her eyes, blinking at the two little faces staring down at her. Then she stuck her tiny fist in her mouth.

"She's kinda red," Teddy said.

I laughed. "You were, too, when you were this small."

"Glad you could make it," Kade said to Blane, holding out his hand. They shook, which I always thought was a strange way to greet each other rather than with a hug, but I knew the reasons behind Kade's preference, so I stayed silent.

"Wouldn't have missed it," Blane replied.

"I'll trade you," Kade said to me, brandishing a Starbucks coffee.

"You read my mind," I said, handing him Lana and taking the coffee. I curved an arm around Teddy, who cuddled at my side, thumb in his mouth. Kade had been trying to get him to stop, but he was only three, so I just shushed Kade.

"Uncle Blane, when are we going to the farm?" Kane asked, walking over to him. It was what they called Blane's house on Nantucket.

"Soon," Blane said, ruffling the boy's hair. "Summer's almost here."

"Oh my! Let me see her!"

We all turned as Mona entered the room with a flurry, followed by a grinning Gerard. Kade had no choice but to hand Lana over.

"It's about time we had a little girl in the family!" Mona crooned. "Kathleen, I saw the cutest little pink shoes in the store the other day—I just had to get them. Then she needed a new outfit to wear them with, of course, so I added two new dresses to her wardrobe. Wait until you see them, you'll just die, they're so sweet."

I grinned.

"Why do I think Lana's going to be the most spoiled member of this family?" Kade mused, though his mouth was tipped up in a half smile.

Blane laughed. "I don't think you'd be able to stop her," he said to Kade.

"Oh, you boys hush," Mona admonished. "Like you're ones to talk. I spoiled you both rotten and I intend to do the same to this one."

Everyone stayed for a while, passing Lana around, and I think Gerard was already making plans to build a barn to house a pony by the time they left. After a final round of kisses and hugs and promises to be good, Teddy and Kane went with them.

"I'd better bug out, too," Blane said.

"Are you heading back to DC?" I asked.

He nodded. "I'll fly out this evening, but I'll be back in a few weeks, once the session ends."

Bending over me, he kissed Lana's forehead, then my cheek. "Bye, Kat." He crossed to Kade and gave him a one-armed hug, slapping him on the back. "Congratulations. She's amazing. You're a lucky man."

"Don't I know it," Kade said, and I was glad to see him give Blane a squeeze back before pulling away. "We'll see you soon."

Blane left and it was just me, Kade, and Lana.

"Chance and Lucy came by earlier," I said. "They brought those." I motioned with my head to another floral arrangement that stood next to Blane's.

"Sorry I missed them," Kade said evenly.

I rolled my eyes. Chance and Kade would never be best buddies, but they'd come to an unspoken truce over the years.

Alisha and Lewis came by shortly after that, then Clarice and Jack, and by the time the day was over, my room looked like a flower shop.

I was tired when we handed Lana over to the nurses and I thought Kade was going to leave, but he ended up sliding into bed beside me.

"This is much better," I said with a sigh, cuddling against his chest as his arm wrapped around my shoulders.

"Thought I'd stay tonight," he said. "I don't sleep well with you gone anyway and Mona offered to keep the boys."

"I'm glad," I said. "I missed you."

"Brought you something," he said.

I glanced up at him. "I told you not to do that." Kade had given me expensive jewelry when each of the boys was born, which was really sweet, but I didn't need more jewelry.

"You'll like this," he said. Reaching into his pocket, he pulled out my locket that he'd given me so long ago. I hadn't worn it to the hospital since they made you take off all your jewelry. He opened it and handed it to me.

"Oh, Kade," I breathed, tears sparking in my eyes. My parents' photo had been moved to the left side and the right side of the locket now held a photo of just Kade and me. "Thank you," I said, leaning up to kiss him. "It's perfect."

He fastened it around my neck and held me as I drifted off to sleep.

~

Seven Months Later

"Don't run!" I called out, but I might as well have saved my breath as Kane and Teddy ran through the hallway of Blane's home, chasing a remote-controlled car of some sort that he'd bought them. I adjusted Lana on my hip and straightened the little red bow in her hair. "Your brothers are crazy," I said to her. She grinned toothlessly at me as though she understood.

I headed back to the library, where Kade and Blane were busy picking up the discarded wrapping paper, bows, and ribbons that littered the floor.

"They tore through that pretty fast," Blane said with a grin.

"Well, you shouldn't have bought them so much," I chastised him. "And the toy drum set is *so* staying here."

"Yeah, that was just cruel, brother," Kade added, grimacing. Blane just laughed.

The doorbell rang. "That must be Chance and Lucy," I said, handing Lana to Kade. "I'll get it."

Christmas dinner had become less formal with little kids running around the house, though we still dressed up. Mona went all out with the candles and table linens, but the boys got heavy-duty plastic cups rather than crystal.

"Dinner's about ready," Gerard said as I passed by. He was uncorking a bottle of wine to decant it.

"Smells wonderful," I enthused. Vivian was helping Mona with the finishing touches in the kitchen.

Sure enough, Chance and Lucy were at the door, along with Billy and their other son, Jared, who was slightly younger than Kane.

"Merry Christmas!" I greeted them, hugging them all. The boys squirmed, but I squeezed them anyway.

"Merry Christmas, Strawbs," Chance said, kissing my cheek. "We brought a bottle of Blane's favorite scotch."

"That's nice. He'll like that," I said, taking it from him. "Come in! Come in! It's nearly time for dinner. I thought you were never going to get here."

"The snow gave us some trouble," Chance said, taking Lucy's coat before removing his own. I hung them in the closet nearby. "Be careful going home. The roads are a little slick and they're expecting more snow tonight."

I shook my head, Lucy and I sharing a grin. "Always the cop," I sighed.

"Hey, I'm just trying to look out for you," Chance protested.

"Come on," I said. "I'm sure Lucy needs a glass of wine." I started down the hall, but just then the doorbell rang again.

I motioned for Chance and Lucy to keep going. "Go ahead to the den. I'll get it."

They continued down the hallway while I turned back and opened the door. I smiled, leaning forward to hug the woman standing in the doorway. She never let me hug her for very long, but I always tried anyway.

"Merry Christmas!" I said to Branna. "I'm so glad your flight wasn't delayed any longer." Branna lived in Annapolis, Maryland, and the weather had caused her arrival to be later than she'd planned.

"Branna, glad you could make it," Kade said, suddenly appearing over my shoulder. "I'll take your coat."

Branna's face softened when she saw Kade and she shrugged out of her black overcoat, revealing a red silk dress. I was suddenly glad I'd worn my black dress with gold threads shot through it rather than the red dress I'd contemplated. Kade gave her a hug, brushing a kiss to her cheek.

"Merry Christmas," she said with a smile. "I brought this." She handed me a box of gourmet chocolates.

"Thank you," I said, passing them to Kade. "Blane's in the den and I could use a cocktail." I hooked my arm through Branna's, leading her down the hallway to the library. We were exactly the same height, even with our heels on.

I opened the door and saw Blane standing next to the fire with Lana on his hip, adjusting the little velvet dress she wore while she sucked happily on her fist.

"Look who's finally arrived," I said.

Blane glanced up and smiled when he caught sight of Branna. "It's about time," he said, coming forward. He kissed her lightly on the lips. "Merry Christmas."

"Merry Christmas," Branna replied. She reached out to grasp Lana's tights-encased toes. "Hello, little one," she said. Lana grinned, bouncing in Blane's arms.

A crash sounded from somewhere upstairs. "Oh no," I said, glancing at Kade. "The boys."

"I'm on it," he said, heading for the door.

"Can you please actually get after them this time?" I called out to him.

Kade looked innocently at me. "Trust me," he said. "I'll put the fear of God in them."

I rolled my eyes. "Yeah, sure you will."

Lana started fussing and I glanced at the clock. "I'd better feed her before dinner if I want to eat, too," I said, reaching to take her from Blane. "Please excuse me."

Dinner was much better than the first time we'd done this, a year after Kade and I had married. That first Christmas, Blane had pleaded too much work to be able to get away from DC, and since he'd only held the office for three months, I'd stifled the protests I'd wanted to make.

The next year, things had been awkward, and it had taken a while for Blane to warm up to Kane, who'd been a little over six months old at the time. He'd been a colicky baby and I'd spent Christmas night pacing in the library, holding him as he cried nonstop. Kade had been out of town on business and though he'd be flying in that night, he hadn't yet arrived and I'd been exhausted. I was nearly in tears as I paced and tried to comfort Kane, feeling helpless and frustrated at the same time.

"Let me have him," Blane had said, startling me. I hadn't even heard him come in the room over Kane's fussing.

I'd hesitated, but had been too desperate for a respite not to do as he asked. I handed over my squalling baby boy, who seemed very small against Blane's bulk.

"Go take a break," Blane had told me. "He'll be fine."

"Thank you," I'd murmured before leaving the room. I'd breathed a sigh of relief, then immediately felt guilty for needing to get away from my child.

Guilt at Blane having to mess with a fussy baby had me returning inside of fifteen minutes, only to stare in stunned amazement at the scene in the library. Blane stood in front of the fire, Kane perched against his shoulder, sound asleep. Blane soothingly rubbed Kane's back.

Seeing the two of them had brought tears to my eyes, and that moment had been a turning point for Blane's relationship with Kane. They had a special bond. Though Kane looked just like Kade, his demeanor and personality were reminiscent of Blane, something that had become more apparent as the years passed.

Branna had joined us for the first time last year. It seemed whatever animosity Branna used to have toward me had evaporated into a careful politeness that grew more easy and comfortable. Likewise, I found my antipathy toward her had faded over time. From what I could gather, she and Blane had been casually together for a while now. Sometimes I wondered if they'd marry, but had never thought it my place to bring it up with either of them.

The boys behaved and didn't spill or break anything this year, and Lana was happy chewing on a toy in her high chair. All four boys went to play once they were finished, leaving the adults to chat. I was seated to the right of Blane, who was at the head of the table, with Kade then on my right. Branna sat opposite me, with Lucy on her left.

We talked and laughed and Blane poured more wine, heaping praise on Mona and Vivian for the fabulous Christmas dinner. It was late when we finally roused ourselves from the table. I put Lana down in a crib Gerard had installed in my old room upstairs back when Kane was born, then joined Mona and Vivian in the kitchen to help clean up.

"Are you ready to go?" I asked Kade when we were finished, perching on the arm of the chair where he sat in the den, drinking some of the scotch Chance had brought. I removed the glass from his hand and took a sip, then handed it back.

"The kids'll probably fall asleep in the car on the way home," he said, sliding an arm around my waist. I rested my arm across his shoulders. "They've worn themselves out."

"Sounds good to me," I said with sigh.

"You can't go yet," Blane protested. "You haven't sung for us."

It had become a yearly tradition, Blane playing the piano while I sang a carol or two. It had felt a bit odd at first, but over the years everyone had urged us to do our usual performance and I couldn't say no. This year was no different.

Blane's fingers ran over the ivory keys while Kade refilled everyone's wineglass. The rich notes of the piano filled the room.

"What'll it be this year?" Blane asked me softly as the hubbub of conversation drifted around us.

I leaned on the piano, thinking. "I don't know. How about . . . 'Have Yourself a Merry Little Christmas'?"

Blane's hands moved seamlessly from the chords he played to warm up into the opening lines of the tune. The song was slow and I took my time with the lyrics.

I rested my hand on Blane's shoulder as the lyrics spoke of faithful friends. He was so dear to me, to our family. I was grateful beyond words for his presence in our lives.

My eyes found Kade's as I sang, their blue just as piercing as on the day I'd met him. His gaze held me captive and I couldn't look away while I finished the carol. I sang another couple of tunes before we finished our performance, then Blane stood, wrapping an arm around my shoulders as everyone applauded and began talking.

"Always beautiful," Blane said with a warm smile. He squeezed me in a hug, pressing a kiss to my forehead.

"That's just because you play so well," I replied. Kade's hands settled on my waist, tugging me slightly, and I turned to see him standing behind me.

"Nicely done," Kade said. I stretched onto my toes to give him a kiss.

Chance and Lucy gathered their boys and headed home after more admonishments about the roads. Gerard left to drive Vivian to the hotel where she preferred to stay when she was in town.

Kade and I had driven the SUV tonight, so I didn't think we'd have any trouble getting home, and besides, we lived just a few miles away. I saw Chance and Lucy out, then returned to the den, where Branna sat on the couch, a glass of wine in hand, while Blane stood by the fire. I went over to him and reached up to give him one last hug.

"Thanks for letting us invade your home," I said. "Again."

"Anytime," he said. "You still having your annual New Year's party?"

"Absolutely," I said. "You're coming, right?"

"Wouldn't miss it," Blane replied.

"I'll go round up the boys," I told Kade. "Would you mind starting the car?" He'd already taken the kids' haul out earlier. God forbid we'd get up in the morning and there was some toy we'd left at Blane's.

"Sure," he said.

"I can get the little one for you," Branna offered, setting her wine aside.

"Thanks," I said. "That would be great."

It didn't take me too long to get the boys bundled up, and I sent them in to tell Mona thank you before she left for home as well. I was passing by the den when I heard Kade and Blane talking. I would've kept going, but I heard my name, so I stopped.

It had been a long time since I'd eavesdropped on one of their conversations, and I felt a niggle of guilt as I did so, but that didn't make me step away from the door.

". . . still in love with Kathleen?" Kade asked.

"Don't be ridiculous," Blane said. "That ended a long time ago."

"Yeah, it ended," Kade said, "but I don't think that did a damn thing to change how you feel. I'm your brother, and I know you."

My eyes widened. What was Kade talking about? Surely, Blane had moved on—it had been years, after all. He'd dated other women after Kade and I had married, and he'd been with Branna.

"Christ, Kade, you think now is a good time to talk about this? On Christmas?"

"What, should I fly to DC and make an appointment with your secretary?" Kade's sarcasm was thick. "Just answer the question."

~

Blane stared at his brother, who gazed unflinchingly back at him.

Well, this was awkward. Blane should have known that he wouldn't be able to fool Kade. Not that he'd tried. They hadn't had a frank discussion about Kat in years, though why Kade would pick tonight of all nights to bring it up was a mystery.

"What do you want me to say, Kade?" Blane asked, lifting his arms in exasperation before they dropped back to his sides. "That I'm still in love with your wife?"

"Are you?"

Kade didn't look angry. He looked . . . pained. As though he already knew the answer and was just waiting for Blane to say it out loud.

Blane didn't want to hurt Kade, but neither did he want to lie. "A part of me is always going to be in love with her," he said at last, his voice quiet. "She changed me, changed both of us, and you know I'd do anything for her.

"But that doesn't mean I'm not living my life or that I begrudge what you and she have," Blane continued. "I'm glad you have a family, that you're alive and happy. I'm not pining away for the past."

And that was all quite true. Mostly. Did Blane lie awake in the dead of night and wonder what might have been? Sometimes. But no one needed to know that except him.

"I know Kathleen loves you," Kade said, and Blane's heart gave a lurch even though logically he knew Kade meant it in a way that didn't warrant the brief hope that had flared in Blane. "She always has and she always will. I came to terms with that a long time ago."

"So what's your point?" Blane asked. There were about a thousand and one other things he'd rather suffer through a heart-to-heart with Kade about than this.

"Are you being fair to Branna?" Kade asked.

Ah. Branna. She'd been there when he'd lost Kathleen, and Blane had been there for her when she'd realized that she and Kade weren't ever going to happen.

"Branna is very special to me," Blane said.

"Are you going to marry her?"

Blane took a deep breath. "Besides the fact that it's none of your business, no, we have no plans to get married." How to explain their relationship? "Branna's a friend, Kade. We've been . . . good for each other. And that's all you need to know."

Kade nodded. "Fine. I don't wanna know the details." He pushed a hand through his hair. "I guess my point, and I do have one, is that . . . we're family. Me. You. Kathleen. And nothing's going to change that."

Their eyes met and Blane was suddenly glad that his brother hadn't taken Kat away from Indy. He could have. Kade could have put as much distance as he wanted between Blane and Kathleen, but he hadn't. He'd allowed Blane to be a part of all their lives—Kathleen's, Kade's, and their kids'.

A look of mutual understanding passed between them. The past was a long time ago, but it felt good to clear the air. If Kade, who avoided talking about his feelings even more than Blane did, brought it up, it must have been bothering him.

The door suddenly swung open and the boys came barreling into the room, looking for their dad. Beyond the door stood Kat. Blane's gaze fell on her. She was staring at him, her expression stark, as though she'd overheard every word he and Kade had said . . .

Shit.

"Here you go!" Branna said, stepping up to Kat with Lana in her arms and jerking Kat's attention from Blane.

Lana was rubbing her fists against her eyes and yawning, all bundled up in her coat and shoes. She looked like a doll-sized version of Kat, with her reddish blonde curls, blue eyes, and little red lips. When she saw her mom, she held her arms out. There was a familiar twist in Blane's gut at this, but his face showed nothing.

"All right, you monsters," Kade said, corralling the boys. "Outside with you. The chariot awaits. No pushing, no shoving, no running. No activity that will result in wet clothes or crying."

Blane shook his head. His little brother—a father now, and a good one at that. Kade had turned his life around.

He followed Kade out into the hallway, watching as Kade took Lana from Kat and then headed outside after Kane and Teddy, who were already ignoring his edicts and hurling snowballs at each other with ungloved hands.

"It was good to see you again," Kat said politely, giving Branna a hug. Branna allowed the gesture, murmuring, "You too." Blane was glad they'd buried the hatchet a while back. He doubted they'd ever be close, but at least they didn't fight anymore. Branna glanced at him as she passed by and Blane brushed her hand with his.

"I'll be there in a moment," he said with a small smile. She nodded before heading back into the library, leaving Blane alone with Kat.

Blane reached into the nearby closet for Kat's coat, which he'd gotten as a gift for her last Christmas. He held it open for her to put on, and she obediently slipped her arms into the sleeves. Blane reached inside the collar, lifting her long hair from underneath. His fingers grazed the back of her neck.

Kat was looking up at him when she turned around, but Blane focused on doing up the fastenings on her coat. She was so little, even after having three children. Blane had deliberated for a long time as to which coat would keep her warm enough through an Indiana winter. The wool and cashmere blend he'd finally settled on was a good choice.

"I'm glad Branna's here," Kat said quietly.

Blane didn't answer. He didn't want to talk about or dwell on the past. It was enough to just be around Kat. His fingers moved slow and deliberately, easily slipping the loops one-by-one over the fastenings.

"I . . . don't like to think of you by yourself."

Blane finished doing up the last loop and lifted his gaze to hers. Yes, she'd overheard all right. She looked sad, and Blane couldn't bear to see that in her eyes.

"I'm content, Kat," he assured her, lifting a hand to cup her soft cheek. "You've given Kade so much—a life he never would have had without you. You saved my brother. If

I didn't already love you, I would for that. Things have a way of . . . working out."

Kat's expression eased and Blane folded her into a hug, savoring the fleeting moment when she was in his arms. They stayed like that until that twinge inside him said any longer would be unwise, then he let her go.

"Don't worry about me," he said, squeezing her hand. He smiled, trying to lighten the mood. "Though I won't pretend I don't like it when you do."

Her lips lifted in an answering smile. "I always worry about you," she admitted.

"I'm fine," Blane said easily, dismissing her concern though a part of him was pleased. "You'd better go. Your husband's going to think you forgot about him."

Kat nodded and took a step toward the door, then turned back to him. Rising on her toes she pressed her lips to his in a quick kiss, then another. Her palm cupped his jaw as she looked into his eyes.

"You're a *good* man," she whispered, her blue gaze intent on his.

Blane was too stunned to say or do anything, and a moment later she was pulling open the front door and hurrying to the waiting car. He stood in the doorway and watched as the SUV pulled away from the house, heading into the falling snow as they drove down the road.

Blane's lips tingled from her touch, her words echoing in his mind.

A good man.

Blane knew his life would have turned out much differently had he not met Kathleen. No doubt he'd be married to Kandi by now, miserable, possibly following in his father's footsteps and cheating on his wife, living for his ambitions and neck-deep in whatever illegal and unethical machinations his uncle would have trapped him in. It was because of Kat and the changes she'd wrought in him and in his life that Blane could still claim he had honor and integrity.

A good man, she'd said.

Blane smiled. Yes, he'd take that.

Closing the door against the snow and the cold, he headed back down the hall, to the warmth of the library, and the woman who awaited him there.

By the time we got home the boys were barely conscious for us to wrestle them into their pajamas and tuck them into bed. Lana was out like a light as I tugged her tights and dress off, pulling on her footed pajamas. I kissed the top of her head, then settled her into the crib on her tummy. She immediately drew her knees up underneath her, sticking her bottom in the air and wedging her fist in her mouth.

Finally, it was still and silent in the house and I went in search of my husband.

I found Kade sitting in the living room, gazing past the brightly lit Christmas tree to the large picture windows beyond. Big, fat snowflakes were falling, adding to the snow already on the ground.

"That's beautiful," I sighed, standing next to him. He pulled me down to sit on his lap and I rested my head on his shoulder. Together, we watched the snow fall. It was like a scene out of a fairy tale, and it got me thinking of how we'd gotten here from where we'd begun. Our fairy tale, mine and Kade's, had been filled with betrayals and blood, villains and victims. But love had flourished, too, and trust, which in the end had overcome all the rest.

"I wouldn't change anything," I said after a while. "You know, if I had it to do over again." I glanced up at him. "Would you?"

Kade's hand moved to tangle in my hair, the strands slipping through his fingers.

"No," he said at last. "Somehow, even with all the mistakes I made, I got the girl. So no, I wouldn't change anything."

His words brought Blane to mind again. He'd said he was content, but maybe he'd just sought to reassure me. Kade would know the truth.

"Do you think he's happy?" I asked. I didn't have to specify who I meant. We both knew.

Kade took a deep breath, his brow furrowing slightly as he thought. "I think," he said slowly, "that Blane's life . . . is exactly what he wants it to be."

Suddenly, I realized just how understanding Kade had been over the years, sharing me and our family with Blane. He had never protested or so much as hinted that he had any problem with Blane being around me or the kids. It was a testament of Kade's love for Blane, and for me.

"I love you," I said, reaching up to brush a lock of his dark hair from his forehead.

His smirk remained as he raised an eyebrow. "I know."

Then he kissed me, the taste of him and the feel of his lips against mine pushing away thoughts of everyone and everything else. His hands cupped my jaw as he cradled me in his arms, my fingers undoing the buttons of his shirt to press against the warm skin underneath.

Kade suddenly stood and my legs automatically locked around his waist. His hands cupped my rear, supporting my weight as he climbed the stairs to our bedroom, and he made love to me on Christmas night while our babies slept in their beds and the snow fell outside.

And it may have been a rocky road getting there, but I wouldn't have traded my happily-ever-after for anything.

The End

ACKNOWLEDGMENTS

Thank you to my wonderful husband, Tim—the finest man I've ever known—and my daughters, Erica and Savannah. Your support and love have made my life a dream come true.

Thank you to my editor, Maria Gomez, for your patience and willingness to push me. Thank you for always telling me the truth and loving Kathleen as much as I do.

Thank you to my betas—Leslie and Nicole. Your enthusiasm for Blane, Kade, and Kathleen have given me the will to continue when I was sure it was absolute crap. I don't know how I would have gotten through the series without your unwavering encouragement.

Thank you to Jennifer Armentrout for your pull-no-punches advice and ability to read really, really fast.

Thank you to Alexandra Ivy for being the shoulder to lean on when I was going out of my mind.

Thank you to my sister, Tonya, for being proud of me and telling me so.

Thank you to my fabulous Snow Angels! I so appreciate your tireless working to spread the word about this series and hook more readers. I love you all!

Last but not least, a heartfelt thank you to Montlake and all the people who work there. I'm grateful for your commitment to The Kathleen Turner Series and for doing all you can to make it the best it can possibly be.

ABOUT THE AUTHOR

Tiffany Snow has been reading romance novels since she was too young to read romance novels. After fifteen years working in the Information Technology field, Tiffany now works her dream job of writing full time.

Tiffany makes her home in the Midwest with her husband and two daughters. She can be reached at tiffany@tiffanyasnow.com. Visit her on her website, www.Tiffany-Snow.com, to keep up with the latest in The Kathleen Turner Series and her other projects.